Energy Barons

A. Dru Kristenev

Energy Barons

E-edition, ChangingWind.Org: March 2010
Second Edition: 2012

Cover Photo: Reclaimed Coal Excavation
    Courtesy of Wyoming Coal Industry

ISBN: 0615647596
ISBN- 13: 978-0615647593

Too easy to lose our way when People's handwork is
prized more than the Maker's.
Axée

Author's Note...

The gears of Washington, D.C. churn out legislation and policy faster than we can keep up. You know it and I know it.

Thus said, I must confess to the fact that since the first draft of Energy Barons was finished in October of 2009, I have attempted to update the manuscript, to little avail. As soon as an addition or change is made, circumstances inside the Beltway flip again.

The point of the Baron Series, as you may have noted, is to start a fire under you, the reader, to do the follow-up data gathering in order to stay ahead of the curve. And curveballs are flying fast and furiously with this administration. Yes, it's practically an impossible task, which is why the website, ChangingWind.org, is there to help out.

Toddy is busy every day, seeking out information that is hard to uncover and making the connections that people like me tend to overlook. The implications of the machinations of influential moguls like George Soros and his patsies are far more subtle than we normal folk can sometimes conceive, not being driven by a devious nature. Nor does the journalistic establishment find it to their advantage to truthfully cover the news. That is a huge indictment, however, there aren't many who report with the integrity the profession once embodied. Being a renegade from the world of newspapers, I make the charge to my own detriment. God bless those few left who beat the bushes for real news and have the chutzpah to report it. Let them dig even further into the muddy depths where only intrepid individuals of Toddy's caliber do not fear to go.

I must extend my heartfelt thanks to the many consultants who gave me encouragement to continue with this charge to write fiction based on good facts that they supplied, though not all agree with my views. Carolyn Boguslawski, dialysis nurse; Mindy Webster Paine, Soldotna, Alaska fishing guide; Steven Laird, coal industry expert; Steve Zollman, rancher and rodeo cowboy; Sean Sullivan, environmental attorney; and others who will go unnamed, from a teacher who has worked among Native Americans for decades; a professor of anthropology whose years of working with

Plains and Plateau Indians gave me invaluable insight; to my many friends among both worlds, on and off the reservation, whom I love. There are more people, too many to mention, who patiently endured my endless questions, guided my research and inspired me, that I am overwhelmed on a regular basis when I contemplate what they have helped me to accomplish in writing the Baron Series, and whom I can't thank enough. To them I must also extend my sincere apologies for license taken and the inevitable mistakes that likely appear in this volume, despite my best efforts to "get it right."

So, read this for pleasure, recreation and entertainment. Perhaps it will also engage you enough to take a more active role in the workings of our nation. A nation on the verge of dissolution should the barons have their way.

God bless,
A. Dru Kristenev

February 26, 2010

Energy Barons

36 And they served their idols: which were
a snare unto them.
37 Yea, they sacrificed their sons and
daughters unto devils.

Psalms 106

Prologue

With the sun's banishment behind the lofty, jagged peaks of the Big Horn Range to the west, the sky deepens in color from azure to indigo, accentuating the growing brilliance of the stars scattered across its vast expanse. Knee-high grass bends in the rising wind as night encroaches over the rolling plains.

Two men hike toward a railroad switch point where one train's powerful diesel engines idle behind a red light, signaling the engineer to wait for the slow passage of it's twin bearing down from the opposite direction. Practically invisible in the leaching daylight, the traveling pair reaches the junction and melts into the shadows as the powerful headlamps of the oncoming train sweep from side to side, washing the perimeters of the track with intense light.

They keep silent watch as the train approaches and begins its passage of the idling locomotive, the sonorous thrumming of the engines filling the air and resonating in their chests. Conversation is impossible in its wake.

As the train lumbers past and the last of the freight cars eventually come into view, the blond man, hair luminous in the reflected headlights, moves to follow the loaded cars. He picks up his speed and, with practiced ease, tosses up a customized grappling hook, catching the lip of the tall aluminum gondola. Rapidly working the braided nylon rope attached to the carabiner on his harness, he pulls himself up, hand over hand, until he is flat against the side of the car, cinched close to the top and gripping the rim with his gloved hands.

The whole process is accomplished in less than a minute while his darker companion observes and rises to catch his own ride aboard the temporarily stopped train anticipating the signal's change.

As the heavily laden train rumbles north, its scores of cars passing at a snail's pace, the engineer of the waiting locomotive sees the light finally changing to green. Throttling up his engines, he trundles from the siding to the main line heading south. The dark hitchhiker goes unnoticed, swinging himself just inside a rattling gondola halfway down the line, fingers grasping the rim.

Pulling empty cars, the southbound train swiftly covers the two miles to reach its destination. The railrider waits for the train to come to a full stop and nimbly climbing over the lip of his chosen car, releases his hook and drops to the ground outside of the brightly lit, batch load out area. Operations at the coal mine are in full swing around the clock, constantly feeding fuel to the power station just a few miles away.

The evening crew, still fresh with only a couple hours' duty under their belts, diligently examine the interior of each car, ribbed sides reaching up some ten feet, before it rolls up to the batch load out where a pre-weighed 100 tons of crushed subbituminous coal is released into each waiting car.

Long before the train has pulled far enough forward for his car to receive its cargo, the railrider has abandoned his conveyance. The shadows stretching beyond and between the silos, blocking the stark, jaundiced light cast by tall sodium vapor lamps, are almost impenetrable, and the railrider slips easily from one black silhouette to another.

Crouching in the darkness, he removes items from his backpack and attaches them at the terminus of the six foot-wide conveyor that delivers coal to the storage silos holding 10,000 tons each, and at the base of the silo where another conveyor belt exits to feed the weigh bin.

Managing to do his work undetected, the railrider moves to the next act in his private production by hiking the two miles alongside the conveyor's length, keeping to the outside shadows. Reaching the transfer point from where the crushed black rock begins its journey through the conveyor, he attaches something to the edifice. He then darts across to slither under a behemoth hauler as it dumps its load of 200 tons of coal into the grizzly to be crushed into 2" chunks.

Affixing a device to the undercarriage of the truck is the most hazardous part of his duty and he rolls away just before a dozen-foot tall tire can mash him beneath its enormous tread.

His tasks concluded, the railrider keeps to the dark edges of the graded road. The few times a vehicle drives by during his westward trek to the pick-up point, he successfully scrambles to find a hollow and lays low, watching furtively until they've gone.

He is more than a mile beyond the electrified fence, a barrier crossed by way of a prepared exit that he carefully concealed after his passage, when he spots his ride. With long strides he covers the ground quickly, grinning grimly as his ears register a booming report echoing from the distant north.

Energy Barons

Chapter I

Allie Maitland was bored.

Not that the comeback of the buffalo wasn't a subject of significance, but animal husbandry wasn't exactly a passion of hers and the
way the experts were covering the topic, it was as dull as if she'd
been sitting in a college ag lecture on barley mold. *Spot blotch*, she
corrected herself in her head. All the years of covering the agriculture beat paid off in little ways, she chided herself. Tonight however, it was the reintroduction of buffalo to the Great Plains states and
how here, in eastern Wyoming, there was no need to worry about
brucellosis reaching the cattle herds. Yellowstone was another subject and she *had* been listening when one of the state ag guys zeroed
in on the infection rate among elk over there and in nearby parts of
Idaho.

It had been a long day, having to rise before dawn to drive up
from Denver and be here by noon. All to cover the conference for
the Post for what amounted to two days. *I guess it's a big deal but
couldn't Gleason have just as easily had me call some of these peo -
ple? Nope, "we need pictures" of the big hairy beasts milling
around a pen or, if I'm lucky, out in some nearby field munching next
to the antelope.*

She tried to refocus on the man at the podium. He was droning
on endlessly about the native grasses that were being cultivated to
regenerate the plains and would feed the herds whose numbers had
blackened the horizon more than a hundred years ago.

Allie was a solid environmentalist. She was a member of the
Sierra Club and World Wildlife Fund, but that didn't mean she was
ecstatic about listening to every little detail about eco-systems. She
was a city girl at heart and her idea of a day in the country was tool-
ing up a winding road in the nearby Rockies, maybe a day hike in

the foothills. *Buffalo culture is not up my Allie.* Her mouth twitched subtly at the stupid play on words that flitted through her mind.

It was closing in on 9:30 in the evening and she stifled a yawn when the lights went out and the microphone died. *Thank goodness for little blessings.* That was her first thought but when the power did not come back on after a few minutes, some of the people seated near her started getting restless. She could hear the doors to the conference room opening up but the only light that appeared were the stingy beams of a few flashlights in the hands of the convention center employees.

That reminded her that she had stashed a small one in her portfolio that contained all her journalistic paraphernalia. Digging down in the depths of the heavy-duty nylon case, her fingers closed around the familiar shape. Praying that the batteries were still good, she pulled it out and flicked it on. It worked and suddenly she could see a little more of her surroundings.

After about ten minutes of stewing as to whether she should pack up her stuff and go back to the hotel or stick around a little longer to see what was going on, a few lights came up and the manager of the center came to the microphone. The woman tapped it to see if there was any juice and heard the clicking through the speakers. Taking that as a good sign, she brought her mouth down to the mike and opened with an apology for the inconvenience of the power outage.

"Unfortunately, as you can see, our back-up system isn't quite adequate to continue tonight's session so we will be curtailing the rest of the event. I have been informed that the outage is region-wide due to a failure at the power plant, so as you leave the center, you will notice that traffic signals and streetlights are not functioning, and most businesses are dark. We ask that you be careful and courteous as you depart the facility. Thank you for your patience and be safe."

The manager made a valiant effort to escape the room quickly but a few of the other reporters from larger media – this was a national conference and some big outfits were covering it – cornered her and started bombarding her with questions about the power outage. Allie was right in the middle of them with her little tape recorder held up to catch the manager's comments.

"I'm sorry that I don't have much information for you at this time. All that I was told was that there had been some kind of accident at the new power plant outside of town."

"Which plant is that?" yelled someone from one of the Cheyenne television stations.

"Flat Butte Station."

"You said that it was a new facility?" asked the same reporter.

"It just came on-line a couple weeks ago," replied the manager, carefully keeping a placid demeanor. She looked at the call letters on the reporter's mike and wondered how they could be so uninformed. The manager remembered seeing a piece about the new plant that had aired on that same channel not two weeks prior.

"What kind of fuel does it use to generate energy?" Allie raised her voice above the others. Being from Denver, she wasn't conversant with local power issues.

"It's a new generation clean coal-fired utility."

"Did they tell you the nature of the accident?" Allie had pushed in closer to get in her follow-up question.

"No. I have not been given any details." She tried pushing through the gaggle of reporters and interested conference attendees. "I'm afraid that I have no other information, so if you'll pardon me, I have other duties to attend to. Thank you," and she gently shoved the little crowd aside.

Allie wove through the group that was basically immobile, yapping among themselves about particulars no one possessed. She caught the shirtsleeve of one of the earlier speakers who was a representative from the Wyoming Department of Environmental Quality. He looked around and down, being exceptionally tall, at a much shorter Allie who was tugging from behind.

She immediately apologized for the inappropriate introduction. "Sorry about the grabbing," the corners of his mouth turned up in a cross between interest in a nice looking woman and humor. "But since you're with the environmental quality office I thought you'd probably know where the Flat Butte Station is located."

He wondered why she wanted to know but shrugged it off as unimportant, turning around to answer her question. "It's outside of town to the southeast off of Basin Road."

She pressed him for clearer directions at which point he asked her why she needed to know. She fished out her press ID hanging from a lanyard that had slid under the flap of her vest.

"Denver Post. I'm just trying to get as much information on the accident as I can." She decided to shoot in the dark. He *was* from Environmental Quality, after all. "Have you heard anything more specific than what the convention center manager told us? Maybe about the cause of the blackout?"

He shook his head. "The only thing that I was told was that there was an explosion at the first generating unit that's only been up and running for two weeks. The other section of the plant won't be ready to fire up for another couple months. I'd venture to guess that they'll be pushing that up as much as possible now." He turned to go then caught her eye as he peered back over his shoulder. "Don't quote me. That was pure conjecture."

She gave him a puckish smile. "No trouble, I don't even remember your name," she said staring directly at his nametag. He laughed as he made his way out the door.

Allie didn't waste a minute but pushed her way through the milling crowd. She was in a hurry to find the power plant and get her claws into a *real* story.

As she searched for her car through the utter gloom that was the parking lot, a few headlights began to snap on here and there among the acres of blacktop, adding a little to the visibility. She was immensely relieved at the fact that her little flashlight was operating, thinking that she had no right to expect it to since she hadn't checked the batteries in ages. *That energizer bunny is my hero.*

Finally, she recognized the row and spotted her little compact flanked by two oversized rigs, a dually and a supercab 4x4. Although she privately thought that most people didn't need such big vehicles, she wasn't foolish enough to expect ranchers and farmers to haul hay on the top of their hybrids, let alone pull horse trailers. As she opened the door of her car she wondered if the two Gigantors on either side had planned their parking strategy just to make her feel dwarfed and inadequate. Climbing in, she laughed at the ridiculous thought, turned on the engine and the lights then started to make for the exit when she realized the county offices were in one of the other buildings.

Taking a detour by way of the county admin building, she checked to see if there was anything going on there, like maybe an impromptu press conference. They *did* have their back-up generator working at the complex.

She slowed down and swung by the entrance, peering into the big windows to see if there was any occupancy. Rewarded with the sight of one man juggling phones and looking harried, she pulled into the closest parking slot and jumped out. With her tape recorder in hand, Allie stuffed a pen and notepad in her faux Banana Republic vest that was layered with numerous cargo pockets.

Allie hurried up to the door, tried it and saw that it was locked. Despite the fact that it was after hours, feeling in her bones that this was a big story in the making, she began a steady knocking until the man put the phones on hold and came to the door. He motioned to the "closed" sign and tried to shoo her away. To know avail, of course. This was Alice Maitland, hot on the trail and she'd be damned if she'd give up so easily. Buffalo patties. She *wanted* this *story*.

The phones were ringing off the hook and the man could see that Allie wasn't about to quit and go home so he yelled through the door, "What do you want?"

She held up her press ID and yelled back, "I need to know what happened at Flat Butte!"

He held out his open hands to either side of his shoulders and answered, "I have no idea. That's what I'm trying to tell *them*!" and he pointed to the phones with their clamorous ringing. He started to move back to the desk, then thought a little and told her, "Try the power plant. The mayor and county administrator are headed over there. You'll get more from them."

She shouted thanks, ran to the car, and finally grabbed her cell phone out of a side pocket of the portfolio.

It's time to see if I can reach Gleason. Allie speed dialed her editor and was gratified to hear a ring tone as she held the phone up to her ear. Her other hand on the wheel, she sped off as quickly as she could, considering the lack of illumination both on the street and from the authorities.

"What have you heard?" she blurted when he picked up.

"About what?" He sounded tired and grumpy. *Napping again. Must've been a nasty day at the office,* which boosted her attitude, glad not to be anywhere near there for once.

"The power outage up here in Wyoming."

"Wait a sec." She could hear a chair groan as he sat down, followed by the sound of typing. She also heard the volume come up on the TV. She'd caught him at home, not that that was any surprise at 10 p.m. "And I thought I couldn't miss a thing, but I sure missed this. When did it happen?"

"Not twenty minutes ago but the thing is, they're saying that it's been caused by an *accident* at the new power station up here. I'm going to check it out."

"Good. There may be a solid story there. I don't suppose you got any good buffalo copy," he mocked.

"Enough to make your puff piece interesting despite the drudge duty. I'm running out to Flat Butte right now. I take it that's okay by you?"

His answer wasn't much more than a grunt. "According to what I've been able to pull up on the national stage, they're reporting an outage affecting everything east of the mountains and parts of South Dakota." Gleason's voice rattled and he coughed off to the side.

"When are you going to get straight and dump those cigs?"

"When I'm old and gray." He coughed lung-deep.

"Hate to tell you, but you've arrived."

"Just get the story."

Wonder if I'm leaving a slug trail on the asphalt. As much as Allie wanted to race out to the plant, she was forced to drive at a snail's pace. Since she didn't know Gillette that well, reading road signs in the black of night was difficult. Luckily, she saw the flashing lights of emergency vehicles and the glow of a fire painting the horizon well outside of town, which helped her navigate to the site. By the time she arrived, the lights had been out for almost an hour. Even so, there were just a couple of other reporters on site, mostly the local media who would have received the first calls.

As she was collecting her tools to join the gathering press, two TV news vans came whipping into the lot and tried to maneuver themselves closer to the buildings. They were rebuffed by the police and company security protecting the line of hastily strung up yellow tape, who warned the reporters to get back to the area where Allie had parked. Although she understood their need to get in the middle of the action, she'd also had too many encounters with the self-indulgent personalities who made a habit of cramming mikes in people's faces. In her opinion, most of them didn't have an ounce of sympathy for the victims and were pretty high on her list of human offal. To a lot of them, stardom was calling. *Should've gone into act - ing. Oh yeah,* she told herself, *that's what they did.*

All Allie wanted was a good story, to get the straight facts and present them well enough that she could earn a little respect. Glamour was the last thing that had interested her when she'd decided to study journalism, popularity having become a bane to her in college, causing her more heartache than she'd imagined possible. Always being the one to stand out in a crowd – running for senior class president and head cheerleader, nabbing both – it was a rude awakening that turned her to seek a field that would keep her in the wings where she could avoid the limelight and advocate for truth. So her need to have a byline above the fold wasn't as crucial to her as knowing she'd researched and written a story well, with clarity and no embellishment.

She pushed the car door shut with her hip and hurried past the TV crews that were losing time setting up, checking light levels and make-up for the most flattering effect on the reporter's onscreen image. Allie gave mental kudos to one cameraman who simply climbed out of the van and just starting shooting. No fuss, no muss.

She covered the distance quickly to reach what looked like an improvised staging area where a couple of official-looking types were standing with their heads together. *Getting their stories straight.* She knew they'd have to offer cohesive facts, particularly with the raging fire being fought as the dramatic backdrop.

The towering smokestacks were starkly lit by power that Allie assumed was being furnished from back-up generators, probably only enough to handle the plant's needs. Ambulances were pulling away and driving at breakneck speed for the medical center back in town. She hoped they'd convene this party soon because she wanted to know what had happened here. The story was important but it was her curiosity that had brought her to this point in her life, her *need* to know.

During the press conference delay, while the firefighting and rescue efforts were being orchestrated, Allie tried to get a couple of off-the-cuff comments from the uniformed guards that were keeping the public at bay. Not that there was such a great crowd rustling around, just a couple news vans and about a dozen reporters waiting impatiently. Her efforts were met with mostly stone-faced negatives in response to everything from attempts to wheedle out a narrative of the accident, to her inquiries about basic procedures during a crisis.

When she was finally ready to give up, a man stepped up to a makeshift podium, a microphone precariously mounted on top. The usual sound check followed and then the information everyone had anticipated... *or not*, she thought.

His comments were almost as bland as the convention center manager's had been and about as nonspecific. After tugging a tad nervously on his tie, he gave a prepared statement that said there had been an unexplained explosion at the one operating generator of the new plant. It was impossible to determine what the cause of the accident was at the current time. There had been casualties involved in the accident of which he had no details. He also said that power would be restored to the community within a period of several hours. Authorities were having to divert energy over the grid from already heavily laden plants in Montana and Utah. There would probably be some latent brownouts and blackouts until the power distribution problem could be fully addressed.

Someone asked how long that would be, to which the answer was, "That is uncertain." Allie shouted a follow-up question about whether it was dependent on how quickly damage could be repaired at this utility or if there were other options available.

His answer was that it would be up to the EPA as to whether they would recertify the recently decommissioned plant to be temporarily brought back online. If not, there had yet to be an assessment of the damaged unit, the completion date of its sister unit still under construction and numerous other variables. Beyond that he had no more information.

With that he backed away from the microphone and disappeared into the administration building leaving the mayor and county administrator to offer platitudes about the accident and sending prayers to the families of the injured. They refused to give any details either, and as the county official stepped down there was a series of distant booms that made him stop in his tracks as everyone turned toward the direction of the thunderous report.

There were several minutes of scrambling around, people running to the offices to get clarification on the noise that was definitely not related to the ongoing blaze that the firemen were battling at Flat Butte.

Five more minutes passed and the Plains Coal Company public information officer stepped forward to the podium and retrained the mike more to suit her shorter stature.

"The sounds that seem to have caught everyone's attention are related to a minor disturbance at the company mine. The nature of the disturbance has not been disclosed but we have been assured that everything is under control. Thank you for your patience and good night." She waved off any attempt by the media to stop her for further comments and all of the officials disappeared inside the administration offices.

The rest of Allie's journalistic cadre were tired and didn't seem inclined to hunt down the cause of the so-called disturbance, being content to hang out at the power plant and hound the company reps for more information. What she was hearing among the broadcast crowd were reports that seemed to cast the power company in a seedy light of obfuscation and misdirection. She heard at least two reporters question the disingenuous comments of city, county and company officials, wondering on-air if the facts, when they were revealed, wouldn't indict the coal industry as irresponsible.

Although Allie had a tendency to agree with the speculation, she was also discouraged at the reckless assumptions they were broadcasting before the facts were in. She, on the other hand, was not satisfied with the lack of information being disseminated and, nothing more being forthcoming, decided to check out the disturbance at the mine.

Catching a stringer from the local paper who also compiled news for one of the radio stations and was headed out, she asked him where the mine was located. Tired and needing to get back to write reports for both bosses he gave her the directions, adding the information that Tyne Hill is the captive mine for Flat Butte.

"Captive mine? I don't think I've heard that before."

"That's when the mine supplies coal exclusively to a power plant. Tyne Hill and Flat Butte are owned by the same power company and it's the coal source for the plant," he said as he stopped near his rig, another ubiquitous Wyoming truck.

She thanked him for shedding a little more light on the industry. "Like they say, learn something new everyday," she said cheerily.

He climbed in and drove off while she bee-lined back to her own little car to find out what was really going on, because her gut was telling her Tyne Hill's "disturbance" wasn't unrelated to the conflagration that, after a couple hours of hot and thankless struggle, the firefighters were finally bringing under a semblance of control at Flat Butte.

Chapter 2

The decibel level down in the pit was always intense. Shovels operated ceaselessly on what resembled sixty-foot high steps that swept around the perimeter of the coal mine. A pair of 120-ton class machines worked continuously on these benches, removing the overburden to lade a fleet of trucks that moved the dirt directly to the reclamation area. It was a smooth operation of 'dig and fill' along the top of the pit and at each bench level, keeping the excavation area at a consistent acreage that virtually migrated across the plain over time. Visions of abandoned open pits where wealth had been stripped from the earth were long gone. The modern pit mining operation left a land without scars, a real home where buffalo would again roam and antelope still played.

On the floor of the mine, smaller shovels than those moving dirt at the higher levels excavated the coal. The noise of the gargantuan 3.5 million dollar haulers collecting the black fuel from the shovels' buckets and grinding up the road to dump their load, was a deterrent to normal conversation outside any of the machines' cabs. Inside those cabs, the operators were in constant contact with a dispatcher who managed procedures from his perch in the dispatch shack, a modular building overlooking the excavation.

Tonight, even though the rest of the landscape was swathed in darkness by the blackout, light plants were geared up, bathing the pit in brilliance, keeping operations running like clockwork.

No one in the pit heard the explosions that ripped apart one of the silos over a mile away. Thirty seconds later when the transfer point blew and one of the haulers down
in the pit jumped and came crashing down onto its side, tires exploding and the cargo bed twisting from the blast, everything came to a standstill.

"Mayday!" was transmitted by more than one shocked operator in sight of the haul truck's writhing demolition. Equipment shut down and radios buzzed with crackling voices taking command of the situation, curtly issuing orders and calling the mine EMTs to rush to duty.

The coal train had stopped in its tracks.

Finding her way to the Tyne Hill Coal Mine wasn't as difficult as Allie had thought. All she really had to do was follow the emergency vehicles' route down the highway to the turnoff which was clearly marked.

Just about two hours lagged between the incidents at the power plant and the mine, freeing up the ambulances that now roared past her when she turned onto the highway from Basin Road. Watching the vehicles speed away as she pulled out behind them made her wonder how "minor" the disturbance really was at the mine.

Trying hard not to overdrive the speed limit while hoping to keep the emergency vehicles in sight, Allie chased the procession for a few miles, having to pull over to the side twice while sheriff's vehicles and a fire crew flew by.

By the time she reached the juncture of Antler Road, where there was signage for three mines to the left, she'd decided that everyone who needed to be onsite had probably already arrived. That thought was a little comforting since the winding two lane road leading to Tyne Hill was narrow and edged by electrified fence, leaving very little space if she needed to make room for another emergency vehicle in a hurry. Her comfort zone shrank further as she read regular postings forbidding any stopping and warning of periodic blasting, although she hardly expected the latter to commence in the middle of the night. Then again, she didn't know anything about how a mine runs so it could be that the sounds heard from Flat Butte were something that had been scheduled in the normal scheme of things.

Right. Then why would there be a convoy of ambulances, police and fire trucks hauling ass to get to the scene. And why would the company PIO do a little shuck and jive after everyone was caught scrambling around in a "minor" panic. As she drove up to a spot in the road that widened out enough so she could view the expanse of the chaos around some silos flanking a rail spur, yellowish smoke billowing into the air and flames leaping from the base of some of the structures, all she could think was, *Oh my... I'd be panicked, too.*

There was a large open lot outside the guard shack and she parked her car on the periphery, keeping out of the way of the emergency crews that would need to get in and out without obstruction.

Fire trucks and EMS vans were parked haphazardly at the accident site with half a dozen sheriff's and state patrol cars wedged in for good measure. Scarlet, cobalt and amber lights strobed through the night sky, reflecting off the silos and surrounding buildings. Allie watched from a distance and was surprised to find that more press hadn't taken the initiative to show up, but she knew it wouldn't be long before a few of the die-hards and spotlight seekers arrived. The word would be out in no time that whatever had occurred at Tyne Hill was a lot more than a small disturbance, it was beginning to look like an incident of some proportion.

Scooping up the tools of her trade, she hurried down to get a better view of the wreckage, weaving among the myriad vehicles parked on the edges of what looked like a combat zone to her. The initial chaotic appearance of the scene was belied by the efficiency of the med techs and firemen performing their duties… wrestling with hoses, tamping down the fires, bandaging the more superficial wounds and loading up the seriously injured for quick transport to the hospital. A helicopter's blades steadily beat the air from the lawn that fronted what she assumed was the administration building. As she watched, she saw a stretcher loaded in by med techs, who then ran back to the mêlée, but still it didn't take off.

Within the brief amount of time that had elapsed since Allie's arrival, two ambulances were already loaded and beginning to move out and back up the hill toward town. A few moments later Allie's attention was diverted by the flashing lights of another ambulance, stenciled with the mine company logo, barreling down a road that descended from the opposite direction. It pulled up next to the mede-vac where another stretcher bearing one of the casualties was rapid-ly carried aboard and strapped in. The door was secured and the helo lifted off.

The panorama was ablaze with flickering light from the fire and the emergency vehicles, plus a hastily erected spotlight that illumi-nated the first responders as they worked. Zeroing in on a tight group of men and one woman conferring some ways apart from the relent-less commotion, Allie quickened her step.

Because she reached the scene so close on the heels of the emer-gency medical and fire teams, Allie slipped by the security which was still in the process of establishing boundaries. So it was with a dimension of surprise that the company officials reacted to her appearance in their midst.

Allie examined the people standing in a circle and decided to waylay the man to whom everyone else seemed to defer. He was of average height, with graying hair, steel-rimmed glasses and a tie that had been loosened and hung limply around the open collar of his oxford shirt. Colors were indeterminate in the yellow cast of the lamps suspended from the buildings that were connected together by, what Allie estimated to be, hundreds of feet of metal tubes meas-uring six feet in diameter. She'd never been to a mine before now and had no idea what she was looking at, though she recognized the black gravel strewing the ground around the structures – coal.

Allie approached the gathering with her usual undaunted stride that, more often than not, would get her through a half-closed door. At 5'5", drab blonde hair and clothes that had gone limp after a long day, she hardly looked like a bully, but when she smelled a story, a bloodhound would have had a tough time keeping up.

The clique widened to almost gawk at the woman whose attire was out of place for a mine. Wrinkled, khaki cotton slacks and a roomy vest that topped a butter yellow shirt. Her hair was pulled back with a kerchief which colors loosely matched the outfit and clunky, comfortable clogs encased her feet. It went against Allie's grain to make a fashion statement and today, she definitely did not.

The group wasn't noticing her apparel. Lines of concern, and wariness as they realized she was from the press, limned every face that turned her way. The man she had targeted with her gaze met her advance head-on and with an outstretched hand, something she hardly expected. There was no smile in his greeting, but considering the circumstances of the occasion, Allie hadn't anticipated one.

Clasping his hand, she introduced herself, softening her attack in response to the dire situation.

"I'm sorry but you shouldn't be here," he said. "I'm afraid that you haven't been given clearance and you can see that this is a dangerous area."

"Just doing my job, same as you, Mr.?"

"Rees Targhee, mine manager."

"Mr. Targhee. I just wanted to clear up some questions about the accident that seems to have occurred here tonight. I know that this is inconvenient but with the regional power outage caused by the problem at Flat Butte so rapidly followed by the accident here, I was hoping that you would be willing to comment on the subject." Allie was trying her damnedest to be accommodating rather than offensive, what with all the smoke and blood in the air. She'd keep browbeating as a fallback strategy if he was less than cooperative.

With a solemn expression he considered his words carefully before answering her.

"As to Flat Butte, the company hasn't determined the cause of the accident." He drew a breath and let it out slowly. "Here, we're just trying to sort out the injuries and the damage."

"Any idea what caused the, what was it? An explosion?" she asked.

"No, we have no idea what happened. It's going to take some time to comb through the debris to reach any conclusions."

Targhee seemed disinclined to elaborate so she prompted him. "I saw an ambulance come down from the road over there," and she pointed off to the side. "Can you tell me what's up there and what occurred?"

Seeing no reason to dodge the question, he said, "The actual excavation site is up that road but we have no information on the series of events other than a couple of our operators were injured and have been medevacked out to Gillette Medical Center."

"Can you tell me how many workers sustained injuries and how seriously they were hurt in the explosion?" She was trying to trip him up to, at least, admitting to there being an explosion. "Was there an accident involving blasting at the excavation? The ambulance coming from that direction would indicate that there was more than one incident."

"For safety reasons and in accordance with mining regulations, there is no blasting after sunset. So, in answer to your question, no, I can't tell you what caused the injuries. However, we have transported four people to the hospital for care. Other than that Miss," and he squinted at her press ID from the conference, "Maitland, I'm afraid I have no other comments at this time. We will be conducting a press briefing in about half an hour over by the guard house."

His attention was snatched by a mud-caked, white Dodge Ram 2500, company logo emblazoned on the driver's door, sliding to a rickety stop about twenty feet away from where they stood. A tall, rangy man jumped out and, eating up the yards in just a few paces, parked himself right between Targhee and Allie, giving her his back and making it clear that her chat was at an end. Before she could say anything, a security officer came up beside her and courteously, but determinedly, escorted her to the other side of a newly suspended length of caution tape where a few other members of the press had finally assembled.

The press briefing was a waste as far as Allie was concerned. She got almost no new information. The only thing the management *did* confirm was that two of the injuries were life-threatening and, in fact, another man was killed in what they never conceded was an explosion. She had pressed them to find out if there had been more than one blast at the mine. Despite all the evasion, the fact that injured people were taken from at least two sites over a mile distant from one another, they couldn't deny the fact that there had been more than one *incident*. They were loath to call it anything other than that or an accident, relying on elusive language in stating they wouldn't know anything positive until after the experts had thoroughly investigated the scene.

At which point she'd pushed them with, "You do mean *scenes*, plural. Correct?"

Targhee, who took the lead on the briefing, acceded to her assessment, but that was it. As he closed the proceeding down, the man who had cut off their earlier conversation stood off to Targhee's side, leveling an irritated gaze at her throughout most of the questioning.

The reporters were drifting back to their vehicles when she caught sight of the local newspaper rep she'd talked to at the power plant. Swinging in beside him, she asked whom the character was with the malevolent stare at Targhee's right.

He turned around to look back with her at the dispersing crowd, and he said, "You mean the guy in the plaid shirt and the rodeo buckle?"

Is that what that monstrosity is on his belt? "Yeah, that guy."

"That's Sawyer Aleman, he's the pit supervisor who was on duty tonight."

"Pit supervisor?"

"The manager who oversees the pit operations." He was dog-tired and wasn't about to describe the workings of a coal mine to the woman who he'd noted was from the Denver paper. The city girl was going to have to look it up on her own. "I've gotta get. This's been one helluva night."

"Sure has. Thanks for the info."

He tipped his head, bringing his hand up as if to touch the brim of a non-existent cowboy hat and loped off to his rig. Allie wondered at the quaintness of a small town and hurried off to her own car. She still had a lot of writing to do before the sun came up.

Energy Barons

Chapter 3

By the time Allie returned to her hotel room, it was almost 3 a.m. and power had been restored. It being too early to place any calls, she switched on the television finding a twenty-four hour news station, hoping to hear something about the power outage, and opened her laptop to write what story she had to make tomorrow's, *scratch that... today's* late edition.

Passing through the limited delegation of press corps at the mine as they had packed their gear to return to town, Allie had overheard a duo from the one news network that had bothered to make the trip, discussing how cut and dried this story was going to be. She'd perked her ears and lingered in the vicinity to listen because she couldn't see how any of it was that simple. The correspondent told her cameraman that the management was obviously hiding something. Everyone knew how dangerous coal-fueled power was and that she wouldn't need to infer anything... the facts would speak for themselves.

Facts? What facts? Allie had walked away ticked off both at the TV twit and because she hadn't been able to coax more out of Targhee when she had him all to herself. No one knew what caused the so-called accidents at two coal facilities in one county, or no one was talking. In fact, hardly any press had even shown up at the mine to investigate what, in her mind, were likely explosions and Targhee hadn't actually denied it. So far as Allie knew, coal didn't combust spontaneously, particularly if there isn't a concentration of inflammable gases – she'd have to look it up. To listen to the correspondent describe the incidents as probably being attributable to power company mismanagement amounted to journalistic misconduct in her book. It smacked of shoddy reporting, or rather, no reporting at all. Perturbed by the thought, she no longer wondered why the public didn't seem to trust the press anymore. *Clearly, because some of them* aren't *trustworthy.*

Allie had a tendency to agree that coal-fired power plants were dirty and in need of being phased out altogether in favor of more green technology, but she wasn't convinced that what occurred at either Flat Butte or Tyne Hill were really accidents that could be sloughed off on the inherent evil of coal power and the companies that produce it. She'd been on the scene before any of the other press and had witnessed the efficient manner in which the mine management handled the situation. From what she could see, everything was accomplished with professionalism and presence of mind. She'd been impressed and was determined to get the go ahead from Gleason to delve into the matter further. There was no way that she was going to let the fly-by-nights sweep a major story under the rug to suit a preconception, even if she shared the basic opinion. Reporting news takes the effort to find the facts, not assume or invent them. With that, she began typing her own story sticking to those facts, meager as they were.

Sawyer Aleman stayed at the mine through most of the night assisting the rest of management to close down operations and assess damage before the authorities had come in and cordoned off the areas. Because of the seriousness of the injuries and the death of the hauler's operator, it looked like it might become a homicide investigation. As soon as the police tape was strung, he was effectively banned from doing much of anything, so he tossed his things in his truck and drove over to the hospital. Going home wasn't an option.

There wasn't anything that he could do at the hospital, either. At first he badgered the admitting office until they told him where the PCC employees were. Two had been taken upstairs and were sedated in their rooms, one was still in surgery. The fourth man, the hauler operator, had been pronounced dead when the medevac arrived and was now laid out on a gurney in the morgue, awaiting the coroner to perform an autopsy.

What Sawyer didn't know was that two workers from Flat Butte had also been admitted and were resting in beds in the same ward as his co-workers. He found out about their injuries when he practically broadsided Rain Brightwater, his friend who was a tech at the new power plant.

Rain and Sawyer's association went all the way back to high school as rodeo competitors from different communities. The amicable rivalry became a partnership in later years, in and out of the arena. Now that Rain had moved from Sheridan down to Gillette, they spent more time hunting and riding the semi-pro rodeo circuit as team ropers. They made an interesting pair, the taller Sawyer with his military bearing and Rain with his black braid swinging across his back when he walked. Rain was a Crow whose parents had left the reservation for jobs in Sheridan when he and his sister were toddlers. The ribbing he received about his name had been unending as he was growing up and he was forever being asked if his sister was called 'Brook,' or something equally as foolish.

His parents hadn't planned it that way, but the name had stuck after his old auntie had caught him wandering by the river when he was four, an otter following him downstream for almost a mile. "Keeping his eye on you," she had told him when he was scolded for leaving the summer camp while the adults were getting things set-up in a sudden downpour. Auntie had found him and watched as the otter floated beside the little boy who alternately played in the stream or walked on the bank. After more than an hour of keeping out of sight, the otter had sensed her presence and paddled off. "He knew you were safe," she would say each time she recounted the story to him and others in later years.

Although Rain's Christian name, chosen by his pastor uncle, was Obadiah, servant of God, Auntie had always called him "Rain Otter" in deference to his guardian all those years ago. Rain had stuck when his given name was too much of a mouthful for the little boy.

When they nearly collided in the hall, Sawyer's stern expression lightened a bit at seeing his friend. They walked past the nurses' station as he asked for the skinny on the accident at the plant. Sawyer hadn't had time to look into any of the details and had heard almost nothing about the incident that had preceded those at the mine.

Rain had been at home when he'd received a call from his supervisor informing him of the problem, telling him that his shift had been suspended for the time being. The plant had to be closed down while the management contained the damage and assessed the operating status of the generating unit. Rain had been asked to be on call in case they needed him for anything, at which point he told his supervisor that he'd be at the hospital to check on his workmates. The men who had been hurt were working the shift that was Rain's usual schedule. He'd gotten the night off to visit with his sister who was in town for the Plains Conference and had skipped out early after presenting her paper on indigenous plains flora. She was a botanist at Iowa State University.

Sawyer dragged Rain with him as he checked on the two patients that were sleeping soundly, reassuring himself that they were all right. Then they went down to the cafeteria to get some coffee while Sawyer waited anxiously to hear about the other survivor who was still in surgery. He hadn't been so lucky.

They sat at a table next to one of the windows that overlooked a small patio, abandoned in the pre-dawn glimmer. Sawyer looked ragged from a night of securing the machinery, assisting management in damage control and even fending off a couple of press reps. He told Rain that they'd been fairly fortunate in not being inundated by the media, though the calls to the office had been gaining in number when he left, the reports finally reaching the bigger news outlets. He'd even fielded a few calls before the office staff was called in early to handle the phones.

"Ol' Rees couldn't have been happier than to see my backside leaving the office," he told Rain, leaning back in his chair to allow his long legs room to stretch out.

"I'll bet. They call *me* taciturn," said Rain. "You taught me the meaning of the word." He looked across the table at his companion, "Prob'ly couldn't wait to get you gone. A PR man, you're not. Unh-unh." He wagged his head slowly and sipped his coffee.

"Charm isn't my middle name? Guess I've been fooling myself all these years."

Rain just grunted in response.

They sat in silence for a while watching the dawn gain a foothold in the sky. It was hard for Sawyer to do nothing. As spare as his motions were, he was still a man who preferred action to inaction, confronting problems head-on rather than letting them stew. In this situation, there wasn't a thing he could do except wait. Wait on the doctors, wait on the investigators, wait on company management, and he didn't like to wait. He ran both hands through his almost ebony hair that made the shorter strands on his crown stand on end, adding to his grim appearance.

Rain looked over at him. "Keep that up and the nurses will run the other direction in fright, man."

"Huh, what?" Sawyer came out of the depths of his reverie, wondering what he could have done, what he should have seen that would have prevented the accidents.

"Your face, your hair. You look like a zombie with a bad 'doo. Why don't you go home and get some sleep."

"After Webb comes out of surgery," he sat forward at the table and hunched over the lukewarm, vending machine coffee. "I wouldn't be able to sleep anyway until I know what the prognosis is."

"Will they tell you?" Always the pragmatist, Rain questioned how much information the doctors would give non-family members.

"His parents and sister are upstairs in the waiting room. I'll find out one way or the other." Sawyer looked at his watch. "They may have news by now." He got up, threw the paper cup into the trash and started out the door. Turning back to Rain, he asked, "You coming?"

Pulling his solid frame out of the plastic molded chair, Rain said, "Why not. The chairs upstairs are cushier."

Putting the finishing touches on the story, Allie's cell rang. Checking the LCD readout, she saw that it was Aunt Ell.

"Aren't we the early bird today," Allie croaked. She was exhausted after pulling an all-nighter with nothing but coffee from the miniscule brewer in her hotel room to prop her up.

"I knew you'd be up since all that action was happening right under your nose. What did they do about that dull conference you were covering? Did they let the bison out of their pens?" Allie was Ellis Akkerman's namesake and she talked more to her mother's sister, Ell, than she did her parents. Her folks weren't all that interested in the day-to-day doings of a gadabout reporter despite their support of her career choice. As solid citizens sticking to their Midwest values in suburban Illinois, they saw Allie's chasing stories as an outgrowth of her rebellious nature. Ell was a more adventuresome character, deciding in her youth to pack up everything and head off to the Big Apple. A career on the Great White Way didn't pan out but computing did. As a senior manager of the information technology department at a multi-national law firm, Ell always found Allie to have a ready ear when the legal eagles couldn't figure out where they'd just sent some important brief, only to have it disappear into the ether. It was still early, even for her, and she was calling from home, nursing her own mug of coffee.

"They canned it. No power and the emergencies at the power plant and the mine kind of trumped their plans. Some of the speakers for the morning session are unavailable now, anyway. City and county officials. Like that." Allie yawned.

"Well, I had to call because I caught the early reports coming out of Washington and my backyard. Flipping through the channels and, lo and behold, the first thing I see are your buddies, the most rabid spokesmen for climate change are busy leading the charge against Plains Coal Company."

"And you are talking about…?"

"You know, my two favorite cartoon characters, Theo Kraegen and Rone Haggerty," Ell filled in.

"What could they possibly have to say about the owner of Flat Butte and Tyne Hill? No one even really knows what happened last night and *I* was there."

"Like that ever stopped these guys from opening their mouths. If there's anything to do with oil or coal they waste no time in hopping on their soapbox about the evils of the energy industry," said Ell.

"No, the evils of black energy as opposed to the green kind."

"Now that's an interesting way of phrasing it. But I'd expect as much from one of their acolytes," she laughed.

"I'm hardly an acolyte. Just think that we need to get environmentally sound energy sources up and running."

"Ha! Now you sound like *those* jackasses. Listen to them your-self," and she told Allie what channel to tune in.

Allie followed direction, just a little miffed at the interruption, but she needed to hear what two of the most outspoken global warm-ing advocates were saying about the incidents in Wyoming.

Kraegen didn't disappoint. As an environmental attorney, the son of a well-loved liberal governor who died at the height of his career, Kraegen was the founder of EcoEarth Legal Center, largest of the environmental lobbies in D.C., and always at the forefront of chal-lenging environmental exploitation. He also had his own weekly talk show on NPR where he regularly took environmental abusers – that's what he called them – to task. At the moment Kraegen was excoriating Plains Coal Company for endangering the environment with poor business practices to anyone who would listen. The injured workers were barely mentioned in passing, other than as vic-tims, during his incendiary attack on PCC management.

"You'd think a lawyer would know better than to level unsub-stantiated charges like that," said Ell. "Could get himself in trouble. Wait. What was I thinking? The ACLU and the press will back him up a hundred percent. Must be nice to have such a vaunted opinion, particularly of himself."

Sometimes Ell's right-wing diatribes would get on Allie's nerves, but she held with her aunt's right to express herself, howev-er much Allie might disagree.

Allie then switched to another channel only to hear Haggerty lit-erally mimic Kraegen's call for a halt to using dirty coal to generate power as a hazard to the environment and the earth as a whole. Ell was right, though. The dynamic duo had wasted no time in depict-ing Plains Coal Company as a villain that would strip the earth bare in the name of making a buck. Between the ex-congressman/attor-ney and Haggerty, the nominee for U.S. ambassador to the United Nations, it was difficult to tell who was leading whom in the call to shut down the coal industry in favor of alternative technology. Technology that, even by Allie's left-leaning standards, hadn't yet been proven to be adequate for the job. Flipping back and forth between the two stations, Allie heard both of them segue into lauding the cap and trade legislation Congress was considering.

Ell must have been reading Allie's mind, when she said, "That's all well and good to want to save the planet from greenhouse gas overload, but what do they plan on replacing the power plants with? Their own hot air?"

Chapter 4

The dark blue compact car would have blended into the gloom surrounding it except for the headlights that swung back and forth across the road as the driver recklessly took the curves too fast as he descended the west side of the Big Horn Mountains. The trace of light that heralded the coming dawn was inadequate to negotiate the turns without risk, particularly at the speed the tow-headed driver insisted on goading the engine.

With only the console dimly illuminating the car's interior, the eager driver couldn't see the sour expression on his passenger's face. He was aggravated with the blond man's impatience to reach their destination and his overdriving the twisting alpine route.

After taking one hairpin turn too fast and nearly sending the vehicle over the cliff, the passenger gripped the 'oh shit' bar, and told the driver to pull over in a voice that was not to be ignored.

The blond man, who seemed barely more than a boy with the halo of yellow curls framing his face, smirked at his passenger and started to slow for a wide turnout ahead that was partially obscured by tall pines and undergrowth.

"What's the problem?"

"You must stop the car," and he bent over, covering his mouth as if to make sure he wouldn't puke on the dashboard while holding his other hand at his stomach.

Approaching the turnout, the driver slowed and started laughing, giving the other man crap for being mountain-bred and not being able to handle a few bends in the road.

"Just make sure you don't spew in the car," he said as he whipped into a semi-circular area, braked hard kicking up gravel, and shoved the gearshift into park, practically giving his buddy whiplash. The passenger flung open his door and ran stumbling to the edge of the turnout, under a canopy of trees that obscured his form from the road.

The blond hadn't yet had enough fun taunting him and followed with a smug air, continuing his jeering commentary along the way. As he came within ten feet of the motion sick man who was doubled over as if to vomit, he was stopped dead in his tracks as the passenger suddenly whipped around to face his mocker.

"I thought you were gonna puke, man," a cocky grin in place and hands on his hips.

"No, you were correct about growing up in the mountains. A few switchback turns are not about to make me lose my stomach contents." He spoke with a singsong accent overlaid by the clear enunciation of British English.

Just then the driver's face blanched as he noticed a gun in his companion's hand.

"What's that for? You can't be that thin-skinned about a little ribbing," he said, a slight tremor creeping into his voice.

"Hardly. I have had to endure far worse epithets from some of your fellow countrymen." He waved the gun to the right of the driver's head. "Turn around and put your hands on your head." He then directed the blond to stand still as he walked to the car and tuned off the headlights and the ignition, closed the door to douse the interior lamp, all the while keeping the gun trained on the driver. "Walk to your right until you can see over the edge. Your foolhardy actions are what have made this necessary."

"What the hell are you talking about?" The young man was nearing panic and trying to keep a nonchalant attitude but his voice was betraying him. "Quit messing around. We still have work to do. That's where we're going, to meet about the next job."

"You think that I do not know what plans are prepared, or to what destination you are driving? You are no longer an essential element. In fact, my friend, you have become a liability. Stop there."

Without another thought and before the blond could protest further, he dispatched the young driver with a shot to the back that targeted the heart. As the driver fell forward, and barely hit the ground, the passenger walked over and plugged another bullet into the back of the blond's head, assuring his execution.

Checking around quickly to verify that the whole episode had occurred without witnesses, the man pushed the body over the edge of the precipice. He watched it tumble down the slope, rolling through the scree, leaving streaks of blood among the sharp rocks that were just barely visible in the pre-dawn glow. He was satisfied when it came to rest thirty feet down, lodging almost imperceptibly in the bracken that wrapped the trunks of a stand of trees.

Securing the gun in his waistband behind his back, he broke off a branch of a sapling and scrubbed the ground where the body had been. He then used it to sweep a layer of dead leaves and pine needles over the blood that had soaked into the ground, finally placing the branch across the disturbed earth as if to mark where the fallen lay, awaiting the certain arrival of scavengers.

The sun was finally up and Allie, after catching a quick hour's nap, slipped through the shower, put on clean clothes and went in search of some breakfast and fresh coffee before reading through her story one last time.

Savoring the steaming brew that somehow tasted better than what the tiny coffeemaker in her room had produced, she made a last quick correction and e-mailed her copy to the paper. Minutes later she was on the phone arguing with Gleason who was giving her a hard time about wanting to stay in Gillette to follow the story.

"So far as I can see, there *is* no story, just a couple of accidents at local power plants and the lights were off for a few hours," he grumbled from his desk. It was early and he was finally settled in with his own black sludge that somehow never tasted fresh no matter who made it or when. This newsroom coffee could rival bitter cop coffee anywhere, in his opinion, and he'd tasted plenty in his time. He couldn't light up like he used to before all the smoking bans either, and he was already jonesing for some nicotine, adding to his foul disposition. "CNN is saying that it was probably some internal accident connected to management problems."

"Yeah, well CNN has it *wrong*," she spit back. "I was there long before any of those prima donnas bothered to waltz down the hill.

By then all the ambulances and the medevac were long gone and it just looked like some kind of fire at the storage silos. The mine manager was close-lipped, but I think it was because there's a whole lot more to what happened out there. *And*, there was more than one *inci-dent*, to use their terminology, and one man died."

"Hey, people die in accidents all the time, that doesn't make it news." He just wanted to get outside for a smoke. All his attempts to quit over the years had been futile. Even his wife had given up and set-up a smoking area in the backyard for him. She just wouldn't allow him to breathe fire around the grandbabies now that they had a couple.

"Look, Gleason, I almost had an admission that these were explosions and we know the so-called accident at the power plant *was* an explosion. Coal doesn't just blow-up from what I can find. It's not as volatile as, say, natural gas." She slowed down and took a breath. "There's something strange here. Let me stay and check it out. One more night should do it and I'll know what's what."

He hemmed and hawed on the line.

"You know how flighty those TV angels are. This is an opportunity to re-assert the importance of daily ink, airing sound bites for the shallow entertainment they are and give the people some *real* reporting."

"I thought the pep talks were *my* job," he sighed, knowing she wouldn't back down and even with all the harassment he gave her, he trusted her news instinct. So saying, Gleason finally relented and told her she'd better not come back empty-handed.

"If there's a story, and I'd bet next month's salary there is, I'll get it."

"You'd better, because that salary is tenuous these days."

While she was loading her nylon satchel back up with everything she'd dumped on the desk in order to write the article, Allie called the power plant to get a comment on the accident of the night before.

Flat Butte administration channeled all the inquiries to the PIO she'd seen there during all the hullabaloo, and she wasn't particularly forthcoming with anything more than what Allie had already surmised. When Allie asked about coming over to get a couple photos of the aftermath, she was told flatly that "the property had been closed to all outside traffic and visitors, only law enforcement and employees were allowed on the premises." At which point Allie asked if the power station was considered a crime scene and the information officer answered with the ever-popular, "No comment." She didn't bother with any pleasantries before abruptly cutting the connection.

"Well, that was rude," Allie said to the dead phone in her hands. The experience made the decision for her. She wasn't going to bother with a call to the mine, she'd just show up and let them escort her off the grounds if they deemed her presence to be a nuisance.

She grabbed her bag with one hand and clomped out the door with car keys at the ready.

Twenty minutes later, Allie was closing her car door and slinging the strap of the portfolio over her shoulder. She already had her little tape player in her pocket where she could easily punch the play button in case she got close enough to get a good quote.

Marching past the guardhouse while the gatekeeper was leaning out of the window on the other side of the shack, yakking with a company security officer who was finally going home after an interminable night, Allie gave thanks for her good fortune. It was pretty obvious to her that the two were exhausted and since the press had made such a pathetic showing earlier, the woman at the window didn't expect any of them to make a return appearance.

Good for me, thought Allie as she passed a huge area that was roped off with yellow caution tape, and pulled the door to the administration building open wide enough to slip through.

Unfortunately, she was greeted with a droopy-eyed woman in her sixties who, despite being fried by hours of handling unwelcome phone calls, was not going to be a pushover.

The woman was short and stout with close-cropped gray hair that was showing signs of having been ravaged by the periodic raking of nervy fingers. She was tired but not vulnerable to any onslaught by worried family, who she handled with kid gloves, or the unwelcome inquiries of the press which she'd been fending off for hours.

Lifting her eyes to meet Allie's, the receptionist's guard immediately went up along with her carefully painted eyebrows that were also beginning to show wear and tear.

Allie pasted her most obsequious smile on her lips and greeted the woman with an amiable, "Good morning, ma'am."

Not to be taken in by genialities, the seasoned front desk matron knew the enemy when she saw it.

"Mornin' back at ya, dear. What can I do for you?" she asked Allie while giving her a wary once over.

"Is Mr. Targhee here?"

"No, I'm afraid you missed him by about half an hour. Is there anything I might help you with?"

"I hope so," Allie paused with a slight smile. She didn't want to spook the older woman with a heavy-handed approach that would garner her nothing. "I was here during all the commotion last night and wanted to get some information about what happened. When I left, things were still unsettled and I thought management would be able to clarify some details about the incidents, now that everything is calmed down a little."

The woman sat back and crossed her arms over her ample bosom. "Look honey, I'm not really sure how you got past the gatehouse. As you can see, everything is under control and the management is not available for comment." She gave Allie a halfhearted smile that clearly stated her intention to say nothing. "All communication with the press, and I assume that you are with the press, is being handled through official channels. And, as you must know, that does not include the office help."

Allie knew full well that this woman was much more than 'office help' but she also could see that no real information was going to be forthcoming from the solid little woman parked in front of her. She mentally shrugged and decided to give it one last effort.

"Can you at least tell me how much damage the operation sustained, if it's been shut down and, if so, for how long?"

"I'm afraid not."

"I know that a few people suffered injury last night. Can you tell me how many people were treated and how they're doing now?" Allie thought perhaps she could eek out something if she used a human-interest angle.

"I'm sorry but we can't say anything about that until all of the families have been notified. As you can see, my hands are tied and I can't be any help to you."

Allie sighed. She was as tired as the woman who sat before her, if not more so with nothing but a catnap in the last twenty-four hours.

"If I may, I'd like to leave my card for Mr. Targhee and I'll get in touch with him later."

The receptionist took the proffered card and read the name. "The Post, huh? Well, I'll give it to Mr. Targhee but I wouldn't hold my breath if I were you."

"That much I got. Thanks anyway." Allie trudged out the door, deflated and feeling ready for some real sleep. Unfortunately, she knew that would have to wait until later, much later.

Being pretty much kicked out of the office with nothing to show for her effort, Allie tossed her satchel on the passenger seat and left the mine without a second thought. She was already on to what she *could* do, which was go over to the hospital to see if she could hunt up any information there.

This time she was a little bit luckier. As she walked into the hospital lobby she overheard the receptionist consoling an elderly couple with the knowledge that their son was doing okay after the mine accident. Allie slowed her step in order to catch as much as she could of the conversation. As she bent over a coffee table, picked up a magazine and feigned leafing through it, she was rewarded with the information she needed. The receptionist gave the couple directions to the room that their son occupied.

Without waiting for the parents to finish their chat, Allie replaced the magazine and went to the elevator, punching the 'up' button. When she entered the car, the two still hadn't left the desk so she felt justified in closing the door and allowing the car to ascend.

Exiting, she looked around to see the nurses' station to the right and some activity down the hall. She felt just the slightest bit ghoulish as she checked the room numbers to find the one occupied by the couple's son. Before she could locate the room, however, she found herself confronted by a slightly familiar figure... the man that the local reporter had identified as Sawyer Aleman.

Allie was pretty good with names and she recalled his without any trouble. The real trouble was that he also recognized her and managed to block her forward progress with his bulk and an expression of uncompromising scorn, which didn't add much to his features that, under other circumstances, she might consider attractive.

She noticed that he was still in the same clothes that he'd worn the night before. A definite sign that he hadn't been home yet, indicating he was probably cranky on top of being generally rude. If rudeness were a deterrent to Allie, she was in the wrong business so she countered with the easiest move and attempted to sidestep him.

Aleman extended his arm as if to bar her way. She wasn't about to push it aside and instead, looked directly into his disapproving eyes.

"Excuse me."

"I doubt there could possibly be any excuse for you to be here," he said, not removing his arm.

"Excuse *me*?" she responded. "*You're* blocking my way, sir," and she attempted to go under his arm.

He just lowered the hurdle and said, "I'm aware of that."

"Do you have a problem?" She stood with her feet apart, arms akimbo and glared right back at him.

"I do with press vultures who attempt to accost sick men in a hospital ward."

"You must be misinformed. I have no intention of accosting anyone, though the same could not be said for yourself." She attempted to go around him again and he just moved into her way.

"Then what are you doing here?"

"My job. Looking for answers and since you are hindering me from talking to anyone else here as self-appointed security, perhaps *you* want to perform that duty." Allie wasn't about to back down, no matter his size and menacing stance.

He relaxed slightly and barked a laugh. "You are persistent." He gestured for her to follow him back down the hall, away from the doorway of one of his fellow workers. He turned around to face her.

"Look, lady. I know you think you need to talk to one of the men down the hall or maybe even their families, but they are hardly in any condition to deal with questions right now," and be bent over and got right in her face. "Particularly from the press."

Not to be put off, she said, "Well, what about you then? You're the pit supervisor, you must know something. At the least, you can tell me if your buddies are going to be okay. I'd like to be able to report that they will recover from their injuries."

He straightened up and swiped a hand around his eyes, fatigue and worry ringing them.

"I can't tell you anything other than the fact that some good men lost their lives last night and these men," he waved his hand back toward the hall, "are my crew members and have a struggle ahead of them. The company will be releasing information at the appropriate time," and his eyes became hard again as he riveted her gaze. "Which is not now."

She placed her hands back on her hips and stared him down. "I am not here out of morbid fascination with survivors of an explosion," at which words his hazel eyes narrowed even more. "... Or whatever happened at the mine." She back-peddled in an effort to get him to back off too. "I'm simply attempting to get a little information to the public. I'm sorry if that offends you."

He sighed and looked down his nose at her. "It does offend me, Ms...."

"Maitland. Allie Maitland from the Denver Post."

"I know where you're from, and for now you're going to have to be satisfied with the fact that men are fighting for their lives and no one is in any condition to entertain your questions. Okay?"

"Okay. I'll disappear if you will at least give me a little information yourself." She stood her ground and waited.

"Will you go away, then?"

"I will leave you to your guard duty for today, yes."

He conceded and said, "No guarantees and no quotes."

She hesitated then shrugged, figuring something was better than nothing.

"Let's start here. This morning while I was trying to do a little research, I caught a number of on-air comments by Kraegen and Haggerty, basically lambasting the coal industry and laying these disast… uh, occurrences, we'll call them," and she looked into his steely eyes trying to win him back with the hint of a smile, "at the feet of Plains Coal Company as being derelict in their duties to provide a safe work environment. Or a safe environment, for that matter. Do you have anything to say regarding their take on the situation?"

To her surprise, he threw back his head and laughed harshly at the ceiling, which garnered him a look of dismay from the nurse entering data into the station's computer.

Allie kept her mouth shut and waited for him to elaborate.

He was quiet for a moment and then looked down his nose at her once again. "I can't imagine why anyone would take them seriously. Haggerty and Kraegen are both primarily political opportunists who have no working knowledge of the coal industry despite however much they disparage it. Right now, coal supplies roughly fifty percent of this country's energy and it's an abundant resource. With the new technology that has been employed in both mining and generating power, it's also one of the most efficient and clean burning fuels we have available. The impression that politicians and environmental lobbyists give to *you people*," he made his contempt for the press obvious, "is that the coal industry is filthy, wastes resources and is deadly to the atmosphere. It is none of the above and science bears that out."

"That's not what I've read over the years. The scientific consensus disavows that, saying quite the opposite and that we are facing a crisis of global warming." Allie stuck her chin out in an almost combative pose, which seemed to amuse Aleman.

"Lady, you need to consult news sources other than the New York Times, CNN and your own rag." He zeroed in on her widening blue eyes, "If you'd look up Sir Monckton's testimony to Congress, the petition that is signed by more than 32,000 climate experts *dis* -

avowing the ludicrous idea of global warming and anthropogenic, i.e. human-caused, carbon dioxide overload in the atmosphere, your concept of consensus would dissipate into the thin air that it is." He could see her digging in her heels and said. "You'll swallow whatever the environmental *oracles* and frankly, outright crazies have to say but won't expend an ounce of energy to uncover the facts right under your nose. You're a reporter, get your due diligence in gear and *really* investigate. You'll see that it isn't the coal industry that's blowing smoke up your, uh, dress."

She huffed out her breath to calm down. Ticked as she was, she didn't want to lose him now. "Okay, so if these guys are so off-base, what did happen out there... at the plant and the mine? You're telling me that the operations are safe and yet there was an explosion at Flat Butte," she looked at him pointedly. "That was admitted. But what about the mine? Two incidents, and don't deny that, either. What caused the accidents?"

Aleman sighed with utter exhaustion, at this point he just wanted her to go away. "We don't know what happened at the mine, but I can tell you that it wasn't due to any negligence on the part of our crews. They know their jobs and they perform them professionally. All I can tell you is that whatever the cause was for the accidents, as you so graciously put it, it wasn't my guys. The circumstances point to something else altogether."

"What circumstances?"

He just ignored the question and began to walk away.

"Then who's responsible?"

"Hell if I know. You're going to have to wait for the investigation results same as the rest of us."

Seeing that she wasn't going to get any more from him, she asked one last touchy question. "Can you confirm how many people lost their lives at the mine and at Flat Butte, because I'm certain you are well aware of those facts."

"Two men died at Flat Butte and one of my operators is gone." He looked down at her for the last time, this time with a hint of pleading seeping through from the back of his eyes.

"Good enough, Mr. Aleman. Go home and get some rest. I'm as good as my word." She hitched her portfolio back onto her shoulder and left him leaning back against the wall, chin sinking in weary sorrow.

It was still long before noon and Allie made one last stop, the sheriff's office.

Since she had been waylaid at every turn, it made sense to try the normal channels and see if they were finally releasing any information. Pulling into the parking lot, Allie dropped her head back onto the headrest for a few brief seconds before climbing out of her little compact, legs leaden with the same fatigue she had seen etched in Aleman's face.

Deliberately placing her satchel on her shoulder once again, she made the short trek to the glass doors and swung them open with a spark of hope that *someone* would give her a comment she could use.

For once, she was in the right place at the right time. The sheriff himself was standing at the receptionary going over some notes with the young woman manning the desk. Allie came up to the desk and, holding out her hand, introduced herself to the sheriff who looked a little sheepish for having been caught in the open. Instead of making a hasty retreat though, he took her hand and greeted her solemnly.

"What can I do for you, Ms. Maitland?"

"I'm just looking for a few comments about the incidents that occurred at the Flat Butte Station and Tyne Hill." She purposefully left the subject open to see how he'd field it.

"There's not much that I can tell you at this time. The investigation in both locations is ongoing, as you must know."

"Well, perhaps you can confirm the number of casualties and injured at both places."

"I don't suppose that's a problem. Two workers died at the Flat Butte scene and one man died at Tyne Hill."

Allie continued to pepper him with questions until she had gleaned enough facts to do a follow-up story. The problem was that everything he told her only made her question more the circumstances of the confirmed explosion at the power station and implied blasts at the mine. After a few minutes he cut the interview short, *if you could call it that, he didn't give me a thing to work with,* she thought as he was making his escape back to his office. The sheriff did, however, tell Allie as he turned his back on her that she would be informed when a press conference was scheduled.

"Come back then."

Right. All I have to do is convince Gleason.

Chapter 5

Dialysis is not an option for people suffering kidney failure, it's a necessity of life. When the blood's cleaning agent shuts down and refuses to work, outside help must be called in to rescue the patient, to keep her system operating. She can feed the body's cells the nutrients it needs but if the garbage collector goes on strike, the body's streets and highways become so choked with detritus that, after a while, all traffic stops. That's when dialysis comes to the rescue. As the street-sweeper, it cleans the blood's accumulation of waste so the patient can carry on about her business, happily functioning despite the non-working organs that just seem to be taking up space.

Kara Lysander looked like the average twelve-year-old and, under normal circumstances, she'd be star center of the middle school's basketball team. At least that's what her mother saw for her future when she first held the tiny baby in her hands at Kara's birth. A girl-child to follow in her mother's footsteps, tall and lithe and running like the wind.

It was not to be.

Years of unexplained health problems continually cropping up baffled the physicians at the local health care center, the only one that was available to the family on the reservation. It's not that they didn't do their best to diagnose the cause of the symptoms, it's simply that the facility was always severely under-funded, under-supplied and understaffed, and their pleas for assistance went unheard by the government bureaucracies in D.C. Needed tests were refused due to limited clinic allocations, and the physicians' hands were tied by the miles of red tape required by every government agency, from Indian Health Services up the food chain to the Department of Health and Human Services and ultimately, the House Energy and Commerce subcommittee that crafts the budgeting legislation.

When the appropriate and expensive testing was finally approved and performed, at the age of ten Kara was saddled not only with the knowledge of being afflicted by juvenile diabetes, but the added diagnosis of failing kidneys resultant from not recognizing and treating the disease earlier.

Kara's future and her healthcare had just taken a drastic turn. Insulin injections, diet control and regular dialysis to help her renal system do its job. A rare blood type and the fact that no family member was a match diminished her chances of a kidney transplant to nil. Maybe Kara wasn't going to be making jump shots in the championship game or racing her older brothers across the ripe hayfields and down to the babbling creek, but she was given a chance to accomplish something great in this life because of dialysis. At least, that was the plan.

The greatest problem faced by the Lysanders in their struggle to provide proper and adequate care for their daughter, was the circumstance of their location, the little town of Parker, Wyoming. They had moved off the reservation years before for work that offered wages sufficient to handle all the added costs, and good jobs were scarce on the Montana-Wyoming border. They'd settled into a pleasant town where they were surrounded by good folks, close to good schools and steady work for Kara's father, Key, but it was hours away from a dialysis center and costs for travel had shot straight to the moon over the past year. Unfortunately Key Lysander's income had not kept abreast of the climbing gas prices. The plummeting economy and the pressure placed on the coal industry to incorporate hugely expensive reforms (Key worked at a local coal mining operation), all contributed to the Lysanders finding themselves trapped. Trapped by circumstances where Key couldn't locate a job nearer a dialysis center, nor could they afford the thrice-weekly trips to Sheridan for treatment.

It had taken a year of diligent badgering and non-stop paper chasing by a newly resettled attorney, a fugitive from the meat grinder of corporate law as practiced in New York, to corner the DHHS. The cogs of bureaucracy turn at a devastatingly slow rate, one that can leave patients on their deathbeds or in a silk-lined casket by the time a dire need is recognized, let alone addressed.

Yancy Collings was a bruiser from the city and it wasn't in her nature to let form-shuffling appointees off the hook. Kara was her client and Yancy never let a case go without resolution, resolution that suited her conscience, which was why corporate law was no longer a feasible alternative for the woman. It actually never had been. It was just a waystation on the journey that landed her in the Billings office of the Constitutional Legal Fund where she finally felt she was doing what she was meant to do… advocate for a cause.

Having grown up in Boston and graduated from an Ivy League school, Yancy was raised with the idea that most people are victimized somehow and somewhere in their lives. She took it upon herself to become a swordbearer for those who required protection from the black chasm of corporate greed. How she leapt from the equalization bastion of the ACLU to EcoEarth, to a brief stint in corporate law in NYC was a sideways move, even in her own mind. If it hadn't been for the cronyism that she saw running rampant among the smug elitists at all the so-called social justice offices, she might have stayed buried there for years. Her bosses had been A-1 a-holes, in her opinion, who weren't interested in justice but in self-aggrandizing posturing as faux white knights. More like wolves in sheep's clothing, she'd told herself. In fact, the majority of the legal crew she'd encountered in any of those offices was equally as mendacious. To this day she couldn't understand how she had stomached the frauds for so long.

The antithesis to fighting for victims, invented ones at best, was to move to NYC and school with the corporate sharks. Oddly enough, the transition wasn't all that traumatic… turned out they all had dorsal fins and did nothing but swim in prey-rich waters, feeding indiscriminately. From her perspective, the feudalistic attitude of nobility had infested both worlds of legal practice and she wanted none of either.

Next step? Billings and protecting real people seeking real justice, not "fairness."

The results of Yancy and the Lysanders' search for a little justice were that Kara now had a home dialysis unit and the regular care of a trained nurse who made periodic visits to their home. A positive outcome from pretty much every angle, to Yancy's way of thinking, and far more rewarding than pleading to save one-eyed newts or "freedom fighters" from reaping their just desserts, i.e. jail time.

Training was intensive for both parents and a couple of relatives to learn how to use the machine dialysis unit. Then the cost to install reverse osmosis, water softeners, carbon tanks and the like in order to remove chlorine and purify the water source was close to prohibitive, but the family mortgaged everything they could to cover it.

The other choices weren't really choices at all when taking into account a twelve-year-old girl's quality of life. Peritoneal dialysis had to be done two-hours, four times a day, every day, seven days a week and involved the practically permanent and unfashionable accoutrement of a bag of solution connected to an abdominal catheter, the kiss of death for a pre-teen's social life. Her parents knew the child would end up burrowing, invoking self-imprisonment and becoming a virtual hermit. The nighttime administration of dialysis through a portable unit that was attached for eight hours at a time also would be a difficult adjustment for any child. The travel to a dialysis center was unaffordable and the weather extremes were a hazard with possible road closures to be confronted in the winter. So the Lysanders felt they had no recourse left except to go the whole nine yards and install a mechanized unit for Kara so she could have the freedom to enjoy what was left of her childhood.

Lately, Yancy had been working with the Lysanders on another aspect of their dilemma. Now that the unit had finally been installed and all the components and family trainees passed by the dialysis nurse and nephrologist to guarantee proper care, there loomed another problem on the horizon, one that they hadn't fully anticipated.

Power.

Wyoming is one of the states that not only mines the coal that feeds fifty percent of the country's power providers, but it is dependent on that same coal for its own energy supply. The plant that generated power for the sector where the Lysanders live was considered decrepit and being phased out, denied licensing by the EPA for failing to meet new CO_2 emission standards. The new plant had just come online a few weeks before but it still wasn't sufficient enough to provide full power for the area until the second generating unit could be fired up. That would not be for another four to six months and in the meantime, the rural areas were subject to rolling blackouts and brownouts. What they soon discovered was that not all of the power cutbacks were scheduled far enough in advance for the Lysanders to effectively plan the dialysis times for Kara. So, a back-up power system had been ordered and was in the process of being connected into the house's electrical system. Since it was a cursory set-up, Yancy was working hard for a fix.

The fix was in the form of a petition to the EPA to reopen the old plant until such time as the new plant could fully absorb the region-al electrical supply load. Yancy's follow-up on its submission gar-nered the answer from the bloated bureaucracy she'd dreaded but expected: it hadn't been received and must be resubmitted. And so she did with dispatch.

The next round of responses consisted of a "Notice of Extension of Time," meaning they intended to hand-sit for at least six months, assuming the problem would evaporate through frustration. The offi-cial statement was "this additional time is required to review your petition and determine if a hearing is warranted." The EPA was exercising its "right to such an extension of time."

Fuming at the agency's gall only fed her fervor for swift retalia-tion. Kara's situation was precarious at best, life-threatening at worst and Yancy was poised for battle on her behalf.

Yancy's time spent swimming in shark-infested waters had been well spent. She'd excelled in learning the game's rules, and precise-ly how to turn them to her advantage. Knowing the exact types of lawyers that were employed at agencies like the EPA – lazy – she drew upon those bitter lessons to expedite the issue that agency attorneys were determined to let die a slow death. She was resolute that if there was any death in the offing, it was not going to be Kara's.

A letter thanking them for the "permission to sue" was composed and bound together with a "Request for Immediate Consideration" attached to Form SF-95 Claim for Injury or Damage. She'd smiled when she'd posted the packet, knowing that denial of hearing or fail-ure to act and expedite the administrative process would be equiva-lent to the federal government granting that very permission to sue.

Yancy used the EPA's extension for time against them by noting within the correspondence that, "the emotional distress caused by the death of Kara Lysander would amount to a wrongful death that the agency had within their power to prevent." By using the threat of a wrongful death suit as incentive to capture the ear of a real decision-maker, Yancy was pulling every string to speed-up the process. She was sure that action would be forthcoming faster than the EPA had originally planned. A good thing too, because Kara couldn't wait on their foibles, time was of the essence.

As if Yancy or the Lysanders needed any reminding of the risks confronting Kara, the lights went out. Again.

This time it was a regional power outage that had already lasted for more than 12 hours in Parker. And it was causing real concern for the family. They'd checked with Sheridan and they were having problems of their own. Kara's parents were already on tenterhooks living under the realization that they had no control over the intermittent power supply. As the time approached when their daughter would need to be dialyzed and still no power was available, they decided to take no chances and follow the advice of the director of the Sheridan dialysis center. They buckled Kara into the old Dodge and left for Billings.

Chapter 6

The dark blue compact rambled up the rutted gravel drive and came to rest near a rustic cabin that stood more than a mile back from the cut-off road. Quite a ways off the beaten track, it was sheltered by the dense boughs of tall pines. The driver's door opened and the former passenger swung his legs out, stood up and stretched. As he did so he could hear the breeze soughing softly as it filtered through the trees' needles twenty feet overhead. The drive over made him think of the valleys of his home where dense forests still climbed the knees of soaring mountains that framed a blue horizon. He scrubbed his hands through his dark and disheveled hair and scratched his chin through two days growth of black beard.

Turning at the sound of the front door swinging open, he saw his contact framed by the cabin's interior shadow. An older man, easily twice his own age, time warped in plaid shirt, suspenders and jeans, looked ready to stable the horses rather than garage a new-fangled horseless carriage.

Leaving the door open, the man walked out to greet his guest, a slightly puzzled expression on his face. He looked through the windows of the car noting its emptiness aside from a few personal items and a sleeping bag.

"Where's the other one?" asked the man as he locked eyes with those of the newcomer, whose virtually black irises were hard and unrevealing.

Shrugging unconcernedly, he replied evenly. His words clipped with the accents of a land half a world away. "He wasn't at the rendezvous point. I assume that he did not manage to escape the detonation."

"I've been listening to the news and I haven't heard anything about them finding an unidentified body."

The visitor simply shrugged again as if to say, 'small loss.' "They may not be releasing all of the information that they have uncovered in the investigation. I have no other explanation to offer though I must say that it is a tragedy that he does not appear to have eluded destruction."

Having no evidence one way or the other, the older man brushed the whole thing aside and gestured for his guest to follow him back inside. "Good foot soldiers are hard to recruit."

In some corners of the world, they are many, the dark man thought as he entered the cabin. "It will not pose a problem. A few minor adjustments should be all that is necessary to implement the rest of the operation."

The older man nodded as he led the way. "I'm sure that you have had to deal with many such situations before. I'm not worried about the project."

Like the occupant, appearances could be deceiving and the building looked to be nothing more than a ramshackle hunting lodge from a bygone era. The interior belied that assumption, boasting all the comforts of contemporary living and being fully furnished with every necessity required to conduct guerilla campaigns, from refrigeration, air conditioning and kitchen facilities to satellite communications and television. In a corner was a state-of-the-art computer station complete with a 36" flat screen to match the dual quad-core processor and all the gadgetry to go with it. Wondering at the energy-hungry appliances and technologically advanced components, the visitor assumed there was ample power to keep it all running. He couldn't see or hear the diesel-powered generator that was housed in a shed a few hundred yards away from the cabin, shielded by brambles and evergreens.

"Sit," said the host. "It's been a long night for you. Here," he pulled out a chair at a dinette in the kitchen. "I have breakfast in the works and I'm sure you're hungry. Eat, then we'll discuss the future."

Chapter 7

Rushing back to the hotel, Allie checked her watch, 10 a.m. *Running out of time.* Without sitting down, she unzipped the laptop carrier and booted up in record time. Something was going on out here in antelope acres and she was going to find out what it was.

With one hand she worked the keyboard to go online, while she dialed a direct line at the Post with the other.

"Mornin' sunshine," came a dulcet voice, drowsy with southern charm.

"Can the fake magnolias, Debra. I need some of your Silicon Valley sharps about now, and I need it fast."

"Well, there's a howdy for ya," she half-laughed. Allie always needed something yesterday. "What can I do for the princess today?"

Debra Chorister was 37, a few years older than Allie, but she was relatively new to the field of journalism. A bean counter in her former life back in California, she'd been growing bored with ten-key computations and bookkeeping entries when things stopped adding up. Inspecting the books she was shocked and troubled to discover her boss was fudging numbers. So she turned him in, packed her bags and went back to school to study journalism, finding that she had a flair for nosing around. New degree in hand, she shopped around to find an entry-level job at a newspaper. What really riled her was that everyone wanted to hire her for accounting positions when she wanted to work a beat, learn the ropes and become a black Brenda Starr, fighting crime with the mighty pen, or computer… times change. The best she could do was land a position as a researcher at the Denver Post, more than a thousand miles from her family, but she had a promise from the boss that she'd get her chance to write. It turned out that Debra was exceptionally gifted when it came to cyber research. She could track and hack just about anything, which is why Allie became her best buddy. At least it started that way. Since their introduction they had become fast friends.

"I think we're on to something hot up here in coalville," Allie said while punching keyboard buttons with her right hand.

"*We*, is it now? That must mean that *we* are going to be hunting pigeons together. What do you need?"

"I want to know what environmental organizations in the area have been high profile in their anti-coal activism. Can you find that? You're so much faster than me."

"Just a sec…" and all Allie could hear was the rapid-fire tabbing of fingers skimming the ergonomically designed keyboard perched in front of Debra in her cubicle.

Debra wasn't far off in her time estimation. Less than a minute later she announced success. "Well, let's see what we've got. There's the usual Sierra Club presence in the capital."

"Nah, they talk and collect money. They're more involved with legislation. What else ya got?"

"There's a group called Green Grasslands that has been particularly vocal about open pit mining and the construction of new coal-fired plants in the plains states," Debra continued calling up multiple windows on her screen.

"That sounds more like it. Where are they located?"

"Like the other, they have an office in Cheyenne. I'm e-mailing the lot to you. Why? What's the gig?"

"It's just something a fella said this morning," Allie's voice trailed off as she called up the pages Debra had just sent.

"What 'fella'? Where?" Debra's interest was piqued now. "This has to do with the fires at the power plant and the mine?"

"Yeah," Allie tried to answer as she was distractedly reading some of the information the organization had posted on their website.

"Give, girl," nudged Debra.

Coming back to the present, Allie said, "At the hospital. The pit supervisor at the mine. He said something about us, the press, only listening to environmental nuts, no, he called them "crazies" and it made me think."

"About what?"

"Oh, I don't know. No one seems to know what originated the blast at the plant and, though they won't call it that, the blast, or plural, blasts, at the mine. It just made me wonder."

"So, what are you going to do? I don't see anything solid here except for a couple of associations where people protest coal, oil, nuclear power and so on and so forth." Debra had her own thoughts on the subject but this wasn't the appropriate time to share.

"Well, nothing's cutting loose up here, so I think I'll pay a visit to Green Grasslands and, if there's time, the Sierra Club, though somehow I think that'd be a waste of daylight." Allie copied down a phone number and address and a couple of names of staff, then closed down her notebook.

"Thank you for the info. I'll call."

"Y'all bettah," said Debra to an empty line.

Next to the hotel someone had plunked down a charming little, fuchsia colored kiosk that Allie imagined would have snuggled well into the California landscape without notice. Here in cowboy central, it might have been viewed as an oddity were it not for the exceptional espresso served-up by the sister-owners. As far as she was concerned, it's placement was perfect for re-caffeinating on her way out of town and Allie asked the barista the fastest route back to Cheyenne. She gladly received her coffee with fairly simple directions that would cut two hours off the west sweeping freeway route. Leaving a generous tip, Allie pointed her fuel-efficient car toward the Wyoming state capital.

When Allie finally parked on the street that fronted the hole-in-the-wall office of Green Grasslands in downtown Cheyenne, she was thankful that she drove a compact car, not only for the gas savings but for the fact that it was easier to maneuver into tight parking and was relatively nondescript. More than once on the road to town, though, she wished it were higher profile. The enormous trucks that were in an even bigger hurry whizzed by, leaving her clutching the steering wheel and straining her biceps just to avoid being sucked into their vortex.

Finding the place had taken some effort. Allie hadn't wanted to pull over so she bugged Debra again and had her direct her street by street. Another thing Allie could have used... a GPS navigation system. Maybe in her next life.

Not wanting to spook anyone, Allie decided against hauling her big satchel inside with her. Instead, she just grabbed her phone, little notebook and slid her mini-recorder into one of her capacious pockets. Most of Allie's clothes sported pockets, as did the jumper she was wearing today. Not exactly haute couture, but then that went against her grain and for this crowd, would probably win her more kudos.

Hiking her purse onto her shoulder, she was ready to meet the locals. *This should be a piece of cake...* which thought reminded her that she hadn't eaten since that muffin and hard-boiled egg this morning. She stifled a yawn as she pulled open the door, a cowbell clanging, proclaiming her arrival.

She immediately took note of the myriad of pamphlets stacked, racked and otherwise displayed for visitors' perusal. The front desk was unoccupied and the phones were silent. Allie felt as though she'd entered a mortuary, and by the look of some of the graphics on the printed material, it could have been. The atmosphere was strangely absent of sound. She'd volunteered for a number of conservation orgs over the years, assisting in offices, and doing outreach and none had felt so... *barren.* That was the word that had eluded her. Then she figured it out. Usually there was some kind of music or nature sounds playing in the background. Here, you could here a mouse skitter.

Almost without warning, a pleasant smile emerged from behind one of the doors immediately followed by the lilting melody of Native American flute.

"It vass so quiet in here, I had to go turn on ze musick," the young woman with dimples intoned as she came up to the counter. "Guut afternoon. What can I help you with today?"

Allie hopped to and offered her hand and an introduction. She told the girl that she was doing a little research on conservation groups, especially those that operate in what might be considered unreceptive locales.

The girl looked at her kind of sideways, as if not really understanding what Allie meant, so she explained it in relation to being in coal and oil country while promoting green energy sources.

"Ah! I understand! Yes, it is strange here in zis town but ze people are very nice."

"Are you the director?" asked Allie knowing full well that the answer was no.

The girl laughed a little more robustly than Allie expected. "Oh no! Zat is Race. Mr. Carson. "He hass stepped out for a few minutes, but I expect him back at any time."

As soon as his name was mentioned, at the end of the hallway appeared an average looking man in his early thirties and developing a bit of a paunch under his belt. *No workout habits here other than fair-weather cycling*, surmised Allie. His blond hair was straight and thinning on top, and his mouth was framed by a pale goatee that was almost invisible until he entered the ambient light of the front office.

"Did I hear my name?" he queried., the timbre of his voice, an octave higher than anticipated. Allie could imagine him singing falsetto in a quartet.

"Yes you did," she replied stretching her hand forward to clasp his. She went through the rigmarole all over again and got far enough this time to ask if she could have a whirlwind tour of the office, learn about their mission, etc. etc.

Mr. Carson was more than happy to accommodate the unexpected visitor, explaining that they weren't the most popular organization in town. He took her through the narrow but spacious structure that had four offices stemming from the main hall with a full kitchen and restroom facilities down the way. Upstairs, all but the bearing walls had been removed creating a large open space where Green Grasslands held meetings and seminars. The walls were draped with images of the wonders of the natural world – alpine meadows and waterfalls, eagles with outstretched wings, buffalo and antelope grazing. Then one wall was filled with photos of discolored foliage climbing steep mountainsides, dead fish floating in putrid streams, and power plants belching forth grimy clouds that fouled the sky-line.

Tables and chairs were stacked in a corner, ready to be dragged into place to accommodate a cramped crowd of maybe fifty people. There was also a whiteboard that doubled as a backdrop for slideshows, and a video set-up.

"Impressive," said Allie as she wandered from wall to wall, examining the photos and art displays.

"Thank you. We've been lucky to get enough funding to keep the office alive. It's a little tough in hostile territory. We sponsor speaker series, too."

She asked questions about their community projects, budget, funding sources and volunteers. Nothing out of the ordinary, as far as she could tell. The place was much like any other environmental group where she'd volunteered in the past. When he took her downstairs to show her through the offices, there was a man on the phone in the back room. She couldn't see him well as they passed the half-open door, but she picked up a snippet of the conversation. The man on the phone looked up to glimpse Allie and Race and immediately changed the tone of his voice and the subject of discussion. She had distinctly heard him mention the initials "P.O.P." twice as if it were some entity, and made a note of it in her head to check it out. Something in her gut told her not to ask Race about the acronym, so she filed away the information as they moved along. The man quickly hung up the phone and left the office before introductions could be made, Allie never really catching a good look at him.

Having arrived just about thirty minutes before the office was to close, Allie asked if she could come back by tomorrow to meet some of their workers since everyone had left before she had an opportunity to speak with them. Race was more than happy to welcome her back and told her to come by around 10 a.m., everyone should be in by then. She agreed, thanked him for the quick tour and headed home to Denver for, what she hoped would be a good night's sleep.

Barely able to keep her eyes propped open, she made use of her travel time by calling Debra, knowing she'd already missed her at the office but hoping that a little robust conversation would keep her awake long enough to pull into her driveway.

"Lucky me. The long lost sojourner cries out from the wilderness," Debra quipped. "Damn," was the next thing out of her mouth as she fumbled the phone and the keys while trying to unlock her front door, keep her purse on her shoulder and hold on to an armload of papers.

"Hey, I'm not that bad," said Allie on the other end.

"No, not you. Just about dropped everything, including the phone. I need another set of hands," she said as she kicked the door closed and dumped her burden on the closest piece of furniture which was the sofa. "Okay, hands free. Now, what can I do for you? Still wandering the open range?"

"I'm headed home and before I nodded off at the wheel, I though I could use you to keep me alert by engaging in some witty dialogue."

"Right. So what *do* you need?" Debra reiterated the question.

"Well, I visited that Green Grasslands office and,"

"And it was a hotbed of radical firebrands calling for the annihilation of despotic corporate greedy bastards."

"Hardly. Pretty harmless bunch, looked like to me, however…"

"I knew it, there's always a "but" hidden somewhere," Debra cut-in again.

"Okay, you're right. This is one of those "buts." I overheard one of their guys talking in lowered tones on the phone when he didn't think anyone was listening and he mentioned something called, um, P.O.P. Can you look that up?"

"If you were from California you'd know that it stood for the long-gone Coney Island of the west," explained the researcher.

"What?" Allie was stumped. "What are you talking about?"

"Pacific Ocean Park. It was an amusement park way back when. Gone for decades now."

"Somehow, I hardly think that's what this guy was referring to. You don't clam up and change the subject when you think someone is eavesdropping if you're yakking about roller coasters and cotton candy," said Allie.

"No, I guess not." Debra seated herself at her computer. "Hold on while I see if I can find anything.

"Whoa, look at this. You can still find info on P.O.P.," said Debra a minute later.

"You can?"

"Oh, I mean the park. I'm looking up your request now. Hmmm, let's see. Yeah, aside from all the "P.O.P." music garbage, we find buried here a few notations about an environmental group called Protect Our Planet."

"Never heard of them," noted Allie.

"Neither have I, but let me scroll through some of this," and she was quiet for a few moments while Allie drove in silence. "Okay, this is what I've gleaned so far. They are a radical... see, what did I tell you... environmental group along the lines of EarthFirst! Seems they got in some hot water more than a year ago up in Idaho."

"Really? What kind of trouble?" Allie was interested.

"Want to try murder and mayhem?"

"What?! Are you kidding?"

"No, I most certainly am not," said Debra, getting a little excited. "Evidently, the trial is ongoing but it had something to do with land acquisition by nefarious means. Pretty hot stuff, according to this."

"It couldn't be connected to some little comment I overheard in passing," Allie said disbelieving. "That'd be just too much."

Debra shrugged to herself. "Well, you're the one whose ears started to itch."

"You're right. Can you e-mail that to me? I'll be home in about an hour and I'll want to scan through it, see if we're crazy."

"We? Girl, you are in this *all* by yourself. I'm just the researcher."

Allie laughed. "Gotcha. I'll call you when I get home."

The second time Allie walked up to the Green Grasslands office, wariness crept into her psyche. What seemed such a congenial little place the day before, the director and staff so ingenuous and accommodating, had been replaced by a whiff of threat. She physically shook her head as if to clear the air of sinister undercurrents, real or imagined, as she pulled open the door. *Has to be imagined. I don't see Race – what an odd name – as an eco-nut.* To her, the director looked like half the mild-mannered environmentalists she'd ever met and worked with. Every one of them driven by a need to curb modern man's penchant for self-destructive behavior, which she compared to an addict, even though she'd had no real experience with one. *Not unless you consider my sugar craving sweet-tooth. Nah, I can stop anytime I want.* She almost chuckled recalling the words as generally attributable to the hopeless alcoholic or druggie. *Yeah, like the guilty always claiming to be innocent.*

Shoving the thought away, Allie caught the German receptionist's eye as she stepped inside, a little shiver of apprehension trailing down her spine. *Geez, get a grip. Could anyone be less menacing than her?* Unfortunately, Allie had opened the door in her mind and compared the plump, placid Ilse to the smiling face of the Nazi Youth. *Stop it*, she admonished herself.

Allie pasted a smile on her lips and offered a genuine "good morning" to the young girl ensconced behind the battered wood desk. The good-humored beam that answered her was enough to melt away Allie's unease as wholly unfounded and, what she recognized to be, plain silly.

"Is Race, Mr. Carson, here yet?"

"Oh yes! He arrived a while ago. You sit," and Ilse indicated a chair by her desk. "I'll go right away," she said, bouncing down the hall. Watching the cheery imp, Allie called herself everything from idiot to delusional.

This time the tour was long-winded, including a PowerPoint of the organization's local and region-wide efforts to educate the community about earth-friendly energy usage and improvements in sustainable technology. Allie took the opportunity to interview the director and Ilse about their duties at Green Grasslands as well as how they had become involved in the environmental movement.

"I don't think of it as a movement so much as a way of life," Carson pontificated. "Having grown up in a city that was struggling to keep a clean water source and sweep out the layer of smog that blanketed the valley, it wasn't hard to realize that I had a mission in life. I suppose that began at birth," he added.

Losing interest since everything seemed to be on the up-and-up and dull as ditch water, Allie felt she had to ask for clarification of his statement.

"My name."

"Yes, I noticed it to be unique. What about it?"

"Have you ever heard of "Silent Spring?" he queried, barely visible brows rising in question.

"You mean the book?" she asked, only to immediately smack the heel of her hand against her forehead. "Oh, no wonder your name tripped a switch in my mind. Rachel Carson... Race. Clever." *Some strange parentage there.*

"Yeah, my folks became environmental pioneers in the sixties realizing that mankind was overwhelming nature, and," shrugging and smiling shyly, "guess they couldn't resist the temptation. My life was foreordained. Kind of like being a priest."

That's stretching it, even for me. "Sent you on your way, to be sure," she agreed.

The back door to the office opened and two men sauntered in who Allie hadn't seen earlier. She was immediately interested in the new arrivals. Mid-twenties, dark hair and eyes, one was approaching 6" tall and the other was closer to 5'8" with a sturdy stockiness that counter-balanced his companion's lankier build. They were speaking in low voices but the accents were clearly foreign. Middle Eastern or further east, perhaps? Allie did notice a British pronunciation from the shorter fellow. *Probably educated in the UK.*

She immediately perked up and asked Race if they were employees. "Is there some kind of international coalition? Ilse is German and these men are from..."

"Volunteers from Colorado State. They've just transferred to Ft. Collins to study Environmental Science. Great assets to the office," he grinned his approval. "But, no. There's no coalition among international environmental organizations, we just seem to draw interest from foreign students. Ilse happens to be attending University of Wyoming, here for the year. I think it adds to our *mystique*," he said conspiratorially, then laughed.

"May I speak to them? I've already gotten a couple of statements from Ilse."

"Why not? A'zam, Jehal, come on over here for a moment," he called the two who were making tea in the kitchen.

The taller one looked up from his mug and finally took note of Allie, his brows drawing together slightly in distrust or disdain, it was hard for Allie to distinguish which. She kept her own reaction in check despite an instinct to step back from the veiled hostility that quickly evaporated into a bland expression making her wonder if she had seen anything at all. Before she could process anything more, the burly man came forward, mug in one hand, and said hello.

He had a fairly pleasant if hesitant manner, something she chalked up to cultural differences, reminding her that he may consider it improper to touch a woman if he was Muslim. Without her usual forwardness, she again went through her rote speech explaining her position with the paper. He didn't show anything other than polite but bare interest in her credentials and a nod in deference to her purpose there.

Race relieved the minor awkwardness by introducing the men by name. "This is A'zam," he said indicating the friendlier man, if you could call him that, "and this is Jehal. They've been a huge help in developing some of our educational outreach programs."

"Good to meet you both. I'd be interested in asking you a couple questions about volunteering here, if you wouldn't mind."

The two appeared uncomfortable with the request but A'zam shrugged and acquiesced, nodding almost imperceptibly. "We must leave for an appointment soon, but perhaps a question or two..." He spoke with clipped precision overlaying a vaguely singsong intonation.

"I'd be fascinated to hear where you are from," asked Allie.

"We are both from Lebanon and are finishing our graduate work at Colorado State University," said A'zam.

"That's quite a journey. You sound as if you were educated in England," she said. "Is that the case?"

"Why...?"

"Your more formal manner of speech and pronunciation, not

American English. Just listen to me," she added with a laugh. "We use too many contractions and shortcuts."

A'zam allowed himself a brief smile, Allie thought as an attempt to set her at ease. "Yes, we have been fortunate to receive some schooling in the U.K., myself more years that Jehal."

"So, why, if I may ask, did you decide to come to the 'Wild West'? This has to be a huge culture shock for you."

"Not really. One city is much like another. It is not hard to assimilate," he allowed himself another upturning of his mouth at one corner. "We are very adaptable."

Despite the underlying aloofness, she was beginning to warm to his charm, minute as it was. Before she was able to go any further, A'zam made an obvious point of checking the wall clock and cut short the interview. "I must apologize, but we are going to be late for a meeting with our advisor if we do not leave directly. A pleasure to make your acquaintance, Miss Maitland."

Allie could do no more than blurt a staccato farewell toward the strange men's backs as they hurried toward the rear entrance.

She had gathered as much as possible and somehow felt compelled to get back to Gillette as quickly as she could spur the little compact, so she re-packed her reporter's utensils in her satchel, shook hands with Race and darted out the door herself.

Popping into the driver's seat, she speed-dialed Debra while she slapped the car into gear. It didn't take long to give the researcher a rundown of her brief encounter of the weird kind with the Lebanese Mutt and Jeff.

"So, what would you like from me this time?" asked Debra.

"Oh… I don't know. I just find their presence odd for some reason. So far as I know, environmental studies isn't a real popular subject for scholars from the Middle East, what with their dependence on oil production,"

"But you said they were from Lebanon. That's hardly an oil-rich country," Debra observed.

"I know. I'm probably *way* off base, here, but between the two, they had quite different accents and Lebanon is practically halved between the influences of Syria and the Iranian-backed Hezb'ollah."

"Talk about jumping at shadows, this is a stretch, even for you.

If your new-found cynicism has any basis in reality, answer me this... what would fanatic organizations from *Lebanon* of all places have to do with eco-bunnies in cow country?"

"Eco-bunnies? Where'd you get that one? Never mind. I'd just like to know more about those two guys. Not that they were shifty or anything... just... I *don't know*."

"That's good enough for me," Debra said. "Let me see what I can dig up from the U. There's probably nothing there, just a couple of Arab environmentalists."

"Right. It might be worthwhile to check in with Sol Greyfisher, too. You have her number still?" Allie felt like she was grasping at straws.

"Of course. Her husband's that wiz kid hermit." Debra thought for a second. "You think he may be able to help with some deep excavation work."

"He's a good one to have on your team if you hit a rock wall, though I don't get his politics. Couldn't hurt to check in with them, back-up could come in handy."

"You never know when more troops may be needed for the sortie," quipped the researcher.

"Something like that. You let me know what you've got when you get it, okay?" Allie deflated. She hadn't realized how wound up she'd been.

"Mm-hmmm, for you anything," Debra jibed.

"Thanks and many more thanks. Especially since it's probably a dead-end."

"We'll just see about that, won't we?"

Energy Barons

Chapter 8

No wrangling. No cajoling. Barely a peep from the minority party in the House of Representatives aside from an outspoken few. Yet the tumult among voters gained force. They were rapidly tiring of the call for more and more spending that was hailed as balm for the ailing economy.

President Cameron Van Schaal had been the fallback candidate in the campaign when the popular Yakub Kasili's meteoric ascent to the White House ended in a fireball, literally. While the investigation into the plane crash continued, Van Schaal became the heir apparent and never lost a step in his race to the presidency, and it was close race. The sympathy vote and the persistent call for "hope" and "change" just tipped the scales, with the press adding a thumb to ensure victory, and securely planted the otherwise has-been senator from South Dakota in the Oval Office.

So it was Van Schaal's 3.6 trillion dollar budget that was causing all the hubbub among at least half of the constituency, prompting a rebirth of the anger that had occasioned the Boston Tea Party in the days of America's forebears. A new cry arose from every corner of the nation that instigated new tea parties protesting the overreaching budget and the unwieldy deficit spending it promised to incur. The Democrat majority ignored the noise and easily overrode the House Republicans to institute the president's budget with nary a sigh.

It was an opportunity for more crowing about the people's mandate and how the budget would usher in a new era of "green." Throughout the presidential campaign the bywords had been "green" technology, "green" jobs, "green" energy production. In order to establish the mechanism to fund these ideas, the president was ramming spending bills through Congress with record-breaking speed and the minority had no input other than to point out the impending doom of overwhelming debt.

No one bothered to listen. Instead, after the budget victory, the familiar voices of Theo Kraegen and Rone Haggerty again mounted a virulent attack on the oil and coal industry while hailing the budget as a triumph in making real progress to address the planet's health. Speaking from the same page, they virtually mimicked one another's words, not that the media took any notice. The press was ecstatically giving every nugget of airtime possible to global warming proponents, and with the new CAFE (Corporate Average Fuel Economy) standards that were part and parcel to the president's budget, a number of congressmen and senators weighed in with their approval.

Of particular notice were Haggerty and Kraegen's vociferous tirades tying in support for the upcoming vote on California Rep. Wexler's Clean Air and Energy Act, otherwise known as Cap and Trade. Touting the legislation that would supposedly clean up excess carbon dioxide emissions, these two and others' faces were plastered wall-to-wall and channel-to-channel, expecting to convince the nation that higher energy costs were worth levying in order to save the earth from man's rapacious appetite for energy. And some of the nation was buying it. The rest was raising unholy hell about pie in the sky technology that, to their way of thinking, hadn't been proven and, in some cases, even invented yet. The White House swept the argument under the rug while peddling the imperative to cut emissions at all costs… to the United States. The Administration hadn't been able to sell the bill of goods to any other nation, despite the Kyoto Accord, which the U.S. never signed, some years back. Instead, the Europeans were back-pedaling as fast as they could and up-and-comers India and China were basically telling Van Schaal to stuff it. Economic recovery and growth was more important than monitoring and going through the motions of reducing industrial CO_2 discharges.

Amid all the happy clamor about the budget and similar legislation that had been slammed, and sneaked according to some critics, through on the Hill, a number of high profile leaders in the Congress took a night to celebrate their success. This gala somehow didn't capture press coverage although a few cable and network news moguls, attended by their on-screen lackeys, were in attendance. It could be because it was held at a private estate near Provincetown on Cape Cod. The curling tip of the peninsula was an area where lifestyles varied and privacy was endemic among the baronage that inhabited scattered holdings.

Sand and sea grass met the lapping, frigid waves of the Atlantic where the power brokers from Washington converged to fete their conquest thus far. Gauche and suave intermingled for one night, tolerating the company to share credit for their triumph. The commoners eyed the wealth of the nobles who deigned to dine with them for the evening, smugly believing that their fortunes were turning. Plebeian to prince, that was the goal of the new power peddlers on the Hill. It was their fervent desire to force aside the patricians at the trough, to trade blue-collar for blueblood. This night's convivial bacchanal would secure their place among the established families and the graced nouveau riche, acknowledged for their wiles and usefulness.

The theme of the evening was "Mandate for Change" and the only face not present, however much he was omnipresent on television screens across the country, was the president. His attendance would have been impossible to keep under wraps and he seemed to be providing a diversion by escorting his wife on a hundred thousand dollar date in NYC. Whether he considered himself cover for the event or above the minions gathered at the soirée, only he knew. In this respect Van Schaal was no different than his campaign predecessor before the plane's plummet forced a democrat ticket change, arrogance was inbred in the man.

There were no guests of honor though one made a brief appearance only to be flown back to the mainland by helicopter after a mere hour in near seclusion with the host and a select few. His visit was such that no other attendees knew of his presence, nor did they pay attention to the rotors beating the air as more than one of the affluent arrived and departed by similar means, the helipad was patterned to accommodate three such aircraft at a time.

A private study was furnished lavishly with Moroccan leather armchairs and sofa, the walls lined with bookcases brimming with exotic tomes and first editions, many signed by long-dead authors. Works of philosophy and scholarship were many, the most thumbed versions tending to a certain viewpoint of which Machiavelli would be proud, *The Prince* showing the same dog-eared wear. It was in this red oak paneled bastion of masculinity that men who never associated in public now met to puff hand-rolled Cuban cigars and swig drams of single-malt scotch. The purpose was to welcome the last senator seated after a lengthy court-battle following a well funded, deviously engineered win in Wisconsin.

There was now a filibuster proof majority that had been the goal of the man who sat in one of the deeply upholstered chairs, studying the other men in the room over the rim of his cut crystal glass. His father's billions, now under his control, had supported and orchestrated the ascension of the new regime in D.C. and it was his bidding that most of the others heeded. Only one man seated in the library, the one born to privilege who owned this shoreline estate, had the audacity to believe himself equal to the multi-billionaire who'd flown in for the brief hour. A foolish fallacy that the wealthier man recognized and scoffed in private, though he would not disparage his host in this setting, rather he raised his glass in a silent toast to those assembled.

The answering smiles echoed sentiments of poorly concealed amazement at the company and sumptuous surroundings, pompous self-satisfaction, or presumptive elitism. They all expected to acquire fortunes above and beyond those already in their control, but the one man, the multi-billionaire, he stood to gain the most. He had expectations of regal proportions the others couldn't fathom.

Raising their glasses in salute to one another, they heralded the future of the carbon credit and coups yet to come.

Chapter 9

It was almost eighteen hours before the power supply came back up at the Lysander home in Parker. By then, they'd gone to Billings for Kara's dialysis, and wasn't that a hassle. Because she wasn't a regular patient at that clinic, the sluggish mechanism of bureaucracy took hours to straighten out the paperwork and provide care. By the time Kara was finished with the procedure, it was late and everyone was exhausted so the family camped out at a cousin's place just outside of town.

The next morning, Key and Mary Lysander left the kids with her cousin and met with Yancy at the Constitutional Legal Fund office, saving her the trip down to their home this go-round. The petition had been submitted to the EPA's regional hearing clerk and placed on the docket with more speed than Yancy had imagined following her unorthodox prompting. At this point, the parents wanted to know what the next step would be. They were at their wit's end, having run out of money to complete the installation of the supplemental generator. This most recent blackout had scared the begeezus out of them being so far-reaching to encompass the whole of Eastern Wyoming, tentacles stretching into parts of South Dakota and curling around the Black Hills.

Frightened for the life of their daughter, they slumped into two snugged chairs that faced Yancy's desk, wondering and worrying what would happen next. Another blackout during a storm when they can't negotiate the roads to a dialysis center in time? Key had his arm draped across Mary's back, his other hand unconsciously rubbing her forearm that lay virtually lifeless in her lap. Despondency had been descending on her with the realization of how precarious the situation could become.

Yancy sat with her hands clasped in front of her on the blotter, files stacked to either side, Kara's within easy grasp. She was sympathetic to their predicament and had been keeping the phone lines buzzing between Billings, Denver and EPA's D.C. headquarters.

"We have a date for the hearing," Yancy wanted to ease their immediate concern with promising news. "It's no guarantee, of course, but I believe we have a good shot at making them listen and take action that will alleviate the immediate problem."

"How long do we have to wait?" Key asked as Mary perked up a little, hope flickering in her eyes. Yancy was trying hard not to be too confident knowing that should the effort come to naught, the devastation could strip them of the small reserve of hope they gripped with an intensity that practically hummed in the air.

"It's hard to say. I expect the administrative hearing to take very little time. It depends on how quickly they render a decision. It could be days or it could be while I'm still standing in front of the judge after presenting the argument." Yancy sighed, knowing the level of anxiety the Lysanders were experiencing. "I'm hoping that it won't be long, but I can't conscientiously tell you one way or the other. I'm sorry to be so vague." She sat back in her chair. Unwilling to leave things dangling after watching their faces drop at her answer, she added, "With luck, though, we'll have an answer by next week."

After seeing them out, Yancy walked in circles around the lobby, trying to work off her own frustration at how long it always seemed to take for the wheels of justice to turn, often enough simply grinding to a halt before a satisfactory resolution could be achieved, if ever. Her interview with the Lysanders was difficult because she had little to offer them in their struggle to meet the challenges God seemed to have dropped on their shoulders. Yancy wasn't a particularly religious person but she did have a faith that continued to drive her to make a difference wherever possible, and today she was praying that this was one of those instances.

As she made a final turn around the carpeted waiting area, a newspaper caught her eye on one of the chairs. The office received the local Billings paper every day, but that was neatly folded on the edge of the empty receptionist's desk, this one looked like someone had brought it with them and abandoned it for the next client to peruse. With nothing better to do except work, Yancy picked it up and skimmed through the stories on the front page. She decided to take a few more minutes, sat back on the lumpy sofa, and opened the pages to check out what was going on in Colorado. It was today's edition of the Denver Post now rescued from Laura the receptionist's quick hand, which would ruthlessly decree disposal.

Opening to Page Three she recognized a name on a story's byline about the power plant explosion and resultant blackout that had rolled across the region two nights before. Allie Maitland. Yancy dropped her head back against the wall, the plump blond bun twisted at the nape of her neck cushioning the contact, and contemplated what it meant to run across her name just when a little publicity might come in handy for Kara and her folks.

Tracking the blackout, huh? Well, here's a sidebar that your edi-tor might pick-up.

Yancy stood up and hurried back to her office. Flopping down in her chair, she opened the paper to the flag and dialed the Post's offices. *Maybe, just maybe we'll get a break,* she thought, the hint of a smile breaking across her face.

Dead-ends and more dead-ends.

At least that's the way Allie felt her exploration was heading. Nowhere.

She didn't seem to be gaining any traction. Little inconsistencies niggled at the back of her mind but nothing seemed to have any roots. A few oddly spaced explosions that couldn't possibly be coincidences; a strange acronym dropped during a *very* private conversation; and two even stranger Arab, or Lebanese if their story panned out, environmental science students. Not much to go on, *nothing to go on,* thought Allie as she sped back to Gillette to follow-up on Carter Gleason's directive to corner the Plains Coal Company execs to get a reaction to the environmentalist condemnation of their business ethics.

He was allowing her to return to the scene of the crime – *if there really was one,* she lassoed her errant thoughts. *Can't be jumping the gun, girl* – to pin down a solid response to accusations made by the

Big Boys Back East, namely Kraegen and Haggerty. They had clout on the Hill as past politicians (some would say, "once a politician, always a politician") who now played the media market as radio host and network entrepreneur. No one actually paid attention to the fact that both efforts were largely unsuccessful money pits. Even so, they were still the ones getting the lion's share of attention. Gleason knew that having Allie call the coal company offices would result in little more than a one-sided "no comment" exchange followed by a rapidly disconnected line before any real answer was ever evinced. The plan was to sic Allie on the unwary and pray for an outcome that would make good copy.

Allie glanced down at the odometer. She was really racking up the miles on this venture and with a pittance of results… so far. She had to stay optimistic. The story had too much potential and not only did her gut tell her so but if Gleason was giving her leeway, there had to be something there, and she was going to find it and flog it until she had the real, printable skinny. Two days in and, like cops would say about a homicide investigation, the more time elapsed after a murder, the harder it is to find the murderer. Well *she* was going to get her man, or woman, or whoever was behind this whole thing, whatever this thing was. *Hell, I don't even know if a crime's been committed!* But damn it if she wasn't going to find out.

Hours on the road flew by in record time as Allie went over the information she had, and didn't have, regarding the incidents at Plains Coal Company's Flat Butte Station and Tyne Hill Mine. Since she'd had far less reticence from Rees Targhee than the PIO at the power plant, she turned off the highway to the east, miles south of Gillette, to go back to the mine. No one was expecting her and she wasn't in any mood to announce her arrival, she just hoped that she'd be able to wriggle her way past the guardhouse. *No guarantees, no disappointments.*

When she pulled up alongside the tidy security kiosk, she was relieved to see that there was a new man on duty rather than anyone she'd already encountered. Drawing on her reserves of charm, which had grown thin with the minimal sleep and maximum wear over the past couple days, Allie affixed the sweetest smile she could conjure up for the occasion. It didn't take much to get over the first hurdle, mostly due to the fact that there was so much bustling activity. The guard assumed she was tied to one of the other groups that had been rolling on and off the property all day long.

She parked in front of the administration building, snagging the last place available. The premises were crawling with uniforms, dark suits and more casually clad mine personnel, and both marked and unmarked police vehicles were haphazardly deposited by the roped-off area. Climbing out of the confined space of her compact's interior, she also noticed a steady stream of traffic coming and going up the hill toward the excavation. Allie was sandwiched between two company trucks and barely had the room to briefly stretch her limbs before grabbing her portfolio and beelining for the front door.

Entering the building just as she had the day before – *was that really only yesterday?* – Allie was greeted by the very person she was hoping to snag for an interview. Blessing her lucky stars, she marched up to Targhee and offered her hand with a pleasantry to break the ice.

"Afternoon, Ms. Maitland. I'll admit that I didn't expect to see you back around here. The rest of the press packed it in and left town," he peered over the glasses that had slipped to the end of his nose.

"Could be the rest of the press isn't interested in actually learning anything," said Allie.

Targhee's eyebrows raised a bit. He didn't trust the media, and after what he'd been reading in the papers, online and seeing on the national news shows, it was no wonder that he'd show some surprise at her reappearance.

"So, what can I do for you? As you can see, things are still in an uproar and the management isn't releasing any statements beyond what you've already received."

"Well, Mr. Targhee, the Post would like to know what Plains Coal Company has to say about the strong words that some high-profile figures have been using insinuating a lack of safety standards being employed in your industry and, in particular, here. You must have some response."

He hemmed a moment considering whether or not to give any comment. Taking into account her diligence, he decided to give her an answer.

"It seems evident that their remarks are based on little or no knowledge of how Plains Coal operates, nor do they appear to have any real interest in learning all the facts. It's unworthy and injudicious to comment without adequate knowledge of what happened the other night. No one knows what occurred, including the outspoken critics, and no one will know until the investigation is completed. I'd venture to say that the credibility of the most vocal critics is questionable when their purpose is fairly apparent." He turned aside to gather some paperwork that was lying across the empty receptionist's desk.

"What purpose would that be?" cocking her head, Allie opened her blue eyes wider encouraging his clarification.

He looked at her with a determined but calm gaze that softened slightly at her apparent interest, his eyes magnified behind his aviator styled lenses. "Don't you think the pressure is on to influence public opinion and further the administration's agenda to downsize the coal industry?" Targhee asked rhetorically.

Allie couldn't comment herself so she made a non-committal noise and moved on. "Can you give me any indication of what did happen? No one's been forthcoming about the cause of the blasts," She hoped he'd have *something* to say other than...

"And they won't be until law enforcement has finished their investigation. We're as much in the dark as everyone else."

...what he said. *Damn.*

"Which agencies are conducting the investigation? Local police, sheriffs or maybe state officials?"

"This is something a little more than the local authorities are usually confronted with so they've also called in federal assistance. All of the events are being thoroughly studied by experts," said Targhee.

"Federal agencies? Do you mean the FBI? ATF? Does that imply that this is more than just an accident?" Allie was trying to keep her excitement in check. This could be a vindication of her hunches.

"I'm afraid I don't have an answer for that, but thank you for coming out here, Ms. Maitland. I'm already late for another meeting so that'll have to do for today." He shook her hand again before disappearing up the hall and into the recesses of the warren of offices where decorum prevented her from following.

Somewhat disappointed at getting so little, Allie couldn't feel as though the effort was completely wasted. Now she knew something big was afoot and Targhee had just whetted her appetite.

While Allie was repacking her satchel, the receptionist returned to her post. It looked as though the older gal she'd sparred with the other morning had the day off and a much younger woman had taken her place. If she played her cards right Allie thought she could cajole something out of this new pigeon, *if* the receptionist didn't figure out who she was.

Double-checking to be sure she wasn't sporting anything that screamed "Press," Allie started to chat up the young woman behind the desk by asking after Sawyer Aleman.

"I'd been told that I could meet him out here this afternoon," Allie grinned innocuously. *Not that he'd give me the time of day if he's here.*

"I don't think he's been in today," the young woman replied, tossing a strawberry blonde braid over her shoulder while she checked a personnel sign-in for the day. Allie tried to get a glimpse of the sheet as the woman's freckled nose obscured the paper that was inside the half-opened belly drawer of the desk. "No, he was here but went home and will be out for the rest of the day and probably the week."

Allie added concern to her voice as she asked, "He wasn't hurt in the accident, was he? We made arrangements for the meeting last week, before all this ruckus," she waved her arm to encompass everything outside the front door.

"Oh no," coral bangs swayed with the negative roll of her head. "He's fine. We just had to pull back operations for a while so the police can investigate."

"That's a relief. Do you know what all is going on?" Allie tried to seem ingenuous. "I mean. I heard something on the radio and read a little in the paper about the blackout, but not much was said about why it happened."

The woman could see no reason not to answer Allie's question. The gossip was flying everywhere. "Well, the explosion out at the power plant has closed that for the time being and since our operations supply the generators, and we've been told to cut back excavating and transport..." she shrugged to emphasize the powerlessness of the situation, "there isn't much anyone can do here except let the police figure it all out."

"All I could recognize were sheriff's deputies and a state police car, but there are lots of vehicles out there. They don't all belong to mine personnel do they, since you said the shop's pretty much closed?" Now she was fishing, hoping the woman had warmed up to the subject.

The receptionist leaned forward, hands clasped in front of her, with forearms and elbows on the desk. "I saw the guy from the FBI when he came into the office to meet with Rees, Mr. Targhee. He was good-looking," she winked. "You know, tall, dark and handsome, but a real city slicker."

"I guess this thing is a pretty big deal. I wonder who he is, where he's from."

"Yeah, it is," the woman sat back, relaxing into her role of informal informant. "I didn't get the agent's name, but he's up from Denver. I guess there's some connection with the EPA on this thing, too. At least those letters were mentioned."

"The EPA? Like a liaison? What would they have to do with all this? Seems kind of weird," observed Allie innocently.

The shoulders shrugged again. "Oh, I don't think it's anything official, though the EPA has refused to reopen the old plant that just closed last month." Her mouth turned down in disapproval. "Seems idiotic to me when everyone needs power until they can bring the new plant back online, wouldn't you think?"

"I'd agree with you." Allie thought maybe this would be a good time to see if she could locate Aleman and see how much more he knew, because she'd bet he was a lot better informed than the receptionist. "Well, if Sawyer is out for awhile, I'm going to need to catch up with him. With everything going on, our meeting must have slipped his mind." Allie had opened her portfolio and feigned rummaging around for something. "I seem to have mislaid his number and address, do you think you could find it for me?"

"Well, we don't keep that kind of information at the front desk, but Sawyer's family has a ranch south of town at Depression Creek and I heard him say he was going back down there today. You could probably catch up with him there. They're in the book." She pulled out the bottom drawer on the right and extracted the local phone directory, handing it over to Allie. "I think you'll find it listed under "Depression Creek Ranch."

Allie shot her a grateful smile that was genuine. "Thanks. This will help so much." Taking out a pen and pad, she scribbled down the number and address and stashed everything back in her bag. Thanking the young woman before practically sprinting, elated, back to her car, she unlocked the door speculating about how gloomy Depression Creek might really be.

Chapter 10

Driving down the two-lane highway, Allie realized how stupid it was to take off to parts unknown this late in the day. After the initial excitement at catching another lead had subsided almost as quickly as it bloomed, it struck her that she'd be coming back to town after dark, navigating unfamiliar roads. *Not a problem, this road is as straight as a beam. Don't see how I could possibly get lost. It's all good,* she reassured herself.

Tired and preoccupied as she was, Allie wasn't paying attention to anything other than the unwavering ebony ribbon of highway in front of her, including the inklings of a storm front boiling up out of the west. Towering thunderheads climbing thousands of feet into the otherwise crystal blue Wyoming sky escaped her notice.

As it happened, locating the Aleman family homestead turned out to be a breeze. Miles south of Gillette she came upon a plainly lettered sign posted a quarter mile before the turn-off, an ornately drawn arrow pointing to the left. Lo and behold, almost exactly point-two-five miles later, the promised road appeared. Allie followed directions, turned left and a mile down the paved road, pulled up to a stop sign. Another more decorative sign indicated that she was on the right track, so she continued onward as the road degraded to gravel and began winding up and around a steep-sided pond of translucent water that spanned twenty acres, nary a ripple disturbing the smooth surface. It had the look of a deep crater, though what had created the waterhole was a mystery to Allie who had never been an avid geology student. Social sciences were more her forte.

Continuing along the road she began to rue her rash decision to drive into unfamiliar country this late in the day, picturing herself missing a curve in the dark and ending up at the bottom of the clear lake. At the other side of the pond, a canal cut through the rim and a rushing creek spilled out onto the rolling plain beyond.

Now I know why it's called Depression Creek. No melancholia intended, unless other folks have ended up under water driving around in the dark. The thought made her shudder despite the lonely beauty of the scene… *in the middle of nowhere.*

Skirting the oversized waterhole, the road brought her up and around a hill, depositing her underneath a typical western ranch arch, the crossbeam carved with the name "Depression Creek." A curious looking brand was burned into either post, and a cattle skull hung from the center. *Shades of Georgia O'Keeffe*, thought Allie shaking her head and rolling her eyes as she drove through.

Even after passing under the simple structure, she continued to follow another good half-mile of road that crested a small ridge, bringing her to half a dozen tidy acres, a split-rail fence delineating the perimeter of the household real estate. A bumpy but manicured lawn that could accommodate a super-sized game of croquet circled the residence. Stretching from one side to the other of the rambling ranch house was a broad veranda, decked with a well-used porch swing and wind chimes tinkling a bright refrain in the rising breeze.

Allie pulled up near the front steps, shifted into 'park' and taking just her handbag after transferring the micro-recorder and notebook from the satchel, opened the door and planted both feet on the ground as the front door swung wide and a trim woman stepped out.

Standing up, Allie vainly tried to brush the imbedded wrinkles out of her clothes. The woman came halfway down the few stairs curious to greet her unexpected guest. She was a bit taller than Allie at maybe 5'7" with thick dark hair pulled into a neat ponytail. Sparkling hazel eyes glinted with good humor, which Allie took as a good sign considering her unheralded arrival.

"Can I help you? You're not lost are you?" asking a little uncertainly, the woman supposed Allie to be looking for something and likely made a wrong turn somewhere along the way.

"I would have been lost if your property wasn't so well marked," Allie said as she came forward, noticing the other's eyebrows quirking up in further question.

"You were looking for us?"

"Actually, I was looking for Sawyer Aleman. I am in the right

90

place aren't I?"

Now Allie really had the proprietress' attention. *A nice looking girl to see crabby old Smart Ass? This has* got *to be good.* "He's been out all day working and won't be back until supper. Is he expecting you?"

"Afraid not. I came out here on the spur of the moment." Allie finally scanned the cloud-darkened sky, "Maybe not a smart move."

The furrows in the woman's forehead smoothed as she made a reassuring gesture toward Allie. "No, no, don't worry. We're used to having odd folks pop in unannounced."

Allie wondered what she meant by that. *I'm odd*, and glancing down at her creased attire figured she would fit the description, *or they welcome anyone who just happened to show up at odd times.* Either way, the woman beckoned her inside with an encouraging smile, saying, "I'm Carly."

"Pardon my poor manners, I should have introduced myself. I'm Allie Maitland," she said as she followed her new acquaintance inside, already feeling an easing of the slight tension in her shoulders. *Passed the first test.*

As she followed Carly into the house, Allie was shown into a large, comfortably furnished living room that was as advertised, lived in. Overstuffed couch and matching wingback chairs showed signs of wear that dated them by a couple of decades of solid use. Handmade afghans were draped across furniture backs and immaculately tatted armrest covers protected the fabric that was tending toward threadbare. The muted floral pattern was a little on the dingy side but the overall room and fixtures were well-maintained and clean.

Carly told Allie to have a seat and offered her a choice between coffee, tea and lemonade.

"I never refuse a cup of coffee," accepted Allie with alacrity. She was in need of another shot of caffeine to boost her mental acuity for the coming confrontation with the caustic Mr. Aleman. He was a tough customer and she'd better be on her toes.

It wasn't long before Allie's hostess reappeared with two heavy ceramic mugs that looked like she'd just plucked them off a Formica counter in a forties diner. Settling across from her guest, Carly started in with some personal questions that bordered on the delicate. Evidently she considered Allie to be Sawyer's love interest, a notion that practically cracked her composure, inconceivable as it was, but decided to humor Carly rather than laugh aloud.

Allie was actually enjoying being on the receiving end of an interview, however bogus her interrogator's assumption, but before Carly could eke out much information, Allie turned the tables on Aleman's sister. At least she *thought* Carly was his sister. The resemblance was there, so Allie facilely led the conversation away from her by *asking* the obvious question. Confirming Allie's guess was all it took to open the floodgates of a sister to happily jaw about a beloved, but admittedly acerbic, older brother.

She had anticipated more reticence from Carly, after all Allie *was* a stranger, but as she rambled on about Sawyer, Allie thought she understood her willingness to talk. Particularly after describing his stint in the Marines and why he'd divorced – the young wife hadn't appreciated being abandoned on the ranch while he had his marching orders half a world away – a woman might pine for female company after living like that for awhile. Although the ranch was isolated, Allie doubted that Carly was that starved for girl-talk. As she rambled, the idea of being crowded by men made more sense.

By the time Carly had reached the part of the story where Sawyer had returned from Afghanistan and gone back to school to obtain a degree in geology from the Colorado School of Mines, Allie was genuinely engrossed. The arrogant jerk seemed more human than she'd thought possible.

The impression didn't last.

The two women amiably kibitzed away what was left of the afternoon when, from the direction of the kitchen, three dusty men in stocking feet tromped in. The first two just nodded their heads at the two ladies in hasty acknowledgement as they passed. The third one stopped dead in his tracks and stared at Allie, briefly startled at her presence. Carly watched amusedly as his features rapidly went from surprise to annoyance, a touch of scarlet slowly slashing along the ridge of his cheekbones.

Anchored in place during the brief struggle to bury emotion, Sawyer ignored his surroundings until a fourth man, examining a new blister on his finger, plowed into him, practically bouncing off Sawyer's rigid back. Snapping his head up, Mickey checked around his older brother to see what was causing the roadblock.

"What the hell? Move it S.A., I've got a date tonight."

Without answering, Sawyer stepped to the side, allowing Mickey to pass, never removing his eyes from Allie's.

"What are you doing here?"

"That's some way to greet a guest, brother dear," Carly's smile widened as she tried to fathom the lightning arcing between the other two.

"She's no guest, she's a reporter," he spat.

Carly regarded her coffee chum with eyes that radiated a new mistrust followed by a growing worry that she'd spilled too much in her blind acceptance. "Oh," said Carly not verbalizing the dangling "*dear.*"

"Mr. Aleman, I'm not here to badger you about your precious job or to get you in hot water. I wanted to get your reaction to some information I ran across that I thought you might find of interest."

"I doubt that there's anything you have to say that I'd think interesting." He wasn't budging an inch.

"Don't be so quick to judge. It may pertain to the *accidents* at the plant and the mine," persisted Allie.

"Phones work just fine out here in the sticks."

"Would you have taken my call?"

He just glared in answer.

"That's what I thought," she said mildly.

"If you have something that could be relevant to the accidents, I suggest you take it up with the investigators. I understand the FBI is handling inquiries," he added flatly.

Allie laughed. "They'd kick me off the property busting a gut with belly laughs at my little conspiracy theory."

"What makes you think I won't do the same?"

"Because you're already hooked." She kept her features schooled even though she felt she was winning this round.

Sawyer hiked an eyebrow and barked a harsh laugh at her audacity. "Yeah, maybe I am. Let me get cleaned up and then I'll consider talking to you."

"Hey, I'll take what I can get," she said to his retreating form.

He wagged his head in amazement as he climbed the stairs.

Carly finally couldn't control her curiosity. "What's all that about?"

"You heard him. I'm a reporter, and I guess good enough of one that I irritate him."

"You shouldn't let that bother you. Everyone irritates S.A. You'll have to stay for supper though if you plan on getting anything out of him. He's going to want to eat first and you can't very well sit out here and stew while everyone is in the dining room."

Since Carly's two children, the usual kitchen crew, were still out with their father, Dan, she accepted Allie's offer to help with dinner preparations. Within a matter of twenty minutes everything was on the table and Allie could hear the tread of the stragglers coming down the stairs one by one, filling in chairs around the dining table. Carly glanced up at the clock for the umpteenth time mumbling her impatience that Dan and the kids weren't yet home when the kitchen door flew open and the latecomers trooped in.

Dan shooed the kids off to wash up while he kissed his wife's cheek with a mischievous smile. She didn't bother to cross-examine him about their tardiness, seeing the muddy knees on the two boys' pants was enough to establish that they'd stayed late at baseball practice. She used her hip to nudge him toward the sink for his own hand washing before sitting down with the rest of the family.

Finally, the boys darted into the room and slid into their seats, receiving loving glares, if there is such a thing, from their mother. The rest of the men paid no attention to anything but the hot food lining the center of the table, passing bowls of potatoes, salad and squash, and platters of meat around before the kids had plopped down at their places.

Dishes piled high with a savory feast, Allie was just about to fork up a bite of roast that was so tender it fell apart as the tines speared it, when a resonant baritone intoned a brief blessing. She quickly replaced her silverware until the head of the household had finished the prayer. It was then that introductions were finally conducted, and acknowledged mostly with simple nods and brusque words between mouthfuls, starvation practically overriding manners.

Father Sam perched regally at the head of the table, a full head of silver hair bobbing briefly with an accompanying smile as Carly did the honors. Clockwise was Carly with both boys on her left, absorbedly plowing through their food as if it would disappear before they could devour it. Sawyer's eldest brother, Cole, occupied the chair opposite his dad at the table's foot. Allie, to his left, was relieved to have Dan forming the demilitarized zone between her and Sawyer, who closed the circle. Absent was Mickey until he dashed through with affable apologies to their guest and, ruffling the nearest boy's hair with a grin, rushed out the back door to meet his date in town.

"Which town?" The ranch seemed a country to itself to someone who was accustomed to strip malls and fast-food joints on every corner.

"Creekside," supplied Dan to Allie's question between bites. "Hardly big enough to call a town but we do have two bars, a café, post office and a grange hall."

"Don't forget the school and feed store," piped up the boy closest to Carly. At fourteen Travis' voice was cracking, not that he noticed or cared. He was eating at the rate he was growing, faster than prairie grass.

"Is it far from here? I don't remember seeing it on the map."

Dan lifted his shoulders, "Depends on your definition of far. It's about fifteen miles down the road." He returned his attention to his food, hunger taking precedence over talk.

Allie noticed how similar were the two older Aleman brothers, Cole and Sawyer. Cole was obviously older, maybe by five or six years was her guess. He showed a fair sprinkling of gray fanning out from his temples where Sawyer's hair was still practically jet-black. She'd swear they were competing for the title of 'surliest.' *Maybe it's just that they're too famished to engage in polite conversation.* At least Sam had a smile while he ate and even took enough of a breath to complement the chef.

As soon as the men had demolished their first servings and were angling for seconds, the banter ensued. At least it did among every-one except Cole and Sawyer, who, if she hadn't known better, acted more like bitter enemies rather than convivial siblings. Allie assumed this was normal behavior since the rest of the family ignored their unsociable silence. The others at the table were brim-ming with questions for her after Carly told them she was a big-time reporter from Denver, leaving Allie to correct the misconception that she had star status. No one heard her. Terry, ten and the youngest at the table, compared her to Lois Lane, comic books still being his choice of reading material.

"Well then, who's Superman? Last I noticed, no one's seen any superheroes in these parts," cut-in Dan, smiling.

"Uncle Sawyer could be a crime-fighter. He's a Marine," Terry answered after giving it consideration. "Right, Uncle Sawyer?"

Sawyer wasn't happy about having anything from his past brought up in the company of a prying so-called guest, but he turned up the corner of his mouth slightly, eying his nephew. "Not hardly, Terry. Crime fighting is a tough job."

"Well, so's being a cowboy and you're a soldier too. So I think you could." The little guy was sticking to his guns. He promptly dropped the whole subject and redirected his attention back to his plate, much to Sawyer's relief. Allie noticed that Cole, on the other hand, had paid the whole exchange little heed except to sniff at Terry's assertion. *Wonder what that's all about?*

Sam picked up on Allie's puzzlement at the two men's animosi-ty. "Don't mind these two. Tired and Grumpy are what we call them after a hard day wrangling," he said light-heartedly.

"Right. They've been fixing fences all day, not a steer in sight for either one of 'em," Carly clarified. "Don't give her any ideas about the glamour of ranch life. It's all chores, all the time."

"Hey, just trying to keep the cowboy mystique alive for our city friends." He winked at Allie.

Cole excused himself and carted his dishes into the kitchen. Before the boys could race out of the room, their mother collared them and put them to work clearing the table, ignoring their whines about KP duty.

She lightly smacked Terry's behind to motivate him, "Kitchen

Police is as close as you're getting to crime busting for tonight. Now get a move on." She wagged her head with a smile underlying the slightest bit of exasperation.

"Must be something living in a house full of men," observed Allie as the two finished their job in record time.

"The testosterone can be suffocating sometimes. Its no wonder Grandma Sarah prefers her own company to dealing with an overload of male egos." She noticed the query in Allie's eyes. "Gram lives in the old cabin. She got tired of the one-upmanship years ago and moved out after making Dad do renovations."

"I can see that not all of it has subsided," said Allie.

Carly looked at her quizzically, then got her gist. "Oh, you mean Cole and Sawyer. Those two are just too much alike. Royal pains in the ass, both of 'em."

Changing tack, Carly took Allie's hand and showed her the coffee making equipment. "Here you go. I'll let you make the coffee for dessert while I clean up the rest of this wreckage. All right?"

"Absolutely. This is something I can probably handle," and she hopped to grinding coffee beans, happy to be of use.

A quarter-hour later, Allie assisted Carly in bringing coffee out to the living room where Dan and Sam were channel surfing and yakking about the commodities market. Sawyer was slouched on the sofa, stocking feet perched on the cocktail table, magazines brushed to one side. His eyes shuttered when Allie entered the room bearing two mugs. She handed one to Sawyer, a tad uncomfortably, as Carly beat her to the punch by serving Sam and her husband, watching Allie and her brother out of the corner of her eye.

Sawyer received the mug courteously, if not with any real enthusiasm, and took a hesitant sip. His eyebrow rose, "Pretty strong stuff."

"I thought cowpokes liked strong, black coffee," Allie injected a little attitude.

"Yeah, but not fifty weight," drinking it anyway, he tamped down the trace of amusement before it crept into his voice.

"Hey, this is the way they taught me to brew it at the espresso bar," Allie hitched a hip. "For your information, we had award-winning coffee."

"So you carry certification as a bonified barista?" He kept the snigger to himself. "I'm impressed."

"*Not hardly,*" she tossed his expression from dinner back at him. "Just trying to work my way through school, though it was a lifetime ago. Bolstered my income with it when I was starting out in the news business." He closed down again at the reminder of why she was standing in his family's home, an interloper making nice with his sister and now waiting on him in his own living room.

Not to be discouraged, Allie followed Carly back into the kitchen to get a couple wedges of pie and deliver them to the men while Carly settled the boys at the kitchen table with their desserts. Cole didn't say much when he came to get his own coffee and pie before restationing himself in the study, surrounded by paperwork.

After dessert, Carly hustled the boys upstairs for their showers, Dan and Sam moved into the den to check out markets on the internet, and Allie grabbed the opportunity to broach the raw subject of her visit, the accidents at Plains Coal, hoping that she wouldn't be shown the door without so much as a 'good night.'

Anticipating the metamorphosis of agreeable guest into meddlesome reporter, Sawyer flicked off the TV and turned cold eyes on Allie. "Well? Now's your chance."

Restraining her aggravation at his open disdain, she plunged in anyway. "Look, I'm just interested in getting your feedback on something. I think you have more facts than you care to let on, so an educated opinion would follow."

"I'm listening." Blasé tone.

Allie abbreviated her tale as much as possible, going over her impromptu visit to the Green Grasslands office in Cheyenne, sketching out the set-up and that she'd stumbled across a mention of an organization called P.O.P. "Ever hear of it?"

"Nope, sounds like candy. Should I have?"

"I honestly don't know, but they were involved in a situation up in Idaho about two years ago."

"And?" He was beginning to lose patience with the roundabout explanation of something that seemed to have nothing to do with him or his place of employment.

She let out a breath and continued with slow deliberation, watching his eyes narrow, already having decided that she was wasting his time and her breath. "From what we've learned, businesses and farms were devastated by a scheme involving this group P.O.P. It's an acronym for Protect Our Planet. People died. The prosecution is ongoing." Hazel eyes bored into hers. She lifted her shoulders, emphasizing her helplessness in explaining the pathetically slow court system. "The ponderous wheels of justice."

He finally perked his ears, unsure of where she was going with all this.

Sighing, "So, I make an innocuous visit to a local environmental group and just trip over a mention of activists. I don't know," she said wearily, "don't you wonder if these were really accidents?"

"Isn't that what the all-knowing press is saying?" Sawyer resurrected his snide act.

"I guess I'm not one of the anointed and omniscient few, because I think something strange is at work here, and I'd like to find out what the truth is."

"That's a new one. Since when is the media after facts? Making it up as you go has worked for *journalists* like Jason Blair." Pausing for a beat, he added, "Until they're caught."

Allie bristled. "Look, I know there are some jokers that have gotten sloppy over the years, but I'm not one of them."

"Sure, you're the one in a million that doesn't allow personal convictions to color your reporting," he snorted. "You've got the ethical rhetoric down pat, but you're still a flaming liberal who has an axe to grind with coal power, just like the lot of them, Googling the internet, accessing slanted websites and interviewing one-sided experts, then self-righteously pounding away at your computers to reaffirm your *beliefs* in print."

She was taken aback at the outburst he'd unleashed before reining himself in, reasserting an outward calm that barely masked the anger vibrating through his skin.

"I've read your stuff. You beat the drum for global warming as much as all the rest."

She pursed her lips, eyes widening in stunned silence. She couldn't deny her political leanings though she was positive they never contaminated her work. "You've read my stories?"

He nodded. "After you started hounding the accident victims, I pulled up some of your bylines. You need to do better research."

Allie's cheeks blossomed with heightened color in outrage. *What the hell does he know about my research?* "I've always been diligent about checking and double-checking my sources," she ground out.

"Your sources are limited then, because the argument for anthropogenic CO_2 polluting the earth's atmosphere doesn't hold water, if you'll pardon the expression. The science doesn't support it."

"It's common knowledge that humanity's output of carbon dioxide is creating the greenhouse effect that is driving up planetary temperatures," she returned the volley.

"Common knowledge or common misinformation?' He swiped a hand through his hair. "If it weren't for the complicity of the media, there wouldn't be such a backlash against more than 32,000 climate scientists that have factually refuted your popular theory. Because that is all it is, a *popular* idea. If you'd take the time to read, I can give you a real bibliography the length of your arm that will not only validate their assertions, but make you feel like a chump for having swallowed Haggerty's fabricated documentary and *news* that he carries on that joke of a network he owns."

Allie breathed deeply to regulate her rapid pulse, she was a guest in his home and it would be unseemly to argue a point at the top of her lungs no matter *how* wrong he was. "All of my work is examined with a fine-tooth comb for mistakes. I do my damnedest to ascertain the facts."

"That's the trouble, *Ms. Maitland*. It's the accepted assumption that global warming even exists that creates the problem. If the majority of the news editors in the world tacitly agree, whether or not the premise is factual, then your work will pass with flying colors. People accept too much on blind faith. Yes, I used that term purposely. The concept of global warming and saving the earth has practically reached the status of a religion."

Before Allie could offer a retort, Sawyer added, "Take a look at the story you brought here tonight. P.O.P.? What are they if not a counterpart to religious extremists if they will go so far as to destroy their fellow humans to promote their beliefs? Remember that it was Hitler's propaganda minister, Göebbels, who said that a lie repeated often enough becomes fact. It's something to think about when considering the power of the press."

She huffed and crossed her arms over her chest, but she didn't disagree with the last statement. The media had a great deal of power and she witnessed its misuse daily though she refused to believe that she was one of those duping the populace.

Allie wasn't given a chance to reply, in any case, because Sam stuck his grizzled head in the door and asked if there was any more coffee. Allie popped up, smiled back at the kindly man who she had difficulty believing had sired the glowering spawn of Satan sitting on the couch.

"If not, I'll make more." She glanced at her watch on her way to the kitchen, feeling at home despite the rough treatment she'd just received at the hands of her supposed host, and realized that she'd better be getting on her way. Although she'd enjoyed Carly, her three 'boys' and Sam, her trip had been pretty much a waste otherwise. Sawyer didn't have much to offer. As she measured fresh grounds into the basket and fired up the coffee maker, it struck her that he hadn't discounted her supposition that these weren't accidents, even if he had trounced her views on carbon emissions. The thought rejuvenated the smile that Sawyer had swiped clean, because he'd inadvertently given credence to her hunch.

As she finished in the kitchen, Allie noticed that the gurgling of the coffee pot overrode another sound that she'd paid no attention to until now. Peering out the window, she saw that it was streaked with steady streams of water reflecting the outdoor lights in channels sliding down the glass. The rain created a steady pounding on the roof that she hadn't even noticed, she'd been so engrossed in her discussion, *make that 'argument,'* with Sawyer.

The next thought was how she was going to see to get back to Gillette in this downpour. Allie wasn't given any opportunity to ponder the driving conditions when the back door burst open and Mickey shot inside, wind-driven rain blasting in with his drenched form.

"Man, it's miserable out there. The sky just opened up and dropped everything it had. I didn't have a choice but to leave early." As his head came up from brushing off rills of water as he stood in the mudroom, his eyes caught Allie's. "Whoops," he grinned. "Hope you've got your overnight bag 'cause there's no way you're making it out of here tonight."

"Are you kidding?" She was abashed at the idea. "It can't be *that* bad. I have to get back and report to the night editor with my follow-up," she couldn't think about the implications. "I had no intention of imposing even for dinner."

Mickey shook his head negating her hopes. "There's a flash flood warning out there and I just made it back before the water starting rushing across the road behind me. You'd be crazy to try to get back to town tonight."

Carly had come into the kitchen as Mickey was describing the road conditions and dripping all over the mudroom floor. "Lord, Micah, did you get washed into the creek?" Turning to Allie, she offered apologetically, "You know he's right. It's too dangerous for you to drive."

Allie's mouth opened and closed, briefly imitating a fish trying to catch a fly rather than capture a wild thought, which was what she was trying to do.

"It's fine," Carly sublimated her bubbling laughter with encouragement. It was hard to do after listening to her brother haranguing their guest. "No need to worry, we've got plenty of room." She figured that having Allie staying under the same roof as her brother might even be entertaining. Trying not to grin, she decided that he was not going to take the news well.

"I'm expected to check in. Maybe I can call from here. I'll grab my cell..." she started for the other room and her purse when Mickey derailed her good intentions.

"The phone's out and so's cell service. I tried calling from town to let you all know about the storm and I couldn't get through."

Allie dropped her head back and just stared hopelessly at the ceiling, hearing the coffee maker burble away. "Gleason'll kill me."

Carly shrugged. "He'll just have to wait until tomorrow."

Chapter 11

A normal day at the ranch and the guys were up early grabbing a breakfast that didn't fit with Allie's preconceptions of country living. No overloaded plates of eggs, meat and potatoes. Quick fix toast, some bacon and coffee, plenty of coffee, and the men made their own. Allie was comfortable with the menu, awkward with the company.

Luckily, she wasn't pressed for commentary. No one was particularly garrulous. Only Sam seemed to be a real morning person among the male population but even he was out the door without much chitchat and Carly showed briefly only to disappear again upstairs.

The storm had passed during the night leaving mud puddles and strings of puffy clouds trailing across the sky, no further threat of rain in the brisk wind that propelled them eastward. Encouraging for Allie, assuming that all the roads were clear of debris.

Checking her cell phone to see if service had been restored, Allie was gratified to see she had a strong signal. Sighing in relief and nursing a second cup of coffee, she tried to ignore Sawyer who hadn't rushed off with the others. Curious as she was about his hanging back, she said nothing and proceeded to check in with Gleason and see if Debra had unearthed anything new.

Sawyer, on the other hand, wasn't really a working partner in ranch operations and he and Cole's tenuous truce was in danger of collapsing at the moment. Sibling rivalry might be a catch phrase with psychologists but even Sawyer had to admit that there were tendrils of truth in the concept, and his arrival back home to offer a hand while the mine was under virtual lockdown wasn't helping things. Being more of a hindrance to family tranquility than not, Sawyer was planning on driving into work anyhow, not caring what

the feds had to say. He'd decided that Allie's far-fetched word association might be worth a gander, so he acted relaxed, slouched back
in his chair, long legs stretched out under the table, mug cradled
against his middle, and eavesdropped on her calls.

The first one was contentious. She bickered with someone that
he assumed was her editor about following-up on a story. He was
impressed by her dogged commitment and amazed at how much lat-
itude her boss would give her. *He must hold her in pretty high esteem
to allow that much cheek. Hell, I can't say hello to Cole without him
thinking I'm giving him lip.* He just sipped at his coffee and listened
as she yielded – or seemed to – a furtive smile appearing as she clev-
erly won the argument, and closed the connection.

Paying her tablemate no mind, Allie speed-dialed Debra. She
wanted an update on the foreign exchange students at Green
Grasslands, because her sensitive gut was rapidly becoming dyspeptic concerning those two. Connecting to the researcher, who Allie
now bestowed the qualifier of 'gifted,' she eagerly pulled her
notepad from her purse and started scribbling as fast as she could.

Sawyer only heard half of the conversation but the tension in
Allie's shoulders as her pen scratched at warp speed spoke volumes.
She was onto something and her non-sequitor from the night before
meant more than he thought.

"You located them in the university's records?" asked Allie.

"Mm-hmm, and those only go back two months."

"That's odd. It means they showed up in the middle of the term.
What else."

"Well," said Debra, "I decided you might have a point about Sol
and her new hubby, so I caught up with them. You would not believe
how fast that man talks. He lost me every other sentence."

"Right. I believe that." Allie didn't buy it for a minute.

"He put me on the right track after I'd found that they're listed
as Lebanese nationals who came in via Puerto Rico. We pieced
together an interesting angle between his following political developments that are what I'd call *subtle* and your little tidbits. It bothered me that they entered from a U.S. commonwealth and not directly from home. They had vacation plans? Anyway, seems there had
been a court case conducted by EcoEarth Legal Center representing

detainees from Guantanamo Bay that were classified as less danger-ous …"

Allie cut her off, "How'd you get to Gitmo from the U? Never mind, just tell me what you got." Sawyer was intrigued by the reference and the shock on Allie's face as she listened.

"As I was saying, evidently just about three months ago, EcoEarth championed the release of five detainees. Toddy, Sol's husband had been following the litigation. Well, they won and the five were sent to Puerto Rico because no other government would accept them, supposedly exonerated or not."

"So the connection is…"

Trying not to lose patience with her impatient friend, Debra went on, "We couldn't track them after that. It's almost like they up and phhtt, disappeared, possibly absorbed into the system, somewhere, after EcoEarth forced their release."

"And this leads to these guys, how?"

"Just the fact that two of the five may look a whole lot like two new transfers from Lebanon. Two students who have no real history before their arrival in Ft. Collins and, ultimately, Green Grasslands, and they just happen to have materialized from the place where the others vaporized."

"So, Lebanon to Puerto Rico and thence to the U. Any ties to the rest of them? And where did they come from, really?" Allie's perplexity was stretched all over her face and Sawyer found the context confusing.

"Toddy gave me some leads that I'm working on. The IDs on the released prisoners don't jibe with those of the students, not that we expected them to."

"People have been on edge about the possibility of these guys being let loose on American soil, and what you have isn't really convincing, yet," Allie mulled aloud. "I'm probably barking up the wrong tree, anyway."

"Remember one of the first rules of good reporting – there are no coincidences," exhorted Debra from behind her computer console. "Don't underestimate that reporter's nose of yours."

As if to punctuate the comment, Allie sniffed her doubt and said, "What would activists and misplaced Arabs have in common, anyway?"

Sawyer couldn't hear what the other person said in reply as he watched, eyes veiled under thick black lashes. Allie ended the call, but his interest was piqued by what little he'd heard. Maybe she was talking about some other story. He didn't think so.

Letting his curiosity get the better of him, Sawyer bluntly asked what that was all about. Allie blew it off. She wasn't in any mood to share after his rude diatribe the night before. Besides, the connections were too tenuous to be talking out of school.

"Look, none of this has anything to do with anything. Don't worry about it." She let the subject drop while they finished their coffee, no one making any real effort at conversation. She stood up and started gathering her things asking where Carly might be so she could thank her hostess before running off.

Sawyer gave a non-committal answer and she hiked back up the stairs to offer her goodbyes while he mused about the tidbits that had dropped. *Not enough to do anything with* but still, it nagged at him.

When she came back down and was getting ready to leave, Allie turned and asked a question. "Have you met the FBI guy who's heading up the investigation?"

"No. Why?" *I was right. It is about the explosions.*

"It always helps to know who your enemies are."

He was puzzled. "He's the good guy."

"Not to a reporter," and she slung her bag over her shoulder on her way out.

On her way back to Gillette, Allie pulled her phone out and dialed Debra one more time.

"Now what?" she answered playfully, acting slightly annoyed at another interruption. "I have other stories to work on too, you know."

"And they take you all of five minutes each," laughed Allie. "Just one more thing. Can you get me the name of the FBI agent in charge of the investigation and the best place to find him?"

"No prob." She clicked away for a few seconds. "Here you go, girl. His name is Roy Esteban and they've set-up a temporary head-quarters at the sheriff's office in Gillette. Good enough?"

"Yes, indeed. Thanks." Allie turned onto the main road, knowing exactly where she was going next.

Energy Barons

Chapter 12

Sawyer had nothing better to do beyond his original idea to go out to the mine, so he pulled on his boots and followed Allie toward town.

Driving onto the main campus of Tyne Hill where the business offices were, Sawyer descended the asphalt road toward the parking lot adjacent to the ravaged batch load out area. He was struck anew by the devastation that was roped off with hundreds of yards of yellow tape. One of the tall silos had a ragged cavity in the side, coal spilling in every direction. Because the silo's store was depleted after delivery to the newly loaded train that was moving out when the blast occurred, debris wasn't spread as far as it could have been. That didn't improve the scene much, part of the conveyor was collapsed and the weigh station had suffered extensive damage, blackened by the fire that had long since been extinguished. He was grimly reminded that this is where one man had died. The others were in the hospital fighting for their lives and he resolved to check on them after tracking down the officials conducting the investigation. Overhearing Allie's half of her phone conversations had built a fire under him to find out what really *had* happened.

Too many questions and he wanted some answers.

Grabbing a parking space alongside other company vehicles and a big black SUV, Sawyer hopped out of his truck's cab and strode up to where he saw Rees Targhee standing just outside the police tape. Not far from his boss' position there were two men examining the rubble at the base of the silo. Two days after the explosion and the FBI were still combing through the remains, piecing together events.

Hanging back, Sawyer and Targhee listened intently to the running commentary between the crime scene tech and the man in the business suit.

"I thought this was an accident," Sawyer said to Targhee.

"From what I'm gathering, it's looking like the explosion can't be tied to any accidental fuel leak, or any other *natural* cause," replied the production manager.

"Ain't nothin' natural about any of this," said Sawyer bitterly.

The man in the suit was crouched down next to a tech from the forensics lab who was indicating a dispersion pattern of coal and concrete building fragments. Hearing Sawyer and Targhee's remarks, he looked back over his shoulder at the two men watching the techs work. Knowing the production manager and shift supervisor on sight, though he hadn't actually met Aleman yet, the suit decided that it might be to his benefit to drop a little information in their direction.

"You're right about the explosion not being attributed to anything natural. There was an incendiary device. We have something that looks like fragments of a detonator."

Sawyer almost opened his mouth with a snide comment about how long it's taken them to find it, but thought better of it. No need to antagonize the man. He and Targhee moved as if to cross the line to better see what the tech had collected, but the suit waved them back dismissively. "I'll get with you later."

The suit turned back to his team member. While Targhee took the agent's attitude in stride, Sawyer was less forgiving, biting his tongue not to make a blistering retort. Instead he stalked off in the direction of the office building, Targhee at his side.

"So, who the hell is that guy?" Sawyer asked over the top of a cup of coffee. The men had adjourned to the kitchen and were discussing the direction of the investigation, not that the FBI had been particularly forthcoming. It was mostly conjecture.

"That's Roy Esteban, the special agent in charge. A real stickler for protocol," Targhee removed his glasses and massaged his temples. "Apparently the man's good at his job. Hauled him in from Denver rather than bringing in someone from the Cheyenne office."

"Yeah, but maybe there's more to it than that. I gathered the EPA is snooping around this too." Sawyer was referring to the fact that the regional EPA offices were headquartered in Denver. "Could there be any connection with that?"

"Don't know. They've threatened to come out and stick their nose into the process, but what I picked up, between the FBI, ATF and OSHA investigators, the environmental bureaucrats have been denied access until the FBI has posted their findings."

"Just what we need, another federal agency strutting their stuff around here," Sawyer exhaled with fatigue and looked over at his boss, the shadows under Targhee's eyes looking like bruises from lack of rest. "How much sleep have you had in the last couple days?"

"Enough to function," Targhee peered across the table at his co-worker. "You're not looking any better, you know."

Sawyer rubbed his own eyes. "I know. Couple of worrywarts. Like that's going to help the guys in the hospital."

They started to get up to head back to the front office when Special Agent in Charge Esteban sauntered just far enough into the kitchen to block the doorway. Ignoring the tactic and determined expression on the man, Sawyer offered the agent some coffee. Accepting the Styrofoam cup of a more aromatic brew than he'd expected, Esteban didn't relinquish his station obstructing the exit.

Targhee took the initiative. "So you're sure it was a bomb that caused the explosion at the load out." It wasn't a question, allowing no convenient obfuscation from the agent.

"Pretty positive about an explosive device. Too many traces left behind." Esteban eyed them skeptically while he sipped.

"So what now?" Sawyer asked charily in his own right. He had no reason to give the fed his full trust despite what he'd said to Allie about him being the good guy.

Bypassing the question, Esteban posed his own. "How good is your security here? I mean, it's just a coal mine, there's nothing to be overly protective about, right?"

"In that assumption you'd be wrong," responded Targhee, knowing that the agent already had the answer. "Mining is dependent on the judicious use of hazardous materials and proper equipment operations. Not to mention the expensive machinery that costs tens of millions to replace, maybe more, depending on what's compromised. I'm sure you're already aware that the whole facility has limited access. Personnel must have proper authorization. This can be a dangerous place and security is tight to protect the community."

"And the company," Esteban added blandly.

"Of course the company," Sawyer put in, beginning to lose patience at what sounded like insinuation. "Liability is huge and operators are meticulously trained."

Esteban leaned back against the doorjamb, cradling the cup at his chest, steam curling up from the hot liquid. Giving the impression of being relaxed, he cocked his head and tossed off the comment, "Sounds like an inside job then, don't you think?"

"That isn't possible," rejoined Targhee. "Everyone here is thoroughly vetted. We're more than careful. We have to be."

As much as the agent was getting under Sawyer's skin, he had to admit how the circumstances looked to Esteban. As if thinking aloud, he said, "There are thousands of acres here, all security fenced." He gave Esteban a sidelong look, "As you must have noticed. But, there are ways to get on the property. It's only happened twice in the last ten or fifteen years."

One of Esteban's eyebrows rose. "Oh?" Then his gaze zeroed in on Sawyer and Targhee as if they'd been withholding evidence. "You've given this some thought. Tell me about it."

Rees leaned forward at the table, replaced his glasses on the bridge of his nose but continued working his temples with his knuckles. "The gondolas. After an accident twenty years ago, the operators at the batch load out," Targhee caught the agent's eye, "where the coal is loaded into the rail cars…" Esteban nodded in comprehension. "… they've been trained for extra vigilance."

"Why? I don't get the connection,"

"Hitchhikers. You know, modern day hobos. Most of them are drunks or guys strung out on drugs looking for some place to sleep it off. They get themselves inside the rail cars and then they can't get out," explained the production manager.

"Again, why?" Esteban echoed himself.

"Have you looked at the cars? The sides are taller than a man's reach and they don't have anything like handholds inside. Once you're in there, you're stuck." Targhee shrugged. "Like Sawyer said, hasn't happened in years but we keep a sharp eye out for anyone dumb or drunk enough to end up at the bottom of one and we get them out before they're buried and pancaked by a hundred tons of coal. Our guys are good, no one gets past them."

"But it leaves the option of hitching a ride," said Esteban.

"How? Like Rees just told you. You can get in but you can't get out," said Sawyer acidly.

"There are ways," he looked straight at Sawyer, "and I'll bet you've already considered the possibilities." Abandoning his barricade of the door, Esteban abruptly dropped his cup in the trash and thanked them for the coffee. Walking back down the hall, he considered Mr. Aleman's curiosity about the investigation. Esteban had been told that the mine crews were given time off. *So, why is he hanging around here? I think I'm gonna have to check on that boy.*

Chapter 13

Allie went to the sheriff's station in hopes of digging a little information out of the locals about their new office-mates, the feds.

No luck. You can't buffalo a buffalo, she found out. Even after listening to hours of data about bison populations and behavior during the ill-fated conference, she hadn't learned enough to deal with the Wyoming natives who proved themselves to be just as obstinate as buffalo. All she got from them was the press conference schedule, which was to take place later that afternoon.

Allie was as impatient as Debra had pegged her. There were few things she hated more than having to cool her heels waiting for anybody when a news story was in the offing, but today, she had zip for a choice. Instead of hanging around the sheriff's office gathering nothing, she went to a downtown coffee shop she'd spotted on her previous trip and settled in for the duration to do a little online research of the county's populace and industry… otherwise known as 'background.' Checking her watch after a long while, she discovered that it was time to pack it in and get to the press conference.

Time had flown by as she packed away informational tidbits about Gillette and environs. *It will only add depth and color to the story*, she told herself as she quickly stuffed her computer into the carryall. *If there is a story*. Refusing to give in to that demoralizing thought she blew through the doorway.

Walking back inside the lobby area of the new sheriff's station, the ever-present satchel swinging from her shoulder, this time she was halted by a deputy to check her credentials, *not like they don't remember me from two hours ago. There are only twelve of us here.* And that was including the television crews.

Despite the nationwide frenzy the incident had riled up about the evils of the coal industry, it appeared that the media were more interested in listening to their own pundits than collecting any breaking news on-site. She gave credit to Fox News for being set-up for a live feed. The network affiliates from Casper and Cheyenne were present, but no other cable stations or wire services were there. Apparently Allie represented the only large newspaper. Local radio and print filled out the rest of the scanty showing. *But it also means that when I break the story, the Post will be back on the map.*

Disgraceful was Allie's other thought regarding the turnout. The death of a Triple Crown champion got more coverage than a tragedy that caused a major power outage and human loss. If the victims aren't considered sympathetic enough by the news media they don't rate a story, let alone a sidebar. *Puppies, babies and horses always trump a power plant worker.*

She was beginning to wonder at her growing skepticism of her fellow professionals' objectivity. Maybe Aleman's accusations had gotten to her. To Allie, news was news no matter what your personal viewpoint, and right now she wanted to hear what the man in charge had to say. And she prayed he had *something* to say.

Without any more adieu, the very person she was contemplating approached the microphone. He didn't tap it or blow into it, assuming correctly that a sound-check had already been performed. He just placed himself behind the mike with the poise of a man used to the spotlight. He looked the part, too. Tall, dark with a fair amount of gray at his temples. Tanned complexion complemented by dark, penetrating eyes and government-shorn hair. Not too young, not too old, just enough age to give the impression of wisdom and experience.

The man introduced himself as Special Agent in Charge, Roy Esteban. After that, it was all downhill. He had virtually nothing new to add about the explosions at Flat Butte and Tyne Hill, even if he delivered his non-news with the proper gravity. By the time he was finished with his update, Allie was silently cursing the lack of progress he had to report and she determined to catch him when the media dispersed after asking a few lame questions that led nowhere.

Melting into the woodwork, which under the circumstances she would have thought to be difficult considering the small crowd, Allie managed to catch up with the FBI agent as he was making his way to the lobby exit.

Esteban hadn't seen Allie before the briefing and, looking her over, assumed her to be harmless enough. She'd junked the earth shoes and cargo pants in favor of jeans and boots, deciding that she may have need to blend in a little better. She figured that she'd be less threatening if she wasn't flaunting her progressive leanings in cowboy country by her usual choice of garb. When she addressed him, Esteban made the decision to be courteous rather than blow her off. This wasn't the kind of crime where he wanted to alienate the press, no matter how innocuous or, adversely, antagonistic they appeared.

"Is there any real evidence that the two blasts are related?" Allie took the direct tactic.

Esteban was taken off-guard, but the flash of surprise didn't register with Allie. He answered the forthright question with aplomb. "Not at this time or I would have said as much in the briefing."

"Would you?" She didn't feel like circling the issue after having to waste time waiting to get to the horse's mouth. She was just praying that he wasn't actually a ringer for the animal's hindquarters. "No one has really made an issue of the fact that the two incidents took place only hours apart. Why is that?"

"Disinterest? Who knows. They're your colleagues making judgment calls on this. We don't speculate."

Refusing to be baited, Allie kept on track. "You said that you have a few leads you're following, do any of them have to do with local environmental groups?"

He rotated his head to make better eye contact. Neither he nor his team had really gotten much beyond the fact that the explosions were rigged, having no real evidence yet to go further, so her question got his attention.

"That's an odd supposition. What makes you think that?"

Ignoring his question, Allie pressed on. She needed to know whether her ideas had any merit or were completely off the wall, so she wanted to see what his reaction would be. "Do you have any idea if Green Grasslands has had any connection with eco-terrorism in the past? Along the lines of radical groups like Earth First! who have had reputed members that acted individually to target polluters, sometimes with violent actions?"

Esteban stopped in his tracks and turned to face her fully. *Where did all this come from?* She'd been walking beside him as he made his way across the room but now he examined her more closely, riveting her earnest gaze with his own.

"What gave you the impression that there could be domestic terrorism involved?"

"I didn't say domestic."

"No, you didn't. You implied eco-terrorism. Either way, it's quite a stretch even for someone with a fertile imagination." He wanted to nip this in the bud. He couldn't afford to have the media running off with some half-baked theory.

With no real answer, Allie moved on. "What about P.O.P.? Protect Our Planet? Have they been operating in the area? Are the groups connected?"

There were still a couple of press reps lingering in the area and he didn't want to have any of this wild speculation seeping its way into some story. Clutching her by the arm, he hustled her through the door and down the hall, depositing her in a small office.

He released his hold and Allie rubbed her bicep, his grip having been more determined than she'd expected in maneuvering her out of the lobby. Standing in the doorway, hands on his hips he gave her his full attention. "Okay, what's this all about?"

"What's your problem? I'm just asking a few questions."

"Some very odd questions." He pointed to the one guest chair in the tight quarters. "Sit down."

She sat.

"What gave you the idea to ask about environmental groups?" He stared hard at Allie, letting her know that he wouldn't brook any evasion, but she was used to getting the "look."

"Like any decent reporter…"

"Right. Where are you from?

"Allie Maitland. Denver Post. As I was saying… like any decent reporter, I looked at the information that has been disseminated and started to do a little research, that's all."

Esteban parked his haunch on the corner of the desk. He didn't believe a word of it. "No reporter just has an out of body experience that makes them follow-up on something that, to the best of my knowledge, has no relationship to the story."

She peered up at him. "How do you know there's no relationship?"

"I'd like to know what makes you think there is."

"That's privileged."

"Like hell it is. This is an official investigation into a couple of devastating explosions at important energy facilities where people have died. If you have some kind of information that could lead to the apprehension of the perpetrators, you need to give it up. *If* you've got anything solid. We could be talking murder here." Esteban had leaned over to get in her face and put the fear of God in her.

It wasn't working.

"I know that. Do I look that stupid? If I had anything more than a hunch, don't you think I'd tell you?"

"No, I don't. I think you're after a big byline and to hell with justice served."

Allie stood, calmly collected her things and started to leave.

"Since you don't have any other information, I may as well be going. If I stumble over anything of interest for you, I'll be in touch."

"Like hell you will," said Esteban under his breath to the closing door.

Esteban pulled his cell phone out, scrolled through the address list, and dialed the Denver office. He wanted information about Allie Maitland and he wanted it yesterday.

This whole day was turning into a bust. Allie was feeling like a desiccated leaf, twisting in the wind and about to lose its tenuous hold on the branch. The afternoon was nearly gone and she'd gotten bupkis from Mr. Roy Esteban, agent extraordinaire. Plopping down behind the steering wheel of her car, she made the decision to try the hospital again. It'd been a couple days, maybe one of the victims would be feeling up to talking to her now. She turned the key in the ignition and jammed across town.

Allie carried only her purse with her hoping to avoid spooking anyone by being saddled with too much gear. She walked blithely down the hall and slipped past the nurse's station undetected, not that she'd expected anyone to confront her. It was visiting hours and the nurses had better things to do than examine all the bodies passing their post, unless they were supine.

She passed a whole family that was clogging the doorway of one room. People were meandering in and out of the other rooms occupied by the blast victims, which Allie saw as a good sign. *Maybe they're up to receiving other visitors, too.* There were five victims on this floor and one that was up in ICU. She'd never even consider trying to reach that man or his family. There was good reason why outsiders didn't have access to patients in acute or intensive care and she had no inclination to buck hospital policy.

Allie circumvented the family members crowding the room where children were chattering happily at the bedside. She was thinking that their mom must have snuck them into the room, but then perhaps rules have changed since she was a kid and had been barred from visiting Grandma's sickbed. Diverted as she was, she barreled right into Sawyer whose mouth instantly turned down at the sight of someone he was beginning to categorize as a prowler.

"Here again? Can't you leave these folks alone?" he hissed.

Allie straightened up immediately and returned fire. "For your information, I have. I haven't spoken to any of them yet. Thought somebody might be willing to give me the time of day now that they've begun recovering more. Obviously, you're not among them."

"I'm also not half blown-up sitting in a hospital bed waiting for friends and family to come by and say 'hey.'"

Allie rounded on him, hands planted defiantly on her hips, her oversize handbag swinging off her shoulder and across her back.

"Look, I'm just trying to find out what happened. It doesn't look like the FBI is doing such a bang-up job on it's own."

"Oh, and you can do better?" Sawyer relaxed his onslaught a little, allowing the corner of his mouth to curl at her presumption.

"Evidently. Mr. Big SAC looked shocked when I made a couple

of suggestions not half an hour ago. In fact, I thought he was going to haul me in for conspiracy or obstructing justice." It was difficult to keep her voice down when she wanted to spit her irritation at the flat disregard she had encountered at the hands of Esteban.

Sawyer stooped to meet her eye, invading her personal space. "Should he?"

"What? Are you nuts? I just have a particularly sharp researcher doing a little digging and whatever I trip over, well..." Allie shrugged, sending the bag down her arm. She grabbed the strap and pushed it back into place, punctuating her pique.

Still blocking her way, he leaned against the wall near the over-flowing room, arms crossed over his chest. "So, what have you *tripped* over?"

"Doesn't sound to me like you're really interested or that you'd give it any more credence than Esteban."

"Try me."

She examined his features more closely to determine if he was just patronizing her or was genuinely interested. "Okay I will, but would you mind moving your oversize carcass so I can *tactfully* inquire about the patients' ability to remember anything?"

Sawyer considered her request. Making the decision to give her a chance, he moved slightly to get out of the way of the neighboring doorway. "All right, but I'm going in with you and if you upset anyone I'm hauling you out."

"Fine," she said shouldering past him. Entering the room that he'd just exited, Allie introduced herself and politely asked if she could briefly talk to the bedridden man about the accident. The man, bandages wrapping his left side and his arm in a sling, looked over at Sawyer, uncertain about the newcomer. He'd already been inter-viewed by the police, company officials and federal detectives. He raised singed eyebrows at Sawyer expecting an explanation.

"No biggie, John. It's up to you to say what you want, or if you want," said Sawyer.

"Are you with her?" John lifted his good shoulder in the direc-tion of Allie, who patiently waited for the exchange to end, not happy about being referred to like a dog in the corner but not want-ing to bully anyone, either.

"No, I'm the bouncer if she upsets you."

John smiled almost shyly and asked, "What do you want to know? The sheriff, FBI, ATF and every agency I can think of has been in here asking the same questions over and over."

"Well, I'll give it to you straight. I'm from the Denver Post and I'm working on some follow-up stories on the accidents. It will help me fill in some of the blanks if a few of the sur... injured could give me their impressions of the order of events." Allie wanted to reassure him, so she added. "I know that you've already been grilled by the authorities, but I'm not here to do anything more than just write an accurate account, and for that I need your help."

John seemed to accept her explanation and sighed, settling back into the pillows piled high behind his back.

"Truth be told, I don't remember that much. You know, everything was pretty ordinary, run-of-the-mill. Filling the rail cars at the weigh station. Everyday stuff." He stopped and seemed to look into space for a minute. "I worked the controls to load the coal into the next car and as it starts to flow, the whole place just blew sky high right in front of me." He looked down at his bandaged chest and arm. "I was lucky. Cal died and Dale may not walk again." John's guilt at surviving washed across his features. "I'm gonna be okay."

"And thank God for that," said Sawyer, placing his hand on John's good arm, giving him encouragement.

"I understand that you lost a good friend and colleague," Allie carefully continued. "I imagine this is hard for you, but as the police probably said, anything you can remember will only help to find out what happened." She paused briefly, "Do you think it was an accident?"

John looked up at her with concern. "I don't see how. Coal doesn't just explode. Sure it burns, burns hot enough to produce the BTU's needed to run a power generator but it's not volatile like a gas, it doesn't just go off like a bomb."

At the mention of a bomb, Sawyer froze remembering the words of the SAC. They found remnants of a detonator. He wondered if Allie knew that. He doubted it. Looking over at her now and seeing the softened lines of her face, he wondered if she was playing the poor guy or really felt badly about having to remind him of the tragic details. He wanted to believe she had a heart.

"That's what I understand," she nodded, accepting his description of coal's combustibility. "Did you notice anything odd… out of the ordinary? See anyone who didn't belong?"

"No. I already told the other guys that if any of us had seen an intruder we'd have reported it right away. Security is really good that way. And we're careful to check all the rail cars before we load. Can't have any old bums winding up at the bottom of a coal car."

Allie looked sideways at Sawyer hoping to get clarification. She didn't want to upset the patient, but could see that her companion wasn't going to give her anything.   "What do you mean? Bums in a coal car?"

John explained the problem much the same way that Targhee had for Esteban, adding that there hadn't been a problem since he started working there.

"Gotcha. Hobos still ride the rails, huh?"

"I guess, though I've never seen any," said John.

"John, I'd like to thank you for giving me your time. Get back on your feet soon." She smiled and shook his right hand with both of hers, squeezing lightly to underscore her good wishes.

Sawyer escorted her out. "Anybody else you want to badger?"

Turning on him with subdued anger. "Don't you get it? I'm just doing my job, trying to piece a puzzle together and write a factual report. I'm not out to make anybody's A-list for Miss Congeniality. Get off my back."

"Only if you'll let me in on what you're looking for. You have an agenda or some inkling of what might have happened. I heard you on the phone with your researcher. What have you got?"

"Nothing that I can really repeat," she blew out a breath and released a little tension. "It's all just guesswork and I don't want to get anyone in trouble if it leads nowhere. Journalists *do* have a responsibility to get the facts straight before they start spouting off."

He snorted in derision. "Like it doesn't happen all the time. I read the half-assed reports that make it to the front page of some of these papers."

"Not in my stories. I make sure I've got it right before it goes to print and so does my editor." She had her defenses back in place.

"One of the last newspaper heroes?"

"Him or me?" Allie tossed her hair over her shoulder in a gesture that mirrored flicking him away, like an annoying insect that wouldn't leave her alone. Sawyer just let it go and trailed her to the elevator.

He stayed stuck to her side all the way out to her car, a fuel-efficient Ford Focus, stopping by the door as she unlocked it

"All right, I'm leaving now. Your security duty is fulfilled."

Ignoring the remark, he made his own observation. "Well, at least you drive American-made. I had you pegged for a Honda or maybe some Korean job."

"I'm from the Midwest. We support our industries," she said matter-of-factly.

"But didn't you know that American automakers don't know how to build anything without government guidance and oversight?" Sawyer couldn't help saying something sarcastic. She seemed to bring out the worst in him.

She gave an unladylike snort. "Typical right-winger. Government is the badass and corporations are the good guys."

The discussion digressed into a mini-argument about the right and wrong of business acumen versus government meddling. He pushed, she listened, but finally put up her hands, warding off the onslaught.

"We can go over this all day. We're not going to agree." For some reason he wasn't leaving her side. "So, what do you want? You can go now. I'm leaving."

"Driving all the way back to Denver tonight? You won't get home 'til after midnight."

"I haven't decided. The paper hasn't really given me an expense account for this story. So if I stay, it's on my own dime, and dimes are getting fewer and fewer."

"I heard the staff at the Post took a pay cut recently due to the economic downturn. It's hard enough that the Rocky Mountain News is gone. Doubt you want to see this paper go under too." He actually sounded sympathetic, causing her to look at him a little quizzically, but she gave him a straight answer.

"Seems to be the way of things. Everyone goes to online news outlets these days."

"You know why print media is losing readership, don't you?"

"You're the expert. You tell me," Allie retorted archly.

"Easy enough." She'd given him an opening and he walked through. "People who like to turn actual pages are generally conservative. The computer is a tool not something they sit down to their morning coffee with, and they've stopped subscribing to newspapers because they have become so liberal in their reporting. The big papers like USA Today and the NY Times, LA Times, etc. don't answer their needs, so they're dying. Simple really."

"Simplistic is more like it." She took offense. "In any case, I don't color my news according to my views. News is news. Facts are facts."

"Unless you view the facts differently. Truth is not the same for everyone."

"What made you so cynical?"

"Coming home from Iraq to deal with media darlings like Cindy what's-her-face. The twit who stood on her son's body to get media attention for something she didn't understand, or even bother to try. And now we have a whole batch of likeminded fools in Congress and the White House ruling by ideology rather than rational thinking." Sawyer just shook his head in disgust.

"That's a damn gloomy look at the world. I'm sorry that serving your country has been such a sour experience…" As soon as it was out of her mouth, she regretted her choice of words.

"You've got that backwards. It's the homecoming that was a sour experience. Serving was honorable. Or so I like to think. This is just a lighter shade of what Americans did to Viet Nam vets when they returned. I thank God that I didn't have to deal with what those men did." His response was more resigned than angry.

"Look. I'm sorry. I didn't want to make an issue of things here. I have respect and admiration for those who go into the armed forces. It's something I don't have the nerve for and someone has to do it."

He looked at her with a sharpened vision. "That's funny. I figured you for one of those anti-war types."

"I'm not a Code Pink person. That's a little far afield even for me. But I'm not too sure about what we've been doing over there all these years, either."

"I'll take that on face value." He hesitated. "If you want, I'm sure Carly wouldn't mind having you spend the night out at the ranch again. She doesn't get into town that often and seemed to enjoy having another female around for a bit. Gram doesn't like company that much anymore."

Allie looked at him suspiciously. She wasn't looking forward to a long drive home or the alternative of dropping another hundred on a room. *Why look a gift horse in the mouth? This one has kind of a nice turn to his if he ever smiles.*

"All right. I don't really want to impose, but you'd save me more than wear and tear on the car, not to mention me. I accept your somewhat dubious offer."

The ceasefire was in effect.

Chapter 14

Theo Kraegen was leafing through files that had piled up on his mahogany desk, the very same desk that had graced his father's office in the governor's mansion three decades before. He'd played that violin until the sympathetic strains of nostalgia, the stories of the beloved elder Kraegen long since gone, had bored the public. Now they were attuned to the modern version of fiddling while Rome burned with global warming. This was his most popular and successful melody and Kraegen was banking on a never-ending reprise.

Not giving the expansive ocean view a second thought, Kraegen sorted through the folders, finally pulling out one stamped with the EcoEarth Legal Center insignia. This file outlined a milestone case for the legal group he'd founded after leaving his seat in Congress. EcoEarth was the defender of the rights of natural resources around the globe, if resources actually had rights. Rational people might argue that insentient minerals, flora and fauna couldn't possibly exercise their 'rights,' but organizations like Kraegen's had built a reputation and power base on the manipulative concept that humanity strips resources of those 'rights' to exist in their natural form.

Lately, EcoEarth had expanded its scope of modern chivalric pursuits to championing the causes of downtrodden individuals, the dispossessed and the politically disenfranchised. This file held the details of such a case that had been won a few months back – the defense of a cadre of individuals accused of terrorist activity. Kraegen was a defense attorney at heart, though proving the innocence of the client was not his incentive for becoming an advocate. It was winning cases that would increase his clout in D.C.

This case proved his influence.

The new president had made no bones about his intent to close the detention center at Guantanamo Bay, a position that had been heavily supported by power brokers like Kraegen. The intense thrust from the left had created a wedge in the door to bring suit for the release of detainees that were suspected of terrorist ties, *but unproven*, added Kraegen silently as he skimmed the file's contents. This case had gone largely undetected, or ignored depending on one's viewpoint, by the press and had been brought to the bench in New York. It had slipped through because of the executive order that the president had signed not a week after his inauguration. With the radically progressive panel sitting on the Second Circuit Court of Appeals, these detainees were given the green light of liberation without any real fuss, *or notoriety*. A point that suited Kraegen quite well and made him smile as he flipped the pages.

Growing censure among the public and some lawmakers to shut Gitmo's doors was raising the specter of where the potentially released prisoners were to be relocated. As Kraegen saw things, this was advantageous to his cause. No nation, not even the home countries of the detainees, wanted them.

So what's a nation to do with the new untouchables? His ego expanded yet a little more as he perused how his legal team had managed to shuffle the freed men through the system with the complicity of U.S. Immigration. How easy it was to get visas for intellectual applicants. *Thank God for the educated fanatic*, he thought as he noted where the new émigrés were dispatched.

Content with the progress of EcoEarth's endeavors, he set the folder aside and shifted his attention to the computer desktop where his assistant had sent a number of files flagged with links to current news.

Kraegen was preparing for his national radio program. Checking his watch, he saw that he still had a couple hours before going on air, plenty of time to decide which drum he was going to beat today. The usual environmental claptrap was what had built his growing empire. He came from enormous family wealth but that didn't inhibit his need to add to that financial base. Like many moneyed liberals, the politics were all about the riches they engendered and the power those riches purchased. More assets equaled more control, and control was what he understood. The trouble was that even Kraegen was low man on the totem pole. There were a select few who wielded power above and beyond his and he didn't like it one bit.

Kraegen used every platform he could find to self-promote and climb to a higher position within the system, a system he was aggressively seeking to change with the help of someone else's greater power and money. Kraegen's plans were to use that man's resources to undermine and, ultimately, supplant him.

He relished reading his own words in print, losing count of how often media mavens quoted him as an expert on global warming, or 'climate change' as the newspeak favored term. Of the files on the computer, there were at least five articles that deferred to his statements on the Wyoming power failure and the coal company that, according to him and like-minded environmentalists, had perpetrated the crisis. Calling the situation disastrous was his own doing and he'd supplied Haggerty with the talking points needed to pound it home. Kraegen had little use for Rone other than as a dispensable tool used to help institute the carbon credit bureaucracy that would make them all that much wealthier.

Rone Haggerty was the scheduled guest for today's show. They would go after the coal industry with renewed vigor and make the case for less being more. *What a crock*, he thought, knowing well that people were still buying it, despite the naysayers, the 'deny-ers.' He made a few notes on the computer as fuel for his radio monologue and went over the questions for Haggerty, all designed to make it look like the man had a clue about CO_2 emissions generated by coal-fired power plants. He thoroughly disliked the political hack but had to admire the way he'd worked the environmental lobby for gain and a sure trip to the U.N. ambassadorship.

Finishing his show prep, Kraegen sat back in his chair and cradled the back of his head with interlaced fingers. Propping his feet on the desk, he thought about how well things were coming together.

Finally gazing out over the vast Atlantic's frothing whitecaps, an insidious smile curved his lips. *Got 'em by the 'nads.* As to whom he was referring by that thought was clear only to him.

Energy Barons

Chapter 15

Another night spent at Depression Creek Ranch turned out to be uneventful and a good deal more pleasant than the last slumber party. Sawyer wasn't as antagonistic toward their guest, probably because this time she'd actually been invited rather than forced by unforeseen circumstances to bunk there. The only tension she encountered was that humming strain between Sawyer and his brother, Cole. A strange relationship that wasn't explained even when she attempted to squirrel information out of Carly.

Allie did find out that Sawyer owned a house in town and stayed there most of the time. He usually spent time on the ranch when extra help was needed for calving, branding, culling cattle or farming duties. On the whole, Sawyer avoided his older brother as much as possible and vice versa.

The relationship between the two men intrigued Allie and her natural curiosity would have gotten her in trouble with either one of them if Carly hadn't quietly suggested that asking questions would instigate some ugliness.

"It's better to just let the boys work things out for themselves," she told Allie.

Allie furrowed her forehead in frustration. "It doesn't look like that's been real successful. How long has this been going on, or, can't you answer that, either?" The two women were cleaning up in the kitchen after dinner. All of the boys except Sawyer had taken off to watch Carly's oldest son's baseball game. It was early enough in the season and Carly had a few other things to attend to so she'd opted to stay home. Allie thought it best to hang with her hostess rather than be odd-woman out among an all-male contingent, even though they'd politely invited her to tag along. Allie had a brother and the paper business still catered to men in many ways, so she was

used to dealing with testosterone, but being the only female surrounded by cowboys she hardly knew, nice as they were, didn't really light her fire. She'd rather indulge in girl-talk and see if she could-
n't get Sawyer's sister to loosen up and relieve her gnawing curiosity.

"Well, being a reporter you understand that there's always a back
story. We just don't talk about it around here. Grudges run deep in
Aleman blood. Must be the Latin side of the family."

"Latin? Your name hardly sounds Spanish or Italian."

"That's because our ancestors dropped the Latin pronunciation a
couple of generations back. The name is actually pronounced
'allaymáhn.' It means 'German' in Spanish."

Allie turned to face Carly, continuing to dry a large casserole
dish. "So you're German Spaniards?" She grinned at the thought.
"That's a mix for around here."

"Oh, I don 't know. About a hundred years ago our grandfather,
a vaquero of German descent from Mexico, moved up here and mar-
ried the daughter of a local land-poor rancher. He brought quite a
few hundred head of cattle from his family's holdings south of the
border. Kind of like a bride price." She shrugged as she wiped down
the counters. "Anyway, things worked out and now we're still land-
poor ranchers, in a manner of speaking."

"This place looks pretty prosperous to me," observed Allie.

"We do all right. Ranching is a tough gig these days. Property
taxes, cost of feed, cost of farming, BLM regs. On top of that you
have to have degrees in chemistry or ag and have basic vet skills to
boot. There are a whole slew of things you have to take into account
to raise beef. The days of the range wars and cattle drives are long
gone," she sighed. "The Old West is ancient history around here."

Being a city kid Allie had no idea how much was involved in
running a ranch. "I never thought about the logistics of cattle ranching in the modern world. Maybe tomorrow I can see a little bit of
how things work. I might be able to sell it as a story to my editor. If
nothing else, it's good background for the other stories I'm doing
about the region."

While Carly considered the suggestion, Allie asked, "Do you
think the guys could handle a greenhorn hanging around for part of

the day?"

"I don't know how much you can learn in a few hours, but, what the hey. We may as well ask. Sawyer's still here and I'd guess he'd go for it." She pulled her towel through a cupboard door handle and grabbed some coffee for herself and Sawyer, handing a third full mug to Allie. Gesturing for Allie to follow her, they went into the study where the middle brother was working on the computer.

Carly gave Sawyer his coffee and plumped down on the couch, perfectly comfortable in the masculine stronghold. Allie, on the other hand felt like a trespasser, but settled in next to her hostess and sipped her hot coffee, savoring it and waiting for the other shoe to drop.

Although Sawyer had been cordial all evening, there was still an aloofness that she couldn't really fathom. What she'd seen of him puzzled her. One moment he'd be brooding, the next he was fired up and passionately defending his beliefs. A man of contradictions who really seemed to be able to get under her skin. *Not a good thing.* But she was here and she didn't want to waste the opportunity to learn something about how cattlemen lived and, she had to admit, more about what made Sawyer *Alémán* tick.

At the moment, his commentary in response to Carly's inquiry about having their guest tour the operation the next day amounted to little more than grunts. It left Allie wondering what the prognosis would be until Carly turned to her and let her know that she'd have the full tour in the morning. Carly then got up and yawned.

"I'm bushed but I have a few things to see to upstairs before the crew gets back." She looked down at Allie who was still seated on the couch. "You're all set for tonight, right?"

A little confused that Carly seemed to be abandoning her in the ogre's den, Allie couldn't muster up anything more to say than, "Uh, sure. I'm fine."

"Good girl. See you in the morning," and as Carly slipped out of the room, Allie could have sworn that she saw the slightest smile tweaking the corner of Carly's mouth. *Sneaky stinker. What does she think she's accomplishing by leaving me at the mercy of Mr. Personality?*

Allie let the air escape her lungs in a slow exhale that, from the tilt of Sawyer's head, alerted her to his awareness of her continued presence. If she didn't feel awkward before, she sure did now. She was stuck. She couldn't just get up and leave unobserved. She either had to say something or, what?

After a few unnerving moments she finally determined to just wish him a good night and pack it in. Before she could rise, he closed down the computer and swiveled around in the chair, pinning her with a celadon gaze.

For some reason, a frisson of panic shot through her. She covered quickly before Sawyer picked up on her discomfiture… she hoped. To her surprise he slid down in the secretarial chair, visibly relaxing with his legs outstretched and crossed at the ankles.

"So, you want to see what it takes to raise beef for a hungry world."

The innocuousness of the statement was the last thing she expected, but the words finally gave her something real to respond to. "I'm here and if you're willing, it makes sense for me to pick up what background I can."

He cocked his head questioningly. "I thought you were here to do a story about the collapse of the coal industry. Why the interest in ranching?"

Allie sank back into the sofa, suddenly tired of questions, both asking and answering. "This is Wyoming. Oil, cattle and coal, all important components of the state's culture and economy. You can't write a good story without the whole story. Know what I mean?"

"No."

Neither do I. "I just want to be thorough and take advantage of a great opportunity to learn something useful. Is that so objectionable?" *I hope he buys this mush, 'cause I sure don't.*

"Nope." He rose from his chair and offered his hand to help her up. "I just hope it actually helps 'expand your horizons.'" He smirked as he held out his other hand to accept her coffee mug. Taking it, he went into the kitchen leaving her standing in the doorway, wondering what had just happened when the back door banged open, the rest of the ranch's male residents making a boisterous entrance. Before she was sucked into the vortex of post-game rowdiness, Allie escaped up the stairs, happy to disappear into her room for the rest of the night.

After breakfast, Cole and Sam left for a regional meeting of the cattleman's association, planning to be gone for a couple days. Dan left for work, Carly took the boys to school and Mickey went into town for tractor parts. That left Allie in the care of her guide and all-around fun seeker, Sawyer.

This is gonna be a hoot, I can tell. Allie rolled her eyes with the thought of spending hours alone with a man who alternately infuriated or intrigued her. *But he knows the business and can be a fount of information, so suck it up and smile,* which she did.

"Was the coffee that bitter this morning?"

"What?" Allie was brought out of her reverie. "Bitter? No, it was fine. Why?"

"That look on your face. I thought for sure it gave you indigestion," he turned to give her a half-grin, "or something."

"Must be the *something.*" She shot back. *It's not the coffee that's making my stomach flip,* she thought sullenly. *Keeping company with a sourpuss would give anyone heartburn.* She wanted to kick herself. *Man, whose stupid idea was this?* Then she recalled that she'd expected to at least have the genial Sam as a buffer. Again, she told herself to suck it up. She'd asked for this, after all.

"So, where do we start?" Allie chirped.

Did she just flip a switch? "In the truck," he replied, walking over to the beat-up, early 1970s Ford. Holding open the door, Sawyer ushered her in with a courtly wave of his hand. "It isn't exactly a royal carriage but it'll get us around."

"I don't need velvet cushions."

"It'd be more fitting to do the tour on horseback, but you need more time for that."

"You also need to know how to ride," said Allie, climbing up into the cab. She had to move a box of pump parts and assorted mechanical odds and ends to make room for her rear on the bench seat.

"Don't ride, huh? Too bad," Sawyer clucked his tongue.

For some reason that put her on the defensive. "I like horses fine. Like most kids, I would have loved a pony for Christmas, but they aren't common pets in the 'burbs. So the chance to learn never came up. Thought I'd get to rectify that oversight once I moved west." Allie grabbed the door for stability as the truck bounced down the road. "I didn't realize I was trading one big city for another. Denver's hardly a cowtown. More bicycles than cars in some sectors."

"Ain't that the truth," he agreed with a tinge of regret. "Well, trucks and ATVs are useful for moving tools, parts," he gestured with his head toward the oil-stained box she'd repositioned, "and feed, but nothing can replace getting out and riding. Clears your head."

Allie glanced at Sawyer as he guided the truck over ruts and dips toward some farm buildings. He seemed a little lost in thought, so she let the silence stretch until he was ready to talk.

He drove her out to a large barn where he pointed out farm equipment, naming off the types of machinery. Disc harrow, seeder, sprayer, swather, hay baler. There were also two horse trailers parked by the side. Inside, she noted two all-terrain vehicles, two tractors, one that was partially dismembered, a couple of covered snowmobiles and various gear that he didn't fully explain, not that she would retain everything anyway. There was too much, even with her mini-recorder to try to pick-up the details. He briefly showed her the tack room that housed saddles, bridles, harnesses and all types of ropes, none of which was familiar to her beyond what she'd seen on the few occasions she had been on a horse, and those she could count on one hand. A veteran horsewoman she emphatically was not.

While he led her around the farm equipment outside he also walked her through the seasons on a working ranch. Starting with the winter months, he pointed out the depleted haystack of round bales.

"All this equipment is for cultivating and harvesting hay to feed stock during the winter. Around here we can have some pretty harsh conditions, so animals that are kept here rather than moved to winter pastures in states with milder weather, feed in ice and snow, where it's relatively clean and dry." Sawyer nodded in the direction of the bales, the small pile dwarfed by the height of the hay shelter rising two stories above it. "This is all that's left after a rough winter. The cows are all out in summer pasture now. We get them out there as soon as possible to avoid scours that can come with the spring."

"Scours?"

"That's when the nursing calves end up with diarrhea from the mud and manure that can get on the cow's udders. Getting them out to clean pasture keeps that at bay. The general rule of thumb is, when the hay pile is shorter than the grass, they go to grass."

"How much hay does it take to feed the cattle over a winter?" Looking at the height of the open-sided hay barn, she wondered at the immense amount needed for a wintering herd.

"It takes about two and a half to three tons of hay per cow per winter."

"That's a lot of hay. How many head do you have here at Depression Creek?"

"Around five thousand," he said candidly.

Her eyes went round. "That's a *lot* of hay. And you grow your own so how much land does it take to feed them?'

Sawyer scratched his jaw. "Well, you can do the math, depending on how much you fertilize you can harvest between three and a half tons to six tons per acre. But fertilizer is expensive and getting to be more so with all the new regulations that have been imposed on the industry over the years, including the cost of energy to manufacture it.

"The cost of energy affects everything. Whether you truck your cattle to warmer climes for the winter or raise, or buy hay to feed the herd. Ranching is a continuous treadmill. Profit margins diminish or stay static from year to year so the farmer and the rancher can't get ahead." He hooked his heel on the lower fence rail and leaned his forearms on the top one, gazing off into the distance, rolling acres of grassland filled the horizon, dotted with clusters of grazing cattle. "Farming and ranching have never been a get-rich lifestyle. It's something that some of us are drawn to do, it's who we are. Husbandry is an ancient and revered calling, one that feeds your family and the world." Sawyer paused a few beats.

"The Patriarchs were strong men, stanchions of an agrarian society who offered sacrifice to God in recognition of the gifts that had been bestowed on them, their families and their people. The gift of provision. We try to live up to that but it gets harder and harder with the crushing pressure coming out of bureaucracies that haven't got a clue."

He abruptly stood up and walked back to the truck, Allie doubling her step to keep up. She couldn't let the comments slide without a question.

"My understanding is that the governmental regulation is in place to assist the sustainability of agriculture and, well, society in general. Otherwise we'd have indiscriminate dumping of hazardous chemicals, over-grazing, water wastage, that sort of thing."

Sawyer halted at the rig and looked at her from across the truck bed, which was loaded with lengths of sprinkler pipe and a roll of barbed wire. "What you're assuming is that farmers don't know what they're doing, that they have no feel for the land or how to use it wisely. Centuries of farming and herding should tell you otherwise. Sure, you're going to run across some dishonest agribiz corporations and maybe a few unconscionable acts by landowners. But for the most part, farmers don't bite the hand that feeds them. You destroy the land, you destroy your own future. Farmers and ranchers are some of the most educated individuals in America. They have to be to understand the use and application of chemical and natural pesticides and fertilizers. They have to be able to vaccinate and doctor their own stock, manage seeds, feeds and the very soil that nurtures them all. Forest rangers, land management bureaucrats and that whole bunch of governmental toadies get degrees based on high-minded theories that, frankly, are constantly being proven wrong when they're actually applied to the land." He climbed back in the cab and barely waited for Allie to get in before taking off up the track.

"Look, my point is that the environmental lobby has brought about laws and regs that seem to be more about controlling people rather than preserving the earth for future generations. The planning commissions do their work based on outdated and faulty data," he glanced at her pursed lips, seeing her need to refute his claims. "I'm not making this up, the evidence is there. Every time they try to *plan* urban growth or *guide* agriculture they eff it up and the situation gets worse. People are a lot smarter than government gives them credit for being. We're actually pretty good shepherds, on the whole, and left to ourselves, the costs of food and energy wouldn't be skyrocketing at the rate it is."

He gave her a stern glance that was contradicted with a half-mocking turn of his lips. "Did you get all that on tape?"

Allie had to laugh. "Yep, every word. Now give me the rest of the tour without the bombastic commentary and we're good."

They spent the next couple of hours going through the rest of the annual cycle. Calving in the spring followed within a few weeks by branding, castrating and vaccinating. Running bulls with the cows to breed for the next year's calving season would usually happen in June. Seeding the fields for hay would occur in the spring, and be harvested and baled later in the summer. During the summer months practical miles of fencing are checked and repaired, cattle and wild game knocking them down over time. Thence to the fall when they go to market, the whole circle of life to begin again when stock is rounded up for winter feeding.

By noon Sawyer had Allie back at her car. She had gathered far more information than she'd thought possible, not to mention getting an earful about interfering bureaucracy. Initially balking at his one-sided opinion, she found herself listening to his words, stated strongly but without the emotional overtones generally heard among the opposition. To her surprise, much of what he said began to filter through as being more sensible than she'd expected.

Allie had a lot to chew on while she drove back to Denver.

Energy Barons

Chapter 16

Cirrus clouds streaming across the vibrant blue of a spring morning sky greeted Allie with promise. She knew she was in for a scuffle with Carter Gleason to convince him to give her more leeway in covering the coal story, but she had conviction on her side. Parking beneath the oddly designed Post building in Denver's city center, a pearly edifice resembling the bow of a great ship, Allie pulled her arguments together as she rode the elevator to her floor. Determined to win her case, she pushed open the door to her editor's office.

He was not a happy camper.

Unlit cigarette hanging off his lip, he glared at her as she closed the door behind her. "Where have you been? I give you one day, you take two and I see on my desk, what? Nada."

"That's because I just e-mailed my story this morning. It took that much time to corner the FBI weasel, and, if you'd read it, he still gave me zip."

"I did read it. Like I said, *nada, nothing.*" He held up the printout of her copy. "What am I supposed to do with this? Stir-fry it? It has about as much substance as bok choy," he flattened the sheets under his meaty fist.

Allie knew she had to find a way to defend the story. They were too close to blowing it wide open. Keeping her emotions in check, she planted her palms on Gleason's desk and stared him down.

"I know this looks pretty lame at the moment." He started to bluster but she cut him off, "*But* I have a couple of leads that we're following up on. If what I think happened *did* happen, we're going to beat out every other news source."

He sat back and crossed his arms over his chest, challenging her to persuade him. "Tell me."

"That's the problem, it's still tenuous." She told him what transpired with the SAC in Gillette, leaving out some of the pertinent details so Gleason wouldn't shut her down. She did go into the point that it looked like sabotage but until they had confirmation she couldn't run with it.

He leaned forward and dropped his head in his hands. "It's a major headline but what we have that's solid hardly rates as a puff piece, let alone a follow-up." He rolled his blood-shot eyes up at her. "Give me something I can use."

"I will."

"In the meantime, cover this local event. We need it for tomorrow." He handed her a sheet with some basic information on an afternoon groundbreaking with the mayor and some debatable dignitaries. Knowing better than to make a fuss, she grabbed the paper and beat feet to her desk.

Lunch hour and Allie wanted to catch up with Debra away from the office. Cradling an espresso, she sat on a well-worn couch at the Tattered Cover, staring past the rows of library bookshelves that lined the warehouse-sized store. She didn't notice Debra until fingers snapped under her nose.

"Daydreamin' again?" an elfin grin crossed Debra's lips. "Girl, you've got to wake up."

Shaking off the cobwebs, Allie smiled in return. "Just trying to get a grip on what we've got."

"Or don't *got*," added Debra. "Yeah. Let's go for a walk. I think a little privacy would be preferable to a hippie bookstore."

"Hippie? What decade are you living in?"

Debra just shrugged her shoulders and led the way out onto the street and down to Cherry Creek, Allie catching her on the steps outside the shop. "I like it in there. Nice atmosphere."

"And too many ears that are paying more attention to what goes on around them than what they're supposed to be reading. We're not discussing the debutante ball, you know."

"You're right. Besides I could use a walk. Too many hours on the road lately."

"You certainly have been the road warrior this week," agreed Debra. They strolled down the street the couple of blocks it took to bring them to what Allie considered a decorative concrete ditch. A path led down to a prettily landscaped walkway that followed the creek skirting the lower downtown area, or 'Lo-Do' to the locals. To Allie's claustrophobic mind, the ten-foot walls that lined either side of the canal confined her in more ways than one. She had to admit that she'd thoroughly enjoyed the vastness of the plains, rimmed to the west by the soaring Big Horn Range, and was beginning to prefer it over this man-made mountainscape of skyscrapers… a mockery of the real thing that formed Denver's picturesque backdrop.

Instead of descending the pedestrian trail, they settled onto a bench overlooking the mini-canyon and listened to the lunchtime walkers confiding to their companions or complaining into a cell phone. Debra tsked at the few runners loping past, commenting that they looked underfed and stringy, health enthusiasts that maybe took their passion too far.

"That gal needs to *eat*," she said in low tones. Debra was in pretty good shape herself but she definitely didn't believe in denying oneself the benefits of life, like real food.

Allie chuckled and almost choked on her coffee. "So, what did you find? Anything yummy?" The talk of food, or lack thereof, made her think of the lunch she didn't get.

"Some pretty interesting doings. When's the last time you talked to Sol?"

"I haven't. Figured you were jumping in as the liaison and since I don't understand much of anything that her husband says…" she shrugged. "He travels faster and further than this meager mind can follow. More like your speed."

"Hmmph," sniffed Debra. "I'll opt to take that as a compliment when it could be construed to mean that I am a socially stunted nerd."

"Hardly. Just far more able to travel the internet research channels than I am. I can't seem to get dialed in very well. And understanding Toddy, well…" she just let it hang.

"Nah. It's just the difference in style. I'm more bookish and you're, well, aggressive."

"I guess that's a nice way of calling me annoying and pushy," Allie winked, "But it works. So what'd she and Toddy have for us?"

"It looks like this P.O.P. is tied into an environmental group called Rural Resources which, it seems, is loosely connected to Green Grasslands."

"They like the catchy names, don't they? Maybe there's a group called Eco-Equalizers too."

Debra looked at her friend suspiciously. "That hardly sounds like you. I thought you were a greenie from the get-go."

"I am, but I don't hang with the idea of using terrorist tactics to make a statement. Our job is supposed to be to cover the stories and do the fact-finding so people can institute change civilly."

"I took you for more of a rabble-rouser," she laughed. "Guess I had you *all* wrong."

Allie snorted. "Right."

"Anyway, turns out Solana and Toddy have been following this P.O.P. group because of its involvement in a land purchase scheme that was cracked almost two years ago by a friend of hers in Idaho. Rural Resources was involved to some degree and now they've located offices in Alaska where something else is going on."

"Alaska? That's got to be the last frontier for the environmentalists. I know that the university up there is very active ecologically speaking, the arts included. I believe there's even a big lobby to curb greenhouse gas emissions, despite what everyone says about Alaska being full of backwoods NRA types."

"Don't know about that. It's no place I've needed to travel. I like the sun too much." Debra leaned her head back to take in some midday heat as if to emphasize her declaration.

"Well, you must like snow too or you wouldn't be here at the foot of the Rockies."

"A girl's gotta make a living. It's nowhere near as cold here as Alaska and we don't live in the dark six months out of the year," she shivered. "Now, that would put me over the edge. I have my skin color for a reason." She slid hooded eyes sideways at Allie in partial jest, "to handle those golden rays." She sighed in pleasure allowing the warmth to seep in.

Getting back to the point of their little conclave, Allie said, "All right then. You enjoy those rays while I reiterate, so what's the big deal in Alaska?"

"Just that it looks like there's some kind of network of activities on the agenda of Rural Resources and it's clandestine partner, P.O.P. It seems to involve mostly straightforward litigation but remember when I first told you about the nasty business in Idaho? A little murder? A little land extortion?

Allie nodded. "You didn't go into detail."

"All we need to know is that there were some dastardly doings in the piney woods of Idaho." She swiped away the past with a flawlessly manicured hand. "The connectors are the fact that pressure groups with eco-backing are taking a gold mine to task instead of a lumber mill, trying to shut it down before it ever goes into production."

"So? Gold mining is notorious for polluting streams and waterways with cyanide, I think it is. Maybe they're doing a good thing here."

"Except for the fact that the plan for disposal of mine tailings has already been okayed by the Army Corps of Engineers as being environmentally acceptable. The permits were issued and Rural Resources and a conglomeration of other groups have been dragging this through the courts to keep the mine from opening and supplying desperately needed jobs."

"I still say they may have a point," Allie's stubborn streak was coming through.

Debra wagged her head in dismay. "Girl, you're a *reporter*. You need to get all the facts before you jump to any conclusions."

"Okay, I'll bite. What am I missing?"

"The fact that this mine is the only real employment opportunity for the local Native population and they have an ownership stake in its production. Alaska Natives have some of the highest unemployment rates in the country. The environmental lobby is doing everything in its power to block a real opportunity for the Yu'pik to make a viable living from their own land." She huffed with the slightest trace of indignation, "And this isn't the first time it's happened. Nor will it be the last."

"Be more specific."

"Ecologically minded people seem to think that Native Alaskans can make an adequate living by saving the salmon, carving totems and tourism. It obviously hasn't happened that way since Congress set them up as corporate entities in the seventies. As Alaska has prospered by basically utilizing its natural resources, environmental groups have grown up to save what's left, though I'd venture to say that because most of the development occurred after the birth of conservationism, the state hasn't suffered as many environmental problems as the lower forty-eight." She looked at Allie, "Of course, that's just my take on the general situation. Anyway, the culture shock still occurred but now the Native corporations are trying to step up for the new millennium and provide for their own. Unfortunately, the eco-lobby is doing everything they can to impede their efforts to improve living standards by developing their own resources.

"The point here is that there's a different kind of discrimination going on, environmentalists vs. everybody else who wants to flex their property rights by making use of what belongs to them, and in the case of the Yu'pik, it's the corporate land that was retained for them by Congress."

"I still don't get the connection, other than Rural Resources and Green Grasslands are brother organizations. I get that rogue members of this Protect Our Planet were caught doing bad acts and now I've heard mention of them in Cheyenne. *And* we may have an actual attack locally. What it has to do with a state a couple thousand miles away… hmmm, I don't know."

"You really think we're looking at intentional destruction of the coal operations. Sabotage." It was a disheartened statement rather than a question.

"Listen to yourself," clucked Allie. "You're the one put me on to thinking it's possible, though I can't convince Gleason of that. And I can't just up and leave to investigate in Alaska, As it is, he doesn't like footing the gas bill for me running up and down to Wyoming for the last week."

"Well, you don't need to worry about Alaska. Sol is heading up there herself. She's particularly interested because of the Native correlation to the story."

"That's a relief. I can call her and see what's going on in the great white north. But I've gotta admit, I'm beginning to wonder how much substance there is to our hunches."

Yancy was on her way down to Denver. The EPA hearing on the petition she'd filed to reopen the old power plant as a stopgap to provide adequate power to the region was scheduled for tomorrow. Despite her pressure tactics, she was still surprised that the Environmental Protection Agency had granted the hearing in the first place. Now she wondered what the chances were for getting a positive ruling from the huge bureaucratic machine.

It had been a couple of days since she'd left a message for Allie about the case, fervently hoping to wangle a little coverage for an issue that could impact everyone living in the affected area, not just the Lysanders.

Yancy had met Allie a few years back while she was employed at the law firm in New York, the one where she'd needed a shark cage to interact with her own colleagues. They'd gotten to know each other briefly when Allie had spent a holiday with her aunt, Ellis Akkerman. Ell had been, and actually still was, the go-to gal for anything computer at the international law office. The three had spent a weekend trolling the streets of the city for girls' night out. Good food, good jazz and a couple of cocktails. Tame by New York standards.

When Yancy zeroed in on Allie's byline, she new it was a natural move to make the contact and see if she could drum up PR for the case. If she could get some coverage it might raise awareness of the need to avert other potential health emergencies like Kara's.

She'd called Ell to get Allie's cell number when she hadn't heard back, then punched in that same number and, happy day, heard a live voice answer the call.

They'd chatted briefly while Yancy laid out the purpose of her trip. It didn't take much to get Allie's animated response. She felt sure her editor would go for a human-interest angle on the power outage story. A few more minutes of yakking and they had an agreement to meet the next day at the newly constructed, widely touted, 'green' building that housed the Region 8 EPA offices on Wynkoop Street in Denver.

The appearance before the administrative law judge was scheduled for 3:00 p.m.   Gleason lauded Allie for turning in an exceptional story on the windbag mayor and his pals at the groundbreaking of an energy-efficient, government parking structure. The punishment had been levied, penance paid and now she had managed to get him to allot a few inches to a blackout feature on the complaint Yancy had filed.

Allie hadn't been given much background before the hearing, but she figured the Lysanders' predicament ought to be a sure-fire tearjerker as an additional story, maybe even garner the front page of the regional news section. On top of that, Allie was hoping the story would bolster her request for more flexibility to continue the investigation, if you could even call it that with the miniscule amount of news it was generating.

Allie *knew* something was going to break, and soon. What she hadn't expected was to walk out of the hearing with a different perspective on the EPA's regulatory process and the widespread effect of its policy decisions. She'd assumed, like most of the media and the public in general, that the agency was beneficent in its actions, doing the work of the people, keeping them safe from polluters.

This was an eye-opener that began to chip away at the foundations of her core beliefs, something that Allie hadn't signed up for and was begrudging deep down. She kept telling herself that she was a journalist and preconceptions had no place in covering the news, particularly since Sawyer Aleman had been so accusatory of the whole profession.

Frustrating as the process was, Yancy had been given the rostrum to make her argument that the failure of the EPA to allow the reopening of the obsolete coal-fired plant would not be a victimless circumstance, but a crime.

What? That was a new one on Allie and she had listened carefully to Yancy's explanation of how the law is written to protect life, not endanger it. Stressing the point that ruling to refuse the allowance of a reliable energy supply to the region would be tantamount to criminal negligence, in that it created a victim by imposing the potential for loss of life, Kara Lysander's advocate laid out her case. A case laying the foundation for an appeal, should it come to that.

In the end, the hearing wasn't overlong, the outcome being a foregone conclusion as far as the judge was concerned.

Claim denied.

The doors of the administrative court closed with a soft whoosh behind them. To Yancy it sounded more like the door slamming shut on justice. Allie found the whole process confusing and was seriously beginning to doubt who or what the bureaucratic judge was protecting. Her mind was telling her that the EPA was standing tough for the earth's health but at what cost? The health of a little girl, and others like her, whose chances of dying had increased dramatically by the decision Allie had just heard rendered? The scales of justice were meant to weigh the merits of both sides of a contention, or so she thought. Today she had witnessed a jaundiced decision rather than a prudently considered adjudication, and it had just shifted Allie's perception of the status quo. Who was really blind here? The implicit justness of government policy, or her and others like her by accepting it without question?

They found themselves walking back to their cars in silence, each contemplating the conclusion of the proceedings.

"Okay, no more brooding," Allie piped up. "Let's go get dinner and you can give me the background on the Lysanders. I've got the details now from the actual hearing, but I need to know more about what led up to this point. Flesh out the story."

"Good enough. I could use a little down time but I ought to get settled at a hotel first. I didn't have a chance to make reservations before coming down."

"What hotel? You can stay with me. It ain't fancy but it's clean." On second thought Allie added the disclaimer, "Well mostly. I haven't been home much this week."

"I'm not fussy and very appreciative for any place to lay my head for the night, so I accept with enthusiasm." Yancy smiled her appreciation.

"Good. Let's go get some grub, or first a drink to soften the blow of the disappointment."

Yancy nodded and Allie took her by the arm and led her to their destination.

While waiting to be seated at a popular gin joint and grill that was just quiet enough for conversation but not so dead as to be abysmal, Allie and Yancy sat in the bar sipping cocktails and going over the details of the petition that was just denied. Allie took notes and even had her little tape recorder going now and again to capture the minutiae she couldn't get on paper fast enough.

"We're actually talking two different issues here," Yancy began to outline the scenario. "Two different government bureaucracies that have so affected this one family's life, it's a blueprint of what is becoming, or threatening to become, standard operating procedure for everyone who lives and breathes in America."

Allie expressed her doubt. "You're saying these policies will affect everyone? That seems an overstatement." She almost regretted using that word as soon as it fell off her tongue, knowing enough about Yancy to realize she wasn't one who was given to exaggeration.

"It does seem far-fetched, I'll give you that," Yancy blew through the implied skepticism. "On one side of this issue with Kara, and other tribal members, is the Department of Health and Human Services. On the other is the Environmental Protection Agency. The Lysanders' case starts with Indian Health Services, which is run by HHS, which is funded directly by the House of Representatives. You might make note of the fact that no funding for government programs can originate in the Senate. That's unconstitutional."

"Is that important?"

"It could be considering the Senate has already overstepped its bounds in this respect with the original TARP bill, but that's another story." She brushed it away, swiping through the air with the back of her hand. "IHS has been seriously under-funded from the outset. Almost all clinics on reservations are understaffed and inadequately equipped. Understand that the treaties, and in this case I take you back to the particular one between the Crow and the U.S. Government of 1868, guarantee certain services and funding in exchange for ceded rights and lands. I'm just skimming the surface here, so bear with me. What has occurred is that Congress has been given the authority to oversee Indian Health by the fact that they allot funds, or lack thereof if you want to look at it that way. The outcome is that Indians generally receive insufficient care and this is what came into play with Kara. She had difficulties from infancy and lack of funding for proper testing led to misdiagnosis of her problem. It wasn't until she was ten years old that they finally figured out she had juvenile diabetes and by that time the damage to her kidneys was already irreversible."

Allie found the tale heartbreaking but didn't comment.

"Kara's story is just one of hundreds, and just to put this into perspective, Indian Health could be considered a microcosm of the heath care agenda that Congress is fighting over as we speak. And that will affect everyone. What HHS and IHS show us is that bureaucracy doesn't manage money very well and the government wants to expand the scope of its influence. In fact, within the House bill, Indian Tribes are lumped into the same category as states. This is interesting because of their status as treating nations, sovereign entities, they should not be considered as equals to the federated states. Their status is legally different, yet in the currently debated bill, Section 1904 of HR 3200 the Congress takes it upon itself to federalize what are supposed to be independent nations. Okay, that's it for my opining."

Allie wanted to ask more questions but realized they'd be at this all night if she didn't allow Yancy to move on.

"What we had to do was go through an administrative process that's taken more than a year to allocate funding for proper care for Kara, to ensure that she has access to life-saving procedures. In her case, it's dialysis. The problem now is ensuring adequate power to run the machines she needs to keep her alive and able to enjoy a fair-ly normal existence."

"Okay, this is where the EPA comes into the picture, right?" Allie wanted to be sure she was on the same page as Yancy.

"Right. Power outages occur often enough throughout the region in north central Wyoming where they live. The Lysanders have been installing a reliable back-up system to power the dialysis machine purchased as a result of badgering IHS. However, it's not complete and, for the moment they're out of money to finish the project. This explosion that destroyed the new coal-fired plant, taking it off-line for the next half year has left the family in a really tough situation. No reliable power in the remote area where they reside.   " A n d now, you were a witness, the EPA has denied the petition to reinstate the old power plant until such time as the new one can come back online. In so doing, they have placed Kara's life in danger, and like-ly hundreds more. This is no longer just a policy battle where the EPA is regulating the emissions of CO_2, this is a direct affront to human rights and, I think, the constitutional guarantee against cruel and unusual punishment as outlined in the Eighth Amendment."

"Whoa! We've just gone from administrative procedure of restricting carbon dioxide emissions to inflicting cruel and unusual punishment? I thought that was limited to prisoners," said Allie.

"It's not so defined. It may be a longshot but this is the direction I'm thinking of taking the argument in applying for a stay on the decision. There's also the Fifth Amendment that guarantees that no person "shall be deprived of life, liberty or property without due process of law.""

"I thought that's what you just did, was go through due process."

"We're still in the process by taking it to a higher court, which is what you do after you've exhausted the administrative process."

"Okay, I think I have enough to go on unless you can think of anything else pertinent to add." Allie was ready to close up her note-book and drink the glass of wine that had been sitting untouched by her elbow.

"No, there's plenty more in terms of challenging the scientific basis for categorizing CO_2 as a pollutant to begin with, but I think that's for another discussion on another day. I'm out of steam." Yancy wilted back into her chair and did what Allie was contemplating, took a sip of her drink.

Forty-five minutes after they'd begun, Allie was stashing her notes in her satchel when the hostess came to fetch them. They trailed the young woman, burdened by the accoutrements of their respective trades, oversized briefcases that looked more like luggage. Rounding the corner to cross the lobby, Allie's forward progress was arrested by a hearty "howdy" that issued from in front of the hostess' station.

Two men dressed in cowboy chic, i.e. clean jeans and fancy boots, were standing before the podium, hats in hand. One had a genuine smile and the other younger and taller man sported an expression crossed between interest and distrust. Allie could quickly see that the uncertainty was meant for her, but Yancy was receiving frank approval from Cole Aleman. Sam's grin was authentic, making it obvious who had offered the timeworn greeting of the West.

Yancy gave Allie a questioning look that was answered by her friend putting both hands out to grasp Sam's and say hello, then take Cole's cool one in a solid clasp.

"I thought you two were off to a cattleman's association meeting. It's being held here in town?" asked Allie.

"Yep. We're enjoying the sights and smells of the city so we can really appreciate our little paradise back home," Sam winked. Taking Allie gently by the arm he opened his palm toward Yancy. "Don't be shy, now. Introduce us to your friend."

"How could I not?" Allie played along with him. "This is Yancy Collings from Billings. Yancy this is Sam Aleman and his son Cole. Gentlemen ranchers from the great state of Wyoming. They and their family were kind enough to put me up during a storm this week and I even received a tour of ranch operations yesterday, supplied by another of the Aleman brothers."

"I guess there's another story here," said Yancy. Looking over the two men, she wondered about the relationship between the Alemans and Allie.

Allie picked up on the curiosity and suggested that Sam and Cole join them for dinner, the invitation coming none to soon for the hostess who had waited, unsuccessfully trying to conceal her impatience. The line was growing in length and restlessness while the foursome got acquainted. To her relief the men accepted the invitation, so she whisked two more menus out of the slot and quickstepped to the table, the now doubled entourage in tow.

The evening took a pleasant but unexpected turn from there. Sam queried Allie about her work, inserting some keen questions about the power plant story. She was cagey about her progress, instead segueing into the purpose of Yancy's visit to Colorado's capital, opening a new topic and mercifully diverting interest from Allie's iffy theories.

Cole's attention heightened when Yancy began talking. He followed her words and was impressed by her concern for her clients, raising his estimation of lawyers, a profession he didn't hold in high regard on the whole. Having daughters of his own, whom he didn't see often enough living as they did with their mother in Montana, Kara's dilemma touched home.

Sam watched his eldest son with a muted smile. Cole didn't take a shine to women, period. He'd been burned so badly he kept a wary distance from any flames, but this new gal, she was sharp, conscientious and concerned. *Not bad lookin,' either.* Apparently, Cole had noticed that attribute as well and rerouted the conversation to learn more about Yancy's personal life. It had been long enough since Cole had made any effort with a woman that Sam nearly laughed a couple of times at his son's abrupt manner. *That'll win her over, all right.*

Allie, on the other hand, was comparing the two older Aleman brothers. It was astounding how similar they seemed to be at first glance but she suspected the two were actually a world apart, and this one was homing in on Yancy with a fierce glow in his eye. *Woohoo, girl. This boy's ready for a chase. Wonder if he brought his lariat?* Allie caught the gleam in Sam's eye as he winked at her again. She shook her head at him almost imperceptibly, feeling like part of a conspiracy and sat back to enjoy the show.

Chapter 17

Cole had a long day on the road. Leaving Denver before dawn, he dropped his dad in Cheyenne where Dan was going to meet him and drive him home. The rest of the hours were spent rushing to get to Montana just in time to be bludgeoned by his ex-wife about his inadequacies as a father. The general complaints were, "You're never here when the girls need you," contradicted in the next breath by, "You're screwing up their schedule. The girls need a routine to function."

He'd given in to the fact years ago that there was no winning with Suzanne. She'd wanted security but she needed to be in the city. She'd settled for Billings and a new husband who worked for the phone company. Cole couldn't complain too much. The man was good with his children but the fact that he only got to see them every other weekend and a month in the summer hardly filled the hole in his heart. If it weren't for his two daughters, he doubted that he'd have the will to continue breathing day after day.

The original plan had been to leave Denver on Friday so he could arrive in Billings early in the day to make as much of his time with Toni and Cassie as possible. Suzanne put the kibosh on that without a second thought. Toni had a playoff game for basketball in the morning and Suzanne had made it clear that he wasn't welcome. He was torn. The whole way up he brutalized himself for not ignoring his ex-wife's wishes and just showing up, but then, he didn't want to make waves that would negatively affect the girls.

Why things couldn't be less acrimonious was obvious. Their past hid too many betrayals to ever be smoothed over. He just prayed his daughters would survive the battle and turn out all right in the end.

So far, so good.

When he did arrive at the door, both girls rushed their dad, burying their faces in his chest for a hug, their mother glowering from the kitchen doorway. She'd never be able to accept his existence because then she'd have to acknowledge her own transgressions. Instead she hated him for the reminder of who she'd been even as she loved the daughters she'd borne with him. It was easier to turn back to her tasks and let the threesome go without a word.

If the bitterness between their parents bothered them, and Cole was sure that it did, cutting him to his core knowing how much it probably hurt them, they were expert at hiding it. And today's agenda was just to shop, play and eat before he returned them to their mother's care.

Shopping was always an adventure with those two. Toni, a budding young woman at fifteen, could be a handful. She was sure what she wanted and sometimes gave Cole a hard time when he refused to give in to her just because something was fashionable. His answer was always, "If it's that important, we'll have to ask your mother." It was a good way to keep from having her walk out with some article of clothing that, in his mind was inappropriate for anyone of age, let alone a teenager.

Cassie, twelve now, was more of a tomboy and would rather be out riding with her dad. Given her druthers, she'd be living in Wyoming with him, so she wasn't quite as mesmerized by the social hype that drenched most of her friends' thought processes. Or Toni, for that matter.

While Toni burrowed through the clothes racks and chatted away on her cell phone, getting the latest gossip from her BFFs, even she couldn't text while pushing aside hangers at warp speed to examine each item, Cassie hung back to talk with her father about the colt he'd given her to train this summer.

Everyone was having a great time.

At dusk, Cole was cut loose. This wasn't the best weekend to be visiting since the girls had a special party to attend that had been in the works for more than a month. Suzanne hadn't been willing to exchange weekends so he made the best of the time he'd been allotted with Toni and Cassie before dropping them back at home to get ready.

Kissing them both, he reminded them that he'd be picking them up for church in the morning and to be ready by 9:30. Quick hugs and rapid yeses were all he got before the girls ran off excitedly and Suzanne closed the door with barely a word.

Now what? It was just about dinnertime and he rated his choices of what to do as lousy and worse. He drove to his buddy's where he usually spent the night on his weekend visitation trips, but the prospect of eating alone and watching TV didn't hold much appeal.

He let himself in the front door with his own key. Russ wasn't often there on weekends so it was an arrangement that was advantageous for Cole. Tonight the loneliness was more tangible than usual.

He dropped his duffel on the floor and went hunting for the phone book. A wild thought had taken him and he decided to follow through before common sense made him change his mind.

Flipping through the pages, he was gratified to see that the listing existed. He lifted the receiver from the phone parked on the kitchen counter and dialed.

Aunt Ell was regaling Yancy with her latest adventure in dietary roller coasters. Ell was a gourmet chef who enjoyed eating and was forever battling with her thirty pound 'hormone hangover,' something of a misnomer since she'd been waging the same war long before menopause had arrived. It was a subject Ell often used to blow off steam and entertain her audience all at once. She had already cross-examined Yancy about the hearing, which made Yancy wonder who was the better litigator. Ell had missed her calling as far as Yancy could tell.

In the middle of one of Ell's always amusing stories, Yancy was beeped by an incoming call. She made her apologies to Ell, promised to catch up again soon and depressed the 'talk' button and said, "Hello."

"Is this Yancy Collings?" A vaguely familiar male voice came through the receiver.

"May I ask whose calling?" She glanced at her watch and noted the time. The action meant nothing really since she hadn't been expecting any calls, let alone one from a man.

"This is Cole Aleman. We just met last night." Before she could answer, he added, "I hope I'm not disturbing you." He tried to soften the initial terseness in his tone. He didn't make these kinds of calls every day, well, ever, if he were being straight with himself.

"Not at all," Yancy covered her surprise with practiced ease.

"I realize this is a little unconventional, but I'm here in Billings. I come up fairly often to visit my daughters."

"That's great." *How lame does that sound?* "So, Cole, what can I do for you?" *Geez, that's worse.*

Luckily he laughed at the question rather than taking it as faintly off-color.

"Actually, I was hoping that I might be able to do something for you." He took a breath. "Look, this is a little awkward since we just met and you hadn't actually given me permission to call."

Oh my, an actual gentleman. "No problem. What's up?"

"As I said, I'm in town to visit the girls but they had an important event tonight so I'm on my own for the evening. You know the single dad syndrome: drop off the kids and then my choices range from hanging with the boys at the bar or tucking in for the night at a buddy's bachelor pad to watch some mind-numbing television."

"Doesn't sound like much of a choice, I agree."

"Neither have any appeal, so I looked up your number and thought I'd take a shot at offering to buy you dinner..." His voice trailed off.

"I had been planning on staying in for the night..."

"Oh."

Before he could talk himself out of pursuing the invitation, Yancy forged ahead, "But I think I could make an exception tonight. I've been working too hard as it is."

"Terrific," he tried not to sound too relieved at her acceptance. That would give away his uncertainty, which he hardly wanted to admit to himself.

The rest of the conversation required less effort, Cole having gotten over the initial hump of asking a woman out for the first time in what seemed like years. He hadn't realized it had been so long since anyone interested him enough and, of all women, he chose to ask out a lawyer. He hated lawyers. Frankly, he just didn't like that many people, period. Hanging up, he began to think that he'd really gone around the bend.

This Saturday was much like any other Saturday for the Lysander family, a morning where the boys helped their dad do chores around the house – mow the lawn, till their mother's garden, fix the screen doors. Kara had her hair-slim, flexible needle moving with rapid assurance on beadwork for a young cousin's wing dress, the little girl preparing to dance at her first powwow this summer. This kind of handwork was soothing for Kara, giving her a special purpose since her infirmity hindered her from being more physically active. She would have loved to be able to participate as a dancer herself, and on occasion she was at least able to join in for the intertribal songs at powwows, but anything more strenuous wasn't feasible. Kara had instead become proficient at beading and her auntie had shown her techniques that she readily mastered, proving her skill as a budding artist in the medium.

Today the visiting nurse was scheduled to see Kara. It had been quite a crusade to get Indian Health Services to send out an LVN specially trained in dialysis twice a month, and today was one of those two appointments. Mary Lysander was always relieved to have the assistance, particularly since the scare of the last week during the blackout. Until they had the new back-up power system fully installed, she would continue to feel edgy about giving treatment.

Right on time at 2:00 p.m. Paula knocked on the front door and Kara got up to welcome the plump Indian woman into their home. Almost as soon as Paula began arriving for the biweekly visits, she and Kara had connected. The young woman was now as much a part of the family as anyone who slept under the Lysander roof.

Greetings and some time to share came first, then Paula got down to business inspecting and preparing the dialysis machine, and hooking up Kara for the couple hours it would take to go through the cleansing process. Kara was ready with her right arm prepped for Paula to insert the needles from the machine into the arteriovenous fistula, the port in her forearm that allowed the blood to flow out of the vein, through the machine and back into the artery. It was pretty much old hat for the both of them, having been through the drill regularly for the last year. Before that time, Kara still had some kidney function and dialysis hadn't yet become a habitual treatment. Most of the time, one of Kara's parents, both of whom had gone through meticulous training, performed the procedure that was necessary every few days.

Because they had a routine, it didn't take that long for Paula to get Kara rolling, guaranteeing that they'd be finished by dinner, when Paula would stay for the evening, just like usual.

At least that's the way things normally went.

Not today.

Just as the process was started, the power was cut and so was Kara's lifeline.

Although Yancy had been in Montana for over a year, she wasn't familiar with the local hotspots, rarely allowing herself to go out and play. Ell ragged on her about self-flagellation, not understanding Yancy's compelling need to atone for some shadow in her past. But then, Yancy didn't really understand it either. She just knew that she had some obligation to fulfill and generally chocked it up to being a workaholic.

So it was that Cole made the suggestion that they meet at Twang's, a citified cowboy hotspot, thinking that they'd both be comfortable there. Her with urban roots, and he being a country boy. One of the first questions she'd asked when he recommended the place was what the name meant. The place may be in Montana, he'd told her, but it was run by an old roughneck from Amarillo, hence the referral to Texas 'twang,' because the guy had one that ran deeper than an oil strike.

Cole had Yancy tell him what kind of car she drove so he could fetch her from her vehicle. The place had a mélange of customers and he'd felt better about walking her to and from her car. That was a new one on Yancy. It made her wonder what kinds of bars this seemingly remote character frequented. It was also kind of sweet. *This guy looks anything but sweet*, she'd thought as she parked and saw Cole sauntering over from the direction of a newer model pick-up that gleamed from a recent washing.

No, this is a tough guy with a touch of cowboy class. She smiled as he stood by the door and helped her out of the car.

They walked toward the entrance where a number of people stood. Most of them shooting the bull about everything from rodeo to upcoming rock concerts. Some were wearing buffed-up boots and others had on loafers. The evenings could still be a little too nippy for the summer sandal crowd. Walking inside, Yancy decided this was a place where she wouldn't mind meeting friends for drinks, had she made the effort to cultivate any real friends since she'd come west.

They hadn't waited overlong to get seated after going briefly into the bar and ordering specialty brews, the place was Texas big.

"I kind of like this atmosphere," said Yancy as they settled into a booth. "Not too country, not too metro."

Cole managed a grin, spare as it was. He wasn't given to being particularly approachable, but he was taking a stab at softening his brittle edges. "I'm glad the choice is a fit. I've only been here once myself and liked it. Good mix of folks."

"That's not an understatement. It seems to draw a real cross-section of Montanans."

"Yep." He relaxed more into the upholstery, tilted his head sideways and instead of elaborating, studied Yancy's eyes.

It would have made her uncomfortable under other circumstances, but she seemed to pick-up on the fact that he was cautious with words. Being the sharp attorney that she was, Yancy inquired about his daughters without sounding like she was taking a deposition. She thought the topic should be safe, hearing the devotion in his voice when they were mentioned during the phone conversation.

It was. Talking about his girls eased them into an evening of sharing affable company, opening doors that both had kept under lock and key for a long time.

Empty plates had been cleared from the table, only dregs remained in their pilsners and they were still engaged, feeling out what made the other tick.

Melodic tones of a cell phone interrupted the conversation. Cole didn't move, the ring tone wasn't recognizable to him. Yancy reached for her handbag. Looking at the readout, she excused herself, telling Cole that she should answer the call, and pushed the green button.

Within seconds her countenance collapsed from a blush of enjoyment to ashen with alarm. Cole reacted by immediately sitting ramrod straight, concern painting his features.

The exchange lasted less than a minute. All Cole had made of it was Yancy trying to calm someone's panicked voice on the other side.

"Slow down, Key. Where are you? Okay, let me get over there. I'm across town but it shouldn't take long. I'm so sorry this happened. Hold on and I'll be right over."

Cole was already up and shoving some bills into the payment folder, leaving it on the table as Yancy grabbed her purse, muttering a 'thank you for a lovely evening, but I've got to go' while in motion, practically running for the front door. At least that's what he thought she said.

With a few long strides, he was by her side and opening the front door to let her through. Outside he was trying to get a coherent answer to his query about what happened, but she wasn't answering. When they reached the driver's side of her car, she scrounged in her bag for her keys, bringing them out and, with trembling fingers, tried to open the door without much success.

Cole put his hands around hers, gently holding her still. "Stop. Just stop, Yancy, and tell me what's going on. Your hands are shaking. Tell me. Let me help."

"Oh God," she let her composure deflate, her eyes welling with tears. "Kara." Yancy swallowed, trying to get a grip on her voice before it broke. "Kara. She's at the hospital. This wasn't supposed to happen." She tried to break his grip on her hands to get into her car. "I have to go. They need me to be there."

"Wait. Kara, that's the girl whose case you were pleading in

Denver."

Yancy nodded. "I have to go."

"Which hospital is she at?" He looked deeply into her luminous green eyes, swimming with unshed tears. "Let me take you. You're in no condition to drive."

If ever Yancy felt that she could give herself over to a solid shoulder to cry on, it was now. Taking a deep cleansing breath before she utterly lost all control, she nodded in agreement. "Okay. She's at the Billings Clinic."

He put his arm around her shoulder and led her to his F-250. Opening the passenger door, Cole held it wide while she swung into the seat, grasping the handhold to pull herself up. Yancy operated on automatic, buckling the seatbelt while Cole closed the door, walked around to the driver side quickly without appearing to hurry.

"I don't know what's the matter with me. I'm a professional. I don't get emotional about cases," her voice was cracking under the strain of trying to keep herself together. She found a tissue in her bag, dropped her head back and dabbed at her eyes, not wanting to redden them. She needed the family to think that she was an unwavering pillar of strength. Yancy gurgled a heart-wrenching laugh at the thought.

"What? Are you going to be all right?"

"Oh yeah," she said bitterly. "Just fine. This is precisely what I was warning the EPA idiots could happen, but I never really thought it *would*." She sighed, pulling herself together. "Damn. And we were so close, you know?" She looked across the center console at him, a cowboy who exuded the kind of strength she desperately needed to convey to the Lysanders. Problem was, she didn't have an ounce of it stored away.

"No, tell me." He caught her eye briefly as he made a right-hand turn.

"They ran out of money with the installation of the new back-up generator almost finished. Another month and they'd probably have the financing together. I'd have paid for it myself even if it wasn't exactly kosher, not that they'd have let me." She almost lost it again. "Oh hell," she said as she wiped her eyes.

Cole didn't say anything, knowing that there weren't any words that would help.

"There was another blackout as the dialysis nurse was starting the procedure and the old generator didn't kick on in time. Kara lost consciousness and they called emergency. I think he said a Flight for Life helicopter got her and brought her here. They have a pediatric diabetes center. It's hard to know exactly what happened. Key wasn't making a lot of sense."

Neither would I if it were my daughter, thought Cole.

They reached the hospital in a matter of fifteen minutes and Yancy practically spilled out of the truck in her haste to rush inside. She wouldn't let Cole take her arm, afraid that having someone to lean on would only allow her emotions to get the better of her. They hurriedly rounded the west arm of the building, going through the doors at the valet entrance.

She checked the directory, then raced to the elevator, repeatedly pushing the button for the second floor. Cole watched silently as Yancy fidgeted while the car rose, she couldn't wait until the doors slid apart. When they finally did, she forced herself to walk at a slower pace so the Lysanders wouldn't detect her own near panic.

Yancy found the family at the Intensive Care Unit. Through the window she could see Mary sitting by Kara's bedside, rocking in her chair, trancelike. Key held her from behind.

The dialysis nurse, Paula, was standing nearby, watching through the window, Kara's two brothers hunched over in chairs lining the wall.

"How is she?" Yancy asked Paula.

"She's not coming around." Her voice was mild, but Yancy could hear the underlying strain. "It was the shock that got her. I tried everything I could to wake her up and watched while the EMTs tried again on the flight here." She didn't look at Yancy, just kept staring through the window.

"We got her here pretty fast. I think she'll be all right." Under her breath Paula added, "Lord, I pray so." That's when Cole noticed the rosary she was clutching.

Chapter 18

A perfect time to book a little holiday by the turquoise waters of the Caribbean. Spring had arrived inside the Beltway, but the weather hadn't cooperated. It had been so cold for the Earth Day rally that people wore puffy down jackets while actual snow flurries whirled around the frozen noses of diehard green groupies. Temperatures had risen since then but not enough to suit the global warming proponents, and certainly not enough to keep Rone Haggerty in town, not being officially tied to government office anymore, or "yet" by the look of things. He was positive that he had the U.N. ambassadorship from the United States tagged and bagged.

It was still a chilly end to spring and a week's jaunt to the isle of Curaçao was just what he needed. This trip was to be on the 'batch.' No Maddy to nag him, besides there was business to do even if his press agent had cultivated the idea of a father-son vacation. He didn't expect to see his wayward offspring for more than an occasional meal throughout the whole week, which suited both of them fine. Haggerty the younger was too fond of extra-curricular activities that were apt to draw attention, making his father all the happier that he indulged those hobbies far away from American shores.

Haggerty was comfortably ensconced in his seaside estate that most people believed was a vacation rental. In a way, it was. He leased it regularly from one of his shell corporations based on the island nation where access to less restrictive banking was a plus. Today, he was preparing to host a limited assembly of representatives from around the globe for a casual dinner party, and all those invited were there to play their hands in the world energy game, poker faces ready. He envisioned himself as an energy broker, believing that this intimate get-together would cement his position as the dealer at the table, watching the ante go up.

By nine o'clock the men, and one woman, adjourned to the lush garden to enjoy the gentle tradewind rustling through the palm fronds overhead. Except for the few Muslims present, who consciously avoided the one female despite her high rank, cigars were lit all around and a rare brandy sloshed in crystal snifters.

A strange council, by all accounts.

Azerbaijan, Venezuela, Brazil, Libya, Iran, Indonesia, Mexico, Colombia, South Africa and Uzbekistan. The nations represented, albeit informally for this conclave, all had a stake in one or more of three commodities. All were suppliers of oil, coal or gold. And they figured greatly in Haggerty's plans to pare the industrial giants down to size.

Of course, Haggerty didn't recognize that his role was limited to little more than that of a figurehead. As much as he construed his guests to be pawns in the game, it was beyond his comprehension to see his own role in the machinations to undermine the status quo.

That hardly bothered the last attendee to arrive. Darkness as an ally, a black limo arrived to disgorge the unimposing man from the back seat. With now-graying curls of short-cropped hair and dark eyes that some would swear could bore through steel, he had the bearing of his father – brusque and, for all intents and purposes, rude. His multiple billions, and leverage of hundreds of billions more, bought him tolerance among lesser beings, the description of which he readily applied to the assembly now gathered.

Haggerty was a convivial host and he was trained well enough in diplomatic circles to coax his guests into accepting the plan outline that was actually engineered by the latecomer, an extortionist with a velvet glove.

Before the evening was through, all the attendees had pledged their countries resources to his cause. They would press their buyers for concessions on carbon dioxide emissions or their product would become more difficult to obtain, further driving up the costs of energy and the one metal with intrinsic value that bolstered the world's economy.   Yes, China was a wildcard having it's own reserves of coal and being unwilling to play the global warming game, but oil was their soft underbelly and even drilling off Cuba's shores would be insufficient for their needs. Russia was making noises about drilling in the arctic, but the billionaire had their number, no matter how pompous was the Russian prime minister. Even the United States was playing itself against the middle by planning to finance, through the U.S Import-Export Bank, Brazil's state-run oil company to the tune of two billion dollars, an enterprise that the billionaire's hedge fund had just acquired over $800 million in shares.

The environmental lobby, heavily underwritten by this same man's unlimited resources, created the circumstances that opened the door to accomplish his goal.

A shift in the balance of power was what the billionaire wanted and he was determined to get precisely that.

Energy Barons

Chapter 19

Who's calling at this hour?

Instead of answering her phone, Allie rolled over and pulled the pillow over her head. *Shut up and go away.*

Whoever it was, didn't. Just before the answering machine came on, they hung up and then called again. Then they called again. Someone who knew how many rings there were before the machine picked up.

She gave up and reached for the phone. "What could you possibly want this early," she bit off the statement with a tone that showed how much she'd rather bite off the caller's head.

"Woooo-oo-oo, ain't we the peppy one."

Allie opened one eye, reached for her glasses and checked the clock. It was 4:00 a.m. "You can't possibly have a good reason for interrupting my beauty sleep."

"You know good and well that I wouldn't call unless it was important," said Aunt Ell. "We all know how necessary it is for your nightly rejuvenation of those peaches and cream cheeks."

"You'd better be talking about the upper set because you're on the edge of being classed with the lower pair real fast," Allie ground out between yawns.

Ell laughed briefly without any real mirth. "I just talked to Yancy."

"Don't tell me you called her first. Have you no compassion?"

"That's why she called me. That girl has too much. I can see why she was such a bleeding heart with that civil liberties group." She paused before continuing. "She knew that I'd be up, so she got a hold of me first, leaving it to me to catch up with you at a decent hour."

"Since when is 4:00 a.m. a decent hour? *You* are losing your mind and I'm going back to sleep."

"*No*, don't hang up. It was too important to leave until later because you're going to need to follow-up as soon as possible."

Now Allie was sitting up. "Okay, give me the scoop," she said brushing wild tendrils of hair out of her face.

"You covered that hearing at the EPA, right?"

"Yeah, ran a good story yesterday, too." Her eyes opened wider with a dawning of worry. "What happened?"

"That little girl is in a coma. All that Yancy was trying to avoid by getting the bureaucrats to bring the old power plant back online? It happened."

"*What?*"

"Yeah, that's what I said. Those damn policy-pushers can be so incredibly s-t-u-pid, stupid." Ell took a deep breath, she was so incensed.

"Okay, I got it." Allie climbed out of bed and went into the kitchen to put on some coffee. "Where's Yancy now?"

"She's probably still at the hospital. She feels just awful and couldn't pull herself away to go home. Said she couldn't sleep anyway."

"I've got her cell number. Since she's still there and obviously awake, I'll call her and get the story." Allie sighed. "This is hardly the follow-up I was looking for."

"But maybe it'll get some of those a-holes off their butts."

Ten minutes later, with a cup of coffee under her nose, Allie couldn't wait for the whole pot to finish brewing, she had her phone in her hand, her tape recorder set-up and was dialing Yancy's number.

A tired and utterly demoralized voice answered the phone. "Yes."

"Yancy, this is Allie. Ell just called to tell me what happened."

"She was supposed to wait for a civilized hour before calling you. So much for good intentions."

"No, I'm glad she called, that is, if you can talk."

"They say no cell phones, but I'm in the cafeteria trying to scrounge up some coffee. At this hour, all that's available is the vended stuff." Yancy sounded disgusted on top of being exhausted. "You ever had coffee from a machine? Ick." Allie could hear coins dropping in anyway.

"Where are you?"

"Billings. They had to bring Kara in on a Flight for Life and I wasn't all that far away, getting some dinner with Cole."

"Cole Aleman? He's there? Never mind, that's another story." She brushed the back of her hand to the side as if anyone could see her gesture. "Are you feeling up to giving me the low-down on what happened? Or do you want to wait 'til later."

"I'll give you the basics now, but we're going to go back to get my car. Then I can call you from home after I have a shower and a real cup of coffee."

"That'll do just fine. I'm going to turn on the recorder and put you on speaker so I don't miss anything. You can fill in the details later, but I want to get the story in for the late edition. That's what you want, isn't it?"

"Oh yeah. We need to do what we can to make sure this kind of thing doesn't happen again."

An hour and a half later and Allie was getting "the rest of the story" only this one didn't have the uplifting end that Paul Harvey's tales always had.

"What do you do now?" asked Allie. "You lost the petition and Kara's paying the price. So, what's the plan? Is there one?"

"I have to go forward with this case. There's more to this than just the Lysanders. How many others are being put into a bind by denial of reliable electricity? It's due to a policy enforcement regarding CO_2 emissions. Energy *is* available but the EPA is shutting off accessibility to implement the new administration's policy. The price that will be paid comes in two forms: less supply and increased cost."

"My question is, how much of the problem is really government agency interference and how much is actual need to reduce output due to dirty energy production? There is a need to reduce our dependence on coal and oil." Allie wanted to keep this factual.

Yancy yawned. "From what I've been able to uncover, the whole purpose of closing down the generating plants comes back to the regulation of greenhouse gases, which relates to your assumption that we are too dependent on what is referred to as non-renewable resources. It doesn't seem to have much of anything to do with true lack of these resources since we are sitting on huge reserves of oil, coal and natural gas in this country, it has to do with CO_2 being classified as an air pollutant. As much as we hear about these emissions on all the media outlets, including yours, after checking into it, the designation doesn't make much sense."

"Come on, Yancy. Everyone knows that global warming is caused by too much CO_2 in the atmosphere and humanity is producing it."

"Is that said as a journalist or a personal opinion?"

"It happens to be my opinion, but facts support it."

Yancy was too tired to argue but she wasn't willing to let this go, the premise of her case stood on the fallacy that Allie was citing as fact. "You surprise me. I thought as a reporter you would have investigated this better."

They were friends but that got Allie's back up. She decided that Yancy's bluntness might be due to a sleepless night and worry for Kara. "What do you mean? The information's out there all over the internet, TV, newspapers. It's common knowledge."

"Allie, I would have agreed with you completely a year ago, but this situation forced me to look behind all the hype and guess what I found?"

"Okay, what," she said flatly.

"That that *is* all it is, hype and hot air. The science doesn't really support it and never has. During the last congressional hearings on the cap and trade issue, Lord Christopher Monckton, an economic and climate advisor to Margaret Thatcher, testified about the lack of global warming. Let's see, what did he say? "The right response to the non-problem of "global warming" is to have the courage to do nothing." He made clear to the committee that the statistics show that the last decade has been one of global cooling and he brought all the charts and stats to back it up." She sighed with the frustration of it all. "I'd say look up his report online. He uses real facts as opposed to Haggerty's manufactured documentary which even the British courts banned from showing in classrooms because of nine, I believe it was that many, falsehoods in the film. They weren't called inconsistencies, either. Haggerty publicized incorrect data and called it science." Yancy took a breath and continued.

"You're dealing with a situation in Wyoming right now that may have something to do with environmental extremism, from what you said last time we were together. You need to read these authors, Paul Driesen, Dr. Patrick J. Michaels, and others and do some more research. Don't leave the topic coverage up to your colleagues. You're too good for that. Even the reports from NASA aren't supporting Haggerty and his tirades on man destroying the atmosphere. Science or no science, they're pushing an agenda that has nothing to do with saving the planet from anyone."

Allie didn't have anything to say to that. She was sitting at her kitchen table with her coffee mug cradled in both hands, beginning to wonder if she'd really missed something. She'd gotten the same scenario from two people now and one used to believe what Allie still did.

Yancy sighed again. "Look I've been learning the hard way. It's not a fun trip."

"No kidding," was all Allie could come up with.

Chapter 20

Heading north on I-25, Toddy Littman relaxed back in the passenger seat of the SUV while his wife, Solana, drove. She was the designated driver in the family, preferring a steering wheel in her hands to peering out the side window at the rugged desert peaks. Generally speaking, it was a six to one one-half dozen choice of catching her flight out of El Paso or Albuquerque, either being almost equidistant from their home in central New Mexico. Actually, there was no choice. Sol had gone to school at UNM and knew her way around the city. Toddy didn't much care. He was the homebody between the two of them, being more suited to the life of a practical hermit before he'd met Solana. Privacy still suited him.

For now, they were emerging from their mountain cocoon because Sol had a burning interest in a story that Toddy had come across in his research. The tale had been flashed across one cable news network then was gone, disappearing to give airtime to more *interesting* news. No one had made the onerous connections that he'd uncovered, and she was determined to track down.

He'd unhappily conceded when Sol insisted on going to Alaska. He was still of two minds about the plan after what they'd been through the year before. Their 'nemeses' may no longer be in the picture but that didn't assuage his concern about his wife's safety. If it weren't for the fact that he was on deadline to complete a promised project, he'd be accompanying her, though whether he'd be a help or hindrance she refused to say. Inscrutability was as indelible in her make-up as was her Native American heritage and, truth be told, Sol had protected him more than the other way around all those months ago. Since returning to New Mexico, she'd insisted on his becoming proficient with firearms and he'd been practicing. After all, she was the investigative journalist, he was just the computer geek. His words, not hers, as she would remind him that he looked nothing like what the self-applied descriptor implied, being tall and well-made with unruly, dark curls.

The biggest problem for Toddy was that he was already missing her and she hadn't even left his side yet. Must be the fact that they were still newlyweds and he was undeniably a romantic, a rarity among men in the modern world and not to be confused with the metrosexuals, who, in Toddy's opinion, *were* confused.

As the sparse vegetation sped by, they discussed Sol's itinerary, starting in Juneau. She'd never been to the forty-ninth state before though she was northwest born and bred. She'd worked in New York and later in Denver at the Post before going back to Idaho and running the tribal paper for a brief period. After the wedding they'd moved to Toddy's place in Ruidoso while she decided what was next in terms of a career move. It was turning out to be freelancing for different news carriers but this little jaunt was solely related to their joint work on ChangingWind.org, Toddy's news-editorial blog.

"I'll call you every day with whatever updates I have, and e-mail may not be available in some spots." She looked over and caught his down-turned mouth in a near-pout. "But you knew that. Why I mention anything remotely computer related is beyond me, you already know the answer," she laughed lightly as he gave her the *"so, and that means.... what?"* look. She ignored it and went on, "The stop by the Juneau office may be superfluous, but since they're the office that's based in the state capital, it's worth a gander, don't you think?"

"I guess it couldn't hurt, but from what I can see there's not much point other than to add a couple more days onto your trip," he grumped. "It would be good to see how closely Rural Resources is in bed with the environmental legal groups. From their websites and the court filings online, they appear to be separate entities, but I have my doubts. A pissant organization like RR couldn't possibly have the kind of dough they need for extended litigation."

"Well we'll see just what kinds of bedfellows they are with the legal eagles and the re-routed Herculaenea Fund funds." She grimaced at her choice of words and Toddy grinned.

"I wish that I could go along and get my hands on one of their computers. Ah, the fun I could have digging through records to follow the money trail. I wouldn't put it past the greenies to disparage the Qagit Corporation in personal e-mails, walloping them for providing a decent living for their people because mining gold isn't *environmentally friendly*." He threw up his hands in frustration, emphasizing the offending words with sarcasm. "Sometimes I get so ticked at the elitist attitudes these people have regarding everyone else. It's fine for them to have their hands in everyone's pockets to support their pet projects, but God forbid they should actually *work* for a living like the Yu'pik are trying to do using what was *ceded* to them by the omniscient Congress." He actually growled as he calmed himself.

Toddy's passion for justice was nothing new to Sol, she had come to appreciate his need to champion those whose rights were consistently trampled by the know-it-alls in office, assisted by the know-it-alls who plastered the media with misdirection and misinformation. Or, in his words, *bullshit*.

The Qagit Corporation, a Yu'pik corporation, was partnered with Corcoran Creek Ltd, a mining company that had the expertise and resources to develop the huge gold deposit that lay beneath Yu'pik land. Toddy and Sol had found the creation of the corporate entities, that all Alaska Natives had been divided into, fascinating and odd in the distinct differences between how the United States government had treated them in comparison to the lower forty-eight tribal nations. No treaties in Alaska. In their place was the Alaska Native Claims Settlement Act of 1971 which created for-profit corporations instead of reservations for the Native people, and a different set of government rules for dealing with them. They didn't treat with Alaska Natives as they had with the Indian nations south of the Canadian border, working around any reference or acceptance of them as sovereign nations by incorporating them and their land holdings.   At least that's the way it appeared to Sol who was definitely *not* an attorney and acceded to her limited knowledge of the law. What she was looking into on this excursion was the pressure being brought to bear by environmental bullies on the Qagit Corp., which had gone as far as the Supreme Court, to abandon its plans to provide local employment by tapping into their gold reserves. Opening the mine looked like a good idea to her. There was a growing demand for gold in a world turned upside-down by the international flood of toxic assets that had managed to bring the global economy to its knees, damaging currencies further by the ill-conceived deluge of stimulus "money," most of which hadn't even been spent, just "allocated." Lord, she didn't get that at *all*.

This was personal for Sol in some ways, being Nez Perce. She'd seen other situations where Native Americans' endeavors to supply good jobs for themselves were being shut down by environmental interests. The hurdles were outrageously expensive because of the never-ending litigation like what had been happening with the Navajo in trying to build a state of the art, clean coal plant in New Mexico. What really made both her and Toddy's blood boil was that they had seen something they believed could be very similar to the situation in Alaska just nine months ago. A small Indian nation in northern Arizona had a healthy gold deposit that they were developing to feed their chronically unemployed people, and the whole operation was collapsed by the environmentalists. Toddy was still working with them to rectify the land lease problems, the project that was keeping him from traveling with Sol this trip.

Changing the mood of the conversation, Solana settled back in her seat, relaxing with one hand flopped over the top of the steering wheel. "I'd really rather drive than be crammed into one of those confining airline seats from hell."

Toddy, mooning over the beautiful, barren landscape, couldn't help but be irreverent. "That'd work. If you want to get there after all the action is over."

When she leaned over to grab the phone, Allie almost lost her balance, just avoiding taking a dive headfirst into her suitcase.

"Y'ello?"

"I never got the gist of that greeting," Sol opened the conversation sardonically. "Is it a mix of 'yeah,' 'yes,' or 'yep' and hello? Or some other equally indistinguishable American colloquialism that I will never understand?"

Allie just laughed as she pulled herself upright, making certain to step around the open luggage that was sliding off the bed and destined to dump all the contents on the floor. She grunted as she pulled the bag back into place.

"What *are* you doing?"

"Packing to make one last foray into Wyoming. That's all the local gods would afford me in return for my incessant sacrificing at their altar," said Allie.

"Hey, you got that much. Count your blessings, I'd say," Sol couldn't resist.

"Ay-yai. Have you any more quips or bad puns before I hang up on you?"

"Nope. Just wanted to see if you've come up with anything more regarding a possible RR/GG connection. I'm up in Alaska and plan on visiting the Juneau office of Rural Resources, the suspected Green Grasslands counterpart, tomorrow morning. So, have you got anything good?" Sol asked hopefully.

"Not yet. That, of course, is why I'm packing to leave, but you can tell me what *you* have. It might help me narrow my search… or something."

"Let's see. The visit to the Juneau office is pretty much a fishing expedition. They were one of the original claimants in the court case to block the Corcoran Creek Mine project up here that may be sitting on the world's biggest gold reserve."

"Let me sit down and take a few notes." Allie went into the dining area and sat at the table, pulling a legal pad from her inexhaustible stack of them on a shelf of her computer printer stand. It was a reach, but she got it and slapped it down in front of her, pen in hand. "You're going to need to get me up to speed on what you're doing up there. All I know is that the acronym P.O.P. made a light bulb go on."

"Where to start," Sol sat back on the hotel bed with her own notes. "I'm not going to go into the Idaho thing other than to say that the RR and P.O.P. association is what brought me to thinking there might be something here. It could be that RR and GG have nothing in common except for this nebulous mention of the eco-dragonslayers."

Allie chuckled at the comparison because she'd met too many

environmentalists that really thought of themselves as knights of Camelot – "might for right." Even though she was pretty much in their camp, their pomposity was sometimes hard to take.

"Unfortunately, these guys aren't particularly an amusing bunch. They don't always stick to lawful means of getting their way. But in this case, the green organizations are going the legal route."

"Well, I'd consider that a good thing," threw in Allie.

"Oh, I agree. If you're going to fight something at least do it in a civilized manner," said Sol. "Well, we have RR working with EcoEarth Legal Center, the Conservation Society and a whole host of environmental groups local and international to bring suit to close down Corcoran Creek and Qagit Corporation interests. The case has made it all the way to where it now sits on the Supreme Court docket. For once, something like this has made it on the fast track to be adjudicated." Sol continued, "We've been looking at corporate board personnel swaps and funding channels to pay for this litigation against the mine, and what we have is most interesting."

"Okay, I'm ready. I think," said Allie, pen poised above paper.

"There are people who have served on both the boards of EcoEarth and the Conservation Society, which funnels money to the legal center. The Free States Foundation funds both EcoEarth and the Conservation Society. Rural Resources has received funding from the Conservation Society also, mostly on joint projects."

"Let me get this straight, EcoEarth is Kraegen's baby and it has ties to the Conservation Society and, maybe Rural Resources, which was connected to this Protect Our Planet," Allie was making notes and starting a flow chart.

"Right," said Sol. "And all of them have received funding through one channel or another from the FSF."

Allie stopped her. "I'm not familiar with this, what'd you call it, Free States Foundation?"

"They never had much of a presence in the United States but are deeply entrenched as advocates for environmental causes and the *underprivileged* in, oh, sixty countries? Something like that. It's also funded by Scirras' money, or at least it was until it got a reputation and it was supposedly disbanded only to be replaced as an entity by the Scirras Foundation," added Sol.

"Good or bad reputation?" Allie wanted to know.

"Depends on how you look at it. They definitely had one for getting involved in local politics around the world, supplying educational material and the like."

"That sounds like a good thing," Allie was confused by Sol's insinuations.

"Well, it is if you want your country's values redesigned by an outside philanthropic organization that dispenses it's own idea of what is just and good for your people through *education*," Solana emphasized the word.

"Okay, I get it. FSF was pushing its own agenda through supplying funds and education that supported its own goals."

"You are sharp, girl!" Sol moved forward. "Scirras' money seems to be everywhere. Not only was it behind the winning presidential ticket last year, i.e. buildingbridges.org, but it's the driving force behind the Herculaenea Fund, which is Scirras' hedge fund. And *it* owns a goodly portion of Altamont Mining which has fingers in the Kirkdale Mining pie, which," she checked her notes again, "has a major stake in Corcoran Creek Ltd. which is leasing surface and subsurface mineral rights, etc. from the Qagit Corporation, the Yu'pik people."

Allie made her go over that again so she could draw her arrows, and they were going all directions across her lined, yellow sheet. She scribbled a big X through the first chart and started over on a new page. By the time she had it right her head was spinning.

"And this relates to Green Grasslands, how?"

"Money from Scirras' backed foundations, at least that seems to be the tie that binds. Where it goes from there?" Allie could feel the silent shrug through the phone. "That's why I'm here and you're going back to Wyoming."

"Okay, so now tell me what this has to do with the litigation against Corcoran Creek?" Allie was still confused but dogged.

"It depends on how you follow the money trail," said Solana. "Altamont has stock in Corcoran Creek through a subsidiary, Kirkdale Corp., that's basically partnering with the Qagit Corporation, the Native landowners.

"Scirras' Herculaenea Fund owns major stock in Altamont and

he also sponsors EcoEarth Legal Center through the FSF. Not to mention supplying funds for the eco-group Conservation Society that backs Rural Resources."

"How twisted *is* this?" asked Allie.

"Even more than you can imagine. As usual, he's playing both ends against the middle. By halting the mining operations in Alaska through the court case if they win, he, Scirras, gains more leverage on the global price of gold."

"How does that work? You said he has interest in the mine through the Altamont connection, which is," and she searched her notes for something that had been mentioned earlier, "one of the largest reserves in the world. Seems he'd want to develop the resource and make money."

Sol clarified, "If they think like you and me, sure, but they don't. By keeping the reserve safely underground they can keep gold prices soaring. They've got unbreakable contracts with Qagit, so even if the Native owners could manage to get permitting to dig, they can't find another mining company to sign on, or the funding to fight the battle legally to get out of the binding contract. Their hands are tied both by the outcome of the case and by Altamont sway."

"So Scirras is betting on the case going in his direction so he doesn't have to look like the bad guy in shutting down a Native employment opportunity."

"That's what we think," Sol was referring to herself and her husband, whose perverse mind came up with this in the first place. "And they're using the Clean Water Act to do it. There are conflicting readings in a couple of the sections within the act that give the Army Corp of Engineers the power to permit a project that might impact watershed, which they did. The opposition is claiming that only the EPA can make that determination and the parties are asking the courts to rule on which is the correct interpretation of the act's language."

"I can't imagine anyone coming up with such a warped, and dastardly, if I can use a Dudley Do-Rightism, plan," Allie was stunned at the intricacies of it all.

"Scirras has got a million of these schemes and they're all unfolding under our noses. There are mines in Romania, Ecuador and places I've never heard of before. Just look at what's been happening since Van Schaal took office."

"Back up a minute," Allie wasn't going to let any declaration about the new president ride without a challenge. "I don't see any connection between the two, and what's so bad about what's been going on? It looks like change is definitely occurring with this new administration."

Sol was flummoxed. "Do you read any of the reports you write? Yes, there's change but just start counting the unemployed which is almost at ten percent, the multi-*trillion* dollar deficit that is mounting daily, the huge bailouts that aren't working, the fact that government is now *owner* of what was private business and is calling the shots. Is that "change you can believe in?" She took a breath before going on. "I'd call it highway robbery of every working American. And *Scirras* bankrolled Van Schaal's inherited campaign through buildingbridges.org."

Although they were friends going back to when both of them had worked at the Denver Post, Allie was trying to keep her cool. Sol hadn't raised her voice but she sure made her views clear. "Well, I guess we're not going to see eye-to-eye on this. There's still a story here, and as much as I can't swallow everything you've laid out…" before Sol could cut her off, Allie said, "*yet*, we need to keep each other informed on what we uncover. *Then*, I'll see what I think."

"Allie, you get any deeper into this environmental pressure cooker and you will find that I'm not crazy at all. In fact I expect the next time we talk you'll be looking at some things differently."

Allie harrumphed. "You'll be the first to know."

Solana laughed as she hung up.

Chapter 21

Roy Esteban had spent the week spinning his wheels, or so that's the way it felt. They'd come up empty trying to track the detonator fragments. It had been composed of common parts that could have been purchased from any number of nameless electronics and hardware stores. He'd even done background checks on all the employees at the mine and the power plant. He found one guy who'd lied about having a criminal record – a weekend spent in lock-up for reckless driving. Even better, that bad boy had a foolproof alibi for the three days before the explosion at Flat Butte where he was a mid-level maintenance worker. He'd spent his time off fishing with buddies where they were all well-known hellraisers.

As for Esteban's favorite prospect, Sawyer Aleman, he had an impeccable history with the Marines, the Colorado School of Mines and at Tyne Hill. He was even a champion team roper on the local rodeo circuit. No motive and his alibis checked out. So much for an inside job.

And Allie Maitland. It didn't take more than meeting her once to see that she was one royal pain. Other than that, going into her past was another dead end, but her comments about possible eco-terrorism were still circling in his head and he was pretty positive she'd known nothing about the explosive device. They still hadn't released that information.

Damn. Nothing on top of nothing.

He sat back in his chair waiting for, what? Manna from heaven? For a supposedly brilliant investigator he was about as useful as a boil on the director's butt and likely to get lanced if he didn't come up with something soon.

He was just contemplating a career change when the last person he really wanted to see barged into his office.

His scowl managed to get even deeper. "Back again?"

"I didn't get enough answers the last time I was here." Allie impertinently dropped her satchel on the floor next to the desk.

"What makes you think you're going to get anything more this time?" He didn't bother to take his feet off the desk.

"Considering you've had a few more days of sifting through the debris, I'm betting you have some leads that you might share."

Esteban let out a bark of a laugh. "With a reporter... You couldn't seriously have thought that I would compromise an investigation by sharing privileged information with you?"

Allie tried a coquettish smile, looking as contrived as it felt. "Wishful thinking?"

He lowered his feet to the floor and sat forward, elbows on the blotter and hands clasped, a teacher driving home the lesson. "You got that right, Ms. Maitland. I don't have anything that I can divulge."

"Ms. Maitland, is it? I thought we might be on a first name basis by now."

Esteban looked at her like she'd lost her mind. "Whatever would have given you that idea?"

"The multiple unanswered voicemails and phone messages I've left with you and just about everyone on your team. I should have known that you were avoiding me since I never received an answer," she said with a good dose of saccharine. "Especially since you've been checking up on me."

He settled back in his chair, crossing his arms over his chest.

"That obvious, huh? I thought we were a little more discreet these days."

"Oh, you are... a little. There are ways of tracking when you're being tracked. I'm sure you and your cohorts know every trick there is," she was just stating facts.

"True. I shouldn't be surprised that someone who comes in here trying to tie terrorist activity to the accidents would have enough computer skills to see what other people are looking into, particularly if she's the target."

"As you said, I *am* a reporter. And, luckily, I have a few resources. So," Allie sat down in the chair opposite him, "what about you? You have resources. What have you turned up? Anything relating to what I asked about before?"

"If you mean the environmental activist, i.e. domestic terrorism, connection. I couldn't say." Esteban wasn't particularly interested in playing any games but wondered if *she'd* come up with something new. *Now, wouldn't that just be too much.*

"Are you telling me that you didn't look into the Green Grasslands - Protect Our Planet link?" Allie's jawline hardened and thrust forward the slightest bit, trying to keep her disapproval in check. "Do you think that I'd toss that out with nothing more than whimsy behind the question?"

"You misunderstood me," Esteban retained his calm, something that was evidently challenging her. "I *said* that I *couldn't* say, not that there wasn't anything to your assumptions."

"So you'll sit here and play cat and mouse with me instead of just admitting that you do have some leads," her anger was spiking a little at his baiting. "You must be able to give me something."

He considered it, deciding that he appreciated her spunk. "Let me think on it for a minute…" He turned to dig out a file that made Allie's mouth water with thoughts of getting her hands on it. Leafing through the contents, he had it open in his lap where she couldn't get a good look at it without standing up and peering over the desktop. A stupid idea she discarded as quickly as it entered her head. "It does seem that there have been a couple of new faces at the local Green Grasslands office in Cheyenne."

"Middle Eastern origin, or even a little more toward the Orient, by any chance?" she said leaning forward, trying not to show her eagerness.

Esteban raised his eyebrow, "Looks like you may have some other source."

"Is that a "yes?""

"No."

"Hell, when are you going to give me a straight answer?" She let her exasperation show briefly.

"Since you mention hell, my guess is when the devil's building igloos," Esteban quipped.

Picking her bag up off the floor, she said, "Funny you should say that. Igloos and Eskimos are the next thing on my list in this investigation." Allie stepped through the doorway.

Leaning forward, Esteban raised his voice just enough so she could hear him as she walked away. "What do you mean by that?"

Allie just shrugged her shoulders, causing her satchel to slip down her arm. She readjusted the strap as she strolled down the hallway. "Call me when you're ready to talk."

He slumped back in his chair wondering how it was a reporter could be one step ahead of him.

Chapter 22

Allie made an effort not to storm out of the makeshift FBI head-quarters inside the sheriff's station. In fact, just a hint of a smile crossed her lips as she heard Esteban's parting question. *That ought to get his goat. All's fair, as they say...*

Her next gambit was to pester the prickly Mr. Aleman one more time. She had small hope in that direction but maybe, just maybe, he's picked up something pertinent being so close to the investigation, as opposed to someone like her carrying the stigma of total outsider and a reporter, to boot. Pulling her phone out of the bag's custom pocket, she called him praying that he'd answer. Although their last encounter hadn't been quite so frosty as their earlier brushes, she wasn't certain that he wouldn't just blow her off.

She exhaled with a puff of relief when he picked up.

"This is Aleman." Cool, professional.

Okay, two can play that game. "Good afternoon, Sawyer. You don't mind my being informal?"

"No. We've spent enough time together under one roof, informality's a given."

"Good. I know that I've already taken too much of your valuable time over the past week, but I was hoping that you might give me just a bit more. That is if you can fit it into your schedule," Allie winced at the obvious ingratiation, but she had to see if he had *any - thing* regarding the story hidden inside that hard skull of his. If he did, she wanted it and she wanted it badly.

Sawyer considered her request with caution. This was a woman on a mission, and although he'd rate their last outing as better than tolerable, he wasn't sure if he should go there again. Allie Maitland was a tough cookie with a stubborn allegiance to her views, but she seemed able to listen and ask incisive questions. Smart but misguided. *Oh, why not? How bad could it be?* It's not like he was booked for anything. The mine was closed and Cole didn't want his help, so he was kicking around his house doing nothing.

"Fine, I can meet you for dinner at Bar B's Steakhouse."

Allie released the breath she didn't know she'd been holding. "That would be great. Where is it?" Sawyer gave her directions and they settled on a time.

She was off and running.

Allie had steeled herself for the worst. Over the phone, Aleman's initial reaction was less than stirring when it came to the potential for a pleasant interview. He'd been brusque and brittle when consenting to meet. Accepting that the 'date' was a working appointment abated her appetite, she'd eat later when she could enjoy her meal rather than choke down her food in hostile company.

The reality of the meeting turned out to be far more genial than Allie had expected, prompting her to set aside her resolve to go hungry. Tension was in the air but the nature of it had transformed from argumentative to something she couldn't quite put her finger on. When she tried to pin down the feeling, she thought better of the idea and pushed it aside without further scrutiny. She was there to work a source, nothing more, and everything else was a distraction. She reminded herself that there was a young girl, comatose in the hospital, whose condition might very well be attributed to the power plant's destruction. *And if somebody deliberately caused this, I'm going to track them down and they* will *pay.*

That affirmation in her mind, Allie got right to the point.

"What have you heard about the FBI's progress in the investigation?" Allie tried unsuccessfully to appear blasé. *Like he'll buy that.*

"As in…?" He threw it back in her court.

"Oh, I don't know." She thought she'd try being facetious, "Maybe they found some odd bits of evidence like fabric from a torn shirt, a lost wallet or, oh, bomb fragments…"

Sawyer's eyes widened and then slitted with suspicion. "Did you get into their files?"

Bingo! "Of course not. " Allie's eyes flashed with eureka fire. "I was right, wasn't I? There was a bomb!" She barely masked her excitement and kept her voice lowered.   His cool exterior back in place, Sawyer considered his response. "I have no official standing, let alone actual information, which makes me an unreliable source," he said pointedly, "but in my *opinion*, you may be on to something."

She turned her gaze heavenward, murmuring, "I knew it." Perking up with renewed confidence in her hunches, tempered by consternation regarding the implications of sabotage, she speared his eyes with her own. "The two incidents couldn't have been coincidental, or *accidental* when it comes right down to it. What do you know?"

"If anything I tell you shows up in print, the feds will have my head."

"As you said, you're not officially related to the investigation." She was perplexed and beginning to worry that she'd get no more out of him, whatever his status. "Why would they?"

He pushed a plate out of the way and leaned his elbows on the table, "The biggest problem I have with the SAC is that he thinks I had some prior knowledge or somehow might be involved."

"That's absurd."

"Of course it is," Sawyer agreed but was inwardly pleased that she couldn't imagine his complicity. "Evidently, because I was speculating on how hard it is to gain entry into the facility, he's stuck on it being an inside job, which it absolutely isn't."

"I'm not so sure he's convinced of that. He did check up on something I told him. Well, once he got around to it after thoroughly examining *my* history, whereabouts, etc." She was disgusted at the thought that the FBI would even remotely consider her a suspect.

"That's what you get for being a sentient being trying to help them see what's obvious." He shook his head. "Makes me wonder if they could find their hands at the end of their arms."

"Come on, Esteban's not that bad, just cautious." For some reason she was willing to throw the guy a bone. "It's to be expected for them to hold their cards close to their chest and to examine every possibility." A light of unrestrained eagerness shone in her eyes. "So, what else have you got?"

"Not much. I think he's working on some theory about using the railroad to sneak onto the premises.".

"And that works, how?"

"You remember John told you about checking the coal cars for bums before loading?"

"Oh, yes, I do. The new generation of hobos." She sat back to think. "I can see that. Any properly outfitted terrorist can get good climbing gear in an area with world-class mountains to scale, practically in the backyard here."

Surprisingly, he picked up on her train of thought, nodding. "It wouldn't be that hard to rope a slow moving train with the right gear." Sawyer mirrored her by sitting back in his seat, mulling over the implications, only he took his beer with him. "What they have to find is the exfiltration route."

"The what? Oh, you mean how they left the property without being seen?"

"Yeah, that's what I mean. So what was it that you said that prompted Esteban to start looking for an intruder?"

She looked at him warily, wondering whether she should say anything, but then decided it was only fair to give a little for what she got.

"The fact that two guys from somewhere in the Middle East have appeared at an environmental group's office in Cheyenne working as student interns."

Sawyer laughed outright. "The liberal doing racial profiling?" then he pinned her with an almost derisive smirk. "So what?"

"You were in Iraq and Afghanistan, right?"

He gave her a warning look not to go there. She ignored it.

"You know how some people are adamant in their beliefs. Unwavering and would go to the death to protect their faith."

"You mean like liberals?"

"Give it a rest, will you? You know what I mean, you've seen it, am I right?" Allie felt a twinge of regret for bringing up what were obviously unhappy memories but pressed on. This was too important. "Look, when you see something slippery and scaly, you go fishing. I went with it. The men I met don't seem to have any history to speak of before two months ago. Or at least it's a history that looks patched together."

Sawyer looked at her harder, asking a silent question.

"I kind of intimated that there might be a connection between eco-terrorism and the, what now looks like, bombings. Esteban ran with it."

"Eco-terrorism and Islamist type-casting?" he scoffed. "That's a leap. Last I heard, Al Qaeda and their colleagues were more interested in killing and maiming infidels, not saving the planet."

Allie leaned forward with renewed fervor. "Not if you're connecting know-how with need. And who's to say that the "Great Satan" isn't fair game in every aspect, such as energy supply? Haven't Arab states used their oil wealth against us before? Hmm, let's revisit OPEC's manipulation of oil prices in the seventies."

"I get the point." He sipped his beer, giving her credit without voicing it.

That was the turning point of the evening. From adversaries they had become tenuous allies, devising ways to compile more information about what both now were sure was sabotage. They shared a driving need to nail the perpetrators for different reasons and were willing to chance trampling official toes to unmask the actors.

Chapter 23

Sawyer arrived at Allie's hotel room door at 9:00 a.m. the next morning, two coffees in hand from the espresso kiosk in the parking lot. He never thought a woman could be so easily won over, always having been told that diamonds were a girl's best friend, or a fancy car or a big bank account.

He couldn't have been more wrong.

The appreciative beam Allie gave him upon spying the cup could have knocked any man's heart out of the ballpark. It took him by surprise how much he liked it.

"Oh thank you! Real coffee, hmmm." She left the door open for him to follow her inside as she went back to the desk, inhaling the aroma as if she were enjoying the bouquet of a fine wine or the scent of fragrant roses. "You have no idea how much a good cup of coffee means to a girl when all that's here are those stale packets of grounds."

"I do now." His voice was level but his eyes registered her enjoyment. "Had I known in the past that this is the way to get a girl, I might have been more successful with the ladies."

She just rolled her eyes and finished packing up her gear for their little outing.

Last night they'd decided that the investigators had been tunnel-visioned on the explosion site and after Sawyer's comment about an escape route, he and Allie decided to check it out for themselves.

It wasn't long before they had climbed into his truck and were heading south toward the mine. After turning onto the company road, Allie paid more attention to the confining miles of chain link, topped with razor wire that would strip the hide off a buffalo, if one were seven feet tall. Security protocol had called for designing the passage with virtually no shoulder to discourage parking along the miles of nearly empty roadway. He slowed to take a closer look at the construction, something he hadn't really taken into consideration before.

"Do you know what to look for?" Sawyer asked.

"I'd guess any kind of anomaly in the fence." She looked at him as he steered toward the right edge of the pavement, still blocking the lane. "It's posted "no stopping at any time." Will we get in trouble for pulling over?"

He laughed. "I'll take the chance." With operations suspended for a while, he knew there was no blasting scheduled and having clearance for Tyne Hill, he supposed that he probably wouldn't be hassled for stopping along the road to examine the fence line.

Time passed without verbal communication, a country station providing soft background from the radio's lowered volume. Allie concentrated on the fence on her side of the road as Sawyer drove slowly enough to get a good look at the north side.

"I'm surprised that you haven't made a complaint about the music, being city-bred. I can't imagine that this is your cup of tea," Sawyer finally broke the otherwise static quiet that had created a huge gulf between the two front seats.

"I'll have you know that I appreciate all kinds of music and living out here, even in the grand metropolis of Denver, you acquire a taste for country caterwauling."

"Is that your idea of appreciation, describing it that way? I'd hate to hear what you have to say about polka, " He grinned slightly toward the open window, not taking his eyes off the fence except to make sure he wasn't drifting into the oncoming lane. They'd only seen two cars, one passing them going the other way, and one blasting around them from behind.

"Just expressing my opinion, though I'd say country has come a long way since the "dumped again, may as well cry in my beer" days. It's practically a pop sound now. And," she briefly turned towards the back of his head, "polka's fine for Lawrence Welk fans but I don't spare words for hip-hop, either. Bone-crunching bass that gives me a headache." She shivered, turning her eyes back to scanning the fence and making a sound conveying her general aversion to the speaker-busting genre.

Sawyer let loose a chuckle that could have been interpreted as a grumble in his throat. "I thought anyone under forty liked hip-hop these days."

"Oh, so you have a penchant for rap?" she smirked.

"Who said I was under forty?"

"It doesn't take much to find out a person's age if you know where to look," she stated factually.

"That leaves me at a disadvantage," he countered.

"And it will stay that way. A lady doesn't reveal her age." Allie's tone changed from amused to serious. "The fence is buckled over here. Maybe we should check it out."

He pulled over and they both walked back to where she pointed. Inspecting the interwoven wires, Sawyer pulled cattle hair that had gotten caught in the links.

"Just some cows scratching an itch. There'll probably be lots more of these. We need to look for something out of the ordinary."

They got back in and after a couple more false alarms, Allie noticed something that looked like earth had been moved.

"Do cows dig?" She thought it was probably a stupid question but asked anyway.

"They might paw the ground some but, no. Stray dogs and coyotes do. What do you see?"

"I'm not sure. Back up."

He checked to be sure there was no traffic coming up from behind and shifted the truck into reverse.

"There." Allie pointed out the window. "It doesn't look like the kind of marks a dog or coyote would leave. I had a dog once who was working his way to China, and his technique definitely wouldn't look like that."

They parked and got out to look. He held her back. "Don't want to mess up any possible evidence."

That miffed Allie. Like she didn't know not to get too close.

She couldn't help her snotty tone, "Maybe you should make sure you don't step on those boot prints, bucko." She crossed her arms and stood to the side, but it was a good thing she said something because he almost didn't see them.

Sawyer grunted his acknowledgment and stepped sideways just

in time to avoid trampling the marks.

Bending down, he examined what appeared to be an indentation in the dirt that was partially covered over, noticing that there were no scratch marks from an animal. *At least not a wild animal.* To Sawyer, it looked more like some tool had been used and the ground was loose.

Pulling out his phone, he fished out a card and called the number on its face. All Allie heard in the brief conversation was Sawyer telling someone that they'd best come out to where he was located. The person on the other end was snippy, but he gave as good as he got and slapped shut the phone.

He turned to look at Allie's questioning face.

"Now we wait."

Which is what they did.

They waited inside the car for twenty minutes until the first of two unmarked vehicles pulled in behind Sawyer's truck. One was an old dirt-brown Crown Victoria and the other, a newer black Suburban. Esteban emerged from the door of the Crown Vic.

He walked to the driver's side of Sawyer's truck and glared at the two occupants, one of who returned the look with equal intensity. Allie found the dynamic between the men fascinating and kept her mouth shut.

"Nice ride, Roy."

"Pull forward fifty feet and get out."

Sawyer shrugged, put the car in gear and did as he was told. Both Sawyer and Allie started to get out. Esteban looked hard at her and motioned for her to stay in the truck, which changed her feelings about the federal agent PDQ.

Esteban walked Sawyer over to where the truck had been previously parked.

"Show me what you found."

Sawyer took the agent over to the spot where the ground had been disturbed and, squatting down explained what he thought it was. He also showed Esteban the footprints.

Without another word, Esteban indicated that Sawyer should move back then went to direct the crime scene techs to go over the whole area. Turning back to Sawyer furiously, he skewered him, eye-to-eye.

"What the hell were you thinking bringing a reporter out here with you? Don't you realize you probably compromised the whole case just by allowing her on the property?"

Sawyer had had a chance to assume calm in what felt like the eye of the hurricane swirling around him, Esteban was so pissed. He shook his head. "I don't think you have anything to worry about. I couldn't have located that alone and none of you seemed to be looking."

"For what? What *were* you looking for?" ground out the SAC.

"Exfiltration site."

Esteban stepped back and walked around himself, combing the fingers from his right hand through his hair, his left hand jammed at his waist.

"Hell, why didn't you just call me?"

"*Now* you're receptive to outside suggestions?" Sawyer asked incredulously.

"Believe it or not, yes." He'd stopped his circling and looked at the other man.

Sawyer snorted. "And I thought you were looking at me as a possible perp."

Esteban glared at him again, then laughed. "If that's the case, you *must* think I'm stupid."

"No, just grasping at straws."

Esteban relaxed his stance and placed both hands on his hips. "Pretty much." He pointed his thumb back towards the truck. "She's too sharp for her own good and simply can't be allowed too close to this investigation. Even if she wants to keep some of this under wraps, any good editor is going to horsewhip the help until he gets a story worth printing, and she's not about to chance ticking him off to the point of losing her job." He took a deep breath and let it go. "Figure it out, man. Reporters are a different breed from the rest of us."

"I'm not sure if I should thank you or curse you for allowing me membership in your club, however temporary, but I will disagree about Allie. I think she's smart enough to stave off her editor long enough to gain you some time. It may be that you could actually use her help." Sawyer surprised himself a little by sticking up for the woman who, right now, was probably ready to rip into Esteban the next chance she got.

Esteban gave him a sideways look and glanced over at the truck where he could see Allie watching them in the rearview mirror.

"All right. I know I'll regret this but," he hesitated then said, "what are you thinking?"

Sawyer considered his response. "That you give her a couple of tidbits that will make the paper happy, make it look like progress is being made. Then direct us on what can't be released. Give her some responsibility as a partner in this sideshow. I don't think you want the details circulated of how the bad guy may have gotten in and then made his escape, so to speak. If you don't you could be looking at a real breach in the dam that will swamp you with PR problems faster than a flash flood on dry plains."

Without answering, Esteban signaled Sawyer to follow him and headed back over to talk to Allie.

Allie had been waiting in the truck, keeping an eye on the maneuverings between the two men, which resembled more of a Mexican standoff than a civil conversation. She was anxious to find out what was going on and infuriated at being exiled to the truck's cab. Seeing the boys finally coming her way, it appeared they'd called a truce and that somehow worried her.

Sawyer and Esteban walked up to the passenger side of the vehicle and stopped to peer in the window.

What's eating him? The SAC was sporting a major frown that would be menacing if Allie weren't so used to dealing with execs who didn't know how to do anything but glower at reporters, even when they sing their praises. Extolling someone's virtues was not their strong suit.

Esteban indicated that she should wind down the window so she reached across to the ignition and turned the key to accessory, punched the button on the door and the window glided down into its pocket.

"Have you called anyone?" Esteban was abrupt.

She was in no mood for his mood. "No. What am I gonna tell them? We found a crinkle in a fence? Get real, Agent Esteban."

That caught Esteban off-guard and he tried to keep a straight face considering her point at how idiotic she would sound. He changed tack.

"I need you both down at headquarters. Don't make any stops along the way. Don't make any phone calls." He bored both of them with his eyes. "Drive straight there and wait for me in my office."

Sawyer looked a little annoyed and confused. *What the hell? Haven't we been accommodating enough to do his work for him?* He shared none of those thoughts, just dispassionately nodded and said they'd be there.

"How long will this take?" asked Sawyer.

"No idea. I should be right behind you." He turned on his heel and walked back to the techs laying out markers and photographing the area.

Sawyer swung open the driver's door and climbed into the truck. Without a word, he started the engine and made a u-turn to head back to the sheriff's station.

"What's all that about?" Allie slid a glance at Sawyer's set jaw.

"As the man said, "no idea." I'm just following directions since otherwise I'd be tracked down like a dog, cuffed and jailed. He doesn't like me much."

"Gee, that's hard to understand. You have such a winning personality."

He looked across at her. "Same back at ya. He doesn't much care for you either."

"Great. Maybe we should start a new club. The FBI's Most Distrusted and Generally Disliked. Has a ring to it, don't you think?"

"I'm sure you'd find plenty of new members if you set-up a website."

"Maybe next week, when I'm finished cracking this case."

His face broke into a fleeting smile as he drove back toward town.

Chapter 24

Esteban must have called ahead because as soon as Allie and Sawyer pushed open the door at the sheriff's station, a deputy materialized immediately to escort them into the depths of the pristine offices of the new building. Within a minute after arriving they'd been herded into the SAC's cramped, temporary digs and informed that the agent was on his way. The preoccupied deputy hadn't thought to get another chair, nor did he say anything remotely like "make yourselves comfortable" which, under the circumstances, wasn't possible. This reception was a far cry from her visit the day before.

Sawyer surveyed the microscopic quarters, "I don't suppose Mr. FBI would appreciate either one of us usurping his place." He looked at the two chairs tucked into the office, one being positioned behind the desk. "I'd better hunt up another chair."

"Make sure they don't arrest you for prowling," suggested Allie. "I got the impression they don't appreciate sightseers nosing around."

There only appeared to be a few personnel about and none were in the hallway, the deputy having disappeared to attend to other more important duties. Sawyer quickly located a third seat around a corner in the hall and carried it back to the office.

"Evaded capture this time," he said, cramming the metal stackable next to the other upholstered chair facing the desk. They then squeezed themselves into the space where they waited.

And waited.

Finally, they heard the click of Esteban's polished wingtips as he strode purposefully toward the office. He may be late as far as his guests were concerned, but he hadn't been lollygagging, the look on his face made that apparent. Sliding behind Sawyer's chair would have been a struggle if Sawyer hadn't given up his seat some time ago to stretch his legs and prop up the wall. Esteban tilted the chair forward to reach his own. Sitting down without any pretense of friendliness, he leaned back on the chair's rear legs until his head rested against the wall, chin down, peering ominously at the other occupants of the tiny space. Crossing his arms over his chest, he silently examined them with an expression that neither could categorize.

Allie was already annoyed and antsy. The remainder of the morning had dwindled toward afternoon while they'd twiddled their thumbs waiting until the fed deigned to make his appearance. And now he had the gall to just sit there like some dyspeptic buddha.

"So, what's the big rush to box us up in this cubicle?" Allie had had enough of the silent treatment. "Talking to us must not have been that important considering your hurry to get here. Maybe your siren wasn't working."

Esteban dropped his chair back to earth. "I was delayed. The team found something interesting that kept me tied up."

Sawyer quirked an eyebrow in question. Allie just blurted hers.

"Like what?" She leaned forward. *This had better be good.*

"Nothing I can divulge at this time."

"Then why even bring it up? You get a kick out of stringing us along just because we're keeping you honest?" She wasn't going to pussyfoot, she'd had it with this guy.

"Is *that* what you two were doing out there."

Sawyer cut in. "No," he gave Allie a warning look not to further antagonize their host. Esteban was the one with the handcuffs and the power to use them. *Didn't reporters ever know when to shut-up?* "We were just following a gut feeling."

"That is not your duty. Not to mention the fact that your actions may have compromised our investigation."

Allie was incensed. "How so? We didn't touch anything or disturb any evidence. I haven't called or communicated with anyone and neither has Sawyer. And it's not like you were taking the initiative to backtrack along the fence."

If she weren't becoming such a nuisance, Esteban might consider being less hardnosed. "The fence line would have been checked before long. Whatever your provocation for being there, no interference is acceptable."

She huffed and sat back.

"We're just butting heads. I thought we were here to be interviewed," Sawyer, keeping his reserve in check, attempted to reintroduce calm.

"You are."

"Well? What do you want to know?" Sawyer sat back down while Allie glowered, unwilling to forgive the agent's inferences and obvious shortcomings.

Without another word, Esteban pulled a tape recorder out of his desk and started the process of finding out what these two were really doing out there.

Another hour squandered.

That was Allie's perspective. They'd answered question after question that seemed to go nowhere until Esteban finally switched off the recorder.

Well that was a perfect waste. In tandem, she and Sawyer started to stand up, but Esteban waved them back into their seats.

"I don't know about you, Agent, but I have a severe case of fanny fatigue. I need to get up and move. If you want to ask more questions afterward, fine, but you know how long we waited for you before you even started the interview." Allie defiantly stood up again. "A little relief would be welcome," and she gave him a twisted smile that could have meant anything. He didn't bother to try to interpret it.

Relenting and giving in to Allie's point, Esteban rose with them and decided it was time to be more hospitable. Polite but cool, he offered to get them something to drink.

"How's the coffee here?" asked Allie, loosening up a bit. "I keep hearing how bad cop coffee is. How true is it?"

"You wouldn't be far off the mark, but these boys try to set a higher standard. It usually isn't five hours old."

"I guess that's good enough for government work," she shot him a sly glance to see if he had any sense of humor. "I'll have coffee, with a little cream. A lot of cream if it's over three hours gone."

Esteban looked over at Sawyer. "Coffee's good for me."

It felt as though Esteban had determined they weren't menaces to society after all and decided to turn down the heat. He got up to fill the orders, but not before warning them about making any calls or contacts, including text messages.

Allie gave him a cross-eyed glance, "Do I look like a serial texter? If you still don't trust us, take the phones." While she was digging for it in her bag, he wagged his head and walked off toward the break room.

Taking the opportunity to work the kinks out, Sawyer and Allie wandered up and down the hall saying nothing as they passed by occupied offices, they'd been talked out.

A few minutes later, Esteban returned, bearing two cups of coffee and a white bag in his hands, a bottle of water under one arm. Setting everything on the desk, he motioned for the two to join him back in the office, a prospect that didn't thrill either Allie or Sawyer at that point. They were tired of the pointed questions and the inactivity.

With everyone seated again, Esteban indicated the bag with his head while he opened his water. Allie peered inside and grinned.

"Wouldn't you know it? Donuts." Sugar was a sure-fire way to give Allie an attitude adjustment. "How'd you know my weakness?"

"It's my job to know," said Esteban, straight-faced.

Allie rolled her eyes. "Is this in recognition of our new status as junior detectives?"

That garnered a twitch of the agent's mouth. Sawyer sat back with his coffee while Allie pulled out an old fashioned and offered him the bag.

He shrugged and grabbed one for himself. "May as well. When in Rome…"

Taking a long swig of water, Esteban contemplated the odd pair seated across from him. While he'd been quizzing them a stray idea had crept into his head, one that he tried to shake off as being incredibly foolish, not to mention a real breach of protocol. He could take some real heat for what was formulating in his mind as he'd fetched the snacks. On top of that, there wasn't exactly a current of trust running between the three of them.

Placing the plastic bottle on the desk in front of him, Esteban eased his way into the subject. His little plan was iffy at best and marginally dangerous at the worst, but he had pegged Allie for a journalist with a real fire for facts.

He was about to give her the opportunity of a lifetime.

Chapter 25

Once again, Rone Haggerty had the mike.

Seated behind the table facing the House Committee on Energy and Commerce, he was insistently stating his case for the need to pass the Clean Air and Energy Act, otherwise known as the Cap and Trade. It was on the calendar for the next week and Haggerty had been invited to Capitol Hill once more to present his argument, only this time Chairman Wexler barred the countering testimony of one of the world's leading climate specialists and critic of the whole global warming premise. The House majority was taking no chances and throwing its weight around by denying the appearance of a competent, and very convincing, refutation of Haggerty's claims.

Aside from his witness before Congress, Haggerty was quietly making the rounds of Democrat, and a few choice Republican, office holders. What exactly he was peddling wasn't making headlines, but to the few who knew about his recent confab in Curaçao it was clear that he was lobbying with a powerful contingent behind him, ready to lock up the world's oil supply and deny the United States access unless a key vote was cast and carried. The worrisome part to most Republicans and a growing number of blue dog Dems was the text in the bill that denied the U.S. access to its own resources, leaving the people with an energy surcharge that could cripple the economy. Either way, foreign oil producers win and the American people would lose.

Tired of being held hostage by foreign oil and their own Congress, the public was becoming vociferous in its opposition to the bill. Clamor was escalating for a different solution and another "Drill Here, Drill Now" petition was in the works to Washington.

There was widespread reaction to the maneuverings inside the beltway that spiked the price of gold and the dollar was taking yet another hit. China was balking at the declining value of the U.S. bonds it held. Squawking led nowhere so they were hedging their bets by attempting to secure eighty billion dollars in gold.

And as if he had nothing better to do with his time, President Van Schaal was gallivanting around the globe, again. This week he was flirting with Indonesia, lauding them for cultivating their coal and oil resources. In the next breath he was commending American sensitivity to the earth's warming dilemma by recognizing the need to scale back energy usage, not that the media picked up on the hypocrisy. He commended the wonders of America's commitment to develop 'green' lifestyles, jobs and energy production, building wind farms and erecting acres of solar panels to drastically reduce its carbon footprint. While on foreign soil Van Schaal was claiming that the economic crisis was actually lessening with every dollar allocated to new government projects, although the stats didn't support the claim.

That didn't matter to his starry-eyed followers who were still floating on cloud nine while unemployment rose beyond nine percent and still, no one could figure out why, with all the billions of dollars that was budgeted by the government for recovery, virtually none of it had been spent.

The future did not bode well for the American people.

Chapter 26

Exhausted by another sleepless night fraught with emotional turmoil, Yancy packed it in, got dressed and went to the office. She'd visit Kara's family again at the hospital later in the afternoon. In the meantime, she was pondering her next step in the case. A few ideas had threaded through her mind before Kara's emergency airlifting to the hospital in Billings, but now she truly had to plow ahead, her client's life lay in the balance.

Oh God, please let this effort not be in vain. Yancy wasn't often given to prayer but the circumstances had ratcheted up her hopes that a supreme being was out there to protect a young girl's life.

Knowing that Ell was at work, Yancy picked up the phone and dialed. Ell had been one of the best sounding boards she'd had over the years, a woman of intelligence, frightful insight on occasion and just plain common sense. Who else to call in a time of crisis? So far as Yancy knew there weren't any "ghostbuster" listings in the local phone book.

"IT desk." Ell's musical voice rang through.

"I'm glad you're in and not off tinkering with one of those dipstick's desktops. They're worse than I am when it comes to computer know-how. I should say know-nuthin'."

"*I'm* surprised you're not in bed with a pillow over your head. You've had a helluva weekend and need the rest, doll."

"Yeah, I tried that yesterday, didn't work then and I *do* have a job. Besides, my mind simply won't allow me to shut down," Yancy said wearily. "That's why I'm pestering you."

"Pester? Are you kidding? You just saved me from having to rescue the insufferable Ri*chárd*," Ell pronounced the name as if it were actually "Dick" and meant the same thing, "from a mess of his own making. Why that guy hasn't figured out that you can't load your own programs onto the company network completely baffles me."

"You know how it is. The more education we get the less likely we are to think," commiserated Yancy.

Ell laughed loud and clear. The onetime songstress' voice could carry across the Hudson River. "Thank God you never reached that level of institutional stupidity. So what's up?"

"Aside from being physically and mentally burnt, I'm laying out my plan of action on the Lysander case and you had such good input when I started this thing, I thought I could toss a few things at you," just a hint of hope radiated through the telephone line.

"I'm all ears."

"You asked for it." From there, Yancy sketched out the plan she'd started pulling together last week. She had already begun drafting the brief based on the Eighth Amendment, which states, "nor cruel and unusual punishments inflicted" upon individuals. Yancy clearly thought that the EPA's denial of electrical power to operate a life-saving device was cruel and unusual punishment. The terrible circumstance that had since come about of Kara actually being on the edge of losing her life due to that very ruling, was probably a demonstration in fact of what she had been about to describe as a possible consequence of the ruling.

She was halfway through composing the paper and was reading it through to Ell, when Ell brought up something Yancy had considered.

"Are you going to cite the Fifth Amendment, too?"

"As always, you are reading my mind. I have it here..."nor shall any person... be deprived of life, liberty, or property, without due process of law."

"Okay, so you're claiming that the EPA's arbitrary decision to not reinstate the old power plant went outside the due process clause," said Ell.

"Yes. It was an arbitrary decision made by a bureaucrat without any public input. The administrative decision that was rendered last week leaves us this recourse, hence taking the case to the Federal District Court." Yancy was quiet for a few seconds. "What else crossed my mind was the thought that the Supreme Court ruling of 2007 that defined carbon dioxide as a pollutant could be challenged within the confines of this case. You know, an added argument that the arbitrary designation of a benign greenhouse gas as a pollutant was a misreading of the Clean Air Act."

Ell nodded, not that Yancy could see her. "The concept makes sense to me but where can you turn after the Supreme Court has ruled?"

"Well, if the argument is made as part of another larger case, it's included within the new case if it actually gets passed up the ladder to a higher court, giving it air when it would probably go nowhere on it's own. I know. I'm grasping at straws."

"You can try it. Crazier things have gone before the Supreme Court, like when they ruled on that CO_2 business in the first place. Let's hope it passes muster when you submit the brief."

"The fact that I made my argument before the administrative judge at the EPA, getting it all into the transcript, gave us the grounds to file an appeal, which this essentially is."

"I say run with it. Something's got to be done for that little girl."

"Yes, I know." Yancy was battling moroseness at being helpless to do anything other than file papers and wait upon the pleasure of the Crown, because, more and more the bloated bureaucracies seemed to be no better than a king's ministries.

"Have you talked to Allie?"

"We chatted yesterday after I got back from the hospital. That family is a wreck and there's nothing I can do," her voice was colored by the despair she had witnessed in Kara's mother's eyes. "I think she ran a follow-up article last night or this morning. I haven't looked it up."

"Well, you keep up with her. This next step will be newsworthy as well. A life in the balance and all. You've got to use whatever leverage you can find and that includes the press. The opposition does it all the time."

"You are right again, Ell. Thank goodness I have an 'in,' which I could thank you for since it was through you that I met Allie in the first place."

Ell made some futzing noise pooh-poohing Yancy's words. "We had a good time and fate worked out the rest. Speaking of which, more or less, you'd best get some."

"Later. I have work to do."

After signing off with Ell, Yancy put a call into Allie to check in with her. *Maybe she's made some progress with her story.*

Allie was finally back at her hotel after a grueling day with the FBI's finest. Her head was whirling with so many thoughts crawling through the Swiss cheese she called a brain, everything seemed discombobulated.

When her phone rang, she swore that she'd hang-up if it was Gleason. She was going to have to come up with something good to get him off her back for a couple of days. Nothing else would work except to ditch work.

Checking the LCD display, she saw that it was Yancy, so she punched 'talk' with her thumb.

"How's Kara doing? Any progress yet?"

"No," Yancy answered dully. "I wish I had something good to report. But two days of 'no change' is not heartening news. I'm headed back over to the hospital in a little bit. I wanted to see if anything came of our last conversation."

"Yup. Got a front page to the regional section. Gleason's hot on the trail for me to get to the bottom of the power outage now that there's a human side to the story. So, I'm back here in Gillette for a final effort to fight for truth and justice. You know, the usual."

Yancy chuckled despite her client's frightening situation. At least someone was working hard to uncover the facts. "Any luck?"

"I don't know. It looks like the Feds may have made some progress, not that I can get anything out of them. I hear that the mine will be reopening tomorrow. Looks like OSHA can't keep them shut down any longer and the investigators have gotten all the evidence they can find. Other than that, I got zip. How about you?"

"That's why I called to give you an update, just in case your boss will want it. I'm filing papers in the Federal District Court tomorrow." Yancy waited to see what the verdict would be from Allie's perspective. Did she think her editor would continue with the side story?

"Great. I believe that I may be able to interest him in the details of it, but you'll have to give them to me. You kind of sketched out some things before but they didn't really play into what I wrote for yesterday's edition."

They settled in for a quick overview of what the brief was claiming against the EPA, including Yancy's theory on the regulation of CO_2 as a pollutant being the crux of the problem.

Although it seemed Allie'd been getting it from all sides lately about the evils of government interfering with carbon emission standards, she still wasn't convinced that it didn't require official supervision.

Hearing Allie's continued reticence to accept the data, she gave Allie even more evidence to chew on.   "Here's an example of why the global warming theory doesn't pan out: a thirty-eight year veteran scientist with the EPA, Dr. Alan Carlin, has just issued a report on exactly what I'm talking about, that the science does *not* support the hypothesis of CO_2 causing global warming. The director of the agency told him that it would not be released. You know why?" She didn't give Allie a chance to answer, the question was rhetorical. "Because it countered the president's policy, not because the premise was faulty, it wasn't. In fact, he was at first forbidden to go public about his report and forbidden to release it. Now however, you can look it up on his website or that of the Competitive Enterprise Institute."

Allie was used to hearing all kinds of wild claims against climate change, but the fact that the EPA, tried to suppress a report from their own agency at the behest of the administration, said more than if the report had been released without fanfare. *What were they try - ing to hide?* The whole idea made her bridle. Allie had spent her adult life trying to shed light on shady subjects and if the administration was involved in this kind of manipulation of data simply by omitting it in order to further its agenda... that really spiked her blood pressure.

"Are you still there?" Yancy thought the connection had been cut.

"Yeah, I'm here and I find the whole scenario incomprehensible."

"Believe it. I couldn't make this stuff up if I tried. I'm not devious enough."

"I know. That's why you were so miserable at the law firm in
New York with all those vultures. I still don't get how Aunt Ell hangs
in there," mused Allie, happy to be distracted from an uncomfortable
subject that effectively trounced all of her environmental values.

"They're not all that bad and Ell has the kind of personality that
finds humor in everything, including the pompous strutting of some
of those peacocks." Yancy sighed. "Anyway, that's all I have for
now. Do you want me to call you if anything changes?"

"Absolutely. We want to keep tabs on Kara's progress as she
recovers."

If she recovers. Yancy hung up without giving voice to her
thought.

Mary Lysander was inconsolable and battling despair.

The tears came now more sporadically after the constant stream
that had rained during the first twenty-four hours of their watch.
Paula had stayed with them and taken on the duty of shuttling family members to and from a cousin's house in Billings. Mary had been
there to bathe, and once for an attempt to sleep through the night.
She couldn't stay away from the hospital but for a few hours at a
time even though there was always a family member with Kara, and
the strain was already beginning to take its toll.

Feeling utterly powerless, Mary kept vigil by her daughter's bedside. She'd watch the doctors come in and read the chart, and hover
over Kara, shining the penlight in her eyes checking for pupil reaction, running a pinwheel over her extremities expecting a flinch or
something to indicate signs of feeling. They'd question the nurses
and even ask Mary or Key if they'd noticed anything. Maybe Kara
had moved her hand when they held it or slightly squeezed back
when they clasped her limp fingers. Maybe her eyelids had fluttered.

It was a 'no' to all the inquiries but one. Mary and Key and now
the doctor had noticed movement under Kara's eyelids. The moni-

tors tracking her brain function had increased in activity ever so slightly, indicating that something was going on inside their little girl, something positive, but not enough to get excited about, the doctor said. Coma patients often move their eyes, thoughts running around in their heads and they do hear. She encouraged them to speak and maybe even sing to Kara. It may bring her back sooner.

Key stood disconsolately at the foot of the bed as he watched the jagged lines spiking across the screen. Looking down at his wife, he saw a stray tear slip quietly down Mary's cheek, hardly noticing as the small woman left the room, white jacket catching a ghost wind in her hurry to continue rounds.

The word from the doctor was optimistic but not enough to latch onto. Key had seen two cousins from different sides of the family, victims of car wrecks and a work accident, who had been in comas. One for nearly a year. Both had left this earth. But before they had gone to join the ancestors he had watched the constantly rolling eyes of his younger cousin, as if he were fighting to get them open, but they never did. He'd lost the struggle.

Key had to take action, but was at a loss. What could *he* do? Waiting around was not something that he did well, he was an impatient man. He walked out of the room and down to the stairwell where he took his cell phone from his pocket and placed a call.

"Axée, what should I do?" He addressed his uncle, an elder of his father's clan, by Axée, a title of respect meaning 'father' in Apsáalooke, the language of the Crow. Axée was also a man of considerable medicine.

"She is suffering," said Axée without inflection.

"We can't tell. Her eyes move, but nothing else. The doctors say that she is stable." As Key spoke to his uncle, his words caught in his throat.

"The Sun Dance is this week. You will dance for your daughter's healing." There was no yes or no about it, Axée spoke with a quiet authority that simply told Key what he already knew he should do. He had already attended two preparatory prayer meetings, sweats in the 'Little Lodge' but he hadn't planned on being a full participant this year. The timing of the Sun Dance was propitious in the eyes of his uncle, and as Key considered it, to him as well.

"Yes," was his only answer.

He returned to the ICU and watched the crumpled form of his wife as she sat half in prayer, half in an exhausted daze, her hand clutching that of Kara's whose own impression in the bed was little more than wrinkles in the blankets outlining her slender limbs. He went into the room and told Mary that he would be leaving in the morning for the Sun Dance. The news was not what she had expected, but she nodded in agreement that he must go and pray for Kara. The corners of her mouth lifted the tiniest bit. It was hope where she'd felt little in that antiseptic room.

"You take Keith along. He should sweat with you before you go to the Big Lodge and be there to support your prayers."

This time Key nodded and smiled, pulling his wife to her feet and hugging her tightly, then leaning over and squeezing Kara's hand before he went down the hall to collect his oldest son.

His eagle-bone whistle would soon crease the air at Spotted Horse Mountain.

Chapter 27

This was Solana's first time in Alaska. She grew up in the mountains along the Clearwater River in Idaho and her grandfather's ranch in the foothills of southern Montana's Absaroka Range, where steep craggy peaks topped by lingering winter snows were a familiar scene. That still hadn't prepared her for the stark beauty of Juneau's vertical backdrop, a virtual wall of granite decked with snow not yet melted despite summer's approach. The Coast Mountains were so precipitous that even a two-lane highway had not yet been constructed from the interior to reach Alaska's capital, leaving air and sea as the only access routes available.

It was a brisk morning, the chill expected by her brain but not her body, which was acclimated to the sunnier weather of New Mexico. Even taking into account the mountain elevation at home, the cool air was still a bit of a jolt. Sol had wrapped herself in a jacket before getting directions to the local Rural Resources office. The hotel's front desk had located it for her on the map, showing her how it was situated along a trolley route, which allowed her to forego hiring a taxi.

Not knowing what to expect when she pushed open the door of the quaint old building that long pre-dated statehood fifty years ago, Sol walked into a pleasant woodsy office complete with an eight-foot Tlingit totem pole. Being Nez Perce and Crow by heritage, Sol had an interest in other Native groups, however she wasn't particularly well informed about the coastal people of Alaska and British Columbia. She knew the names of many, Tsimshian, Tlingit, Haida, Kwakiutl, Bella Coola, but she wasn't familiar with their cultures and histories. She'd scanned the art thinking how much more there always was to learn.

Her purpose in visiting the Rural Resources office had been to get a feel for the personnel and their involvement with the Corcoran Creek Mine case that was soon to be heard by the Supreme Court. The name of this organization figured prominently in the briefs she'd read, and re-read, not having her husband's legal mind that soaked up lawyereze without a second thought. She'd figured she was also fairly safe in making a personal appearance at the office. The times she'd managed to catch national attention the year before were long gone and had zip to do with the outpost of Alaska. She doubted these people were interested in anything that didn't have to do directly with their little war on industry in their pristine state.

Evidently, she was right. The office staff was helpful and amiable but hadn't a clue about the news coverage she'd received, which was a good thing. If they had, they'd probably have shown her the door without a word wasted.

What Sol encountered was a batch of nice folks who were almost patronizing in their treatment of her. Not that she could really complain. They thought of themselves as genuinely working for the benefit of all Native peoples, guardians of the environment, intervening on their behalf. As if Indians and Alaska Natives should just fish and carve pretty masks for the benefit of tourists in order to feed their families.

She admitted to herself that she may be hypersensitive having been forced to deal with some well meaning, but seriously misguided, white Americans over the years, but Sol thought environmentalists were the worst. The Rural Resources staff came close to condescending in their attitude when she came in the door, though she doubted they were aware of their behavior, and she wasn't about to point it out, either. Luckily, they expected a five-foot-ten Native American woman to be stoic, so she played the part. Made it easy to get away with being only marginally sociable.

Afterward, she'd walked the streets downtown for a while, stopping for a late breakfast and a well-deserved latte before heading back to the hotel and going over her notes and making phone calls.

"Stereotyping comes in quite handy on occasion," she told Toddy when they talked later on in the evening. "Makes it so I don't have to act nice for folks who think I should be surly."

"They couldn't have been that bad," he laughed.

"All right, so I'm overstating it a little. But they were relatively pompous in their need to be understanding of my ethnicity. When are people going to get over that?" She actually said "sheesh," which only made him laugh more.

"So, do you think there's any connection between these people and the group in Wyoming?" He went back to the purpose of her visit.

"Not that you'd know. They put on the "peace be with you" BS so thick I thought they were all going to close the interview with "namaste" on their way to yoga class."

"What have you got against yoga?"

"Not a thing. I just wish that they'd understand that practicing an art of meditation doesn't miraculously imbue them with superior brainpower. Though with these people, they seem to think that being in touch with the earth, or having compassion for it rather, makes them able to view the uninitiated as lesser beings. It's back to the old "revere the Native connection to Mother Earth" without knowing how Native cultures view the earth and its bounty, and that all of the cultures don't see things exactly the same way. I have to admit, it's pretty irritating."

"So I see." Toddy couldn't help himself from laughing again, Sol could get so ticked at other people's good intentions. "What else have you got?"

"Not much," she admitted, "though there were also a couple of students from the U, one appeared to be Chinese and one was Middle Eastern or maybe even Pakistani. They weren't very talkative. The Middle Eastern guy, in particular, wasn't interested in being cordial. There was a map of the Alaska Pipeline that was taken from a satellite photo in one of the back offices. It had a number of colored tacks along the route, but that could mean anything, there were a lot of maps around. The staff had a lot to say about saving the lake from desecration by the mining corporation. It came across as if they were saving the Yu'pik from themselves." She exhaled her exasperation. "At times it was hard to be civil."

"Knowing you, I can see that."

"What? I'm not the picture of stoicism you see in the hundred year old photos of my ancestors?"

"Hardly. Since you're not in the room and I can only imagine the evil-eye I'll get for saying this, but I'd call you a red-hot mama."

It was her turn to laugh.

They talked about the gold market, Toddy bringing up the recent news about China looking to purchase eighty billion dollars in gold. "Check this out, an interview of an Illinois representative by Fox News gave us this about China, and I quote," she could hear clicking on the keyboard to bring up the text. *"They funded a second strategic petroleum reserve and they plan to buy eighty billion worth of gold. That's two Fort Knoxes. Both of those investments only make sense if you expect significant dollar inflation."* That'll give you something to think about, especially when Scirras now has his hand in what we think may be the largest gold reserve in the world, right up there within a few hundred miles of where you're sitting right now."

"More like eight hundred miles, but who's counting."

"Damn, Alaska's a big state. The fact is that it behooves Scirras to see that gold stay underground. Just like DeBeers does its best to keep gem quality diamonds from flooding the market and bringing down prices, he's interested in controlling the price of gold. Another fact is that China's hunting for gold, and the amount they want to purchase to hedge their bets against the dollar's inevitable demise, the way Van Schaal is ballooning the debt by one trillion after another, may not be available to them."

"Can't anyone act out of common decency anymore?" Sol was tired of all the politicking that she saw as wholly destructive to their country.

"Not if all you're interested in is power and more power," said Toddy. "Anyway, I've got an idea on why Scirras is trying to keep a lid on the gold market besides the usual hedge against paper currencies."

"Okay, give."

"Not yet. I have to research it further to be sure I'm not cruising down the wrong alley looking for scraps. I'll let you know when I've got something more solid."

"Fine. I suppose I can wait," Sol feigned a pout.

"You're one of the most patient people I know. You have to be to put up with me." He sighed. "I miss you."

"I know, Toddy. I miss you too, but it's only a few more days."

"Good, because I'm not good at waiting."

"Don't I know it, and I love you too."

After hanging up, Sol's mind was running a mile a minute with all the talk about Scirras and the gold market. She started reading through her notes from her one-woman sortie to the Rural Resources office. Something was bugging her about the visit aside from the sweet-elite attitude that was so like what she'd encountered far too often in the past. They were obviously doing their part in the area of diversity as well, bringing in foreign students as interns.

She sat back on the bed, her notepad in her lap. She was picturing the two young men from distant countries and the setting of the back room. All those colorful satellite maps of Alaska's vast wilderness, dwarfed spots of civilization at odd places along the coasts, rivers, or deep in the interior, and one map that hosted a staggered line of equally colorful tacks.

Energy Barons

Chapter 28

Books and files were strewn across Yancy's desk, papers and post-its protruding from between pages and stuck to manila folder faces. Left elbow planted in front of the computer screen, she was bent over the desk, running her hand through her hair while following a line of print in one of the tomes with her right forefinger, making certain that she fully understood the precedent before citing it. The brief was basically complete, she was just checking her work so it could be submitted by the end of the workday.

The phone rang, breaking her concentration.

"Yes?"

"Yancy, it's Cole."

She came up for air, setting aside the convoluted language of the ruling, and answered with a bloom of pleasure that caught her a little off-guard. Their outing on Saturday had ended with disaster, her heart plummeting to depths she hadn't thought possible. She almost cringed now as the memories of that night swamped her. Kara lying almost lifeless, creating hardly a bump beneath the covers of her hospital bed, and Cole, whom she barely knew, staying by her side and keeping her crumbling façade glued together, almost. The hardest part of the whole scenario was for her to accept that she had really needed someone to lean on, just that once.

And Kara's not even related. She amended her thought with the acknowledgment of the fact that the Lysanders had practically become family. *She might as well be.*

"Cole. It's good to hear from you. You know, I must thank you for being so willing to shuttle me around Saturday. I shouldn't have imposed on you that way."

"No trouble. Things happen, and you don't have to be family to care deeply about someone."

Is he reading my mind? "Even so, the evening was a bust."

"Well, that's why I called."

Oh-oh.

"Just wanted to see if you were willing to give it another shot," Cole's voice was controlled, bracing himself for possible rejection.

Yancy sighed audibly, relieved at not having chased him away for good. "What did you have in mind?"

"I'm on my way to town for Toni's game, decided that I needed to be there. I'd like to know if you'd have dinner with me afterward."

"That sounds like just what the doctor ordered." She groaned, ruing her choice of words, picturing Kara's family camped out at her bedside.

He seemed to pick up on her train of thought. "How is the little girl, Kara? How's she doing?"

Yancy was taken by surprise at his uncanny ability to hone in on her thoughts. "There's been no real change, but we have hope she'll pull through." *She has to.* "There's not much we can do but wait. I'm working on the next phase of the case as we speak."

"So you could use a break."

"Yes, indeed. This kind of paperwork, with so much riding on how well I make the argument, it induces headaches of monumental proportion. Suing the government isn't as easy as it looks."

Cole chuckled. "Makes my life seem simple by comparison."

"Nobody's life is simple," Yancy disagreed, "unless you're a Buddhist monk. And I'll bet they have tense days like everybody else."

"How do you figure?"

"Maybe they get stressed when they can't get centered? Or worry they'll step on an ant? Or stress over raking their sand garden unevenly? Who knows? Everyone has stress. It's just whether or not you give into it, and monks are probably excellently trained to ride it out most of the time."

"The decision's been made then, we'll do a stress-free evening. No ants and no rakes."

"I'm in."

Preparations had been going on around the flat meadow at the knee of Spotted Horse Mountain. The encampment encircled the site where the Big Lodge, Ashé Isée, would be raised the day of the Sun Dance. RVs, tents and tipis were scattered across grass acreage that had not yet browned in the coming heat of summer, with two large tents erected for the kitchen and as a mess to feed the numerous helpers and family of the dancers.

This was where the feast would be prepared for serving at the closing ceremonies. Steaks from the buffalo chosen to give his meat for the occasion would be served with fry bread and fruit, watermelon sliced and given to the participants to refresh them after three days without water or food. In the Big Lodge, prayer and dance would be their sustenance, their offering.

Key and Keith were met by Axée, who examined his nephew and son. He could feel the beleaguered air and see their discouragement. Axée nodded, affirming that the seventeen year-old was ready to take on responsibility. He would fare well as support for his father during the three-day ordeal. The ritual supplication would be arduous, strengthening and cleansing for Key. A rejuvenation of spirit that would nourish him so he might convey that strength to his family, feeding hope.

Tonight they would sweat together and prepare.

Tomorrow, Key would enter the Big Lodge and appeal to the Maker for Kara's life.

Chapter 29

The latest update on the power plant and coal mine explosions, meager as they were, had been filed with the Post for the next edition. Allie was the first to break the story, the FBI scratching her back for being cooperative about her and Sawyer's little discovery on Tyne Hill property.

She had finally gotten the official word from the feds that they had recovered bomb fragments at both locations. They were unwilling to say which direction the evidence pointed – to an intruder or an insider – but she did get a statement from SAC Esteban that no group or individual had taken responsibility for the crimes, which had now been classified as homicides.

Driving south toward Depression Creek, Allie was talking, or rather arguing, with Carter Gleason.

"We're finally making a breakthrough here. You have to give me one more week to cover all the angles."

"Happy as we are that you got the *exclusive*," he said almost snidely, "you know as well as I do that they gave you as little as they could get away with. We can't afford to have you traipsing around the Wild West looking for a bomber under every haystack. That's what law enforcement is for," Gleason was on the verge of losing his temper. "And if you've forgotten, you carry a pen, not a badge."

"I expected you to say, 'not a gun.'"

"Well, one of those, either."

"How do you know?" she retorted. "Maybe I've been holding out on you."

"Hah! When you start carrying, I'll flush my cigarettes," he snorted derisively.

"Then you'd better get yourself some nicotine gum, because hanging out with feds and cowpokes can make a girl decide it's time to pack a pistol."

"Whatever," he chortled, knowing that she was blowing smoke, "the answer is still no. We need you to cover the water rights case at the district courthouse. Now that you've been getting comfortable with legal mumbo-jumbo working that EPA case, you're an asset we can use *here*." Gleason wasn't budging an inch and all Allie could think was that she had to find an out. She couldn't be tucked away inside a courtroom for a week to listen to even more lawyers hashing it out in front of a judge. She'd go nuts. *And the killer might get away.*

"Anyone can cover that. It doesn't take a law degree to figure out what that fight is about, farmers versus environmental advocates." Allie was not going to let this go. She *had* to stay on the story. "Then give me a week off. I need the time to track down the details."

"I don't know," but he was wavering. She'd been giving them something where everyone else had zilch.

"Come on, Gleason. What do you care? You're not losing any money since I don't have any vacation time available. Put it in as unpaid leave."

He considered her suggestion. The paper could use a good break and money was tight for the whole industry, so he couldn't justify paying her to stay in Wyoming. "I guess. We can put someone else on the court coverage. But you'd better come up with something good."

"Don't press your luck since this is on my nickel, not yours." She eased up a little. "But, thanks. You'll be the first to hear."

Allie nosed her car into the rail fence encircling the pasture closest to the house. Climbing out of the car, she was cornered by one of the dogs that bounded toward her from out of the blue and hopped up to try to slather Allie's face with her tongue. She'd met this one, Cowzer, on the tour Sawyer had given her of the ranch the week before. There were two other dogs, a border collie and a blue heeler, but they were lazing in the sun, their work done for the day and couldn't be bothered with a new arrival.

Cowzer served as honor guard for the rest of the parade, which had included the other two now-crashed cowdogs plus Sawyer and Rain. The men were making their way back from the corral where they'd just unsaddled their horses after riding part of the northeast quadrant, checking fences for breaches.

Allie hadn't met Rain and was intrigued by the yin and yang the two of them embodied. Sawyer was tall and lean with vestiges of military bearing visible under his rangy stride. Clipped manner to match his clipped hair.

Rain was close to his opposite. Shorter by several inches, dark hair swinging across his back in a long braid, with a brightly woven Pendleton vest buttoned tight around a solid middle. Barrel-chested, but not running to fat.

Seeing her park and be accosted by Cowzer, they followed the dog's lead. Sawyer introduced the two as Allie gave in to the dog's insistent begging for attention and scratched her behind the ears.

"Bringing in reinforcements already?"

"I was thinking we might need them," said Sawyer after giving the dog a command to lie down. "I'm not so sure about Esteban's priorities. He's withholding information and he's asking an awful lot from you." He looked up from the now complacent dog to the woman who he was sure didn't have a complacent bone in her body. "He's not giving you the full tale."

"And that worries you," she said, accepting his assessment of the agent. "Okay, I'll roll with that conclusion, but, I am supposed to be an 'investigative' reporter." She looked the two men over, the Indian Warrior and the Marine and shrugged her indifference. "May as well have a little support, but all I'm doing is my job."

"It would help if your instincts weren't telling you that these folks could actually be dangerous," said Sawyer, pointedly.

Rain allowed just one eyebrow to lift the least bit. "Are you sure about that? I thought you were just talking about some environmental group that has an office down in Cheyenne."

"We don't know what's really going on down there and apparently neither does the FBI." Sawyer hissed his indignation, "Homeland Security is so hell-bent on chasing veterans and conservatives, they're forgetting about the lunatic fringe on the left."

Allie narrowed her eyes with exasperation. "We lefties aren't all that bad and those people at Green Grasslands seemed nice enough. We're probably way off base here."

"You're backing off now? After you put the bug in Esteban's ear about the two Al Qaeda look-alikes you saw at the office? Make up your mind."

This time both of Rain's brows shot up.

Aggravated, Allie put her hands on her hips. "I don't know what to think. The facts are the explosions were planned and carried out by some unknown person or persons. When those two characters were hustled out the door it just kind of got my hackles up. Doesn't mean I'm on the right track. Maybe they were just in a hurry to get to class."

Sawyer gave her a look as if she was acting stupid, and knowing full well that she was anything but.

Rain interrupted. "I don't have the whole story here. Why don't you tell me what you have and maybe it will begin to make more sense. From what Sawyer has said, this FBI agent thinks you opened a can of worms."

"That's not the half of it," grumbled Sawyer.

Walking up the porch steps, they parked their behinds on the available seats, Allie choosing the porch swing. She pushed off with her feet and talked, creating a cadence in her movement that wove into her voice. Sawyer and she described what they'd discovered and how Agent Esteban had come up with a plan, of sorts.

A plan that left a lot to be desired as far as Sawyer was concerned. He didn't like it and that's why he'd asked Rain over.

"You want my opinion? Is that why you're bringing me up to date with this FBI scheme?" Rain wasn't sure about the purpose of the show-and-tell.

"I was uncomfortable with the idea from the outset," said Sawyer. Allie gave him a look that pretty much said, *butt out*, which he ignored. "He doesn't have a back-up plan were something to happen. He's shorthanded."

"We don't need a back-up plan," said Allie. "I'm not doing anything other than visiting, doing a few interviews for a story and getting what information I can. It's all legal and on the up-and-up."

"No one said that it wasn't, but if there's even the slightest chance that you were right and these people are capable of violence, then you need a fallback. And I can't do it, wouldn't fit in. I'm too…"

"Obviously conservative? Right-wing? Look like a gun-toting yahoo?" Allie couldn't help the sarcasm. She was irked at his interference.

"All of the above," Sawyer said straight-faced. Rain let a smile slip.

"You, however," Sawyer caught Rain's eye, and his mirth dissipated, "would be perfect." Both Allie and Rain looked at him for an explanation.

"Perfect for what," asked Sawyer's roping partner.

"You don't appear threatening and eco-types assume that all Native Americans are on board with their agenda of saving the earth from evil mankind."

"We are," deadpanned Rain.

Sawyer moved on knowing that Rain was yanking his chain. "Groups like Green Grasslands are always in need of volunteers. It wouldn't be that odd for you to sign-up as a helper while you're in-between jobs."

"Don't you think I'm a little old to be an environmental groupie?"

"No. They'd probably be grateful for the help and volunteers can range in age, grandmas to teens. Plus with a down economy there are folks looking to be involved while they hunt up something else," continued Sawyer. "Not everyone sits on their tail while they collect unemployment."

Rain considered the proposal. "It's a stretch, but not far from the truth since Flat Butte is closed for the moment and I don't have a job to go to."

"I don't think I'd mention that you're temporarily laid off from a power plant," added Sawyer.

Allie listened to the two, speechless at the planning that didn't include her. "I don't need anyone looking over my shoulder," she sputtered, leaning forward in the swing and skewering Sawyer with her glare. "I can take care of myself."

"Do you know any self-defense?" He asked.

"I'm just getting a story. I don't need to be a judo expert," she shot back.

"I'm surprised. Most women these days have some kind of training, just in case," Sawyer was pushing his point.

"Um, I took a couple classes in college. Aikido, mostly."

"And you didn't keep up with it," He made the statement, already knowing the answer.

She just gave him stinkeye as a reply.

"I rest my case," said Sawyer. "Rain would be good to have around."

Allie exchanged Rain for Sawyer in her sights. "So you and Chuck Norris are sparring partners."

"No. Just a wrestler and cow wrangler," his calm exterior belied an inner strength that made Allie think twice.

She gave up. "What does Mr. Fed think of this?"

"I haven't discussed this with him and I don't think it's a necessity at this point."

"I haven't met this Agent Esteban," said Rain. "Someone else interviewed me after the explosion."

"Even better," Sawyer said thinking about the set-up.

"Uh-huh. And how many Indians work at the power plant besides you?" Allie posed the question.

"None."

"Then you can figure that the agent who took your statement will recognize you if he happens to pull any surveillance duty on this detail."

Rain looked from Sawyer to Allie. He couldn't help himself and said straight faced, "We all look alike to paleface."

Allie threw up her hands in frustration.

Moving on, Sawyer told him, "They don't have any other leads, which is why Esteban is willing to give the idea a try and find out if it's a dead end. It could all be a waste of time."

Rain shrugged. "No way of knowing."

Everyone sat back and mulled over the whole concept. Sawyer was adamant Allie not be alone in a potentially dangerous situation. Allie was peeved but chastened some by the realization that she didn't have the skills to defend herself, not that she thought she'd need them. Rain appeared unconcerned.

Rain finally broke the silence. "When do we start?"

Energy Barons

Chapter 30

The sheriff stood at the edge of a precipitous slope, gazing out over the canyon that dropped away from the sharp bends of the road curling around the mountain. Behind him the coroner was examining a body that had been hauled up from the bushes fifty or so feet below him, just beyond the highway turnout.

He'd already interviewed and released the couple who found the gnawed remains just yards from where their child had tossed his ball over the side. Not that they had actually gone to get it, they'd just followed the arc of its flight through the air, thinking they might be able to retrieve it. When they'd seen where it landed and were considering climbing down, they also caught sight of the half-concealed body, jean clad legs barely visible from under the bracken.

The cell-phone coverage was spotty, if not nonexistent, along the western slopes of the Big Horn Mountains so they'd flagged down a passing trucker and had him call in the report on his CB radio.

All the technology in the world and we still can't communicate half the time. It made the sheriff even more thankful for long-haul truckers, and particularly the ones who plied this lonely stretch of highway.

As to whom the one-time pretty boy was, now laying lifeless inside a body bag, they were still combing the environs for a clue, anything that might fill in the blanks since his pockets had been empty. The sheriff had called the state police and they had arrived an hour behind him with a crime scene investigator in tow who was now doing his job with meticulous patience.

They'd been lucky that the area hadn't been trampled much since the body was dumped. This turnout didn't normally get much traffic, people generally making their way over the mountain having little need to stop. At least, that was according to the coroner's initial estimation of time of death, which was hard to pinpoint being several days at the earliest.

Turning the body over had made it obvious what had been the cause of death. Two gunshots, one in the back and one in the back of the head. The doctor wasn't sure yet which had sounded the final death knell, but by the looks of things, she assumed the headshot was likely the secondary bullet wound.

"So, a possible execution? Or the assailant just wanted to make sure the guy was dead and shot him a second time," the sheriff had asked the coroner as she was zipping up the bag.

"At the moment, your guess is as good as mine. We'll have to see what the crime scene experts come up with to fill in the blanks."

"Yep." The sheriff hooked his thumbs in his belt as he watched the criminologist carefully setting out markers and photographing the slope where it looked like the body had rolled to its resting place. Scavengers had been through the area and dined on the carcass, leaving a ragged mess of bones and tissue partially encased by the torn clothing. The sheriff had a lot of respect for the coroner for not losing her lunch, but then she was a veterinarian by trade and had seen all kinds of damage that animals can wreak upon each other. He was happy to have the body finally hidden away from sight, enclosed in the carrier for removal.

The tech called the sheriff down to where he was kneeling over a small mound of disturbed earth a good thirty feet away from the body's resting place. He wanted the lawman to see what he had found in the underbrush.

"At first glance, this looked like an animal had buried something, maybe bones or flesh for later consumption," said the crime scene investigator, a fellow who had been working the Gillette explosions and happened to be at the state police offices providing interface between agencies when the call had come in. A lucky break as far as the sheriff was concerned. If the FBI tech hadn't been there, they'd be waiting well into the night before someone showed up from the state crime lab. "But I don't think any coyote dug this, it's too uniform and I think contrived to fit into the general landscape. I've already got photos so now I'm going to dig out whatever might be here."

"Yeah, might be nuthin' too," the sheriff nodded as the tech carefully removed the earth with a brush to eventually reveal a wallet. "Whoever dropped this guy must have figured no one would look over here." He removed his hat and scratched his head. "Even at this distance from where the body was dumped, they must have thought we wouldn't look further than a few feet. Must not watch much television."

The tech stood up, opening the nylon billfold with his latex-gloved fingers. He was pulling out a laminated card. "We removed some covering dirt up there," he lifted a shoulder to indicate the turnout at the top of the incline as he extracted an ID card. "I'd say the shooting occurred up there and the body was rolled over the edge. The killer must have thought it was concealed well enough under the brush, which it wasn't, so this may have occurred at night. There was a fair amount of blood on the ground at the turnout that was covered by loose dirt, gravel and branches that were artfully placed to obscure the spill. It's hardly even visible now after, oh, I'd say at least a week. Would be easy to overlook."

"So maybe that's why he didn't take a lot of time to hide the wallet," said the sheriff. "Though why he didn't just drop it off a cliff further up or down the road, depending on which way he was traveling, beats me."

"Hard to say. If he hasn't killed before, he might have thought it was safe enough in the middle of nowhere."

"Yeah, who knew some kid would have a hissy fit and pitch his football over the edge." The sheriff shook his head, "So what've we got here?"

"A Colorado driver's license with a Denver address. Nice looking kid, too." He then pulled out a university ID from behind some other cards, membership to REI and a video store, and held it up for the sheriff to see. "Must have been cutting classes."

Energy Barons

Chapter 31

Her short visit to Juneau concluded, Solana was buckled into a barely tolerable plane seat on a puddle jumper she'd caught from Anchorage, and was now winging across the forested wilderness toward the Qagit Corporation lands in Western Alaska.

She was a little on edge and her stomach wasn't handling the flight very well. Sol had never suffered from motion sickness before and she assumed the queasiness was due to the schizophrenic winds buffeting them around the sky. For some reason this trip had been hard on her, which was unusual, having a resilient constitution. *Probably the stress of flying in this puny plane.* The thought filtered past as she peered out the window at the wavering horizon. She preferred four wheels on the ground.

It wasn't much longer before the pilot broadcast that they would be landing at Orthodoxy airport. The aircraft was so small that he could have just looked over his shoulder and announced the plans to the six passengers without the help of an intercom. She supposed that everything had to be run in an official mode.

She looked back out the window to see miles and miles of trees covering the humps of mountains like hair on the back of a Rhodesian Ridgeback, spiking skyward and coating every surface of the rough ground. Except where the 'airport' was carved out of the forest. It was more like a landing strip in the bush. As they approached at a fast clip, the pilot engaging the braking mechanisms bringing the nose up and tail down that pushed her back in her seat, Sol decided it *was* just a landing strip, and a short one. She gripped the armrests with white-knuckling concentration as they struck the tarmac, nose wheel making contact after the back landing gear, and bounced down the runway until they stopped by the main building.

The five other passengers unclipped their seatbelts and stood up to gather their belongings. She hadn't had the opportunity to speak with any of them during the flight due to the loud noise level of such a small aircraft. Among them were three Alaska Natives, probably locals; a corporate executive by the looks of his styled hair and neat manicure who was dressed down for the bush; and his companion looking more comfortable in his plaid shirt, jeans and boots. Both of them were ready for mud.

Sol had made arrangements to tour the Corcoran Creek mine exploration site that had been in the development stage for a decade. At last contact, she was to meet with some executives who represented the different parties in the enterprise, Kirkdale and Quagit Corporations. The plan was to stay the night at Orthodoxy, an outpost with little to recommend it to travelers aside from being only twenty miles from the planned mining operation. Corcoran Creek Ltd. had a little office in town where she expected to meet with the company reps and they'd ferry her out to the site to give her a tour.

Sol grabbed her overnight bag and deplaned, following the others down the steps. She noticed two helicopters parked on the tarmac near one of the two hangars, one was marked with the CCL insignia.

The other passengers knew where they were going, so Sol tagged along after them toward what looked like an oversized shed that turned out to house the airport offices. Inside the building were management offices, maintenance headquarters, a miniscule waiting area and a bathroom.

Sol dove for the restroom, just managing to bolt the door, drop her bags and close the stall behind her just before she tossed her breakfast.

Chapter 32

Even driving the back way, or more direct route, from Gillette to Cheyenne took a few hours, which meant another early start with not much more than an espresso grabbed from the fuchsia kiosk for breakfast. Allie had never been one for a hearty morning meal anyway, so this suited her fine. It's just the lost couple of hours of sleep that made her cranky. She'd never claimed to be a morning person.

In which case, the best way to start her day wasn't necessarily by taking a call from Aunt Ell. After shifting her eyes off the road long enough to check the readout on the phone, she considered ignoring the insistent song it played as a ring tone. No matter what melody she chose, and she'd tried everything from Mozart to 'La Bamba,' they were all irritating to her sensitive ears. Or maybe it was just the fact that calls always interrupted her thoughts when she most wanted quiet.

I could always put it on vibrate or silent mode. She negated the idea knowing that she had to stay connected to the great big world at every minute of every day or she wouldn't be any good at her profession. And after this last week of hearing from so many people whose opinion she had come to respect, she was beginning to question her journalistic competence in one sense – her assumptive attitude toward climate change.

Giving up on the concept of solitude as the vast plains sped by her window, she punched the 'talk' button with her thumb.

"I was beginning to think you were going to let it go to voicemail and ignore me altogether."

"I gave it serious consideration," sarcasm creeping into Allie's voice.

"It wouldn't be the first time," Ell laughed heartily. "Around here, I'm no one's pal until after I've fixed their problem and then

I'm forgotten until the next crisis." She switched subjects in a heart-beat. "Tell me what's going on."

"Nothing much," said Allie. "Just tootling down the road on my way to Cheyenne. Another interview. No great shakes."

"What's in Cheyenne? Oh wait, not those environmental toadies you talked to before."

"Yup. The very ones."

"So what's the big deal there? Wasn't once enough time to waste with them?" Ell gave the whole global warming crowd short shrift as being a few cards shy of a full deck. Or maybe she equated them with the jokers. Allie figured either description would be accurate according to her aunt.

"It might have been if someone didn't think it was worthwhile seeing what the deal is with a couple of exchange students." Allie hadn't told Ell much about her last visit. Frankly, she couldn't remember if she'd said anything about the quiet Middle Easterners.

"So? Exchange students are a dime a dozen. What's so interesting about these? And don't give me any runaround. I can tell something's up." Ell's voice became a stern command. Allie figured she could either fork up the details now or get a tongue-lashing until she did. Ell could read her better than anyone and was like a pit bull once its jaws were clamped, she wouldn't let go, particularly if she sensed a problem. Besides, who would she tell? A secret is one thing Ell could keep. She'd proven it time and again when Allie was working on a sensitive story.

"Fine." Allie exhaled, "These two students from Lebanon, sup-posedly, were at the Green Grasslands office when I was there before and they kind of gave me the heebie-jeebies so I had Debra check it out."

"And?"

"Well, they seem to have come out of nowhere a few months ago, and then I was working the power plant explosion story and, well, I guess my imagination ran wild."

"I can see why," said Ell.

"Really? No one else could, especially the FBI agent spearhead-ing the investigation."

"You told him?" Ell was incredulous.

"Yeah, and he shot it down at first, but then looked these guys up," said Allie. "Desperation probably. They had no leads. Anyway, he took a look into my candidates for mad bombers of the year and came up with nothing either."

"So why are you going back to the office if there's nothing there?"

"To see if we overlooked anything."

"What do you mean, 'we'?" Nothing got by Aunt Ell.

"Okay, this is really off the record, *anyone's* record."

"Gotcha."

"The SAC is sending me in to do a real interview and story on the beleaguered little environmentalists struggling for justice in the big, bad land of coal and oil, just to see if there might be something odd going on there." Allie wasn't sure how much to spill.

"Why the hell doesn't he do it himself?" Now Ell was teed.

"I'm a good choice for, uh, undercover, if you want to use the word. No one will think twice about my getting a story, and at the same time I'll feel out if there's anything strange going on under the placid environmental façade."

"And if these people *are* tied to the violent explosions that *killed* people? Then what? Do you have any *idea* what you could be getting into?" Ell's voice was beginning to get shrill and Allie wondered if everyone down the hall at the law office could hear her.

"Calm down, there's nothing to worry about. All I'm doing is going in, watching them do a few good deeds in the neighborhood and interviewing the employees. No biggie."

"B. and S." Ell lowered her voice until it was almost menacing, the rage was evident and Allie wasn't sure if it was aimed at her or the indomitable Esteban who Ell knew nothing about. "This is *not* a good idea. My suggestion is that you just keep going straight through to Denver and tell that SAC to get his head out of his ass and do the investigating himself. He has all the resources he needs."

"Actually, he doesn't," Allie was defensive now. "They're shorthanded and I'm already known and trusted by the office. It's a sensible idea."

"It's an effing *stupid* plan. You are not trained for this sort of thing."

"Think about it, Aunt Ell. I really am. Remember all the under-cover stories I've done in the past? This is just another one of them."

"No, it's not, and I'll tell you why. There was never anything to unveil in those situations except some corruption, a little money passing. No violent behavior."

"And there probably isn't any here, either." Allie was done. She didn't want to argue anymore. "There's nothing to worry about. I'll be fine. It's just a story, that's all."

"It had better be, because if anything happens to you, I will be out there to wring that agent's neck myself."

Allie knew Ell was as good as her word, too.

Gently rolling plains stretched away to all sides as Allie closed the distance to Cheyenne. Endless acres of spring grass were slowly slipping from the bright green of young growth to ripening shades of gold, while the cultivated grain fields were still caparisoned with a deeper viridian signaling another month to maturity. A few creeks tumbled across the terrain, lined by great cottonwoods, sentinels that stalked the banks and shaded the fresh water cascading past with the last of the spring runoff.

Any other day it would be a soothing view. Allie's exchange with Ell had made a chill of foreboding crawl up her spine, whisking away the calm she had been struggling to grasp. *Thanks again, Auntie Ell*, she thought sardonically, then switched to thinking that maybe Ell was right to make her take stock of the situation and not be a blithering idiot. Sawyer had expressed concern too, so maybe she'll take their advice and enter with caution.

Okay, done. I'll be careful if it'll make everyone happy. That was enough to settle the matter for her.

For now.

Allie consulted Esteban's detailed directions that she had scribbled down the day before. Once she entered the city limits it didn't take overlong to locate the address on a four-lane boulevard that partitioned a suburban business sector. The modest stucco building was framed by shade trees and shrubs neatly planted to disguise the dated architectural design.

It didn't look anything like a federal building to Allie, more like a neighborhood insurance office and as she pulled into the parking lot and read the sign, that's exactly what it said it was, an insurance agency. No mention of the Federal Bureau of Investigation anywhere.

She re-checked her notes to see if the address was correct. It was. *What's with this set-up? They can't afford regular offices?*

She nosed into a space in a mostly empty lot, a mid-nineties Jeep and a subcompact stood segregated from visitor spots, ensconced under one of the fully crowned maples, its broad serrated leaves stretched toward the sun. Dragging her bag out of the car and slinging it over her shoulder, she walked up to the plate glass door. Swinging it open, Allie entered a small, unremarkable lobby area done over in brown and dun with a carpet to match. She figured it was a good color choice to disguise tracked-in dirt.

Looking around, she was confused as to which way to turn. The few offices were designated as those of the insurance agent, an accountant, and a real estate attorney had hung a subtle shingle. There was also another door at the end of a short hall that declared it to be the office of the building's management. Before she could decide which door to try, Esteban emerged from the management office.

Bewilderment must have shown on her face and Esteban ushered her through the door before she could ask any questions. Without stopping, he showed her through the outer office, past a receptionist who was juggling phones and typing at warp speed on the desktop computer.

Allie couldn't hold her tongue any longer. "What's with all the clandestine operations? Doesn't the vaunted FBI have a regular office in town?"

"Yes, downtown, but we do some of our work out of here. Keeps the nosey parkers away."

"Like anyone's that interested," she grumbled under her breath as he indicated a comfortable chair of faded burnt orange upholstery circa 1978.

"Have a seat."

"Well, this is roomier than the last joint but it seems like every place I see you, you're in some temporary arrangement. Makes me think you don't have much of a budget."

"You'd be right in that assessment. We don't." He seated himself on the other side of the desk. "Everything's been cut with the current economic downturn, even national security."

"You'd think that keeping the country safe might take some precedence."

"That may be what most people would expect, however the current administration doesn't see things quite the same way as some others." He studied her as he decided how much to say. She'd already made the commitment to help with the investigation and apparently had kept her role in this to herself, so she'd been proven as trustworthy. *To a point.*

Determining that it wouldn't make much difference to his employment prospects one way or the other. He was heading this investigation for now, but his last two assignments had probably put his career into a tailspin, his bosses not being thrilled with his plain speech over the past months.

"There have been some policy changes in Homeland Security and the Justice Department that I'd be hard-pressed to agree with."

"What kinds of things? I'm not taking notes and don't see how this necessarily affects the story, but I'm curious about a seasoned agent's opinion."

"Like a lot of people in law enforcement, I'm not too thrilled with the lack of interest in what I perceive as protecting our citizenry. Western states, have always been a portal of illegal entry. Living and working in Colorado and Arizona this last decade, it's evident to me much of the bureau's work has been related to that problem. Identity theft rings, drug trafficking, fraud, even counterfeiting."

"I thought that was under the purview of the treasury department," Allie was interested in his opinion. She didn't do many stories where police were forthcoming about their views on their work.

It was always straight business. *Probably afraid of what might end up in print.*

"It is, but we run across it in related investigations and there can be peripheral involvement. The problem is the lack of border enforcement and keeping a vigilant attitude regarding illegal entry into this country, we've left the barn door open and the crimes I often deal with are the result. We're allowing a dilemma to grow and worsen by lack of implementation of the laws we have on the books. They're there for good reason."

Allie cocked her head, examining his features and evident Latino lineage. "You're Hispanic, right? Esteban's a Spanish name. Don't you feel some compassion for the poor Mexican workers that come north because they want to work, to earn a living?"

"It has nothing to do with heritage. My family has been here for two generations and my grandmother was adamant about speaking English and learning American ways, becoming citizens. And yes, to answer your question, most people want a chance at a good life, to be prosperous, but there are proper channels to entering this country legally. They were established for a purpose, to create a cohesive culture, not the divided one that we've become." Esteban sat back in his chair. "By being compassionate and giving a break to some you open the floodgates to everyone, including those who would jeopardize national security, maybe even work to destroy America. You can't have it both ways. Terrorism is a threat that is not going to up and disappear, no matter what euphemism you use to describe it."

He cradled the back of his head with his hands, elbows jutting to each side in a pose of relaxation, as if they were just chatting when she knew that the next thing on the agenda was to see if security *had* been breached.

"Just look at why we're here, right now." Esteban left the thought open-ended knowing that she could fill in the blanks herself.

Energy Barons

Chapter 33

The House Energy and Environment Subcommittee meeting was in full swing conducting another hearing on the cap and trade legislation, Wexler's baby. As usual he was running the meeting with a heavy hand, doing his damnedest to curtail uncomfortable inquiries by some of his committee members toward the witnesses he was depending on to produce beneficial sound bites for the press. He'd already forced the decision to bar the testimony of the international economic and climate expert whose clear views and supportive facts reject the concept of global warming. The decision left Rone Haggerty free to make any unsubstantiated assertions he cared to with a has-been congressman the only mealy-mouthed witness present to refute his claims. It wouldn't matter how persuasive the countering argument might be, that it was being delivered by that particular messenger chosen by legislation opposition, would be enough to kill any meaningful media coverage.

Toddy had kept one of his many televisions tuned to C-SPAN trying to keep track of the absurdities that issued from Haggerty's mouth. One minute he was answering the congresswoman's questions about his profiteering from the institution of a carbon tax by saying he had invested every penny from his endeavors so far into non-profits, and the next he was accusing her of being anti-business.

Which is it, fool? Of course, Toddy had the answer right in front of him on the computer screen, a Bloomberg report about how much Haggerty had really made since leaving national office and that it *wasn't* invested in non-profit ventures at all.

"How this clown gets away with this, I have no idea." Toddy was talking to himself since Solana was still in Alaska. Muttering a few choice oaths under his breath he pulled up a few more sites to see exactly what and who were lining the soon-to-be U.N. ambassador's pockets, because he sure was living the good life and was all set to enjoy more ill-gotten gains were the bill to be passed.

In the wee hours, Toddy was contemplating some of the remarks that Haggerty had made the previous day, including one that had been picked up by national news. He could not believe how Haggerty had answered one of the questions regarding his business investments in 'green' technology, which had been a reference to the carbon credit enterprise where he was a partner. The man's answer had actually been to say that he would have to dance around the question. How the committee let him get away with a comment like that was utterly beyond Toddy's comprehension.

The dialog had occurred hours ago and now Toddy was writing his latest post for ChangingWind.org addressing the ludicrous nature of Haggerty's testimony and how only one representative, a coura-geous congresswoman, had the gonads to pigeonhole the guy. Haggerty utterly misstated, *read that as 'lied'*, thought Toddy as he typed a mile a minute, about his incredible growth in fortune from net worth of a measly $2 million to his current level of wealth in excess of $35 million.

And then he has the chutzpah to sit there later and say he was going to dance *around the issue! I have to get that quote.* Toddy started going through every site he could to hunt up the transcript from the testimony for that particular exchange.

He was thwarted at every turn. He'd found a couple of bloggers who'd managed to capture some of the testimony, but not the one that he'd heard and was now nowhere to be found on the internet. *They're getting faster at covering their tracks.*

Going to the official congressional website for the sub-commit-tee, he pulled out all of the stops to get at that transcript.

No go.

All that was available was the official written statement that had been filed by Haggerty and had no resemblance whatsoever to his actual testimony. When he finally got through to the webpage that was supposed to contain the official transcript of the hearing, there was only one word emblazoned across the top of the page.

Forbidden.

What the hell does that mean? So much for an open and trans -parent government.

He was ticked and sent Sol an e-mail about the situation. It had occurred to him that one might have to purchase the transcripts, but he saw no link or access to a website for that purpose.

It also occurred to him that the transcripts might be protected. To him, that constituted a crime against the people. Especially if Congress were intentionally withholding committee deliberations on plans to glean every penny possible from citizens through the popularly called "Cap and Tax."

As he typed his message to his wife he went even further with the correlative language as it struck him.

To get a perspective on how energy and commerce really coincide (and why the committee goes under that title), just look at the terminology having to do with exchange of wealth. It all equates to power, and I mean both kinds, electrical and force. Currency = current, the flow of energy and money, a means of exchange; Resistance is used in both instances to indicate opposition to the flow of energy or to a powerful foe or force; Capacitor and capacity — one's an electrical component that stores a charge and the other is the maximum amount that can be taken; Circuit Court; Closed Circuit, etc. The Energy Economy emulates the Energy Circuit, society mirroring physics.

Going further, using the principles of nature creates justification of government's decision to rule, to claim the authority of God. You could even go so far to say that government thereby takes on the role of the adversary of God.

Power and energy are interchangeable and currency is the means of transfer of power. We're witnessing the reinstitution of a feudalistic society. The energy barons keeping the serfs in line.

The door to the back office in the Green Grasslands storefront was closed to accommodate an employee conference. More like a showdown than a discussion, two men were facing off across a round table that sometimes doubled for a desk.

A´zam sat back in his chair, feet planted firmly on the floor, arms crossed over his chest almost defiantly as he looked at the other man with an attitude of indifference.

The room's other occupant, a man in his mid-thirties with a dark, fashionably scruffy mane, was leaning back in his seat, rocking back on the heels of his hiking boots. One hand gripped the rim of the table and the other somberly twirled the ends of his lush mustache. He speared A´zam with a determined, cerulean gaze, crystal eyes that were hard, punctuating his position in their relationship.

This was their first real meeting after A´zam's return from a short break away from the office, ostensibly to study for finals, the semester at the university being at a close. They were to be working together on the finishing touches of a project Mustache had begun at a local school, and now that A´zam's partner was gone, in another capacity as well.

It was a rather sudden change in personnel that required the two of them to join forces, another student had left without giving notice. It was a loss for the office but not an unusual state of affairs. Students were often flaky and just disappeared at the drop of a hat, something better having come along. The older man shrugged off the loss as the usual attrition of volunteers but his eyes bored into the foreigner's, letting A´zam know that he wasn't clueless, even if the other young man's rapid dissolve into the surrounding universe was unexplained.

Mustache was suspicious but not overly concerned, he was just clarifying the situation with the exchange student seated across from him. That *he* was not to be so easily replaced.

An almost imperceptible nod from A´zam signaled his acquiescence to Mustache's point and they both leaned forward to pore over a map that was spread across the table separating them.

Chapter 34

Allie concluded her meeting with her controller. The concept sounded a little weird in her head but she recognized that she was now an unofficial operative rather than just an observer.

Doesn't that make me an informant? Great. I have just graduat - ed into the realm of sneaks and snitches.

She drove directly over to the Green Grasslands office after making a quick call to Race Carson while she'd been sitting in front of Esteban's desk. That way he knew everything that was said and wouldn't have to second-guess his newest 'agent' who, from his brief experience with her, he knew was impetuous by nature.

The director greeted her with a wide smile, ecstatic about the prospect of any publicity.

"I apologize for not being able to sell the story to my editor the last time I was here. Now with the cap and trade bill finally on the House floor, I was able to make a convincing case that environmental awareness is ripe for coverage," she told Carson as he shook her hand and guided her toward his office. "So, I was hoping that I could tag along on some outreach projects." She lifted her shoulders in a gesture of conciliation. "Show what you do here to help educate the public about carbon emissions and using renewable resources. That kind of thing."

"I think that'd be a great idea. It's already late today but let me introduce you to our senior project manager. I don't believe you had the opportunity to meet him when you were here before." Instead of entering his office, he had Allie follow him further down the hall to another office.

The door was ajar and Carson pushed it open wider, gallantly allowing Allie to precede him into the room. The office was furnished with multiple workstations tightly tucked into cubbies. They were all empty but one.

A nice looking man about Allie's age looked up from the computer screen that bathed him with a tepid bluish glow. The Green Grasslands headquarters had been outfitted with all compact fluorescent bulbs that left much to be desired as far as lighting went. Even during the day the offices were relatively dim. Allie hadn't gotten around to changing bulbs out in her own home and after being in a number of offices where they had gone all CFL, she was reconsidering the idea. *Some environmentalist you are*, she reprimanded herself.

Seeing that he had company, he stood and accepted the interruption by holding out his hand and giving Allie an affable grin.

"Toby Blaine. How may I serve you today?" He had a jocular tilt to his lips, which Allie could just see under a thick brush of a mustache. She immediately noticed that he was a handsome man, though his hair could use a trim as it curled over his collar in the back. Then she reconsidered, realizing that the shaggy cut style was in vogue. Almost six feet tall, his flannel shirt was open to reveal a t-shirt that sported a Greenpeace logo that fit his torso perfectly, and a fit torso it was.

"Allie Maitland, Denver Post. I believe that you have just been volunteered to be my guide and general babysitter for the next day or two." He lifted an eyebrow in question toward Race. "I hope that suits your idea of service."

"She's here to do a story about our work in the plains states," said the director as he grabbed a chair and offered it to Allie. He then settled into another one and Blaine dropped back into his. "Evidently, the paper thinks it's the right time to bring attention to environmental awareness, what with the energy bill in Congress right now."

"Denver Post, eh?" Blaine looked at her curiously. "And you couldn't find a group like ours in that big city of yours? I'm surprised."

"I've been assigned to the Wyoming beat for a while and, voilá, here you are, right where I need to be. Particularly since Wyoming is a state rich in the resources that are under discussion by the current legislation, it made sense to pick-up another viewpoint." She gazed archly at him over the top of the monitor. "Does that work for you?"

He nodded his head toward Carson. "If it works for the boss, it works for me," and he gave her an appealing smile. At least, it would have been charming if Allie didn't sense a smidgen of insincerity hidden beneath the luxuriant whiskers that framed his upper lip. She shrugged inwardly realizing that having to show a reporter around could be an inconvenience, no matter how good the press, and sloughed off the impression as just that, a reaction to being pestered when he had work to do.

As the director was rising to leave, it struck Allie that the offices seemed pretty empty. Even their receptionist was missing for the day and she asked Carson about it before he slid out of the room to take care of some other business.

"The place seems pretty well abandoned today. Where's the rest of your crew?"

"Most of the volunteers had classes this afternoon so, Toby and I have been holding down the fort in the meantime. There should be a full contingent here in the morning." Carson started moving toward the door. "I shall leave you in the capable hands of our best lieutenant," he indicated Blaine, "while I take care of a few things that can't wait since it's already near closing time. Catch you in the morning, Ms. Maitland."

"Allie, please. And thanks for the help. See you in the morning."

He nodded as he ducked out leaving Allie with the project manager, who was kicked back in his chair. "So, where should we start, Allie?"

"I know that I was dropped on you out of nowhere, but if it's all right, I'd like to get a quick rundown of the operations so I'll know where to start."

"Sure. Shoot."

"Okay, how many people do you have working here?" she asked as she pulled a pad out of her satchel and clicked open her pen. "Last time I was here, I met," Allie dropped her head back and thought for a couple seconds, "Ilse. Right? The receptionist."

"Uh-huh. She's at school this afternoon. Finals," offered Blaine in explanation.

"I'd practically forgotten. Well, probably conveniently set the memory aside. Test Anxiety and I were roommates in college."

He laughed on cue rather than Allie feeling a real sense of amusement. *Must be my delivery.* "Anyway, there were also a couple of exchange students who I met on their way out. Is everybody in class, today?"

"Pretty much. Volunteers have their own schedule. Race and I are the only actual employees. Ilse gets a small stipend through Americorp, which helps us out tremendously. The two students are gone. One's back on campus and the other has transferred."

"I also noticed another person whom I didn't have an opportunity to meet. Just heard a voice in a different room" She looked up at him with a sideways glance. "May have been you."

He gave her a beguiling smile.

Oh, this boy is good. He can turn it on and off like a faucet.

"May have been, though I don't remember your coming through here. I could have been busy or just out of the office. We have other occasional volunteers. Might have been one of them. What else would you like to know?"

"Perhaps you can give me some information on your current projects," suggested Allie.

"Let's see. We have two garden programs in operation at local elementary schools. The kids get a chance to dig around in the dirt, learn about companion planting, etc. This may be a rural state, but the kids who live in town don't often have that much contact with horticulture." Blaine gave her a look as if to say, *know what I mean?* without actually speaking. "We're also erecting a windmill at the high school."

Allie perked up. "That's great! Maybe I can tag along for that as well as a couple of other things. It'd make good copy and be a terrific photo op."

"Sounds good to me." He glanced at his watch and let a brief frown cross his face. "I hate to be rude, but I have a previous appointment that I really shouldn't miss." He stood up and shoved his hands in his pockets   . "We can pick this up tomorrow and I'll drag you along to all the boring events of the day. Will that be all right?"

"Absolutely," and she held out her hand to shake his. "I'll look forward to it." *And to seeing if there's anything else going on in this sleepy little office.*

Energy Barons

Chapter 35

The office had become oppressive. Yancy had almost finished the paper but was having trouble keeping her mind on her work. Standing up, she pushed her chair away and stretched with a need that was so deeply ingrained her joints popped as she reached to her furthest limits.

"That's it," she said aloud. "I can't concentrate. I have to get out of here."

Not waiting for her conscience to make her park her bottom back in the chair, she pulled on her suit jacket and grabbed her purse off the coat tree on her way out the door.

Barely pausing to tell the receptionist goodbye, Laura stopped her in her tracks.

"Who lit a fire under your feet?"

"Nobody," Yancy wasn't in the mood for small talk. She'd had enough just trying to put together a brief refuting petty arguments from the opposition in one of her many cases. "I *really* need some fresh air and," she finally glanced down at her wrist to check the watch, "it's about closing time anyway." She looked across the lobby at Laura. "You already filed today's papers and everything else that's pending is under control, so I'm going to the hospital."

Laura shook her head and gave Yancy a look that frankly disapproved of her getting so involved with the Lysander family. Oh, she understood Yancy's caring. The problem was, she cared too much. So much that it was getting difficult for her to curtail her worry and concentrate on the other cases piled on her desk. Yancy hadn't been slacking, but Laura could see the bluish tint under her eyes indicating likely insomnia.

"You've got to start taking better care of yourself, Yancy," chastised Laura, who was particularly good at mothering, she had six children and had already accumulated fifteen grandchildren before the age of 55. "Or you'll be no good to anyone, least of all that little Lysander girl."

"Yeah, I know. That's why I'm out of here. Gonna go get some coffee, visit with Mary and go home and just chill for once." Yancy was trying to be convincing. Whether it was for Laura's benefit or her own, she couldn't say.

"You do that. You need the rest."

"Will do, mom. See you tomorrow." And she fled out into the late afternoon sun.

An hour later, Yancy finally made her way down the hall to Kara's room. She had done just as she said she would and went to a coffee bar long enough to have a drink, listen to some soft jazz and read through the day's paper. She wanted to restore her calm before rushing off to the hospital, flying in with a face lined with concern that would only distress Mary more. She'd bought a couple of specialty drinks that she knew Mary and Paula liked and carried them with her, breathing normally now, no panic in sight.

Yancy placed the drinks on the deep sill of the window in Kara's room. She'd been moved to a regular room now that she was stabilized. She had yet to react to any outside stimuli, but Kara was no longer sitting at death's door, she just wasn't responding to anything outside of her own mind. Her eyes roved beneath their lids and she was breathing on her own, but nothing else moved. She was as still as a porcelain angel.

Mary rose from her seat by Kara's side.

"No, no Mary. You don't need to get up for me." But Mary just came over and hugged Yancy, who had become far more than their lawyer, she was a member of the family.

The gesture took the breath out of her, and she embraced the tall woman who seemed to have shrunken with the past week's trauma, her frame becoming bonier than Yancy remembered. Mary's emotions soaked Yancy. The intense fear, anxiety, devotion and distant hope all boiling to the surface as she held on to the lawyer, who guarded herself as best she could while extending her own compassion. Yancy just held her thinking that maybe Mary was actually the stronger one, supporting Yancy who was having her own trouble dealing with the circumstances, trying to be useful when her mind was everywhere but on her work.

Mary pulled back and offered a wan smile. "Thank you for coming, and for thinking of us." She took the cup from Yancy and inhaled the scent steaming from the opening. "How did you know this is just what I wanted?"

"A wild guess." She handed the other cup to Paula who also thanked her as she took a welcome sip.

Before Yancy could ask about Kara's condition, Mary said, "So far, there's been no real change. The doctor was here a little while ago but didn't really say anything before she left."

"She did say that Kara's vital signs all looked good. There is reason to hope," Paula added. She gestured for Yancy to follow her into the hall for a minute. "Kara has been responding we think. Mary is pretty sure that Kara squeezed her hand a few times and the movement of her eyes has become more active."

"That's positive, right?" Yancy was encouraged.

"Yes. It's a good sign that she may be starting to emerge from the coma, but it's not assured." Paula looked back at Mary who regained her seat by her daughter's side. "We don't want to get too confident."

Examining Paula's own concerned features, the young woman showed the wear and tear of the last days.

"Have you been home since this happened?" Yancy knew the dialysis nurse had become close to the Lysander's but she also presumed the woman had more than one patient.

"Not yet. I was able to take some days off, but I will need to return tomorrow. Mary's cousin has arranged to take a few vacation days until Key returns. That will make it easier for everyone. Besides," she looked at Yancy across the top of her coffee. "I had to wait until someone could come get me since my car is still at Mary's house."

Yancy had forgotten that Paula had flown in with Kara and the EMT's on the helicopter. She'd been staying with the rest of the family at the cousin's. Her weariness was evident though, and Yancy felt real gratitude for Paula's presence, knowing how much it had helped Mary.

"Where is Key?" Yancy made a quick inspection of the hallway. "You said he'd left? And Keith, I haven't seen him, either."

"They've gone to Sun Dance," said Mary, overhearing the question. She had decided to come into the hall and stand for a little while, stretch her legs.

"I've heard of that but don't know anything about it. It's a spiritual ceremony, isn't it?"

"Yes. Sun Dance is a time and place for sacrifice and prayer for healing medicine, making a vow to *Akbaatatdía*, the Maker. Key will fast and dry up for Kara, pray for her recovery." Mary looked at Yancy. "It's something he can do for his daughter. The doctor's are doing what they can here."

"Every prayer is a blessing," said Yancy with meaning. "You know that mine are with all of you."

"Yes. The work that you do to help us is God's work too." Mary pressed Yancy's hand briefly but with fervency before returning to her post at Kara's bedside.

Spotted Horse Mountain's rocky peak was suffused with the last glimmers of daylight, painting its stony face with the ruddy tones of the sun's descent behind the taller crags to the west. Under the growing shadow, the dancers were preparing to enter the Big Lodge and begin their vigil.

Inside Ashé Isée stood the center pole, a forked cottonwood tree thirty feet tall, crowned with two branches still bearing leaves, supporting the majestic head of the Buffalo, suspended to face West, and the Eagle perched near the branches' convergence. Sage had been given to the Buffalo, tied below the great nostrils, to savor the fragrance of the meat of life. Willows had been bundled and tied to the fork of the tree, depicting the water of life, the water which flows through the land of the Apsáalooke.

The perimeter of the lodge was encased with cottonwood brush, creating only one opening to face the sunrise. Here the dancers would enter after dark had fully descended.

Key was dressed in an ankle-length buckskin skirt that had been passed down for generations, hidden for a time in safekeeping from government agents when they were commissioned to destroy vestiges of Indian culture. An elaborately beaded belt circled his waist with running horses. Around his neck hung the eagle-bone whistle, a gift from his uncle years before. This would be the first time it would be winded at the Sun Dance.

Blankets draped over men's arms and around women's shoulders, they had gathered separately on the west side of the Big Lodge awaiting formation of the lines that would encircle the structure twice as they start their spiritual trek.

The drum's song filled the air, the heartbeat of the earth accentuating the voices carrying across the night wind, aiding the dancers as they began their prayer journey.

Energy Barons

Chapter 36

Solana stepped out of the restroom, a foul taste still lingering even after repeatedly rinsing her mouth. She popped in a piece of gum just as she noticed a man standing by the one window that overlooked the landing strip's apron. Even that small opening revealed a dramatic backdrop of evergreen spikes marching up the slopes of the Kuskokwim Mountains.

Hearing the door close with a squeal that alerted Sol to the fact a shot of WD-40 was called for, he turned and greeted her in the center of the confined waiting area. He stood a couple of inches shy of Sol's brow, making it possible for her to look straight over the top of his head were she to raise herself a tad onto her toes. Patient confidence shown in his impenetrable, brown eyes that were flecked with the gold reminiscent of the vast reserve that lay beneath the surface short miles to the north. In his fifties, she guessed, he was obviously Native, high cheekbones, almond eyes. The straight, black hair interwoven with strands of gray was shorn just above his collar, and a thin wisp of facial hair at the upper corners of his mouth framed a welcoming smile.

Extending his hand, Sol grasped it self-consciously chewing her gum, trying to be discreet as she cleansed her palate. The queasiness hadn't completely dissipated but she felt far better than she had ten minutes earlier.

"Solana Greyfisher?"

"That would be me, much as I might care to deny it on some days."

He chuckled at her light-hearted greeting. "Farley Ranger. It's good to meet you."

She tilted her head sideways and narrowed her eyes as if trying to capture a thought that skittered away before she could nab it.

"Why does that name sound familiar?"

His eyes twinkled. "I've heard that from a few visitors from the lower forty-eight. Mostly older people, though." He let the inquiry die at that. "When the corporation forwarded your communication I remembered your name from last year. Made national news for a bit."

"I was hoping everyone would have forgotten that by now." Sol would rather forget the whole ordeal herself.

Sensing her discomfort with the subject, he reached for her roll-away. "Let me get your bag. I'm the catchall guy for the mine, general tour guide and on-site public relations for the Native interests. You corresponded with the Qagit Corporation and they sent you to me." He started for the entrance assuming that she would follow his lead, which she did, slinging the strap of her computer bag over one shoulder and her purse over the other.

"Well, I appreciate you affording me the time to show me around," she said as he held the door for her, making their way toward a mud-encrusted four-wheel drive Dodge Durango. "I've tried to follow the progression of this lawsuit since I found out about it, which wasn't long ago and I'll be interested to get an inside view of the proceedings."

"I don't know all the intricacies of the case, just the basics as it pertains to the mine's development," said Farley as he opened the rear hatch and loaded Sol's luggage. "I leave the legal talk up to the lawyers and they leave the mine operations up to the experts, until, of course, the squabbling interferes with the planning and getting things up and rolling."

"Legal interpretations can lead to a real quagmire, can't they," Sol pulled open the passenger door and slid onto the seat.

"Hmm-mm," was Farley's only response. He turned the key in the ignition and made a u-turn on the well-tended gravel road. "I can take you by the bunkhouse first, if you'd like to drop your things."

"Thanks, but that won't be necessary. I'm ready to go now, if that suits you."

He didn't supply an audible answer, just a nod that Sol almost missed. She was fascinated by the wide, unhurried flow of the river they were following toward the edge of Orthodoxy, all half-mile of it. The town felt more remote than any place she had ever been, cut-off from the rest of the world except for the broad bend of water, the surface reflecting sapphire in the sun, and the tiny airport tucked into the farthest corner of the community.

A couple minutes later they pulled up in front of a small enclave of modular buildings that were huddled at the end of the combed roadway. Farley popped down from the SUV and swung Sol's door open. Her eyes widened briefly as he neatly scooped the computer case out of her hands before she could plant her feet on the ground, facilitating her exit. Uttering her thanks for the help, she accepted the return of the bulky bag and accompanied him up the steps into a building that looked as much like a construction office as it did a 'downtown' headquarters for a multi-billion dollar mining outfit.

"Our set-up is pretty informal here," he said as he led her through an outer reception area that was furnished with three desks, two of which were littered with stacks of files, and rolled maps and blueprints, the third was occupied by a plump, little Yu'pik woman. Sol did a double take, swearing she was seeing a replica of her Nez Perce kinswoman who'd played the mild-mannered secretary in "Northern Exposure." They exchanged polite smiles as Sol followed Farley's lead down the long narrow hallway to the open door of what was posted as his office.

He held out his hand, palm up, indicating that she find herself a comfortable seat from among the choices of a sofa and three chairs that matched a small rectangular table. Sol chose the side of the table with two seats and dropped into one chair after unceremoniously depositing her bags into the other. Leaning over the computer bag, she unclipped the flap and extracted a yellow legal pad and a pen.

"I expected you to be more high tech," Farley nodded at the capacious case that he assumed also housed a laptop.

"When it comes to interviews, I'm still old school though I do use a tape recorder when permission is granted." She raised her eyebrows silently asking the question.

Nodding his assent, she rummaged inside one of the pockets and removed a small digital recorder.

"Not that old fashioned, eh?" he said noticing the advanced gear.

"Makes it easier to transcribe. Don't you just love the 21st century?"

"Depends." Farley was noncommittal, which caused Solana to lift her brows once again. "There have been great strides in technology, but I admit to having conflicts about the benefits versus what's been lost."

"You don't mind do you?" she was referring to turning on the recorder.

He shook his head in answer, giving her permission to power up. "Connections to our heritage are being lost a little each day. Preserving the culture and language is important but it is also important that we, as a people, are able to sustain ourselves in the modern world, and sustenance lifestyles simply aren't possible anymore. I regret the loss of some of that but embrace the opportunity to move ahead."

"Don't you think there can be a balance between the two?"

"Yes, I do. Sometimes I think the greatest challenge is to appease the non-Natives rather than our own people." Farley gave her a sly look, "And that's off-the-record as my personal opinion. Going back to the old ways just isn't an option, and anyone who believes that Native people can compete by living as we did a hundred or more years ago isn't being realistic."

"You sound like a pragmatist."

"Some would call me a traitor, and most of them would not be Yu'pik." He scrutinized Sol. "You've lived and worked in big cities, if I remember anything from the interviews last year. I think you understand what I mean. We have a culture to preserve but a people to adequately feed, clothe and house."

"And this is where an enterprise like Corcoran Creek comes in," she prompted.

"Yes. What we, as shareholders in the Qagit Corporation, have as assets are the land, what lives on it, growing, walking, flying and swimming, what flows across it and what lies under it. In this time, what is buried beneath the land is of value. It is our mission to protect the earth that gives it and to use the resource wisely."

Solana nodded as she wrote a few key words as references to locate quotes on the recording. "Tell me something about the organization of Corcoran Creek Ltd. How the partnership is structured."

"It's not really a partnership in the sense that Qagit actually owns any portion of the mine, it will receive royalties. The Native corporation has leased the surface and subsurface rights to Corcoran Creek who operates the mine, or will, once the permits are allowed to take effect. Right now, the process is bogged down by a number of environmental groups that are refuting the authority of the permitting agency."

"That would be the Corps of Engineers, yes?"

"Yes," said Farley. "The dispute that has now gone all the way to the Supreme Court is a matter of which agency can actually grant permits for treatment and disposal of the tailings. It comes down to the language in the Clean Water Act and how it is interpreted. Corcoran Creek contends that it went through the proper channels with the Corps of Engineers and the opposition says that it's the EPA that has the authority. It was a done deal until the environmental groups like Rural Resources and Eco-Earth got involved."

"That brings to mind the plans for a clean coal-fired power plant Qagit had proposed to supply the region as well as Corcoran Creek." Sol asked, "Where does that project stand now?"

"Discarded. The same environmental groups were vocal about shutting down the prospect of supplying not only the operations of the mine, which require somewhere around 130 megawatts, but the whole area with more inexpensive power. Four years ago, the difference in prices between Anchorage and here was more than $300 dollars per 500-kilowatt hours. The power plant would have reduced that cost significantly. Instead, the company has been forced to institute a plan for turbine diesel generators, which require miles of pipeline laid above ground and below the permafrost. Added to that, there will be a wind farm that will produce only eight percent of the needed electricity, none of which will really benefit the surrounding communities." Farley removed his arms from across his chest and scratched his temple. "The opposition is only bent on building road block after road block to the mine."

"Do you believe it has to do with preserving the environment?"

"I would like to think so, but at this juncture I would say that it's more about shutting down anything to do with bringing prosperity to the region. The plans for the coal plant were sound. The environmental studies that have been ongoing for a decade show there is ample provision for protecting eco-systems." He looked at her earnestly, "We have no interest in destroying anything. We want to provide jobs and sustain the earth at the same time. We believe that both can be accomplished."

"How much employment will Corcoran Creek open for shareholders?"

"The current workforce is ninety percent Native and is expected to remain around that level as operations get underway."

"That's an impressive number," Sol commented as she made a few notes.

"It's desperately needed here. Yu'pik unemployment is the highest in the state. This is just one of the reasons that Corcoran Creek has such widespread regional support."

"Excluding the environmentalists," added Sol.

"They aren't regional," said Farley. "They represent outside organizations, some of them international."

"Which means they have unlimited coffers to support the legal challenge."

"So it would appear. I don't know who funds them, but the money seems to keep pouring in. The legal costs to Corcoran Creek have been staggering, and the challenges keep coming."

After asking if she was ready for a drive, Farley went to the break room and grabbed a couple of drinks while Sol repacked her bag. Loading themselves back into the Durango, they headed upriver to inspect a gold cache that would have impressed King Midas.

Driving from Orthodoxy to Corcoran Creek took Farley and Solana on a winding route that left the river behind after eight miles. Once the road moved inland, gaining hundreds of feet in elevation, it dwindled to little more than a one-lane logging road as it rounded some tight curves. The graded surface had a number of spots with depressions that Farley expertly avoided. Solana asked whether tanker trucks negotiated the road.

"Yes, along with big rigs hauling equipment, lumber, and all kinds of supplies, they handle this road on a regular basis. You can pretty much set your clock by them, the way the delivery schedules run. The drivers know these roads really well. People don't get stuck too much and if they do, everyone has a CB. Cell phones are less than worthless up here."

Sol had checked her own before leaving the office. "I noticed." Toddy might be upset that he wouldn't be receiving a call tonight.

"Some of the executives have satellite phones but the cost is outrageous. There's one at the office for restricted use, but you probably noticed this rig is outfitted with a CB, too."

"It is kind of hard to miss." The apparatus was mounted under the dashboard and the extended antenna on the front, right fender rippled with every shimmy and bounce of the truck as it trundled up the uneven road.

"The best insurance there is around here."

Farley steered the Durango around a last turn, coming out onto a straightaway that made a steady descent into a long valley populated with a miniature hamlet of metal structures. A wide swath was cleared through the center of otherwise dense growth of spruce and birch, a helipad situated to one side was straddled by a company aircraft, its rotors stilled. This was the predevelopment site where exploration had been ongoing for the last decade.

There wasn't much to see at this stage of development, Farley told Sol. "Feasibility studies were just submitted that estimated more than a million troy ounces of gold are expected to be extracted per year over the life of the mine," he said.

"And how long is that?" Sol asked over the top of the car door as she pulled a small notepad out of her bag to jot down pertinent data.

"Twenty years at the bottom end. Maybe longer."

"That's twenty million ounces of precious metal," she slowly wagged her head in amazement.

"Closer to thirty million ounces, is what I read in the reports."

"That's more than I can imagine. Kind of like the concept of trillions of dollars in deficit spending," she smiled briefly. "I can't picture either one." It was out of character for Sol to take a poke at politics during an interview but for some reason, she hadn't been able to resist.

Farley laughed unexpectedly. "That's why our governor has been such a shot in the arm. She doesn't mess with the idea of out of control debt."

"Too bad she's decided to get out while the gettin's good," said Sol.

"Can't say I blame her with how her family's been savaged," he commiserated. "You know her husband's a shareholder."

"I remember reading that. Kind of brings it a little closer to home." Sol was interested in Farley's comment. The best her relations had done was to induct last year's Democratic presidential nominee into the Crow nation, her grandmother's tribe. Something that really didn't impress her much since the candidate hadn't impressed her, an opinion that had caused her quite a bit of trouble. "I also understand that the governor had submitted a document to the court in support of the Corcoran Creek project. It must be good to have the administration's solid support."

"It's sensible for the state to support the mine development. It means employment for a region in dire need of jobs and it's revenue for the state," he said as they walked toward some buildings that resembled barracks. "I'd do the same."

He gave Solana the nickel tour of the facilities. He'd been right when he said that there wasn't much to see. There was housing for a 150-person workforce, operations support buildings and an airstrip. Farley gave her an overview of the open-pit plans and explained that so far geophysical surveys had encompassed some thirty linear miles, and almost a million feet of drilling and half a million of trenching, all accomplished in the exploratory stages. Many miles of road had been constructed to facilitate development and the environmental studies that had taken ten years to finish, which included the plans for power and transportation provision to the mine. Environmental Impact Studies were now complete and the permitting process was well underway, some of which was part of the legal challenge that had sparked Solana's interest enough to investigate personally.

They got back into the Dodge and he drove her over a few miles of the laid road to visit a couple of the outer sites where drilling had occurred. In all, the tour took less than two hours, but it was enough to give her a good idea as to how meticulously the operation was being handled. The plans and development that had already been completed took every precaution to minimize effects on the environment and preserve habitat for the local wildlife.

Sol was impressed by the Corcoran Creek facility. This was not the gold mine of the past where the prize was extracted from the earth without forethought, leaving a scarred wasteland of potential poison for later generations to clean up. This was a sound, carefully planned and executed mining operation that would leave minimal marks on the landscape and bring prosperity to a poverty-stricken Native population... the best of both worlds. Not perfect perhaps, but near as could be when it came to both protecting the land and utilizing its resources.

Seeing what sensible, scrupulously studied work had been done to retain the natural features of the earth and its inhabitants, only served to feed Sol's distrust in the massive environmental lobby that had pulled out all the stops to prevent the Yu'pik from realizing a benefit from their land.

The thought had left a different kind of sour taste in her mouth, the result of contemplating environmentalist hypocrisy.

Farley and Sol returned to the office and he showed her a brief video on the computer about the mining process. The presentation explained how gold was extracted from the matrix through crushing and flotation, separating the heavier metal from the bearing ore, pressure oxidation and carbon-in-leach recovery. Part of the video went through the recovery process, explaining CIL, elution, electrolysis, and water and carbon granule recycling. It also covered refining, disposal of tailings, and land reclamation. All of the technology was state of the art in consideration of tough safety standards and environmental protection, all while retrieving ninety percent of the gold from the matrix.

The mechanization of contemporary gold mining was a far cry from the gold rush days of pack mules, sluices and panning. The uses of gold also had come a long way. No longer was it just a precious metal with intrinsic monetary value, it was used as an integral component of electronics, communications and power conduction, the things that make the modern world run efficiently in a never-ending cycle of globally transmitted information. Even this tiny, isolated hamlet in the upper reaches of Alaskan frontier was tied into the constantly spinning world of data transfer.

Nearing mid-summer, the height of the sun so far north wasn't a reliable indicator for a southerner, so by the time they concluded the gold mining lesson, the clock showed evening had arrived. Sol was famished, the nausea having long since subsided.   Orthodoxy didn't offer much in the way of dining and entertainment. It did, however, have a small restaurant that served the area residents, few as they were, with solid fare. The little place doubled as a company café when there were residents staying at the housing in town and Farley ferried Sol over there for dinner.

He had a house a little way down the river but his wife had gone back to her village to visit with elderly parents, leaving him free to accompany Sol for dinner. The short warm season was a good time to travel and take care of business in the city, Farley explained, revealing his plans to meet her in Anchorage for a holiday during the coming month. They'd get to stay with one of their daughters and enjoy the grandchildren for a couple weeks.

"I have to admit that I'd have a difficult time living this far out in the woods," shared Sol. "As it is, we do live on a mountain but it's only half an hour from town." They'd settled in to enjoy a simple but hearty meal that she hoped she wasn't wolfing down, hungry as she was. "Guess I got spoiled living in the city for so many years. I like the rural lifestyle but I'm not good at rustic anymore."

"Even going away to school for a while never managed to work the bush out of my system. We're happy to be here and make a good living," said Farley. "Not many of my people have been so lucky around here."

They finished dinner, after which he showed her to the visitor's quarters in the company housing, dormitory really, on the property adjacent to the offices. Before he left her for the night, Farley made plans to pick her up early for a boat trip upriver to tour the planned dock area where the pipeline would terminate.

First, they'd fish.

At 7:00 a.m. Farley was assisting Sol aboard the twenty-two foot Thunderjet boat at the private dock that fronted the Corcoran Creek Ltd. offices. The boat showed signs of substantial use but wasn't battered by wear. The company maintained three watercraft in the boathouse for the purpose of inspecting waterside facilities, such as the preliminary development of the supply dock located upriver from Orthodoxy, and the occasional recreational outing for visiting dignitaries and executives.

Farley had already loaded the fishing gear for their little excursion, planning to have her back in time to catch the daily flight out early in the afternoon.

It had been years since Sol had gone salmon fishing. Back home, family made an annual pilgrimage to the Columbia River where they would avail themselves of their Native fishing rights. She'd only accompanied them one year while she was home from college and hadn't been back since, but she remembered that summer as one of rekindling an ancestral connection to the river that the Plateau Indians had established over millennia of feeding their people from its bounty. Today, seeing the state of the art graphite rods next to an oversized tackle box, she was looking forward to trying her hand at a more modern version of catching salmon.

Farley situated Sol in the passenger seat and fired up the engine. Jet boats were the best form of transportation on the northern glacier-fed rivers that ran in shallow passages braiding across a wide plain, channels woven with shoals. Quieter outboard motors required a deeper draft to avoid becoming mired in a waterway whose depth vacillated with the shifting silt brought downriver from the mountain headwaters near the Denali National Park.

The Kuskokwim was seeing the first arrivals of the Keta salmon, and the frontrunners of the Chinook were also beginning their upstream swim to spawn. Keta, commonly called chum or dog salmon, the last name referring to their sharp teeth, were more prevalent on this river than the Chinook. Nor was the dog salmon considered to have quite the flavor of the King. Chinook, also called King salmon because of their size, were the aggressive trophy catch that most anglers paid the big bucks to take a shot at landing. Guides on the many slow-moving, unspoiled Alaska waterways made their living taking sport fishermen out in hopes of posing for that sought after photo op, holding the 'big one' that didn't get away.

Sol sat back and enjoyed gazing out at the banks of green spruce and spring leaves of the white birch and aspen rushing past as they sped upriver. The half-hardtop of the craft protected them from the cold morning air, diverting it over and around the windshield. The engine created enough noise to forestall any conversation as they traveled in and around the sandy shoals that separated the stream into ribbons of varying depths.

Farley ran upstream a number of miles before slowing to nose into the muddy shore, pulling forward enough to plant the bow onto the shingle. He climbed onto the transom and pulled open one of the seat boxes, extracting tall rubber fishing boots that would accommodate each of them. Sol accepted a pair gratefully since she hadn't traveled equipped to stand in a couple feet of silty water. The sneakers she'd donned that morning would have been sucked into the soft riverbed, never to be retrieved.

Farley, doubling as the company fishing guide, gave Sol an abbreviated lesson on the differences between lure and bait casting. As a novice to the sport, she paid avid attention but realized the likelihood of her catching anything on a quick and dirty trip like this was pretty slim, not that that was going to stop her from taking on the challenge with zeal.

The hours slipped by far too fast for her taste. Nor had it taken her long to decide that she and Toddy should make plans to come back to Alaska and try their luck together.

By the time Farley started to pack up the gear, there were two Keta and a good-sized King cozying up in the fish box at the back of the stern.

The real world was calling.

Chapter 37

Uncertain whether to feel hope or dread, Yancy left Mary to continue her watch over her daughter. There wasn't much she could do at the hospital, and on the way out Yancy listened to Laura's phone message, the muted vibration of her cell ignored while checking on Kara's progress.

Nothing new there. Laura had left a pleasant sounding nag about paperwork that, the boss had reminded her, he wanted on his desk first thing in the morning. The response to an appeal was on deadline to be filed with the court by Friday. Time was growing short.

Sighing but actually relieved to have something to keep her occupied, she put the car in drive and headed back to the office. The other option was to knock aimlessly around the house, which is what Yancy knew she would do if she just went home,

Twenty minutes later, she was seated in front of her office computer, sipping one last espresso for the day. *Just a final boost to get me to the finish line.*

The brief was basically complete, all she really needed to do was re-read the content and make sure she had all of the precedents and cites in proper order. It would have one last read-through in the morning when her supervisor and office manager gave his final okay for submission.

This was one of many cases that really perplexed her. They'd won a sharp victory for the plaintiff, an environmental group that was nominally supported by a local tribal agency. The problem for Yancy was that a rancher would be forced to abandon use of 160 acres of valuable land in order to save a wetland. A move that would incur severe financial stress.

In this case her gut told her they had represented the wrong side. As sensitive as she was to environmental issues and tribal interests, she couldn't help but to feel that the law, as it was interpreted here, was seriously misguided and justice far from being served.

The problem with this particular disagreement was that the wetland had not existed previous to the diligent construction of a new beaver dam on the rancher's property, backing up a creek just long enough for the environmentalists to swoop in. They immediately claimed damage to the eco-system when the rancher began to dismantle the artificial barrier after the beavers had abandoned it, which they were wont to do.

Yancy knew that the structure was temporary, causing the stream to pool in the pasture, a stream that was dry half of the year. The plaintiffs knew it too. It was obvious to her that the wetland was a freak of beaver industry, not a permanent duck pond, but she'd been compelled to represent the complainants all the same. It wasn't within her purview to pick and choose most of the cases the office represented but this was one that stuck in her craw.

It raised questions about the wisdom behind so much legislation that was continually being added to the books, laws whose intent had been so corrupted as to become a burden on the citizenry rather than a protection. Some of the language was crafted in such a fashion as to make the application practically impossible in any rational sense. She'd also run into a few federal statutes that were virtually indecipherable due to contradictory language within the whole of a cumbersome, convoluted text.

So here she was, responding to an appeal that made more sense than the law upon which the judge had ruled and, unfortunately for the rancher and his family, correctly applied in accordance with its content.

Yancy dropped her forehead on the desk.

Who was she really representing? Just because it was the law, did it make the outcome right or just? It was becoming more and more common to have environmental or public benefit groups run roughshod over individual rights by invoking bad bills that had become law, and occasionally even the Native organizations backed the wrong horse. At least, that was the way it appeared to Yancy and she was the one who had to labor through all the verbiage in order to craft the arguments.

Most of her clients were good people like the Lysanders who had legitimate concerns about the encroachment of regulation after regulation which, in their situation, had placed a young girl in grave danger.

Where should the line be drawn? Bodies were piling up as people were losing their livelihood, being placed at risk of not being able to provide for their families no matter what their color or creed. It was beginning to look like everyone was under attack. But who was waging war? More and more, Yancy thought that our own government was creating the rift between humanity and the environment, and that distressed her deeply.

Man is not an opponent to nature, he is an integral part of nature.

She wondered when we were going to figure that out.

Chapter 38

It took some doing, but Allie, her arms and shoulders precariously balanced with her cargo, used her backside to bump the passenger door closed on her Focus without dropping anything. *I could never be a waitress.*

The box of a half dozen oversized scones from a local organic bakery Esteban had recommended had also put a minor dent in her finances. It was her idea to arrive at the Green Grasslands office with something to sweeten her intrusion. She figured it couldn't hurt to bribe the staff with sugar.

Okay, honey and molasses. The bakery didn't use refined ingredients. Even as an eco-friendly lib, Allie liked her unhealthy foodstuffs even if it meant she had to struggle to keep her weight in check. There were some things she was willing to forego, but the pleasure of the occasional poppy seed muffin or some triple-mud chocolate decadence was beyond her will power. Today's little yield of all-natural scones, which she kind of thought was an oxy-moron, was going to cost her in the workout department, particularly since she wasn't home for Debra to chide her about getting to the gym, Allie's least favorite place.

It had been the researcher's idea to get their butts in gear and tighten things up, adding the reminder that neither one of them were getting any younger. Allie had a particular dislike for forced exercise. She'd been active in high school and college, cheerleading and tennis, even the occasional dreaded Lacrosse game, the word still made her wince, but Debra's recent prodding had produced results. Allie could say that she was in the best shape since college and probably, her life.

So what're a few calories for the sake of peace and justice?
Pushing the front door open with her hip, Allie negotiated the

entrance with caution. Box of goodies in one hand, coffee in the other, her reporter's paraphernalia in her satchel on one shoulder and her purse dangling on the opposite side. The only other bit of equipment that was new to the ensemble was a cloisonné pendant that Esteban had insisted she wear. It wasn't quite her style but it was fashionable in a Ming Dynasty kind of way, not just cheap junk.

Allie stepped inside and the door slowly closed behind her. She was greeted by Ilse, who was seated at reception, the German student's cherubic face lighting up at her entrance. Peering down the hall, she noticed the director was in his office. The only other body that she could see was Rain warming a chair at a desk behind the counter. He gave no sign of recognition as she pushed through the door, just looked up briefly without expression, taking note of another person entering the room.

"Oh look, breakfast! A guut thing too. I wass late and had no time to eat this morgen," Ilse clapped her hands as she rose from behind her desk. She was bright and energetic and given to a tendency to slip into her native tongue when the words were similar to the English.

Deciding to be accommodating, Rain came around the counter and helped Allie with her burden. "Nice gesture," he said blandly. "Thanks for the thought."

"Hey, no problem. Figured I'd try a little persuasion to ease myself into the office clique. Donuts always do the trick at the paper." She turned to him, "We haven't met. I'm Allie."

"Rain," and he nodded before going back to alphabetizing a stack of papers for filing.

"Isn't that a cute name?" enthused Ilse, which almost made Allie cringe, knowing that Indians often had namesakes that had meanings and weren't meant to be 'cute,' not that she knew the significance of Rain's name. There was also the fact that the man didn't lend himself to the description Ilse had applied. 'Still' was the adjective that crossed her mind, as in waters running deep, but never 'cute.'

Ilse opened the box and practically squealed with delight. Dark haired with a generous roundness to her figure, Ilse plainly liked to eat. "These are wonderful. Much better than donuts. Danke," she said as she selected one and returned to her seat where she already had a cup of coffee.

Hearing the commotion, Race Carson emerged from the director's office and greeted Allie. "Good morning. You certainly didn't have to go to the trouble," he added, spying the carton.

"No trouble at all. I was raised with the notion that sharing is a good thing."

Ilse concurred with a nod of her head and a full mouth, the corners of which were uptilted in a charming smile.

"We definitely appreciate the offering." Carson reached into the box and took one without noticing what kind it was.

Guess he's not too picky, thought Allie as he motioned for Allie to follow him as he made his way back to his office.

Breaking one in half first, she snagged a scone for herself before joining him. They sat down and she munched while he explained the plan for the day. He'd decided to pair her up with Toby, the fellow she'd met the day before. The odd Mr. Mustache. Allie was to accompany the project manager to the elementary school where he was scheduled to make a presentation about clean energy. It would be a good opportunity to listen to the spiel, watch their procedures for public outreach programs. Maybe even help out, if she felt so inclined.

"I should probably just observe for right now. I wouldn't mind participating in the future, down the road. For now, I'm supposed to document your message, educational programs, how things are done and the general workings of your office," she explained. "It would be a little inappropriate for me to get involved while I'm officially representing the paper. But I will be of some use by shooting photos. I can forward some of the shots to you after the story's submitted."

"Sure. I hadn't thought about policy conflicts. Look, the fact that you're here is great. We're always looking for some good publicity. In this state, we need it," Carson chuckled before he bit into the pastry.

"We should be able to afford you some of that. The schools are always looking for inexpensive ways to expand their curricula," said Allie. "I imagine they really appreciate members of the community offering to supply useful environmental science projects for the students."

He silently agreed as he chewed. Swallowing, he then elucidated on the programs that were ongoing at the local schools. "We'll be going to the high school tomorrow to do the final assembly of a windmill for their environmental science class. Toby has a helper from Lebanon, another exchange student, that accompanies him on the more physical projects."

"Is he one of the young men I met when I last visited?"

Race angled his head, looking toward the corner as he combed is mind for the memory. Eyes lighting with recollection he said, "Yes, I believe you did meet him."

"I notice that you encourage foreign students to work here. Is there a conscious recruiting effort, or is there just a natural draw to work at Green Grasslands?"

"We actually help sponsor some of these kids to come over to study here at University of Wyoming and also down at Ft. Collins since it's not too distant from here. An hour down the highway." She caught a quick flicker of chagrin cross his face. "Of course you know, you've been driving back and forth from Denver." He playfully smacked the side of his head as if to knock a little sense into it.

"Right you are. Even for me it's only a two-hour drive to Denver. Not a bad jaunt."

As they continued to jaw about the programs and student participation, Toby came into the office, a napkin wrapped scone in his hand. "Hey, thanks for bringing these in. Some of us are lax about the most important meal of the day," and he raised it in salute. "I was just checking in with the boss," he added with an engaging smile.

"We'll be leaving in about fifteen minutes. Do you want to ride with me or follow in your vehicle?" Toby took a big bite after asking.

"If you don't mind, I'd like to ride along with you. Get more of a feel for your perspective of the program. You know, badger you with questions. The usual reporter thing."

Mouth half-full, he disarmed her with a captivating grin, lessening her guard. Maybe she'd misjudged him the day before.

"Finish up and we'll hit the road. The program's at ten."

Chapter 39

The yellow police tape was history.

Operations at Tyne Hill were at less than half-capacity. The damaged vehicles had been cleared away from the pit and excavation had resumed. Repairs were underway at batch load out and a bypass system had been rigged during the interim.

The major hurdle yet to overcome was the reopening of the Flat Butte power station. Without the consumer, product had nowhere to go. Corporate headquarters was in the midst of beating the bushes for short-term buyers and lobbying hard for the reopening of the old plant. The need was evident in the community, witnessed by the immediate economic fallout that was only beginning, causing temporary layoffs that could lead to permanent job losses. A larger problem loomed as the federal energy policy was intent on phasing out coal generated power. Not a happy scenario for the coal-rich state of Wyoming and the coal-fired economy of Gillette.

Sawyer was back on the job in the supervisor shack. With everything moving at a cut-rate speed, he was finding his senses dulled by the inactivity. The usual adrenaline he'd pump by overseeing the fast-paced traffic of haulers was slashed to one hauler servicing one shovel. There was no point in producing more coal than could be moved on the market.

The corporate office had released a statement saying they were lucky that the physical damage to the mine hadn't been as severe as first estimated. *If you could call three good men dead 'lucky.'*

He'd been back to the hospital only to find that one other man from the power plant had lost his battle to recover and now he was worried that Allie had obliviously walked into a potentially dangerous situation of her own.

Yeah, there was no real evidence that anything devious was

occurring at the environmental enclave in Cheyenne, but then there was enough circumstantial data to inspire suspicion in the FBI agent's mind. That was enough to make Sawyer doublethink the reporter's vulnerability. Esteban appeared to be a levelheaded guy.

So why the harebrained idea of sending Allie to do his dirty work?

He was uneasy with the whole thing. When his relief came in, he took the opportunity to call Allie and check-in with her. It would probably irritate the hell out of Esteban that he was sticking his nose in 'official business,' but Sawyer needed to mitigate the doubt clambering around inside his head.

The call went directly to voicemail and he swore under his breath while he dialed Rain.

"Yes."

"Never one to spare words, are you?" Sawyer commented when the cell phone was answered on the third ring.

"Nope." Getting up from behind the desk, Rain told Ilse he was going outside for a minute to get some air. She turned sideways in her seat and smiled acknowledgement, holding the office phone to her own ear while she took notes from a teacher whose school was on the project schedule. He was thankful for the opportunity to get some fresh air. Tedious hours of filing wasn't the kind of work he was built for.

"Tell me."

"Nothing to tell." Rain answered as he stepped out the back door.

"Where is she?"

"With some guy, Toby, at a school."

"A little more information than that would be nice," coaxed Sawyer, even though he wasn't in the mood for being nice himself. He felt frustratingly ineffectual.

"They're at Box Elder Elementary where this Toby, who is the project manager here, is doing a presentation on green energy for the kids. She's tagging along like any good reporter."

"Tell me about Toby, then."

"What do you want to know? A character sketch or his inseam?" taunted Rain.

"Both would be helpful," said Sawyer. "A description and your take on his personality."

"Haven't seen enough of the guy to say anything about his character."

"Okay, impressions then. You have a shrewd eye."

Rain obliged his friend. "He's one of those charmers. Good looking enough to catch a lady's eye and knows how to use it. You know the type. The six-pack and the smile. Throw in a little fashionable grunge. He's got the little receptionist reeled in. I'd bet he's pretty good with a crowd, too."

"What about Allie?" The brief description made Sawyer's skin crawl for some reason.

"You're worried, aren't you." It was a flat statement, no need to question something Rain already knew.

"You'll have to tell me if I should be or not," said Sawyer. "I'm miles away and have no idea what's going on, if anything. But if there was enough doubt about your new workplace to instigate an FBI inquiry, then I'd say it's common sense to keep an open mind on the subject. He *does* think there's a possible connection to eco-terrorism."

"You agree then." Rain said without intonation.

"You must too or you wouldn't be frittering away your time with some silly ass environmentalists," Sawyer accused acidly. "What have they got you doing anyway? Sweeping out closets? Cleaning toilets?"

"These are compassionate white folks," Rain deadpanned. "They let the Indians file papers."

Sawyer snorted in a cross between laughter and derision for the well-meaning, misguided souls. "And are we learning anything new in all those papers you're handling?"

Rain grinned a little into the phone. "Only tidbits here and there. But I did run across a file for a couple of Lebanese students doing work in Environmental Science at CSU."

"I'll bet Mr. Fed would love to have copies of those."

"I'm working on it."

"Call me when Allie gets back or if you come across anything else. I'm at Tyne Hill today so I can't take calls while on the job. And... Rain, thanks."

Rain just clicked off without additional pleasantries. Sawyer understood his friend's terse nature. It mirrored his own most of the time.

He didn't trust anyone else to shadow his unofficial operative. Too much was riding on what could be considered a lapse in judgment were his superiors to get too much of a whiff of what he'd done. Skirting the rulebook wasn't anything new to Esteban but this was the first time he'd allowed a tenderfoot inside an investigation. He was vacillating between kicking himself for his stupidity or congratulating himself for using the best resource available.

With each passing minute he was leaning more and more toward the former choice. What had he been thinking? This little recon mission was instigated more to rule-out a hunch than to prove any insidious activity at Green Grasslands. Still, these people might be connected to a terrorist cell. They could also be a completely benign batch of greenies, but he wasn't betting on that. In fact, he'd just bet a woman's safety on the possibility that she could ferret out information that, in some parallel universe, pertains to his investigation of a couple of not-so-random bombings.

Whatever. All he could do was wait it out for today and then reassess the situation tonight while hoping and praying that he hadn't misjudged either Allie Maitland or the potential to catch some bad guys. Bad guys that were most likely someplace far away from here. *Yeah, you keep telling yourself that.*

In the meantime, Esteban would do most of the stakeout work himself since this was less than a two-day op. She was just to tag along, do her regular job of asking innocuous questions and report to him. He wasn't known in the Cheyenne area, being a transplant from Denver brought in to oversee this investigation, so he felt it safer if he did the legwork himself. They'd reached too many dead ends in Gillette and this was the next best option.

Keep telling yourself that too, menso.

He stayed well back behind the beater truck that one of the Green Grasslands employees was driving. Allie occupied the passenger seat, not that he could see anything at this distance, well, besides the billowing plume the tin can on wheels was belching every time he accelerated.

Some environmentalist he is, spouting all that oily smoke. Piece of junk needs a ring job. Esteban followed the couple thinking, *I guess potential terrorists don't make a lot of money these days*, as he pulled into a parking spot on the street.

Allie had texted him from the Green Grasslands office to inform him of "Toby's" plans to present a program at Box Elder School, so Esteban had known where they were heading. *Nothing dangerous in that, or dubious other than the fact that they were propagandizing the kids*, in his humble opinion.

He took a sip from the cup of coffee he'd brought with him, figuring that he had plenty of time to sit and wait. And think.

The reporter had asked him about border security and if we shouldn't be compassionate toward underprivileged illegals coming to this country looking for work. He'd tried to answer candidly taking into account his own background, a heritage that she'd mentioned.

Esteban had been raised by children of Mexican immigrants who'd followed the law, worked hard in the fields, saved enough money and eventually started their own business. His family had lived the American Dream and they'd striven to pass down their strong belief in that dream to their children. He felt his parents had done an exceptional job to that end and were proper models for anyone hoping to immigrate to the United States. His siblings were successful entrepreneurs and teachers. Esteban's own faith in the promise of America had propelled him to enter law enforcement because he wanted to play a role in making certain that the dream stayed alive for the next generation.

A generation he hadn't made any real effort toward adding his own progeny.

One divorce and no kids, and he had no plans to find another woman to make his life miserable. That was the way he saw things.

Most of the time he avoided thinking about the loneliness of his job, and the singlemindedness with which he'd pursued his career. The marriage may have been wretched, but he also knew that he couldn't lay the fault of that completely at her feet. She'd wanted to see him more, or at least a few times a week. Unfortunately, that wasn't going to happen with the schedule the bureau had him working at the time. It's not as if he hadn't forewarned her that the first years would be hard, being moved around and tested.

It was after she left, of course, that he was finally dispatched to a permanent position in Denver. Too little, too late.

How he'd ended up in Cheyenne was another matter altogether. The resident agency was a relatively small office and they found themselves short-handed when all hell broke loose in the Powder River basin. The supervising agent was out on medical leave and it was unknown when he'd be back, or if he would be back at all, considering his ongoing battle with prostate cancer. Poor bastard hadn't been lucky enough to catch the problem early and the treatment was worse than the disease, from what Esteban had heard through the grapevine. So the higher-ups, in all their wisdom, had plucked Esteban out of his Denver digs and thrown him to the media wolves. He didn't know who was luckier, him or the cancer patient.

He pulled himself out of his reverie and watched as lines of children were marched from the multi-purpose gymnasium/cafeteria toward a feeble looking garden area the classes had planted in the back forty, behind the playground.

Taking another sip of lukewarm coffee, he waited some more.

Chapter 40

Mid-afternoon in Washington D.C. and things weren't going quite as planned. The congressional switchboard was awash with irate phone calls from every sector of the nation, yelling at the top of their lungs trying to get their representatives to listen.

The Clean Air and Energy Act was coming to a vote and the American people were not happy about what they were hearing over the airwaves, on their television sets and through the internet.

It was like listening to a football game at the close of the final quarter. The score was tied and there were only seconds left to make the winning play. The latest reports had the tally at 210 to 210 with fifteen members of the House still undecided. Both sides were cheering and cursing a blue streak at the TVs and computer monitors hoping and praying that the Congress would do the right thing. Of course, what the 'right' thing was depended on an individual's viewpoint when it came to the Cap and Trade. The pollsters held that antagonism for Wexler's bill heavily outweighed the proponents.

The speaker of the House was beginning to worry that her mojo was slipping. Some would argue that she'd never had any to begin with, just a heavy-handed club to keep the majority in line. Today, her sway was in question because the walk in the park vote was turning into a street brawl and her anger was brewing. At three a.m., three hundred more pages had been furtively added to the already cumbersome bill that now surpassed a thousand pages, not that anyone had read the initial draft let alone the final version. Just like the stimulus package that, earlier in the year, had swept through Congress without members bothering to read the bill, this legislation was being brought to a forced vote before anyone could even skim the additional pages.

That didn't stop the speaker from bringing the whole charade to a halt by extorting enough members to assure that their vote would emplace the largest single tax hike in history, utterly gutting the U.S. economic base... an economy that was already reeling under the daily expanding trillion dollar deficits that Van Schaal had engineered with the complicity of a Democrat Congress.

No wonder the public was screaming with outrage.

Yancy had her car radio tuned to one of the popular national talk hosts. She'd begun listening over the last year during the long drives that took her from one rural outpost to another to visit clients, becoming a habit that could be classified as either an addiction or an emotional outlet.

At the moment she was listening to the talk jock hammer the Congress to take a stand against even more taxes and the outrageous wildcatting of Congress. She couldn't decide if it was more appropriate to call it wildcatting or tomcatting. One insinuating drilling the public wherever and however they could to strike oil, AKA cash for their coffers; or the other definition that would suggest screwing anything they could get a hold of, which in this case was the public.

When did I get to be so cynical?

She was slightly heartened when she'd heard the latest polling showed a neck-and-neck horse race coming down the home stretch, offering just a little hope that the Cap and Trade legislation would be blocked. She knew only too well that her cause was tied to preventing this boondoggle from passing. If it were to be signed into law the hope of challenging the fallacy that CO_2 emissions were causing global warming would be nothing more than a pipedream. Key and thousands upon thousands of workers tied to the oil and coal industry would lose their jobs – those industries being heavily targeted by the bill.

And Kara. Poor, dear Kara is already fighting for her life.

The thought of the losses that could pile up because Congress wasn't paying attention to the destruction they were determined to incur was settling heavily on Yancy's heart.

She'd already decided that she was doing nobody any good by hanging around the hospital waiting for either a miracle or a tragedy. Mary and her family needed encouraging smiles and the despondency that was closing in on Yancy had made her throw her things in the car and take off down the road.

She let her mind block out the voices on the radio and tuned into the urgent one in her head as she followed the long sweeping curves that skirted the southern Montana mountains. Realization was filtering through that her efforts in the Lysander case were likely to go nowhere should the Clean Energy Act make it all the way through Congress and the Supreme Court get a facelift.

As Yancy turned off I-90, she heard that the bill passed the House in a squeaker of 219 to 212.

"Damn! Damn, damn and damn!" She pounded the steering wheel and vainly tried to calm her frustration with the arrant idiocy that seemed to have overcome her fellow countrymen. She recalled how recently she had believed the same foolishness and, unfortunately, understood how people have been misled.

What's that quote? But for the grace of God go I?

Except she *had* gone there and now hoped with all her heart that there were others who would figure it out too.

Taking a huge gulp of air and blowing it out in a measured exhale to dispel the feeling of futility, Yancy turned her car to follow a dusty two-lane highway that would take her to Spotted Horse Mountain.

Rone Haggerty breathed a sigh of relief as he hung up the phone.

After spending only a couple of minutes trying to sound unperturbed by the close call in the House, all the while gloating for the sake of the man on the other end of the line, he was sweating through his collar. That man made him nervous.

Haggerty knew exactly where his bread was buttered. He had climbed a steep cliff to get the Cap and Trade passed, spouting so much claptrap had been a huge drain even on his enormous capacity to circumvent facts. The finagling he'd accomplished had garnered him some hefty profits that under most circumstances a man's conscience might balk. That is, if he had one.

He shrugged it off as meaningless in the long run.

All to good purpose.

His ambassadorship was as good as sealed. Van Schaal couldn't possibly disregard the wishes of Scirras. Not if he planned on getting re-elected.

Of course, there was still the test of passing the legislation through the Senate. Haggerty hoped that wouldn't be as tough a sell as the House version. The democrats were numerous enough in the other chamber to slam it through. Of course, that's what they had thought when dealing with the House. It ended up being anything but a cakewalk.

He wiped the drops from his neck with a handkerchief as he launched into devising a new strategy to clear the next hurdle.

Scirras was running his plans through his head at warp speed. Like his father, ordinary men simply couldn't keep up with him nor did he expect it of them.

The next step was to speed correlative legislation through the Senate. It was obvious now that they were going to come up against some serious opposition, but it wasn't anything that he couldn't handle with ease. His deck was stacked so well that he was certain he could force any one of the senate majority members to fold in quicktime. None of them had the intestinal fortitude to stand in his way and he knew it.

Haggerty was foolish to believe he was furthering his own agenda rather than suffering the usage of a pawn. Scirras considered whether the man would ever realize the true ineffectiveness of the United Nations to which an appointment as ambassador would be of little point and less power. *Men and their fascination with titles and office.*

Recalling how the campaign was still unfolding in the west, he was reassured that all was moving forward as expected. It had been a stroke of genius to cull experienced operatives from the discard pile for the more difficult work.

Each task required the proper tools. But the task he had in mind wasn't yet complete.

It would be soon.

Energy Barons

Chapter 41

Toby Blaine and Allie arrived at the Green Grasslands office just as the cork popped and landed across the room, champagne spilling in a frothy gush.

"Whose birthday?" she asked as they pushed through the door, just avoiding being hit by the exploding missile.

"Everyone's. The energy bill passed the House and it was a close call," Race Carson enthused as he handed a glass of bubbly to Ilse.

Grinning impishly, he offered Allie some champagne. "It's almost after hours."

For once she was in a quandary as to what to think after all her recent conversations with Sawyer, Sol, Debra and even Yancy, corporate refugee and lawyer to the downtrodden. The discussions had prompted her to do a little more digging on her own and what she found disrupted her long-held beliefs. What was discussed in numerous studies, congressional committee meetings, at U.N. conventions and in the classrooms, which provided the meat of mainstream news stories, didn't reconcile with the scientific research that had emerged over the years since the controversy had begun. As much as spokesmen like Kraegen and Haggerty had to say, it was becoming evident, even to her, that there was no consensus among scientists.

Shaking off her indecision, she accepted the plastic flute with a smile and joined in the merrymaking, noticing that her accomplice, Rain, wasn't present for the party.

Allie was interested to see that the last of the two "Lebanese" students, A´zam, was in attendance and decided to get acquainted.

She collected two plates of the cake Race had purchased at the last minute for the celebration.

"Couldn't find one with green icing," he'd joked, as Ilse was slicing it.

Allie delivered one to A´zam. Assuming that he probably didn't drink alcohol if he was actually Muslim and not the Christian that his records showed, she didn't want to take a chance of making a serious gaffe. *I suppose he might not eat western confections either. Oh well, in for a penny, in for a pound...*

"Would you care for some cake?" Allie asked, attempting to be as inoffensive as possible, much as it went against her grain. Her style was more like a tugboat than a genteel luxury liner, push or pull to get answers. "Looks pretty good to me."

"Thank you," he accepted the offering without flinching.

So good, so far. "I was hoping that you might be here. If you're willing, I'd like to find out a little bit about your studies and your stay here in the States. I think the experiences of a foreign student working with an environmental organization would be an interesting addition to the overall story."

"There is not much to say about me beyond what you learned when last you visited. My life is quite dull, really."

She laughed lightly. "That's hard to believe. You're well traveled with an international education. I've never had the opportunity to go to Britain let alone the Middle East. I'm envious."

"Travel can be as much a bother as an adventure," he said affably enough, eyes on Allie, waiting to see if she would pounce.

She ignored his quelled wariness. "Tell me how environmental studies in Colorado and Wyoming are of interest to you. Is there a correlation between the eco-systems here and back home?" She tilted her head in a way that suggested a question about the concept's plausibility.

"No. My studies here have more to do with the effects of global warming on this particular region of the world. My thesis is related to carbon emissions in areas more reliant on coal-generated power."

"Is there a way of measuring that?"

"Most of the work is qualitative rather than quantitative, incorporating interviews and anecdotal information collection."

In other words, hearsay. "That sounds fascinating. How long will it take you to complete your studies?" inquired Allie.

"I had already completed much of the work through internet and other correspondence, as well as telephone interviews before leaving for the United States. This is the final stage of my data collection."

"Meaning that you will be here for only a short while?"

"I have a limited visa, but it should be sufficient to finalize my work." A´zam added, "In answer to your question, yes."

"And your companion, the young man I met when I was here before, Jehal. I understand that both of you are from Lebanon. Has he gone home, then?"

"No, he has transferred to another program at a different university." He wasn't sure where she was going with this line of inquiry.

"How interesting. Are there many exchange opportunities in the States, then? It seems that you are in demand." Allie grinned as she complimented their popularity.

"The number is growing. Environmental Studies is an expanding field."

"I suppose it is important to your own country, too, having suffered years of decimation from the political strife," she prompted him to give her more about his homeland.

"Yes, things have been difficult. I believe that every nation is struggling with the effort to control its effect on the environment. It has become a subject of global importance." He gazed over at Toby nonchalantly, giving the impression of having other commitments. "You must excuse me."

"Yes, of course. Well, I hope that your stay here has been a pleasant one," said Allie, hoping to sound neighborly. "We try to be hospitable."

He nodded, almost imperceptibly dismissing her as he turned away, spoke briefly to Toby, dropped the untouched cake into the trash, and left. She joined Toby before he headed out the door too.

"He seems a nice enough guy. Not real talkative," she observed. "Have you worked with him much?"

"Not yet, though I'd agree that he's a 'good egg,' if you'll pardon the Britishism," he said with a good-natured mimicry of A´zam's accent.

Allie gave him a cross-eyed look of amusement. "That's a new one on me."

"Which?"

"The 'good egg,' of course," and she laughed gently at her feeble attempt at a joke. Somehow she wasn't feeling all that jocular.

Blaine was polite enough to smile. "You'll get your chance to see our A´zam in action tomorrow. We'll be raising the wind turbine at the high school and I assume that you'll be covering it. Am I right?"

"You bet. I'll be there. Digital camera, will travel."

Offering her goodbyes to the few left at Green Grasslands, she hitched her satchel back onto her shoulder and left as well. Climbing into the car and turning the key in the ignition, she punched Esteban's cell number into her phone.

He didn't bother to tell her that he was just down the street from her as she pulled into traffic. Instead, he gave her directions to a café and told her to meet him there in fifteen minutes.

"Okay." She spoke to dead air.

Finding the wine bar wasn't a difficult task and Allie walked into the dense jungle atmosphere right on time. The contemporary café was loaded with greenery, giving it the feel of what they used to call "fern bars" in the eighties.

Maybe it's a good place for clandestine meetings. You can hide behind the elephant ears.

Allie let the door close, Esteban catching it as he casually entered behind her. Without overmuch in the way of greeting, he moved ahead of her to meet the hostess, who found them seats in a corner booth. The waitress arrived in a flash, taking orders for wine. Chardonnay all around.

They were now buds having a drink after a rough day at the office.

"Funny, I would have taken you for a red wine kind of guy, or beer," said Allie, taking a sip and savoring the white wine over the inexpensive brut that had burned going down her throat. She'd tossed most of that out along with the cake.

"I'm trying to play the part of the not-so-macho Latino." His face split in a rare smile that actually showed teeth. "Is it working?"

"Not in the least. So, what are we doing here?"

"You are going to kick back and tell me about your workday." He slid back into his seat, trying to look less intimidating in his official FBI uniform. That wasn't working for her either.

"First, I'm hungry," and she ordered a couple of appetizers from the menu.

"Not much time for food today, huh?" asked Esteban, appearing a little more relaxed in his role of work pals.

"Not unless you consider dry cake and cheap champagne a meal." She took another sip and he quirked an eyebrow, egging her on.

It didn't take long to explain the little party at the office after she'd outlined the couple of schools they'd visited. Details of the latter excursions weren't really necessary since they were essentially repeat performances of 'green' education. Esteban was more interested in her dealings with any of the office denizens, which she answered with detailed descriptions and what little information she'd been able to glean about histories. She didn't bother to mention Rain.

When she got down to the celebration for the passage of the Clean Energy bill, he shook his head.

"Strange to make a big deal out of a piece of legislation."

"It's kind of a 'liberal' thing. I've seen it a lot with Democrat rallies. If you live for saving the earth and you believe this bill will do that…"

He interrupted, "Bizarre."

She bridled just a little, "I was going to say that you celebrate. Evidently, you don't agree."

"I probably shouldn't interject my personal opinion, but I've always been given to the concept that politics shouldn't be about 'feeling good' or emotions. Which is what you're describing."

Allie considered a moment. "I suppose I can see your point. It did seem more like winning the NBA championship. I guess it's a good thing they didn't go to the extent of running in the streets, overturning cars or setting them on fire."

He shrugged. "Yeah, we'd have to arrest them for that. What else?"

Allie went into her conversation with A´zam.

"Lebanese, huh?"

"Right. He didn't mention his homeland once so I couldn't ascertain whether he knew much about Lebanon. And he has more of an East Indian-like accent rather than what I'd call typically Arabic, though the British English really overtook any nuance. But I'm no expert."

"You're doing what we discussed, observing. We'll see how things go tomorrow." He looked at her carefully. "If you still want to go ahead with this. You know that you don't have to. So far, it doesn't add up to much."

"No, no. It would look bad if I bailed right when the big photo op comes up. They're erecting the windmill at the high school tomorrow."

Examining her from his partial slouch, he determined that Ms. Maitland had the staying power to finish the job, not that he was really certain what they expected to achieve. So far, things appeared pretty harmless. He nodded affirmation.

"Then let's get you settled for the night." Esteban gave her verbal directions to the motel that she committed to memory. "Just go straight there, in case you're being followed." He stood and paid the tab.

"You think that's likely?"

"Not really, but we may as well be cautious,"

When Allie pulled up at her new accommodations, she was a little disappointed at the neglected appearance of the motel.

"Does this place have running water and flush toilets?" she remarked as Esteban unlocked the room and handed her the key.

"Sorry it's not the Ritz, but it's better on the inside than it looks." He carried her bag inside. "Shabby chic."

Gazing around the room, Allie agreed that it was serviceable and clean.

He explained that the motel was well situated for observation purposes, though he didn't go into detail.

"If it's so easy to watch, maybe it wasn't such a good idea to walk in together."

"Not to worry. You weren't followed. I doubt there's any suspicion anyway." At that he showed her the sparse amenities and warned her not to go out.

"I thought you said no one knew I was here, or even cared?" she said archly.

"Better safe than sorry. There's a number to call next to the phone if there's anything you might need. But don't go out on your own. We don't know if these guys are really on the up-and-up."

"You don't say. I thought they were just a bunch of eco-chumps according to you."

Esteban gave her an unexpected grin as he let himself out the door.

The only word Allie could think of to describe the day was taxing.

Under normal circumstances, she could ride in on her white horse of truth, get the story and disappear into the sunset, leaving everything in print and ready to move on to the next big story. This time, she was playing a dual role that, despite her incessant, internal denials, made her edgy.

Just one more day and we'll have the skinny... or not.

She flopped onto the bed and flicked on the TV. At least the cheap quarters came with a television, and a remote that wasn't chained to the furniture. Having been warned not to go wandering the streets alone, she dug through her overnight bag for shower items and went to wash off the garden grit.

Feeling refreshed after her cleansing, Allie set-up her laptop and began outlining the story as it stood so far, which was duller than dishwater. It was looking like she may have given up a week's pay just for a long shot at making the regional section. *We'll just have to see if anything pops tomorrow*, she thought, trying to be optimistic.

Since there was no inspiration floating around her not quite run-down motel room, she called Solana, hoping she was in a location that had cell service. Maybe something had broken loose in the frigid north. *Yeah, like a glacier calving due to global warming.* She thought there were glaciers in Alaska, then nodded her head 'yes,' reminding herself about the cruises that visit the iced shores of the inland passage.

"Allie? What's the scoop down there?" Sol was at the Anchorage airport, waiting for her luggage to roll off the conveyor.

"So far as I can tell, there ain't one. What about up there in twenty-four hour sunshine?"

"It's not quite like that, but close where I just flew in from. It's almost that time of year when full dark never comes. As to a story, just getting the basics on that gold mine and the court case to shut it down. The usual."

"Tell me anyway. I'm bored." Allie laid back on the bed to listen to Sol's tale of her northern trekking.

She went through her visit to Juneau and the Rural Resources office. Before she could move on to the tour of Corcoran Creek, when she made mention of the foreign exchange students, Allie halted the account.

"What's so odd about that?"

"You said one was Oriental and the other Middle Eastern," said Allie.

"And?"

"Well, one of the Arab students at the Cheyenne office of Green Grasslands was "transferred" just last week. I don't want to sound like a conspiracy theorist…"

"You do," affirmed Sol.

"… but I wonder if it's the same guy."

"I don't know where he hails from. He was part of a group that was looking over a map of the Alaska Pipeline that had some areas marked by colored tacks. I don't know why, but it struck me odd. Just being paranoid, likely," said Sol.

"I don't know. There's a map of a natural gas pipeline running through Wyoming in this GG office that also has a few tacks on it. I thought it was a little strange but, what do I know? They're probably just getting ready to file some kind of injunction claiming that the route goes through an area that's sensitive to some endangered species."

"Watch it. You're beginning to sound like me," laughed Sol.

Allie harrumphed. "There *are* situations where species are negatively affected by developments such as a pipeline or tract housing."

"Who're you trying to convince? Keep at this, girl, and I think you may see another side to the environmental issue, and it's not all as benevolent as it appears."

"We'll see," said Allie a little less skeptically than she would have answered a week ago.

"Let me know if you find out why they're following a map of the pipeline. I'd be interested," said Sol.

"Will do, and the same goes for you."

Hanging up, Allie got back to work, wondering about possible correlations between the offices, or if there was one. There had to be more than a couple of Arabic students in U.S. colleges. *But two working with environmental groups? Since when has the environ-ment been an important issue in the Muslim world?*

It was a query that she couldn't answer.

While she was surfing the net, hunting up any connection between Arab universities and environmental studies, she received a phone call. Expecting it to be Debra, or maybe even Carter Gleason – he wasn't one to leave her alone, even on vacation – she picked up without looking at the readout.

It was Sawyer.

She wasn't sure if she was happy to hear from him or not. After not fifteen seconds of being mother-henned, she'd decided not. She'd already been put through the wringer by Esteban, no matter how laid-back he'd tried to appear at the wine bar, and she was in no mood to suffer a third degree from Sawyer.

"Look Sawyer, Esteban has already dragged me over the coals. Once was enough."

"I'll let you go after you give me a rundown of what happened today and where you are," he insisted.

She had the choice of giving in or hanging up and she wasn't particularly fond of the idea of being rude. Sawyer had been a big help thus far. She gave up and took him through a brief description of her otherwise lackluster day. He said nothing through most of it, letting her talk, only interrupting rarely to ask a question.

"So, that's the long and short of it," Allie wound it up.

"It does sound anything but exciting," he conceded. "Now tell me how the FBI has splurged for a night on the town," he said, trying to lighten the mood a little.

"I was told quite pointedly that there would be none of that. Scolded, actually, and advised not to leave the room."

Sawyer was quiet on the other end for a beat.

"Tell me where they have you holed up."

"I'm sure it's against FBI policy to disclose the whereabouts of a protected witness," she jibed.

He didn't take the bait. Instead he badgered her until she did exactly that, whether the FBI liked it or not.

Allie was done with trying to locate anything interesting on the internet that tied together environmentalism and Islam. The sites ranged from Muslims blaming western civilization for the earth's evident demise, to others praising Islam as an eco-friendly religion, espousing great support for Earth Day. She even found a couple of webpages that blamed the big three religions, Christianity, Judaism and Islam as the culprits behind earth's destruction.

She closed up the computer, bagging it for the night, and started to get ready for bed when someone knocked on the door.

Not being ecstatic with the room situation in the first place, and already feeling a little creeped-out by A´zam and Sol's report, Allie cautiously looked through the peephole expecting to see Esteban checking up on her. She saw Sawyer standing in front of her door.

Now what?

Aloud, she said as she opened the door, "What are you doing here?" This was beyond exasperating.

"Making sure that you're okay," he said matter-of-factly as he pushed his way inside the door.

"I don't know how much better off I can be if I have the FBI watching over me."

"Then why didn't they stop me from coming inside?" Sawyer closed the door behind him. "They can't be everywhere and I didn't notice anyone around when I drove up."

That gave Allie a moment of concern, but then she quickly recovered her nerve. Placing her hands on her hips, she challenged him, "So what do you think you're going to do?"

"Spend the night."

"What?" This time she did lose her composure.

"You heard me. I even brought bedding," and he opened the door to grab his sleeping bag, which she hadn't noticed in her shock at seeing him on her doorstep. He dropped it and a small duffle inside, shut the door again, locked it and shot home the deadbolt.

"On this floor? You've got to be kidding." She was still practically agape at his audacity.

He looked at her with amusement. "Don't you think I've slept in about every kind of place there is? Cowboys don't usually rent a condo when they're out on the range."

She couldn't help herself from feeling a little sheepish. This was a man who had served in the wilds of Afghanistan, let alone slept under the stars on the Wyoming plains. Regaining her poise, she brushed aside her blunder.

"Fine. Just make yourself at home, why doncha."

He gave her a half-smile and said, "I think I will."

Energy Barons

Chapter 42

The office was dark except for this one room in the bowels of the building, where light was trapped in the recesses of the hallway, unlikely to escape through the windows lining the sidewalk along the boulevard.

The evening had grown old as two figures hunched over a round oak table, diagramming strategies for the next exercise. A detailed map was spread across the surface, creases in the paper adding shadows to the printed features of the terrain, every paved road and jeep track discernible. The team leader was tracing the stretch of pipeline that carried natural gas from Wyoming to an energy-starved California. They reviewed every element of the plan thoroughly, ascertaining its precise implementation, leaving no possibility for mistakes.

The message filtering down from the upper echelons was clear. They'd have one chance to get it right.

Time was becoming a precious commodity and the need to move soon had been specified to the leader, pressuring him to move up the schedule of operations. The situation in Washington, D.C. was growing more tense daily and the Senate was wavering in its course on their version of the Cap and Trade. It was necessary to provide justification for taking the low road, the easy street to profit-taking that the uninformed citizenry was unlikely to protest, having no clue the true identity of the profiteers.

The barons had spoken. The means of oil and natural gas transport must be discredited as so hazardous to the environment that the engineered public outcry would drown out the opposition. The mainstream media, as always, was prepared to lead the charge.

Now it was up to a small contingent of saboteurs, these two men among the ranks, to execute the chaos necessary to get the ball rolling.

A´zam entertained his own motivation for participating in the exercise. Although he played the underling in this enterprise, he knew whom he served and the co-conspirators did not serve the same master. In his opinion, the so-called leader was no more than an unenlightened ass. He was all business in planning and accomplishing the mission, but his purpose was not the same. To be led by one's emotions was, to A´zam, the journey of a fool. His supposed compatriot's insistence that the earth was endangered by man's greed and resultant flood of pollutants was puerile.

A´zam knew with certainty what the other could not understand. He knew just how dangerous man truly was, mostly to those of his own species, and not in a disembodied sense of releasing invisible gases into the atmosphere. No, man had the capacity for ruthlessness far beyond the other's comprehension or experience.

"How long will this journalist be accompanying us?" he asked.

"Not long, I think," answered Blaine, twisting his mustache as he often did when stressed. "Tomorrow she'll go with us to the high school while we complete the windmill. That ought to be enough for her story, and then she's gone."

"She was very interested in my history. Uncomfortably so."

"Is the fact that she's a woman a problem?" Toby thought the Arabs that had come through the office were far too sensitive about having contact of any kind with the gentler sex. It was laughable. Any man worth his salt wouldn't let a woman bother him one way or the other. They must feel threatened. Why else cover women from head-to-toe in a burkha?

"No, I have become accustomed to the approaches of immodest women in the west, barbaric as it is. She is curious to the point of being inappropriate."

Blaine just sneered under his mustache, unseen by his teammate.

"Get over it. That's the job of a journalist, to be annoying. You know that."

A´zam shook his head. "It was more than that. She was asking questions that did not seem proper. She appeared far too interested in my stay here, and asked after Jehal who was with me when she visited a week ago. She asked about my home as well. Her inquiry seemed to imply that I was not who I appeared to be."

Giving A´zam the benefit of his clear gaze, Blaine said, "You aren't."

He straightened up, crossing his arms over his chest, considering. "She may be more astute than we thought." He paused. "All right, maybe we'd better watch her more closely tomorrow. Make sure that *she's* who she appears to be."

Energy Barons

Chapter 43

Rounding the last hill that deposited her amid acres of flat grassy fields spreading beneath a solitary butte, Yancy was questioning her decision to come here.

Last night, all her essential paperwork completed and submitted for her superior's perusal and ultimate approval, Yancy had made the trip back by the hospital.

She just couldn't seem to stay away. She'd tried to distract herself with novels, television and exercise over this last week but nothing had diverted her mind from Kara's plight, so she'd found herself back in the hospital ward on the second floor. Suddenly, she'd felt as useless there as she had at home or work.

When Yancy had exited the elevator, she'd been faced with the sight of family members swarming around Mary, her mother seated by her side in the waiting area despite the late hour. An aged uncle was inside the room holding vigil by Kara's bedside. Over the last year, Yancy had met many Indians and this man had the aura of one they would say possessed great medicine.

The scene was one she had been loath to interrupt.

Questioning whether she should stay with so many good people caring for the Lysanders, Yancy had stood rooted in the hall struggling with indecision when one of the elder aunties had come over to her. She had taken Yancy gently by the arm and led her to an alcove in front of a window, the lights of Billings glittering beyond the double-pane.

Yancy had said nothing. No words rolled off her tongue that could express her helplessness, yet the woman seemed to understand. Seeing the need to be useful pooling in Yancy's eyes, she had told her that there was something she could do for Kara and for herself.

The old woman had gone back to the waiting room and taken a blanket striated with the bold colors of sunset. She had placed the blanket over Yancy's arm and had told her to go to Sun Dance and make a gift of the mantle to the lead dancer – the *akbaalía*, the medicine man – running the ceremonies.

Giving Yancy directions to Spotted Horse Mountain, she had told her simply, "You will know what to do."

Now Yancy was here and she didn't know what to do.

She knew that the ritual was one to be respected as a place of sacrifice and prayer. After speaking with Mary, she had taken a little time to look up some basic information about Sun Dance, not that the web is the best place for information about a revered ritual among many of the Plains Indians. Mary's words had opened the door to understanding a little of the purpose of Sun Dance, enough that what Yancy had gleaned from the internet made some sense to her. But now she was here.

Yancy parked her car with the scores of other rigs partially ringing the dance grounds some distance away. She climbed out of her sedan taking the blanket the auntie had given her for the *akbaalía*, straightened up and just… listened.

The drum and keening voices glided toward her on the crest of the drifting wind that caught her hair around her shoulders. Finally, she awakened to her surroundings, as if she were emerging from an echoing well. Brushing strands of hair from across her face, she noticed the arrival of a few others and trailed them toward the source of the music.

Approaching *Ashé Isée*, she could see the Big Lodge standing open to the sky, sheathed around with verdant cottonwood cuttings apart from the entrance that faced the sunrise. A small crowd of people clustered by the opening, the elderly in camp chairs, one person huddled in a wheelchair. Behind them stood supporting friends and family of the supplicants inside the lodge. The gathering was varied in composition – old, young, infirm, healthy.

Despite feeling strange and out of place, Yancy was drawn toward the warbling voices overlaying the staccato beat of the booming drum encircled by seated players, their arms rising and falling in precision, as if connected by a mesmerizing, unseen thread.

Seeing that she was not the only non-Native present, Yancy advanced, joining the group of observers.

The song charged the air with power, awe pulsing. Eagle bone whistles called to *Akbaatatdía*, the Maker.

As the afternoon faded toward dusk, she began to understand her pilgrimage to Sun Dance. Why God had brought her here, to this place.

Raising her eyes to the fleeting clouds, Yancy set free her own prayer for Kara.

Energy Barons

Chapter 44

Awkward was the understatement of the year when it came to describing the situation in Allie's motel room. With Sawyer rolled up in his sleeping bag on the floor, Allie felt like she was living in a glass house, constantly under scrutiny. She should have felt reassured having her own personal guardian, a man who had kept treacherous foes at bay on inhospitable shores, in scorching deserts and rugged mountains.

None of that mattered a whit. There was a man whom she barely knew, keeping watch next to *her* bed. That didn't equate with assurance or comfort, because this was anything but comfortable.

As a result, she'd slept fitfully, alternately awakened with the unseemly thought that she might be snoring to even more improper speculations of what it would be like if he abandoned his place on the floor and climbed into her bed.

Mentally slapping herself for even entertaining such preposterous half-dreams, she'd turned over, tried to banish the thoughts and capture some actual sleep, without any real success.

Waking before her, Sawyer was already in the shower before she pulled herself out from under the covers. He was still in the bathroom when the phone jolted her out of the depths of a steamy dream, immediately afraid that she might have prattled in her sleep.

"I see you have a guest." It was Esteban. She could swear there was a smirk in his remark.

"An uninvited one," she snarled, not particularly happy with either one of the men who had invaded her world. "And how did you know?" She could here the water running and wondered if Esteban could too.

"Did you think we'd abandoned you?"

Chagrined, she asked how long he'd known the room was a double occupancy.

"Since he arrived." Now she could tell he was covering his amusement. Some straight-faced FBI goon *he* was. "I hope you had a pleasant visit," added Esteban.

"It was an encounter of the peculiar kind and wholly unexpected, which you probably knew," she said, insinuating that the place was likely bugged. "So I suppose you are also aware that he didn't trust you to be vigilant enough."

"Worried about you?" The chuckle was only a hint.

"I guess." Allie tried to blow it off as being of no real account. "We played cribbage all evening and he slept on the floor."

Esteban said nothing more than what would pass for a grunt. *Typical*, thought Allie.

"I suggest he head out before you go to the Green office to connect with your subjects."

"You make it sound like this is a scientific experiment." She sighed. *This whole thing is such a pain.* She reconsidered. *Two pains... in the tush.* "I'll tell him you said so." She heard the bathroom door open, "Actually, you can tell him yourself."

Sawyer emerged dressed only in his jeans, rubbing his hair dry with a towel, a question on his face.

"I hope you left me some hot water. Here, it's for you," Allie thrust the phone at him while she grabbed her clothes and tromped off to the bathroom.

"Hello," Sawyer said into the phone, wondering what had fired up his roommate's temper.

"Esteban."

That answered that.

"What are you doing there?" asked the FBI agent.

"What you aren't. Keeping an eye on your little spy."

"What? You don't trust us to do our job?" He couldn't help being snide.

"You, I trust. It's the wildcard you have holed up in this mangy hotel room," said Sawyer.

"Man, I hope she's out of earshot or *you're* gonna get an earful."

"She already woke up on the wrong side of the bed. I suspect that's your doing," accused Sawyer.

"Probably. Look, you need to get yourself gone before she leaves for the Green Grasslands office. Your hanging around is only an additional hazard to the arrangement."

"Like she couldn't have a boyfriend come to visit?" Sawyer regretted the words as soon as he said them.

Esteban ignored the unintended innuendo. "That's not the point, other than the fact that a good reporter is not going to bring her gigolo along on a story, it could crush the rapport she's established."

Sawyer couldn't argue with the fact that he couldn't very well show up as Allie's fan club, but he was determined to keep her within view until this whole thing was over. He couldn't explain why he felt this way to himself and he sure as hell wasn't going to try with Esteban. "Look, I'm staying until this thing is closed up, one way or the other."

Esteban was combing his hand through his hair on the other end of the line. This is just what he needed, some rigid ex-marine getting into the middle of things. It was on the verge of becoming an unholy mess. Using a reporter as an informant had to be one of the dumbest ideas he'd ever conceived. "And how do you propose to do that?"

"You let me ride with you."

"No way. No how." Esteban was proud of himself for keeping his tone restrained when he really wanted to let fly an obscenity.

"It's that or I follow her on my own," Sawyer knew he was walking the line but determined all the same, not that he could figure out why he even cared.

"And risk getting arrested for interfering with an investigation?"

"If this were an official operation, you might have me over a barrel. But it's not and you don't. I'm riding with you."

Esteban could hear the stubbornness in Aleman's voice and knew he couldn't win. Sighing in defeat, he acquiesced and slapped shut his phone, muttering that expletive he'd been holding back.

Wisps of milky cirrus skimmed across the otherwise cobalt sky. A good day to raise a windmill, thought Allie, the winds were high aloft, not raking the plains. *Lucky. There's nothing like trying to put*

up a windmill in a gale.

"Blow ye winds a-afterward," she sang to an old folk tune, remembering her grandfather's tenor intoning the heartbreaking melody of a pioneer going west to make his fortune only to meet a tragic end.

Once again tugging open the front door of Green Grasslands bearing gifts – Allie didn't want to wear out her welcome – she twisted to block it open with her hip, half backing into the office. Today she'd downscaled to Entenmann's and a bag of apples, not even organic. Her pocketbook had reminded her she was on unpaid leave and the FBI wasn't offering to spring for breakfast, just a moldy motel room with a surly houseguest. So she'd settled on plebian vittles.

Besides, even I can handle only so much sugar.

"Oh. You are so-o guut, und kind! You did not have to supply us with morning fare each day," Ilse smiled widely. "But it iss appreciated. Hmmm," she hummed as she ignored the apples and opened the box, removing a donut, hard-glazed with chocolate.

"I just want to do my part. It's good of all of you to allow me to tag along on your projects," Allie schmoozed, which wasn't one of her better qualities, but she was working on her technique. "Are Toby and A´zam here yet?"

"No. Toby called und they are on ze way."

With little to do but wait, Allie meandered around the office sifting through the newspapers and brochures, and examining the exhibits since she had the time. She roamed down the hall toward the open office doors, poking her head in to get a better look inside. As she moseyed by the director's office, Race waved at her, unable to pull himself away from his phone conversation. She smiled, waved back and moved along.

The door to the back room was ajar and she decided to take a peek, pushing it wider. Allie entered casually, checking out the wall art, which consisted of topographic and geological survey maps. There was a folded document on the table and she decided to take a look.

Hey, the door was open, nothing private here, right? For some reason, the hair on the nape of her neck itched as she opened up what was another map.

It was the same one that had been on the wall the day before. The colored pushpins had been removed but she followed a barely perceptibly traced line that traveled west through southern Wyoming, intersecting with numerous other lines crossing north, south, and east through the center of the state. This particular line had three areas marked in red. A hurried glance at the legend showed that the lines indicated oil and natural gas pipelines.

Skin crawling with warning, she mentally noted the locations of the crimson blots before quickly folding the map back over. Telling herself not to be stupid, that there was nothing sinister here and she was just letting her imagination run wild, she sauntered out of the room just as Toby walked in the back door with A´zam close on his heels.

For an instant, she froze, a shot of panic rocketing through her. It was gone as fast as it had come and she greeted the men with a blasé smile, uncertain if they'd noticed from where she'd just exited. *Not that it matters. There was nothing to see. Mm-hmm. You keep repeating it and maybe it'll come true.*

Toby hailed her affably enough, but A´zam's inscrutability unnerved her. His expression was hard to read. A vibe of distrust, or was it carefully concealed disdain?

"Ready to head out?" asked the project manager.

"Yep. Got all my gear up front. Brought in some munchies if you want or are we in a hurry?"

"No. We have time and I could use a cup of joe. Come on," and he guided her back down the hall to the lobby.

A´zam said nothing, silently maneuvering around Blaine and Allie with a nod of his head that sent shivers up her spine.

Eerie guy.

Chapter 45

Landing at Anchorage International Airport this time around Solana hadn't been in a hurry to catch a connecting flight, giving her time to properly take in her setting. Juneau's backdrop had impressed her and the largest city in Alaska could do no less.

From the rear seat of her taxi Sol had been able to gawk unabashed at all the snow-capped ranges ringing the basin, the city situated at the base of the Chugach Mountains climbing high above its eastern flank. The clarity of the evening revealed Mt. McKinley to the northwest, twilight shades of cerise, vermilion and crimson swathing it from summit to foot, towering over the peaks of the Alaska Range. The Kenai Mountains were visible to the south, marching down the peninsula of the same name along the Cook Inlet, which the city straddled at its northernmost point.

When she had taken possession of her hotel room, Sol had entertained herself for the better part of an hour, sipping a glass of wine while drinking in the glorious view from her balcony. The late spring night hadn't descended into total blackness for long but that hadn't disturbed her sleep, tired as she'd been.

This was a new day and she had work to do. Sightseeing wasn't going to be part of the agenda, but she had resolved to come back with Toddy to do just that. Maybe they'd drive the Alcan Highway. *Why not?* Wouldn't that be a kick, though they'd need a month or two to do it right.

Without warning, her stomach flip-flopped and redirected her thoughts to getting through the interview she'd arranged in less than an hour. Pulling herself together, Sol scooped up her bag and left.

Arriving in an area of downtown where the buildings ranged from statehood era to postmodern, Sol entered the sanctuary of yet another Rural Resources office. The businesslike atmosphere was nowhere near as welcoming as its counterpart in Juneau. The sign on the front door had even indicated a resident attorney among the occupants.

No surprise there. From what Sol had read online this was the headquarters from which most of the officious legal work emanated. On the wall to the right of the reception counter were listed the co-habitants. Name, title and corporate association. Rural Resources appeared to be joint tenants of the space with, of course, EcoEarth Legal Center. *So, they're in cahoots. Conspiracies at every turn*, she taunted herself.

The older woman who came to the counter was a no-nonsense character dressed in Coldwater Creek bush trendiness, if there was such a thing. Reconsidering her first impression, Sol decided that she just *looked* older. Weather-beaten was the better adjective because she was probably about Sol's age, who clocked in at thirty-seven. Evidently, she spent much of her life outdoors and, for all Alaska's beauty, if you didn't take care of your skin, you'd be a leathery fifty by the age of thirty. On top of that she exuded attitude and didn't appear all that thrilled to see Sol.

Stuffy old biddy.

Sol reproached herself for not being charitable. The biddy had yet to say a word. Pasting a smile on her own face, Sol took the first step by introducing herself.

"Yes, I remember you called to see about speaking with some staff members about our work here." No offered hand or name. Sol had pegged her right. Biddy. *She probably prefers grizzlies to humans. Like that guy who got himself half-eaten by a monster bear in Kamchatka a few years ago. That's what happens when you try to hug nature. It doesn't return the sentiments.*

"I'm glad that you were able to accommodate me. It's a long trip from the southwest." The woman managed a half-hearted smile that pretty much said she wasn't interested where Sol was from and would prefer that she went back without delay. Accommodation was the last thing on the receptionist's mind from her drab reaction. Sol raised an eyebrow to prompt some kind of answer.

Seeing that the intruder was intent on staying, the woman deigned to speak.

"Well, we're glad to be of help," her tone said she was anything but. "I'm Tommie, the director's assistant."

"What an unusual name. It has a great ring for a woman," said Sol. "Commanding yet delicate."

That actually mitigated some of Tommie's tension. "Short for Tomasina, which has always been too much of a mouthful. I'm more the simple type."

"Will you be my guide today, then?"

"You are stuck with me by default, I'm afraid. Most of the management is out of the office," said Tommie, still not giving much in the way of personality development.

"So, where do we start?" With that Tommie came around the counter and led Sol on the grand tour of Rural Resources Anchorage.

As they trekked through a fairly spacious complex, Sol inquired about the co-operative tenancy of the two entities, Rural Resources and EcoEarth. Not much explanation was supplied other than the fact that the two often worked together on environmental issues. Nor was Tommie apt to elaborate on the actual work that the attorney did. He wasn't in, in any case. He was busy filing an injunction at the state courthouse just a few blocks away. Tommie also wasn't interested in sharing the details of that lawsuit.

In fact, she wasn't interested in sharing much of anything about the two groups. Sol's obvious Native American heritage wasn't of any particular interest to Tommie. This group had a differing viewpoint on the Native connection to the environment than most other conservation groups she'd encountered. The public displays and exhibits had more the sense of shrines created in reverence for the untouched earth rather than being plainly informative or even scientific in nature, which was the least she'd expected. Most often there was some kind of veneration for the ancient wisdom of Native peoples among many environmental organizations. The essence of this office tended toward a commercialized non-profit religion, a bustling mission to save blessed earth by blocking the spread of civilization through litigation. Prayer meetings equaled legal strategizing. This was an enlightened faith.

Tommie was cordial enough to give Sol an overview of a couple of the reclamation projects in which Rural Resources was taking an active role. Even these projects that targeted old mine dumps threatening salmon runs, were given a hasty once-over. She plied Tommie with questions, but it didn't appear that her guide was all that well versed in the details. *Ah, so that's the answer to the haughtiness... she has no answers. Easier to be snotty than informed.* Nor did she know much about the lawsuit against Corcoran Creek, other than basics. It was evident from some of Tommie's comments, however, that this office was deeply involved in the case.

Coming back down the stairs, they were starting up the hall when Sol was surprised to glimpse the same Middle Eastern exchange student she'd seen just days ago in Juneau. He ducked into one of the front rooms before Sol could approach, but she was certain this was the same tall fellow from the other Rural Resources office.

Sol turned to Tommie and asked if it was all within a day's work to hop between the two offices.

Looking a little puzzled, Tommie asked her what she meant.

"The young man who just disappeared into that office as we passed. I met him briefly when I visited the Juneau branch a few days back," explained Sol.

"Oh, the exchange student. He's a specialist on oil distribution. He worked in the field in his home country before coming to the states to get an advanced degree in environmental science," she finally opened up a little. Apparently his contribution to the office was esteemed. "He's a huge asset. His knowledge of the industry is well beyond what most of our staff or volunteers can offer despite the fact that the environmental impact is different here. You know, coming from arid deserts to lush forests and frozen tundra. They are quite dissimilar eco-systems."

"I can imagine. I don't suppose he'd care to field a few questions about his experiences?" asked Sol hopefully.

"Doubtful. He shies away from people he doesn't know, particularly women. It's a cultural thing, I'm told."

"Quite. I fully understand. Too bad, though." She tried another tack, "Can you tell me what he's working on?"

"To my knowledge, he's been assisting the senior organization members and legal counsel to understand the movement of oil through pipelines. Weaknesses and strengths of the structures, etc. Something of a resident expert helping them to make their legal arguments in cases that are pending."

"That is interesting. It's disappointing that he won't share some of that with the media. Most of us are pretty sympathetic to the cause." Which was the truth. It just didn't happen to be her general viewpoint.

"He has his ways and I've been given direction to leave him to his own devices." Instead, Tommie showed Sol around the couple of open offices and conference rooms as they headed back toward the front of the building.

One room in the back boasted a number of satellite maps of Alaska tacked to the wall, including detailed charts of major mining operations and a couple of the Alaska Pipeline snaking through the interior. One even had similar colored tacks embedded along the route as did the map in Juneau.

Sol would rather avoid drawing too much attention to her interest in the wall decor but felt that she couldn't let the opportunity slip. "Tell me, Tommie, why do some of these maps have pushpins while others don't."

"Some of these maps depict projects that the legal committee is in the process of investigating. I'm not sure what the tacks indicate. Ecologically sensitive areas, perhaps?" She shrugged it off as being of little interest and led Sol back out into the hall.

Sol thanked Tommie for her time and expertise, this time receiving a faint smile and cool handshake before walking out the door.

Just as she was leaving the office, Sol turned to see the oil distribution expert emerge from one of the doors and move up the back stairwell. She was perfectly happy to depart such a grim place. If these people were truly engaging in the gallant fight to save the planet, they were sadly lacking the one sentiment that Sol thought would be most needed to be successful… Hope.

Returning to the hotel, Sol tried to decide what to do next. It was still early and she had the afternoon to blow. Unloading her gear onto the desk, she remembered her conversation with Allie just last night. It brought to mind the off-hand comment about it being the same guy from Wyoming that had showed up in Juneau. As preposterous as it sounded yesterday, seeing the man in two places in one week made her rethink that assumption.

What if it was the same man? He just happened to be some kind of expert in oil distribution and what is one of the things they produce in Wyoming besides coal, cattle and cowboys? Oil.

She checked her watch. It was eleven-thirty in Anchorage, which made it two hours later in Mountain Time.

Okay, lets' see if there's something to this little cabal, and she punched in Allie's number. She had to wade through the latest of her friend's horrific choices in ring tones. This one was Richard Harris crooning poorly about MacArthur Park. *What is she thinking? Maybe this whole deal is melting her brain like the song's icing in the rain. Somebody should have left him strung up on that pole in "A Man Called Horse."* As much as Sol liked the actor, this was a prodigious travesty as far as music went. And it went on and on. Finally, Allie's voice said to leave a message. *Thank God.*

"Allie. Remember that Middle Eastern student we discussed last night? Well, you may have hit on something. The same guy from Juneau was at the Anchorage office this morning, and, believe it or not, he's an expert in oil distribution who's getting an advanced degree in environmental science. *And*, there was another map of the Alaska Pipeline marked with colored tacks. Could be nothing but I think you ought to tell your FBI guy. Oh, and by the way, *please* dump that awful ring tone. It's nauseating." Which was something Sol understood better than she ever thought possible, feeling her stomach roil again.

It couldn't have been that *bad.*

Chapter 46

The minor contingent of eco-warriors didn't leave the Green Grasslands office until well after ten a.m. by which time the two occupants of the dirt brown Crown Vic were already getting on each other's nerves.

Esteban was beyond pissed about the whole situation of having an unwelcome companion warming the gunfighter's post. He'd kept his mouth clamped except to imbibe a little coffee now and again. Assuming that they were going to be cooped up in the sedan for hours, he wasn't interested in having to go hunt up a restroom at some inopportune time. His companion was a dozen-year veteran of the Corps who had pulled all kinds of filthy duty in the world's backwaters and mud holes of Afghanistan and the Middle East. Esteban figured Aleman for being able to hold his water for weeks at a time if the command to do so had come down from on high.

Well, hell. He's here now. I may as well get used to it.

They sat side-by-side sipping cold java in a parking spot that wasn't the best but, considering the circumstances, was as good as it got. Esteban had followed Blaine's decrepit, air-fouling rig, Allie ensconced in the passenger seat, to the high school where the truck had driven on campus and around back of the main buildings.

He couldn't very well follow the guy onto the school grounds, which left Esteban out front where he couldn't see what was happening. That was no good.

He continued to drive around the block trying to get a better view of the pick-up. Locating an area where he could observe the truck, there was no place to park without being so conspicuous that someone might call the cops. That was the last thing Esteban needed in this sideshow he was calling a surveillance op.

He settled for a spot where he and Aleman could see some of the activity between the hidden parking area and the garden plot where the support pole had been placed, ready for the windmill to be mounted. They'd be able to see any comings and goings, as well as when the truck left campus.

It would have to do.

Allie and Toby climbed down from the cab of the worn out truck as A´zam drove up in a snappy Hyundai mini-SUV.

I wonder how he rates such a spiffy ride when the good 'ol boy is stuck with a menace to the ozone layer, thought Allie, watching the Arab student get out of the car. She stood back while the guys began sorting through tools and equipment piled in the truck bed.

A few minutes later a cute young thing in her early twenties, light brown hair pulled back in a shoulder length ponytail who looked like a teacher's assistant to Allie, arrived with a flatbed cart steered by a couple of strapping seniors. They'd come along to assist the men from Green Grasslands, shoulder the burden of loading and unloading the heavy supplies and transport it to the construction site.

Peering out the windshield, Esteban and Sawyer caught sight of the threesome. A woman, closer to a girl in appearance by what they could discern, was leading two male students built like football players, guiding a heavy-duty cart from a shed in the direction of where the truck and pony-sized SUV had disappeared behind a building.

The next thing they saw was the whole troop, including Blaine, the Middle Eastern student and Allie, heading from their parking area toward the garden which was positioned behind the gym and way off to the side of the track. They abandoned the cart to sit unattended next to the pole, whose base had been sunk in the garden's midst, and entered a nearby building. More like a Quonset hut, to Esteban's thinking. *Probably the right age to be one, too.*

Nobody left the rounded metal structure for some time, though a group of underclassmen straggled in from one of the main campus buildings.

"They must be conducting a lecture for the classes," said Esteban glancing down at his watch.

The sound of his voice breaking the enforced silence would have made Sawyer jump if he hadn't spent so many years waiting patiently for all hell to break loose, which, all too often, it had.

"It's taking awhile," added the agent after assessing how much time had passed since the last class had entered.

"You know teenagers. Can't keep their focus worth a damn. They'll probably be there for a good hour, is my guess," said Sawyer

Esteban eyed his unauthorized partner amusedly. "Can't keep their mind on the environmental catastrophe that they're expected to prevent? Why would you think that?"

"What teens have you ever known, yourself included, who could think of anything other than their raging hormones?"

"Sex or the environment," Esteban weighed his hands up and down. "Hmmm, which topic would occupy them most. You have a point," he conceded. "How many times do you figure the guys from the Green office will have to repeat themselves?"

"At least a dozen." The ice finally broken, both men chuckled at the thought of the environmentalists trying to keep a bunch of attention deficit high school students engaged with the concepts of utilizing wind power.

Eventually two groups of fifteen or so students poured out of the building, obviously weary of sitting inside and listening to the mechanics of green technology, definitely ready to get back outside and enjoy the sunshine. With a bit more liveliness than what they'd entered with, the classes maundered over to the neat garden, which was now overshadowed by a telephone pole sans the creosote coating. The teacher's aide and a tall man, likely a science teacher, herded the kids to move with more alacrity.

A ladder was propped against one side of the pole. The other had a line of foot pegs solidly imbedded in a pattern all the way up to the top. Through the binoculars, Esteban watched while Blaine had the teacher's aide shoo the kids into a circle around the cart where the windmill lay, ready for assembly and installation.

While Esteban and Sawyer watched from the distance, Blaine and A´zam pulled components off of the cart and began assembling the housing for the motor. A fair number of the boys and maybe five girls were attentive to the work being done. The rest of the students yakked among themselves, a few of them milled around the perimeter of the circle. The male teacher and the young aide kept an eye on the crew. Allie was moving around the edges shooting photos.

It took maybe half an hour to finish assembling both the cover and the blades. Taking what looked like the motor, Blaine put it in a backpack and gave it to his partner who slung it over his shoulder. A´zam climbed the ladder and Blaine donned a harness reminiscent of equipment worn by telephone linemen and scrambled up the pegs on the pole. Meeting at the top, Blaine adjusted the harness for support, then accepted the motor from A´zam and attached it to a footing that had already been mounted. While he was securing the motor, he sent A´zam back down to the ground to connect the dual blades and housing to an apparatus so the whole thing could be hauled up by a rope and pulley device.

Sawyer couldn't see all the detail work, but it looked like the team was well rehearsed for the operation. He assumed they had either practiced or they'd done this kind of work before.

The assembly was lugged up the pole with A´zam guiding it from the ladder. Once near the top, they managed to get the blades and housing into place, tightening bolts and checking it thoroughly before moving back down the pole.

As Blaine slowly made his way down the pegs, he carefully examined the wiring and insulated cable attached to the length of the pole.

The diverted students' attention returned when he hit the ground, greeting him with sporadic applause. The whole process had taken a good hour and Blaine appeared pretty whipped as he disconnected the harness.

Although there wasn't much wind to speak of, after the team checked all the connections and went inside a nearby shed, the windmill began to drift with the breeze, the blades turning listlessly.

This time there was a more resounding round of applause from the small crowd as Blaine came out and began speaking to the kids one more time, his sidekick standing by the shed door.

At that point, from what Esteban and Sawyer could see, the demonstration was at a close. It looked like the guests thanked the students and teachers, dismissing them back to their classrooms. The aide directed the same two boys to help load the tools and whatever else was there back onto the cart.

The surveillance team watched as the six remaining figures walked back to where the cars were parked beyond their vision. A few minutes later, the teacher's aide went with the boys as they returned the cart from whence it had been retrieved and headed back into the school building. Some time later they observed the Hyundai drive out from behind the building and peel off back toward the Green Grasslands office, A´zam at the wheel.

Ten minutes later, the beater truck pulled out and Esteban put the Crown Vic in gear and trailed behind the rig, it's two occupants just visible through the dirty back window.

Energy Barons

Chapter 47

Time was ticking by, minute by agonizing minute, as Sawyer and Esteban twiddled their thumbs waiting for their spook *du jour* to resurface from the depths of environmental sublimation, i.e. the Green Grasslands headquarters. They'd been cooped up in the big sedan watching as nothing happened.

No Allie.

"What could possibly be taking her so long?" Esteban was edging toward frustration. He'd left a voicemail, knowing she had probably neglected to turn her phone back on. The Ford Focus was still parked up the street idly awaiting its mistress' return. "It's doubtful she went anywhere. Any change of plans and she would have alerted me."

"You've seen her when she's on a story. If she thinks there's a possibility of unearthing new facts, you know she won't let go until she hits pay dirt," said Sawyer.

"That must be her most endearing asset," said Esteban, flippantly.

Eying him askance, Sawyer wasn't sure who the agent meant to poke fun at, Allie or him for having taken an interest in her welfare. "She's probably got them all cornered with her tape recorder and notebook drawn, frightened for their lives, or bad publicity."

Esteban wasn't buying it. "Not amusing. We had an agreement that if she was running late, she'd call."

"She's a reporter, not a messenger," laughed Sawyer, though without any real conviction. He was becoming troubled by her absence.

Pulling out his cell phone, Esteban said, "I suppose I could check again…"

He was interrupted mid-sentence by the bleating of the phone he'd just extracted from his belt carrier. Assuming it was Allie, or hoping so, he didn't bother to check the LCD window, just answered the phone.

It wasn't Allie. It was the lead criminologist that had been working on the Gillette bombings.

"Special Agent Esteban. I've been looking for you."

"You got something new?"

"You might say that. I got hauled in almost as a fluke on an interesting find up there in the Big Horn Mountains. A family traveling to Yellowstone just happened to trip over a dead body along Route 16, in Ten Sleep Canyon. Looks like it'd been there for a good week."

"And this has to do with…?" Esteban was wondering where this was going.

"The tests just came in and the lab found Semtex residue on his clothes and his hands. Well, hand. One of them was missing. Chewed off by some coyote or other scavenger."

"So, you're thinking this could be our guy," said Esteban.

Sawyer was paying attention now, wondering whom the agent was speaking to.

"*One* of our guys. He was shot in the back and the head. Looks like an execution. Headshot was to assure death," added the crime scene tech.

"Any I.D.?"

"Yeah. His driver's license gives a Denver address but turns out he's a student at CSU in Fort Collins."

Esteban's jaw clenched in apprehension with each new morsel of information the tech imparted. Explosives, executed and student ID. "What else?"

"The sheriff up here did some checking and the kid was volunteering someplace down where you are now. You are in Cheyenne, right?"

"Yeah. Where was he working?"

"Some environmental organization name of," and he paused to look at his notes to make sure he got the name right, "Green Grasslands."

"Shit." Esteban was hard-pressed to speak civilly. This was turning into the worst scenario possible. "And you're just calling me now? You found the kid, when." It was a demand, not a request, which really caught the CSI off-guard.

"Couple of days ago. Like I said, we just got the lab report. That's why I'm calling you."

Careful not to let his temper loose again, Esteban told the investigator thanks for the information and hung-up.

"What was that all about?" Sawyer was catching every one of Esteban's vibes, and they weren't making him happy. "Because it wasn't Allie."

"No. It was the lead crime scene investigator from the bombings." He took a breath. He didn't want Aleman overreacting. He gave the other man in the front seat a good once-over and realized that wasn't likely. He'd read the former marine's bio. Keeping a cool head under fire was something he'd been noted for. "Evidently, he was asked to accompany the sheriff to a scene in the mountains since he was nearby and available."

"And?" Sawyer was attempting to stay composed when he knew he wasn't going to like the answer.

"... And it turns out they located a dead body by the roadside that just happened to have a college ID card in his wallet and explosive residue on his person." He pierced Aleman with a steady gaze, daring him to maintain control. "And they traced him to working here as an intern."

"Here? *Where* here. Green Grasslands?"

"Yes."

"Hell," said Sawyer so coldly a frigid wind seemed to blow through the Crown Vic. "Where's Allie?"

After the space of a few painfully silent seconds, Sawyer punched a number into his cell phone and held it to his ear. Patience nearly gone, he willed the ringing to stop and a voice to answer.

"You're not calling Allie," stated Esteban, still trying to decide if he should try her phone. The stakes in the game had just changed dramatically.

"No."

"Who, then," demanded the agent.

"A friend," was all Sawyer would say.

Esteban just lifted an eyebrow and waited.

"This is Sawyer. What's Allie doing in there?"

Esteban was perplexed by the question Aleman had posed the person on the other end. He formed the word "who?" with his mouth but Sawyer ignored him.

"She's not here," said Rain after picking up. He was busy at his filing chore in the front office.

"Not there? We saw her drive up with that guy in the truck." He could feel a whicker of anxiety run across his skin.

"That's a woman named Lydia. She's a helper here and a teacher's assistant at the high school." Rain said, the trace of a question in his voice.

Sawyer ended the call with a curse.

Chapter 48

It was a good day's work.

The kids had drifted in and out, their attention span not much better than a gerbil's, but they had responded well on the whole and a few of them were completely absorbed by the activity. Before closing up the whole session, Blaine took a minute to explain that there was one element left to the project. He'd told them that the next seminar would be to participate in the installation of the battery bank that will store the energy collected by the wind turbine, connecting the system components and bringing it all online. Their teacher would walk them through the schematics before they observe completion of the project.

The teacher's aide stood aside while Toby directed the two boys on reloading the flatbed cart with the tools and remaining equipment, A'zam helping here and there. The group then walked back to the parking lot, the boys drawing the burden and leaving Toby and A'zam to catch a little break. As they neared the vehicles, Esteban lost view of the entourage.

Allie had been busy taking notes and recording some of the initial lecture. She spent most of her effort shooting photos during the demonstration, pausing to write down what the two men were doing at the top of the pole. She had real respect for their professionalism and agility, but mostly with their ability to work at twenty feet above the ground, harness or no.

She wasn't a big fan of heights, and definitely wasn't interested in getting in any precarious spot without a safety net. Even a cherry picker wouldn't do the trick for her. She may swing by the seat of her pants when it came to her job, but always with two feet planted on terra firma.

About halfway through the installation process, Allie was talking with the aide, a nice young woman working on her teaching credential, when she felt her phone vibrate in her pocket. She reckoned she'd check the message when things wound down, after she finished interviewing Lydia and before they packed up. After watching the two men handle the group of distracted kids, she was less apt to believe that they were some kind of closet terrorists, and the thought of checking her voicemail simply slipped away after a while.

Toby put the final touches on the afternoon by releasing the brake to allow the windmill to catch what breath of air there was, letting the blades spin uselessly at the top of the pole. The system wouldn't be fully operable until the battery system was installed. With that, the students were released back to their classes and they prepared to call it a day.

Allie watched as the two young athletes took care of repacking the truck. While Toby and A´zam shook hands with the boys, thanking them and the TA, she remembered her phone and pulled it out to check the message.

The Green Grasslands employee and intern were tying down the equipment and stowing tools as Allie listened to the voicemail. A´zam looked up and saw her expression change to one of consternation.

He reached over and tugged on Blaine's sleeve, nodding in her direction. Barely above a whisper, he said, "Something is not right."

Blaine's eyes followed A´zam's to witness the shadow of concern fall across their tagalong's face. His gaze narrowed slightly as she turned her own on the team as they finished their task and climbed down from the truck bed.

A quizzical turn to her head, Allie decided there was no time like the present to follow-up on the suggestion that had been left on her phone. "Have you heard from your friend, the other exchange student I met last time I was here? I sort of assumed that you are friends, both of you having traveled all the way from Lebanon." Her attempt to sound innocuous didn't really ring sincere, even to her ears.

A´zam nodded agreeably. "Yes, I believe I told you that."

"That's right, you did." Allie acted as if he'd jogged her hazy memory. "You do keep in touch, don't you?"

"Occasionally. Lebanon is a small country." She noticed his lack of inclination to enlarge on the topic.

"As I remember, it was mentioned that he had been transferred. Did you mean to a different office or perhaps another school? I'm curious about how the exchange program works." *Hopefully that'll cover the reason for my questions*, though she hardly believed it, feeling his uneasiness. "If I write this well, the story might prompt the interest of other educational institutions to investigate and expand program possibilities." *There, that should help.*

Wariness crept into A´zam's eyes, making them appear black in the afternoon sun.

"He has finished his study for this year and was invited to join another program," supplied A´zam, hoping that assuaged her inquisitiveness.

"That's terrific. Did he move to a different state? Is the new program also with Green Grasslands?"

"He is like me. We go where we are asked to participate and can be of the most use." She could sense his resistance growing, not that that ever deterred her before.

A´zam thought to curtail any further questioning by adding, "He can be of little help to your story since he is no longer in this office."

"Oh, I didn't want to disturb him in his new position, I was just interested in whether there is an established network of groups that sponsor student interns." Allie wasn't going to be dissuaded from this line of inquiry. Sol had left some very revealing news on her phone and Allie thought her friend was on to something. Allie's gut being what it was, she knew she couldn't allow herself to let the subject go.

Allie also had a tendency toward tunnel vision, so while she focused on the Arab student, she had completely lost track of her chauffeur.

"I'd heard there was a program up in Alaska. I don't suppose your friend transferred up there. I mean there must be a dozen places to choose from." *Pretty lame, but maybe I can skid by on that.*

Toby had been standing next to the pick-up, leaning his hip indolently on the tailgate. As calm as he appeared, his mind was running laps trying to decide what their options were because he'd already concluded that there was a real problem brewing here. Her questions seemed to have much more of a point than the frivolous spin she was attempting to put on the nature of her snooping.

Taking stock of the situation, he noted that they were secluded from any classrooms or offices, completely out of view in an area that was virtually a dead-end loading dock. All of the other parking spaces were empty and there were no windows facing their direction. Allie had her back to him and was thoroughly engaged in her conversation with A´zam.

It was a make or break moment.

Reaching into the still open toolbox, Toby extracted a vice-grip and clocked the reporter before he could entertain second thoughts. Allie collapsed to the pavement in a nerveless heap.

A´zam just stared at Blaine for the briefest of seconds, accusation fleeting in his eyes, rapidly replaced with acceptance and resolve.

They didn't speak. Blaine reached back into the toolbox and removed a handful of plastic cable ties he kept for binding parts together to ease hauling. Giving half to A´zam, they trussed Allie's wrists and ankles and lugged her over to the Hyundai, loading her into the rear.

A´zam went into the back seat and grabbed a couple of rags he kept for general use. Today they'd come in handy as a gag and blindfold.

The Green Grasslands staff didn't take time to discuss the new dilemma.

"You know where to go," said Blaine succinctly. "I'll cover for you at the office. Scram."

Closing the SUV's rear hatch that was darkened with privacy glass all around, A´zam pulled his keys out of his pocket, jammed them in the ignition and drove out of the parking lot without argument. He turned toward the office and made his way swiftly down the block without actually speeding. As soon as he was half a mile away, he turned off toward the edge of town.

Toby waited patiently until Lydia reappeared. She was finished for the day and had been expecting to catch a ride back to the Green Grasslands office with the exchange student.

Sitting on the tailgate as if he hadn't a care in the world, Toby got up when Lydia rounded the corner, surprised that A´zam was gone and the project manager waiting in his place.

"The reporter, Allie Maitland? She had some more questions for A´zam but needed to get back to the office to get the story submitted. It seems her editor was riding her to get back to Denver. So we decided you could ride with me since I wasn't in any hurry." He shrugged his shoulders. "Nothing else pending."

He rose to his feet and closed up the rear.

"That's fine by me." She smiled and hopped in the passenger seat.

Energy Barons

Chapter 49

Westbound on Interstate 80, the Green Grasslands intern was staying well within the parameters of the posted speed limit. The last thing on his to-do list was an impromptu visit with a state patrolman during a traffic stop. His current conveyance wasn't as stylish as the little Hyundai had been, but it also wasn't as conspicuous as a bright, bitty import job would be zipping through rural Wyoming. The Oldsmobile Calais was ancient by new millennium auto standards, but it was reliable, easy to service and roomy where it counted – the trunk.

After rolling away from the high school, A´zam had taken a circuitous route through town before pulling up behind a boarded-up grocery store. Stowed in the waiting vehicle had been supplies, including food, water, extra clothing and a first aid kit. The kit had a few extras that weren't standard equipment. Next to the snakebite anti-venom and epinephrine were a number of doses of various narcotics and antibiotics. Removing a vial of a strong sedative, he had prepared an injection for his passenger.

He'd popped the rear hatch just as his hostage was groggily rolling her head, trying to focus on her whereabouts. He administered the shot, heading off any feistiness but knowing it wouldn't take full effect until after he'd be able to get her up on wobbly legs just long enough to make the transfer to her new quarters, the boot of the '85 Calais. He removed the restraints from her ankles to move her, attaching new ties after forcing her into her new accommodation. Once entombed in the carpeted compartment, he had double-checked to be sure she was losing consciousness, and dropped the trunk lid.

Glimpsing the clock on the dash, he calculated when his team member would be underway. Taking into consideration Blaine's need to make excuses at the office, cover tracks at the residence and switch his own vehicle at a preset location, A´zam presumed he had a few hours head start.

Evening was rolling in across the plain like a midnight tide as he motored up the sparsely populated highway. The dose he'd given the reporter would keep her under well into the early morning hours.

With all their bases covered, he settled in for a long drive.

Chapter 50

Parked in front of the last known address of one Toby Blaine, Sawyer and Rain considered their options. Using his volunteer position at Green Grasslands, Rain had surreptitiously collected pertinent information on the current personnel at the office, including the project manager.

Trust was more a character flaw than a quality to Rain. It had to be earned. Holding his temporary position too briefly to give any of them a pass, he'd managed a peek at all their files.

The German girl appeared flighty enough, but Rain wasn't inclined to rely on appearances. Stupid people didn't earn places in highly competitive exchange programs, politically correct ones with the grade point average did. As for the director, his assessment of Race Carson was one of personal conviction to a benevolent concept, no matter how asinine. Head in the clouds rather than being firmly rooted to the earth that he so fervently wished to protect. The Lebanese student's story didn't wash with him either, and although Rain himself stayed aloof in a sense, A´zam was wary, a prowler.

Toby Blaine was the joker in the deck. Rain's assessment was that the man played his part to a tee, a consummate actor. Seemingly genial and helpful, there was an undercurrent of leashed brutality. Occasional flickers of his eyes indicated the bubbling rage.

Only the girl, Lydia, seemed a true innocent bent on being a good teacher of the latest scientific trend.

Rain had compiled mental dossiers on all the cast members in what had become a real life mystery and shared them with Sawyer on the drive to the house. A clandestine operation wasn't what he'd signed up for, but he'd been prepared to accept the circumstances all the same.

Sawyer, on the other hand, had allowed his own good judgment to be sidetracked by the effusiveness of Allie's personality and professional drive. Once they'd found that escape route at the mine property, he should have been ready to intervene more forcefully when Esteban hatched this hare-brained plan, not that he'd have any sway with a woman he'd virtually just met. And one that made it her business to aggravate him.

In the end, he'd felt partially responsible for the reporter and inserted himself into the mix. Now the worst situation had actualized despite his best intentions, and he was driving himself crazy thinking that he hadn't done enough to prevent it. *Who am I kidding? This drama was going to happen with or without me.* All that was left was to use his head and locate his self-appointed charge.

Despite Esteban's insistence that Sawyer stay out of it, there hadn't been much he could have done to keep his ersatz partner on the sidelines. It wasn't as though he could force him to sit in the car while Esteban had gone inside the office to ask questions, which would only set off alarms if any of the bad guys had still been in residence, and with Allie going missing, any one of them could be involved.

Instead, he had punched in the number of the Green Grasslands office and asked for Allie, saying he was from the local paper and wanted to catch up with the reporter he'd heard was in town from the Post. Esteban figured he could pawn off the call to her as a "how-d'you-do-and-how-can-I-get-a-job-at-your-paper?" if he needed a cover for not calling her cell. As it turned out, the receptionist hadn't been curious about why he'd phoned. All Ilse had said was that she was told the nice reporter had to get back to Denver immediately and hadn't come in to say goodbye, the project manager making her apologies.

"Is he available? Maybe he can answer my questions," Esteban had asked, hoping that she wouldn't inquire as to his reason for wanting to talk to Blaine.

"I'm so sorry, but Toby hass already left ze office too. He dropped off anozer person and vass gone soon after. Iss zere someone else who can help you?"

Esteban had pleasantly declined, his scowl belying the tone of his voice, and had closed the connection.

His next move had been one of sheer desperation. Turning to Sawyer, he'd said, "Who do you know in there?"

At that point, Sawyer decided it wouldn't help to be evasive and told him about Rain, watching all the while as Esteban's eyes had narrowed in concealed fury, only to be put away as quickly as it had arrived. "Call him and get him out here. I want to talk to him."

Sawyer phoned Rain without complaint. Minutes later Rain had met them down the street and given Esteban the rundown of everything that had occurred that afternoon.

Allowing only a minute to assess the situation, Esteban told Rain and Sawyer to go back inside and play it cool until someone from downtown came to take everyone's statements. He was going back to the high school. Sawyer decided it had been best not to bicker, much as he wanted to. Esteban had already pulled out his phone and started calling in reinforcements as he sped away, abandoning the pair on the sidewalk.

Intending to follow directions, Sawyer and Rain had gone back inside, playing off Sawyer's introduction as a friend who'd come by to meet his buddy at the end of the day.

They'd hung out for ten minutes when a female agent and an impossibly young g-man arrived from the FBI office. She'd shown her credentials, and gotten down to business talking to Race, Ilse, Lydia and Rain as the only staff members present. Agent Sonya Draper had given Sawyer a warning glance to make sure he stuck around and kept his mouth shut. Evidently, Esteban's time on the phone had been well spent and his briefing thorough.

Sawyer played his role as one who had been caught up in unforeseen circumstances and kicked-back to watch the woman do her job with authority, while the puppy she'd brought with her wore a grave mask and took notes.

An hour and a half later she'd concluded her inquiries and could do nothing to keep Sawyer and Rain any longer. After a quick chat with Esteban, she'd pulled the two men aside, directing them to the downtown FBI office to await the SAC's arrival.   S h r u g g i n g , Rain and Sawyer had left and promptly headed in the opposite direction.

Precious time had been wasted and Sawyer was not about to fritter away the rest of the night when Allie had been kidnapped. *Or killed.* He didn't want to picture her languishing at the hands of some unscrupulous thug.

The reluctant thought had occurred to Sawyer as Rain had driven them out to exchange vehicles. Sawyer had brought his own form of backup, stowed in his truck, and he wasn't about to go poking around an unknown property without it, in case the tenant had malicious intent.

Finally stationed in front of the Blaine residence, they were contemplating their next move. The house was dark, the carport empty and the few vehicles on the street were shadowed in the deepening dusk. No one seemed to pay attention to the dusty pick-up that was parked in front of an obvious rental. The front lawn was overgrown but the place didn't look trashed, just unkempt.

"It's now or never," said Sawyer as he climbed out of the cab, Rain hopping down from the passenger's side and strolling up to the driveway, staying out of the line of sight from the porch. Sawyer walked up to the front door and knocked, expecting the place to be vacant, but preparing himself with a story just in case Blaine answered.

After receiving no response to his raps, Sawyer peered in the windows and walked around the side of the house, looking for another entrance. Rain joined him, pointing out a back door that he'd already scoped out.

The backyard was nothing but patches of weeds surrounded by a broken down, wood plank fence that offered just enough cover from neighbors' prying eyes. The light fixture above the door showed an empty socket, leaving the stoop darkened in the growing gloom.

Sawyer pulled a handkerchief out of his rear pocket. It was a holdover habit he'd picked up from his dad, and used it to try the knob. Finding it locked and noticing it's age, he decided he could probably jimmy it without much trouble. Muttering something about a misspent youth, he had the door open in less than a minute.

Electing to take the plunge, despite knowing that they'd leave some trace of their passage, they entered cautiously and peered around the dim rooms. Sawyer had brought his flashlight from the truck and he flicked it on.

The place felt vacant.

There were some odd pieces of furniture. An old sofa and chair in the living room, a table and two chairs in the kitchen-dinette, and two bedrooms, each with old bedsteads that looked to have been there for more than forty years. No bedding, knick-knacks. No pictures or personal items. The place had been cleaned out, even the waste baskets had been emptied except for a few odd bits of trash that seemed to have escaped notice. Lying on the floor by one on the beds out of plain sight, they'd easily be overlooked by someone in a hurry.

Sawyer bent to pick them up one by one, using the edge of his handkerchief. He didn't want to contaminate the interior any more than need be. They were sales slips from a local grocery store.

Rain found another bit of paper under the bed, crumpled and discarded near an empty trashcan. "Not too careful, was he," he said as he picked it up. "Must've slipped out of the trash when he took it out," he added as he opened the sheet with a pen while holding it with a tissue.

"Gotcha." There was a highway number and what appeared to be a rural route address.

Sawyer looked over his shoulder. "Could he have made it any easier?"

"Not if this has any relevance," said Rain.

"Yeah, I know. But it's all we've got. It's worth following up."

Rain nodded and carefully recrumpled the paper, delicately laying it back where he'd found it.

They left the way they came in.

Energy Barons

Chapter 51

Stygian ink enveloped her senses, muddied her reason. Ephemeral awareness telling her she was in a black hole.

As her thoughts gradually crystallized Allie wondered if being sucked into black holes was anything like tumbling down a rabbit hole, because she was beginning to feel like Alice through the looking glass, plummeting headlong through an endless warren.

At least my name fits.

Except this black hole was constantly rumbling and shifting, tossing her around like the worst kind of carnival ride.

It took effort to grasp that she was immobilized, blind, and cotton-mouthed with tendrils of nausea launching an assault, induced by the inexorable rocking. A headache of epic proportions building to perfect the experience. The pressure behind her eyes grew in intensity as she became more aware of her accommodations, making that rundown motel look like paradise. She decided that this particular room shared quality ratings with a dungeon mounted on a centrifuge.

Rolling from side to side, Allie was uncomfortably twisted, lying halfway on her back with her legs folded up, flopped to the side. Scrunched into quarters so tight that she couldn't extend her legs, her hands were bound in front of her, wrists and ankles screaming for release from the pain inflicted by cutting restraints.

But she couldn't scream, or yell, to get anyone's attention. The gag blocked any sound other than a gurgle escaping her parched throat.

Her perception returning in fits and starts, Allie tried to piece together the events that had brought her to this, being trussed up like a pig to a barbecue. The last recollection Allie had was that of a sun-drenched afternoon and a school parking lot. Her memory was toying with her because, for the life of her, she couldn't figure out how she'd gotten here.

Other than what felt and smelled like the trunk of a moving car, where was here?

Allie wasn't the only one trying to figure out how they'd ended up in this jam.   Having hours to contemplate the circumstances that had led to this impasse, the Calais' driver was exerting real effort to control his agitation and growing anger. Anger that could interfere with their true objective. Yet it was increasingly difficult for him to abate his fury with the 'team leader' for orchestrating this fiasco.

A'zam revised his thought. It was not a fiasco yet. They had the reporter who seemed to be unconnected to anything other than the newspaper. She was just a journalist whose curiosity had gotten away from her. The likelihood of anyone missing her for a day or two was slim from what he'd been able to find out about her. He hadn't been idle during his time away from the office and had done some research, learning that she had a reputation for being a go-getter with an obstinate streak.

He also had found that she'd been working on the power plant and coal mine bombing story. Whether or not that had anything to do with her interest in Green Grasslands had seemed far-fetched, until the last questions she had posed before Blaine cold-cocked her with the vice grip.

In some small corner of his mind, A'zam could understand the other man's quick response, however it was cool heads that should have prevailed. The right answers to her prying would have appeased her enough to send her home with a nice story about the community organization and its efforts to educate students about green technology. Not that he personally cared one way or the other about the issue. That wasn't why he'd been dispatched to the Great Satan's heartland. Now, his mission stood in jeopardy all because one foolhardy American could not weigh the facts and avert his own impulses.

There was nothing for it at this juncture except to finish out the farce, but he determined to mete out proper judgment on Blaine for endangering the assignment with his impetuous act.

Energy Barons

Chapter 52

Interstate 80 was four lanes and a barren median of practically deserted divided highway. The more miles Sawyer put between them and Cheyenne, the less traffic plied the asphalt strips that, now that nightfall had taken a sure hold over the landscape, were invisible beyond the illumination of his and fellow travelers' headlights.

He and Rain had rolled directly from the Blaine address to the freeway, knowing they were already hours behind the kidnappers, which infuriated Sawyer. He'd been silently castigating himself for allowing Esteban's wishes any influence over his better judgment. While the SAC was fiddling with trying to find evidence at the high school, the perps had taken off with Allie, he was sure of it. And he'd been playing nice at the Green Grasslands office. *Damned procedur - al bravo sierra.*

As they plunged deeper into the plains night, Sawyer and Rain were discussing how best, or even whether, to inform Esteban of their destination.

"This is probably a total waste of time," Sawyer was trying to focus and sound rational when he felt anything but.

"Then who better to chase ghosts?" said Rain.

"True." Sawyer was mulling over the options open to them. Esteban had ordered them to FBI resident agency offices downtown. By now the SAC must have figured something was up if they hadn't yet shown. Sawyer wasn't interested in having the agent bully him into returning to Cheyenne and he'd be damned if he was going to turn around. He *knew* that they'd gotten a solid lead and he needed to be there to help Allie. There wasn't anyone else she could depend on. The feds had proven that they couldn't find their ass with both hands, or she wouldn't have been abducted in the first place. *You don't know that she was kidnapped. You haven't a scrap of evi -*

dence. Yeah, he amended in his head, *unless you add up her disap-pearance with that of two men whisked into thin air and a cleaned-out rental property.*

Talking as much to himself as Rain, he said, "I suppose we could call the guy."

"The FBI guy?"

"Yeah. We're already on his shit list."

"If you're right that the address we're following is probably useless, why drag them in? We'll check it out and the feds are free to follow the evidence at the scene."

"And what if we end up in the bad guys' front yard? We won't have anyone at our back when we get there." said Sawyer.

"Do we need anyone?"

"Considering they've already blown up both our workplaces and killed one of their own *and* we think they have Allie." He managed to withhold the concern from his voice. "She may already be dead and all I've got is a 20 gauge and my service pistol."

"You forgot about my .45," Rain said flatly.

"I didn't know you had it here."

"It bothered you enough to have me play volunteer at the Green office. I figured I shouldn't come to town empty-handed."

"That doesn't preclude our being outgunned."

"Any reason that should stop you?" Rain looked over at his friend, the panel lights revealing newly etched lines of worry around his eyes.

"Hell no."

Chapter 53

An old Subaru 4x4 beater was rounding the last curves in the road, Toby's mustache a thick, black slash across his upper lip in the reflected light of oncoming traffic.

Berating himself for his precipitant action in walloping the reporter over the head, he hoped that it had been the right thing to do. Hearing her voice take on a sharpness that hadn't been evident before A´zam had noticed her checking messages on her cell phone, he had acted on an impulse to protect the cause at all costs.

Good or bad, what's done is done, but Toby wouldn't blame his accomplice for trying to take him out. Just like he suspected A´zam had eliminated his previous partner, the missing intern. Yeah, he was sure A´zam knew exactly where the kid had gone.

Energy Barons

Chapter 54

Debra Chorister's phone rang, an unusual sound in her flat on most evenings. Debra was a loner, though not necessarily by choice. She just hadn't given the time to cultivate many friendships since coming to Denver, building a new life was occurring in increments.

Lifting the receiver and saying 'hello,' with the lilt of a question, she was surprised to hear Sol's voice on the other end.

"Have you heard from Allie?"

"That's a fine how'djudoo. As few calls as I get, I expect a little cordiality," she said lightheartedly, unaffected by the brisk question. "But to answer you. Unh-uh, not in the last couple of days. I hadn't expected to hear from her until she got back, which should be tomorrow."

"She should have returned my call after the message I left for her."

"A juicy tidbit?"

"Maybe, but it could be a danger signal, too," a rill of worry in Sol's voice.

Debra immediately switched gears, becoming concerned. "She hasn't landed herself into a tight spot, has she?"

"I have no idea, but the info I left might prompt her to show her hand before checking with her resources, which is why I thought maybe she'd called you."

"Okay, quit beating around the bush. What was it? Keep this up and I could have a panic attack."

"You're not the type."

"You got me," granted Debra. She may not be high strung but she took a sip from her wineglass anyway. "Tell me what's what."

Sol wasted no time in explaining what she and Allie had discussed the night before and the possible correlation she thought could exist between the Rural Resources offices and Green Grasslands. "It's just a little too coincidental for my taste."

"I'm no gourmet, but it smells like something's rotten in Alaska's icebox, and it ain't fish." Debra sat back on the couch and thought for a minute. "Any idea how many of these guys might be involved in the plan? Assuming there is such a thing. Damn, the whole thing sounds sinister."

"I rather think most of the office workers have no idea what might be going on under their noses, as you said, if there even *is* anything *untoward*." Sol gave the word emphasis, feeling like she'd been swept into an Alfred Hitchcock thriller. "But if there is, Allie may have been dropped smack into the middle of it."

"What about you? You made the connection. Could you be vulnerable?" Debra was leaning forward now. *That is the last thing I want to contemplate. Two people I know threatened by terrorists on American soil.*

"I doubt it. I didn't mention anything to anyone other than Allie. Didn't ask any leading questions – learned my lesson last year. Nor do I have a face that projects every emotion that my little brain can produce."

"Stoneface Sol."

"Gotta play the part," she said laughing. "Don't let anyone know what you're thinking. It's safer that way." Turning serious once again, she said, "And it's not one of Allie's best qualities, she doesn't hold anything back. So what do you know? She didn't tell me where she's staying or all the details of the story."

"I know she's gotten in up to her eyeballs with that SAC working the Gillette bombing case. Hounding him every chance she got."

"Can you track him down and see what's going on? She should have returned my call and I'm on my way home. Got my info so there's no reason to hang around."

"I'm on it."

"Leave me a message on my cell, *whatever* you find out. I'll be flying into SeaTac before I catch the final leg home."

"Will do."

Voicemail.

Sometimes I hate voicemail, and this was one of those times. Anxiety was clawing at the base of Debra's spine and Special Agent in Charge Roy Esteban couldn't be bothered to answer his damn phone. She hung up after leaving a brief but urgent message.

Debra was a realist. She knew what Allie had been working on and the possible funny stuff that could be going on at that office of so-called do-gooders. Idealism had a propensity to lead some people to commit unsavory and illegal acts, all in the name of humanity. If there was anything Debra hated more than voicemail at the moment, it was the passion of fools, because no matter how much someone tried to spin bad behavior into benevolence, it was sin. Every once in a while her Catholic roots would sprout up, like now. Except she read 'sin' as in 'missing the mark.'

No, she thought, *that's being too charitable, it's being a half-assed moron who thinks he has the power to save God's earth. Talk about arrogance.* And the information Sol had left for Allie could be a blessing or a curse when it came to confronting that kind of sin, depending on whether that girl could restrain her enthusiasm. She knew Allie was a steamroller when it came to uncovering the truth. Considering consequences wasn't her style. Not a good thing under the circumstances.

Spouting a few choice words she hadn't learned in Sunday school, Debra looked at her watch, it was still early in the evening. She decided the hell with it and made the call to take action.

Throwing a few things in a travel bag, she flung open the hall closet and, rummaging around in the back depths, extracted a sleeping bag. *Just in case,* she thought as she grabbed her stuff and hauled it downstairs. Debra tossed everything in the ancient Bronco II that managed to keep running with almost 200,000 miles under it's timing belt, the car was on its third one, and hit the road.

All the way to Cheyenne she kept trying to get through to Agent Esteban, punching redial every fifteen minutes, to no avail.

Pushing the compact four-wheel drive to it's limit, two hours later she showed up at the downtown FBI offices in Cheyenne only to find out that Agent Esteban hadn't even been working out of that office. He'd been dispatched directly to Gillette from Denver and was peripherally involved with normal operations at the resident agency.

Finagling her way inside had been a work of art. The lobby looked like any small city office building except for the addition of a metal detector and a security guard that didn't look like a rent-a-cop. Being after normal business hours had made her incursion difficult, to say the least. She had to do some fast-talking about a pending emergency to get past the guard and gain access to the elevator.

Well, this is *an emergency.*

He called and warned that there was a visitor on her way.

Once inside the doors, however, the gloves came off. Debra harangued the skeleton contingent manning the office until they got Esteban on his cell phone. Using the press as her protection to keep them from tossing a black reporter – okay they didn't need to know she was just a researcher – out on her behind and invoking the wrath of the media, they threw in the towel and got him on the line.

When he answered the call, just to make sure he understood the importance of her information, Debra raised her voice loud enough that Esteban could hear her above that of the woman attempting to conduct the conversation.

It wasn't one of her proudest moments but Debra didn't care. This guy Esteban had put her friend in a risky situation and Debra wanted answers, even if it got her arrested for interfering with an investigation, or whatever else they could think to charge her with, like being a public nuisance.

"Where's Allie? I have imperative information about your case," she yelled over the words of the woman sitting at the desk.

Fearing she'd gone too far, Debra was confronted with the prospect of finding herself in handcuffs when the woman called over another agent who tried to get Debra to pipe down and leave. She adamantly stood her ground about this being a life-threatening situation. Then she stared the agent down telling him she'd sue him personally if he touched her.

Esteban heard the exchange and couldn't decide whether to be annoyed or amused. The reporter might be crazy, but for some reason he didn't think so, and if she was anything like the over-ambitious Ms. Maitland the manure was going to be hip-deep.

"Put her on the phone."

The young woman reluctantly handed the receiver to Debra, who thanked her politely and accepted it from her hands. The woman was astounded at the turn around in the blink of an eye.

Without preamble, Esteban asked, "What kind of information?"

"First, do you know where Allie is?

He hedged enough that she caught on fast. "She's gone, isn't she," Debra accused.

"We haven't determined that. Look if you have information…"

"I do. A colleague left Allie a voicemail on her cell phone that might have gotten her in trouble. Where are you?"

"Just tell me," Esteban wasn't in the mood to play games, but then neither was Debra.

"No. I need to talk to you face-to-face and if you don't tell me where you are, I'll find out. I'm damn good at my job."

Somehow, he didn't doubt the boast. "I could just have them hold you there as an accessory."

"Accessory to what? Helping solve your case?" Debra poured on the belligerency she'd cultivated out of necessity as a child growing up in dicey neighborhoods in L.A.

"Then as a danger to yourself and public safety," he replied with an affected calm. "You wouldn't dare because I guarantee you will rue that decision."

Pinche… Could this get any worse? At this point, he decided to drop the hardball attitude and take what he could get because this investigation was practically a shambles, and his unofficial inform-ant was missing.

Caving, he got her name and pertinent information, had her show all her ID again to the agent who was on the verge of cuffing her and locking her up, got confirmation that the woman was who she said she was, and finally told her where to meet him. She handed the phone to the woman with a bare thank you and lit out the door.

So much for my image as a retiring, bookish computer nerd.

Energy Barons

Chapter 55

Having a lightning ability with directions, Debra located the high school in no time flat and drove up the campus road, more like an alleyway, into the partially concealed parking lot. There was a string of official looking vehicles but no light bars bathing the area in strobes of red and blue. She assumed that they wanted to keep the whole thing low-key. *I'm about to blow that pipedream out of the water.*

Braking behind a dingy Crown Vic flanked by two other unmarked American make cars, Debra flew out of her door, barely remembering to slam it closed behind her. Pigeonholing the agent she was looking for wasn't difficult, Allie had described him well, tall, imperious with a real snot-nosed attitude.

She went straight at him, fire in her eye and a determined set to her jaw. No one was going to mess with her.

Debra plunged into the icy water. "Do you have any idea where Allie is?"

Esteban didn't know what he'd expected after talking to this Chorister woman over the phone, but it wasn't what challenged him in a sleek, amethyst tunic, the silk rumpled from her long drive. It was like going head-to-head with a panther, and he was beyond caring what anyone thought of him or the whole mess he was holding.

"Why don't you just tell me what you know and then we'll see where we go next," he feigned complacency.

Debra huffed as she halted in front of him, all five feet, three inches quivering with fury and fear. Esteban could sense her tense energy and he could see that this was Maitland's champion, willing to face down anyone who might be endangering her friend's life.

After a few more breaths, Debra clenched and released her fists as if relieved to discard the protective stance. Looking him hard in the eye, she relented, making the decision that he should be trusted. How else was she going to find Allie? Opening the data floodgates, she told him what Sol had passed on about the voicemail.

The SAC kept his expression schooled, but the concern became evident in his eyes as he listened to the possible correlation between the three environmental offices and the "Lebanese" student showing up at both locations in Alaska.

"Give me this, ah…" he tried to reiterate the other journalist's name.

"Solana Greyfisher-Littman," prompted Debra.

Esteban wrote down her name, "and her number."

Debra complied and then asked again. "Where is Allie?"

He decided to come clean. This woman didn't need any more games. "Right now we don't know. We're trying to compile whatever information we can."

"What about the other *Lebanese* student? Is he around? Have you questioned him?"

"How did you know about the Middle Eastern students to begin with?" He arched an eyebrow, suspicion returning.

She looked at him like he'd just grown a horn out of the center of his forehead. "Who do you think identified them in the first place?"

Esteban's eyes widened briefly with surprise that swiftly altered to newfound respect for this petite woman's abilities and chutzpah. She wasn't about to be deterred by anyone she deemed as thwarting her friend's rescue, including the vaunted FBI. Without another word, he turned to another agent to ascertain the status of APBs on both Blaine and the Lebanese intern. The words had barely passed his lips when another agent who'd driven in from the Casper office called him over to examine an object he'd just uncovered. It was a crushed pendant.

Chapter 56

Yancy was back in the office checking e-mail after blowing off the day to drive to Spotted Horse Mountain. Observing the Sun Dance had imbued her spirit with a much-needed serenity. Feeling rejuvenated and redirected, she'd picked up some coffee on her way to making a quick stop at her desk before going home and succumbing to physical exhaustion.

Barely settled in her chair, she opened the mail program and saw something from Ell labeled *Urgent!*

So why didn't she just call? thought Yancy as she opened the missive, remembering too late that she'd forgotten to turn her phone back on after leaving the Sun Dance.

What's going on out there? I haven't been able to reach Allie. She promised to call and keep me updated on her assignment, and she doesn't renege on things like that. The paper said, "What assignment? She's supposed to be on vacation."
Have you heard from her? Call me soonest.
Ell, not to be appeased.

Without another thought, Yancy picked up the phone and dialed Ell's number who'd be home, late as it was in NYC.

"Akkerman here."

"It's Yancy. I got your e-mail but have no idea what you're talking about."

"I haven't talked with Allie today. She promised to call and I've heard nothing."

"When did you talk to her last?" Yancy wondered how urgent

this could be. Ell didn't get upset about nothing, though she could be excitable.

"Last night."

"What is that, just twenty-four hours? Allie could be out for a drink with her friends."

"No. She wasn't at home. Not that she told me everything but she made it sound like she was hot on a story. Only thing is, the Post doesn't seem to know anything about it."

"You called her boss?" Yancy was incredulous. "What did she tell you that made you call her employer?"

"Don't get pissy with me. I *know* Allie."

Yancy decided to let the attitude ride. Ell was fearful for her niece and it was well after midnight for her. "Did you talk to her editor?"

"No, just his assistant. It was late and he wasn't in. Still, she doesn't disappear."

"How can you be sure that she's disappeared? Even the authorities wouldn't consider her missing yet." Yancy tried suggesting calm alternatives. "Maybe she's somewhere that doesn't have cell service. Most of the west is splotchy service at best."

"I know, but for her, that's no excuse. She keeps in touch when she says she will."

"What do you want me to do?"

Ell was sliding a little toward frantic. She had an inborn flair for melodrama that Yancy attributed to her theatrical aspirations.

"Oh, I don't know," admitted Ell. "I just have this gut feeling that something's wrong."

"What about her folks? Have they heard anything?"

"Are you kidding? Allie doesn't talk with them that often. Not that there's a problem, it's just that my sister doesn't understand her daughter's need to chase news. Allie talks to me." Ell painted the facts without rancor.

After talking with Ell and getting very little actual information about Allie's story, she'd even tried the "I'm an attorney, you can tell me" argument that fell on deaf ears as Ell cited that Yancy wasn't *her* lawyer, Yancy agreed to try to find out what she could. Evidently Ell had promised Allie not to talk about the assignment and she was nothing if not loyal to her niece.

As frustrating as it was for Yancy, she made her own promise and hung up from an oddly distraught aunt.

Before long a telephone network had taken on a life of its own.

Yancy put a call into Cole. The tidbits she had extracted from the tight-lipped Ell led her to think that the *big* story was related to the Gillette bombings. Knowing that Cole's brother Sawyer worked at Tyne Hill and that he had hosted Allie at the ranch sent her down that path of inquiry.

It ended up being a box canyon, but she did extricate a promise from Cole to try to reach his brother, which she knew wasn't easy for him. It hadn't taken much to discern a real rift between the two after the couple times she and Cole had chatted about life in general. But he promised due diligence all the same.

After following through on his agreement, Cole began to get concerned because Sawyer wasn't answering his phone either. They may not like each other much but they always managed to be civil and didn't ever refuse to communicate. Cole also knew that his brother had managed to get himself involved with the newspaperwoman somehow. From Carly's comments, he even had a suspicion that Sawyer had grown rather fond of the reporter. Now if that wasn't a kick in the hindquarters, he didn't know what was. If there was one thing the two brothers had in common, it was the swearing off of involvement with women, *any* woman. The thought of which made him reconsider his own feelings about the woman who had just called him.

Shoving that whole line of thinking aside, he tried Sawyer one more time.

On the other end of things, Sol had contacted Debra when she hadn't heard back from Allie. She didn't know that the researcher would toss everything to the wind and drive up to Cheyenne herself to confront the FBI agent. Once there, Debra had put a real bug in Esteban's ear, which was already buzzing at not being able to get a hold of Sawyer who was not where he was supposed to be.

Round and round it went.

Chapter 57

The car slowed down and made a sharp turn, bumping up a track that was leaving bruises on top of her bruises as it ground up a steep grade. The road, if you could call it that by the feel of the washboard under the tires, had to be a few miles long, it seemed forever before the car came to a rocking halt.

Her hearing was unimpeded and the sound of a key being inserted and turned in the trunk lid filtered through the fuzz that comprised her disoriented thoughts. Seconds later, the sensation of cold crisp air flowing over her face, a blanket having been thrown over the rest of her body at some point during the journey, snapped her to attention.

A pair of hands shook and pushed her, urging her to sit up, something she couldn't accomplish on her own after lying immobile for hours, her limbs deadened. The prodding was insistent, though applied in silence. Unable to speak because of the gag, her head throbbing, she just lay there. Finally, with a whoosh of breath, expelled with obvious aggravation, the man rolled her closer toward the opening. Allie assumed it was a man by the size and grip of his hands, and the smell. His odor oozed stale sweat that had long since overpowered a fading aroma of soap. Reaching in, he grabbed her, and with unexpected strength, hoisted her over his shoulder in a fireman's carry.

Allie thanked the Almighty that her bladder wasn't pleading for relief. She'd had few liquids before her abduction – *This* is *kidnapping, right?* – and supposed that the clanging in her head was probably due to dehydration. *Or the drugs he gave me.* As woozy as she was, she knew she had to have been drugged. *This is not a concussion talking.*

She mentally kicked herself to concentrate on the problem at hand, which was *not* whether her headache was caused by pharma-ceuticals or a solid whack with a blunt object. Allie forced herself to focus on where she was and how she was going to get out of this mess. While being jounced up a few stairs and through a door, she tried to pay attention to her current surroundings. There wasn't much to zoom in on other than the smell of dust, some pinesap in the air and the scent of some other greenery, leaves, grass, and throw in some wood smoke. A fireplace? The hike through the house, or cabin, or chalet for all she could tell, was short and she soon found herself callously dumped in her new quarters, which were much roomier than the trunk she had previously occupied. Anything beyond that, she couldn't discern. No light, little sound except for squeaking floor boards as her captor walked through the building. And no heat. Allie was cold, her hands and feet numb.

Retracing what she could recall, she decided there was no time like the present to go over the few details of her compulsory holiday. No matter how hard she tried, she couldn't pinpoint how long she'd been unconscious, which meant she had no idea how long they'd been on the road or how far they may have traveled. There had been no special sounds besides that of the creaking trunk and the tires singing over the macadam; no odors except fuel and dirt. She was just as lost with or without a memory. Then she thought of that silly ass pendant Esteban had slung over her neck. She had no idea what it did, not that it mattered now. The necklace was gone, just like everything else, leaving her blind, incapacitated and abandoned in some corner of Wyoming.

Even that wasn't a sure thing. This might not be Wyoming.

Her mind skittered away, floating on the dregs of some unknown drug. Images of ruby slippers, a star scepter and a hairy little mutt…

I don't think we're in Kansas anymore.

The road out of Rawlins was a straight two-lane highway, unde-viating in its westward course. Sawyer had stopped to fill the tank at a lonely gas station on the periphery of town before launching deep-er into the unknown, at least as far as Allie's whereabouts was concerned. He'd considered calling Esteban from a pay phone while at the pump but changed his mind at the last minute, blowing town to make the best time they could around the southern flange of the Big Horn Mountains.

He'd decided in Cheyenne that he needed to take the chance of waiting to notify the FBI agent. The last thing he wanted was to give up the info only to have Esteban put him in irons and sit on the intelligence while he checked every other thing first. He and Rain were on the trail of suspected kidnappers with nothing more than some scribbled locale that could be just another dead end. Even if it was, there was no way he'd allow himself to be sidelined. He and Rain had gotten a good head start and couldn't be too far behind the bad guys. *If we aren't following a phantom*, he chastised himself.

After the SAC had dragged his feet through the whole affair despite Allie's leads and badgering, Sawyer wasn't about to let her suffer because procedure took precedence. *Lousy bureaucrats... humanity's bottom-feeders.*

He had no allegiance to anyone or anything right now except the reporter's safety and he'd do what was necessary to try to ensure her return. Not that he knew why. Nor was he willing to go down that road, cutting off that train of thought before he ended up driving himself nuts. Like any other mission he'd been on in his past life, he took his role as protector seriously.

Seeing the lights of Rawlins dwindle to a distant glow in his rearview mirror, Sawyer decided it was finally time to make the call.

Glancing over at Rain, he took a card out of his breast pocket and handed it to his co-conspirator. "You call Esteban on your cell and tell him we got a lead on where the kidnappers might be heading. Just give him the likely location and don't answer any questions. Maybe suggest he find Blaine and let him figure out the rest. I don't want him knowing that we found the information at that Green guy's place. It'll cause more problems than a Mastiff mounting a Chihuahua."

Rain indicated his approval of Sawyer's reasoning by pulling out his phone and punching in the number handwritten on the back of the business card.

Esteban hadn't recognized the number on the readout, but

answered anyway, unwilling to chance missing any clue, no matter what its origin.

A minute later Rain had broken the connection after imparting the information Sawyer had suggested and declining to answer the barrage of questions the agent had thrown at him. Almost immediately, the phone rang but Rain hit 'ignore,' an enigmatic grin flitting across his otherwise passive expression.

"We're hours behind these guys," said Sawyer as he gave the truck as much gas as he thought he could get away with and not have the local law haul them to the side. "Let's hope one of us gets there in time."

This time it was Sawyer's phone that rang, not that it hadn't been rattling off periodically as Agent Esteban had tried relentlessly to get through. Without removing his eyes from the road, he handed the phone to Rain to check and see who was calling.

"It's Cole again. You may want to talk to him if he's that insistent," said Rain.

"Yeah, yeah. He's probably just doing Esteban's work by being his lackey." He shrugged and reached for the return of the phone. "What the hell," and he pushed the 'talk' button.

"What is going on? I've been trying to reach you for the past hour."

"Nothing."

Cole grunted his disbelief. "Since when do you refuse to answer your phone? Never mind," and Cole commenced telling him that Yancy, an attorney friend of the reporter had called him trying to find her. "She thought maybe I'd be able to catch you to see if something's up, and then you weren't answering."

"So what's the connection between you and this lawyer gal? I've never known you to hanker after a professional woman," Sawyer gave the term 'professional' the kind of emphasis that had dual meaning.

"This is hardly the time," answered Cole coldly.

Sawyer exhaled. "Tell me about it."

"Then you know what the hell is happening," he accused. "Where are you?"

"No place that matters."

"It does if you've gotten mixed up in something," said Cole.

"The only thing I'm "mixed up" in is keeping track of your friend's friend," Sawyer was trying his damnedest to be vague.

"Then Yancy's fears have merit? This woman, Allie, she's missing."

Sawyer sighed. "Yeah."

"So what's that got to do with you?"

"Hell, Cole, you wouldn't believe me if I told you. Suffice it to say that she may have gotten herself dragged into something nasty. I really can't say any more." Sawyer paused. "Tell your new girlfriend that the authorities are doing everything they can to locate Allie."

"Shit, Smart Ass, that's not enough to tell her friend and family! I know you have more than that."

"Yeah, but I'm not gonna be the one to compromise an investigation."

Cole was skeptical. "Oh, so now it's an investigation? What in the name of God have you been up to?"

"Trying to make sure Allie didn't get too involved in something that's over her head and I'm doing a piss poor job of it." More angry with himself than anyone else, Sawyer hung up.

Rain's contribution was simple. "That went well."

Energy Barons

Chapter 58

Reacting to the call he'd just received on his cell phone was not an option. As much as Esteban wanted to express his frustration with emphatic cussing, he controlled the impulse. Debra Chorister was standing at his elbow, not backing off an inch. Her dedication to her friend was admirable but it didn't defer the problem he now had of another amateur wheedling into the investigation. *An amateur who, if she hadn't identified the Lebanese/Pakistani/Iranian, or whatever they were, students this investigation would be nowhere.* He clawed his fingers through his hair. *Who'm I kidding? That's exactly where we are, nowhere.*

He looked sidelong at the diminutive interloper. If she was as good as she appeared to be, he'd adopt the next best strategy. Put her to work.

After a couple of unsuccessful attempts to reach both the anonymous caller, by redialing the number displayed, and Sawyer, neither of whom answered, Esteban made his decision… he was going to the location the caller had supplied. The voice sounded very like Sawyer's Indian friend who he had met at the Green Grasslands office, so he presumed the two were together going off half-cocked. Even taking into account Aleman's history in the military, it wasn't a kosher situation. He peered down at Debra, standing so close he could feel her vibrating with tension.

"Are you willing to be of some assistance in finding your friend?"

She gave him that inner city, "are you stupid?" look. "Why in the Lord's name do you think I hunted you down?"

He almost smiled at the terminology. That was *his* job to hunt people down. "Good. I'm sending you back to the FBI office. You can man the computers to help us with locale and any other information we may need to find Ms. Maitland."

"Don't you have people already doing that?"

"Not with your track record. This is a provincial office."

She shook her head, "No, I want to be there when you find her. You're understating your staff's qualifications to get rid of me." She skewered him with eyes as deep and resolute as umber wells.

"Maybe, but you're far more valuable at data collection, research. That's your specialty, right?"

She nodded in confirmation.

"I need you to be where you have all the hardware *you* need to get me what *I* need, and that's information. The Cheyenne office is short-handed and you just became our newest recruit." He was serious, and he knew he was going to get a royal reaming for this decision.

Calling over one of the two other agents on the scene, Esteban told him exactly what he wanted for Debra at the office. Balking at the suggestion of allowing an unauthorized gatecrasher to access office computers, he said that he'd have to check with his supervisor.

"I am in command of this investigation, which would be nonexistent if it weren't for this highly competent woman's work." Esteban locked eyes with the much younger agent. "Just do it. I'll handle the protocol." *Or the demotion, which is more likely.* He turned his back on them and Debra followed the agent unhappily but resolute in doing what she could to help Allie.

Esteban went to his car, dug a Wyoming map out of the glove box and spread it out across the hood. He found the general location Aleman's friend had given over the phone and noted that it was centered in Fremont County. The Johnson County sheriff was handling the dead Green Grasslands' intern case since the body had been dispatched in his backyard. Figuring that the suspects, who he assumed had kidnapped the reporter, and this case was just overflowing with assumptions, were on a more direct route, he traced his finger along US 287 out of Rawlins. He was certain they'd be traveling that way.

Esteban placed a call to another resident agency of the FBI, small as it was, located within an hour or two drive of the probable destination of the suspects. The supervisor answered, sounding harassed and out of breath. The call had been forwarded to his cell phone and he was out on a call. Before Esteban could explain the situation and request assistance, the agent informed him that he was in the middle of a breaking incident on the Indian reservation. There'd been a biker brawl involving some Natives and a touring motorcycle gang in Riverton. A couple of stabbings, gunshots and just one incredible cluster. He was obviously in no mood to be accommodating, nor was he able to be. He was inundated.

When Esteban explained the situation and possible kidnapping, the agent shut him down with, "No real proof and no warrant? What do you want from me? I'm up to my eyeballs in bloody bikers. Get the sheriff in Fremont County. You know how small our office is, we don't have the manpower and no way can I get anyone out there for hours, at this rate. Call the sheriff."

Esteban rang off pissed as could be. Not that the agent wasn't right, he was. It's just that he was hours away himself with little to nothing to go on and the probability that a woman's life was in peril.

Instead of fuming, he called the Cheyenne office and had them get a warrant issued for Toby Blaine's last known address ASAP, which the caller had hinted would be beneficial. The agent he'd sent to the Green Grasslands office to depose the employees had come back with little on either Blaine or the Lebanese intern except for addresses and phone numbers. The A´zam character had a flat in Fort Collins and she'd hunted someone down to check it out, but both she and Esteban concurred that he wouldn't have gone back there. The Blaine house made the most sense since both of them were AWOL. With issuing the warrant in the works, he studied the map to see how close to Lander he could get with a small plane and to order an SUV ready for him at the destination. He saw that Riverton was marked with an airport, but he called the office to check on a field in Lander, which he thought he remembered had one, and told them to charter a flight in an hour, knowing it would probably take two, hoping beyond hope that he could get the paperwork in hand and be gone in such a short time.

Without further delay, he left the last agent on the premises in charge of the scene and rushed back downtown to follow-up on entry to Blaine's residence. Esteban had nothing but his own gut grinding, telling him that the information they needed to nail down a reason to race off to central Wyoming, and the enigmatic location, was hiding inside that house. And he was sure Aleman and the Indian had found it.

He prayed that they hadn't corrupted the evidentiary chain. They were going to need everything clean and forthright to back up any decision that might lead to an arrest when the time came. Because he knew damn well that the ACLU would be more than ecstatic to deep-six the case by protecting the rights of a terrorist over that of a kidnap victim.

Arriving at the downtown office, Esteban found Debra ensconced behind a computer bank, another civilian employee, a computer tech, by her side watching her every move.

"Anything new?"

The fresh-faced agent he'd sent back to shepherd the Post researcher answered. "The local police found a vehicle that matched the description of the car driven by the intern abandoned behind a closed-up grocery store on the north side of town. It had been cleaned out of identifying information, you know registration and all that, but they found pocket-sized printed material that was stuck in the front passenger seat track. The owner didn't take the time to check every corner, apparently."

"So, what was it? Any help to us?"

The kid nodded enthusiastically. "Oh yeah. It's a torn page from a prayer guide to the Koran. They got it to the lab right away to check for fingerprints and we have prints from the Green Grasslands office to match against."

"Warrant on the way?"

"Agent Draper is collecting it now. She'd put the judge on notice hours ago in case we got something to move on."

Esteban tried to keep his jangled nerves in check by going through the calming gestures of filling a mug with coffee he really didn't want. What he wanted to do was chase the thugs who he was sure had scooped up his informant.

"Good," he said evenly, "Is that it?"

This time Debra cut-in. "No, your agents had gotten a license number on the beater driven by a... Toby Blaine. I hac... I got into some files and located the registration on both vehicles, the truck and the Hyundai. The first one is registered to a fella in Jackson, looks like a shell corp., the other one is registered to a trust. I'm guessing a holding company. I'm trying to track the property through the trustee. These can be pretty convoluted and hard to confirm details." She turned her attention back to the screen, fingers flying across the keys.

Esteban's mouth twisted in an ironic smile. The Chorister gal was worth her weight in gold. With luck they'll have a connection between all the players sooner than he'd thought possible.

Agent Draper came through the door waving the warrant for Blaine's address, on the phone with a state police detective. "They just located the truck. It's alongside a junkyard just outside of city limits. It's Blaine's ride."

Esteban turned to the female agent, "We need the map from that environmentalist office that had the marks on it, the one that Maitland had mentioned to the Greyfisher woman." He noticed the little researcher's shoulders stiffen at the mention of Allie.

"Already got it. The director gave us permission to remove it from the premises and we bagged it as evidence." She shrugged, "You never know."

Replacing the coffee mug on the counter, he pulled out his phone and dialed the Fremont County Sheriff again to update him and get him on standby for the address in his jurisdiction. He was racing out the door as he finished the call.

"Let's roll."

Energy Barons

Chapter 59

After passing off her assignment to Cole, Yancy continued going through her e-mails and phone messages. Among the short pile of slips that Laura had paper clipped together and left in the center of her desk, was one that immediately caught her attention. Notice had been received from the Federal District Court that her petition to reinstate the old power plant had been granted.

Far too little too late.

At least for Kara, thought Yancy as she aimlessly shuffled the messages. The damage had been done as her client lay wasting away in a hospital bed, comatose and hope rapidly dwindling. She pictured the frail figure, one hand enveloped by the gentle grip of her mother's fingers, waiting to feel a faint sign of recovery.

Still, having stood outside the eastern entrance to the Big Lodge, open to greet the dawn, she recalled the dancers approaching the center pole, offerings of tobacco, the shrill of eagle bone whistles, the reverberating drum and crying song. The sacrifice of water fast. It reminded her of the sense of rightness she'd had in praying for Kara, and the renewed hope she'd felt.

Maybe it wasn't too late after all. If not for Kara how else would Yancy have begun the court battle that may be of help to others, though she knew that it wouldn't be long before she'd get notification of the EPA's appeal, and they would appeal. That was the way of things. But even that thought would not deter Yancy from taking small satisfaction in this little victory, short-lived as it must be.

She began gathering her things to leave the office, debating whether to go directly to the hospital to inform Mary and her extended family of their triumph thus far, hoping that it would hearten them despite Kara's current condition.

As she was reaching for her handbag, her cell phone trilled and she put down her briefcase to fish it out of its pocket. Checking the display, it told her that it was Cole.

"Any news?" she asked, hopeful that it was all a mistake and Allie was already touching base with Aunt Ell.

"Not much," he hesitated before continuing.

The pause didn't bode well to Yancy. Goose bumps ran down her arms.

"And what I did hear wasn't the best."

She sat back down, "You'd better tell me."

"I finally caught up with Smart A... Sawyer, and he confirmed your friend's suspicions. It looks like Allie is missing."

"Missing?" Her purse fell from nerveless fingers. "How can that be? Ell just talked to her last night?"

"All I know is that Sawyer and his buddy are following up on some information and the authorities have pulled out all the stops to locate her."

"Does anyone know if she's had an accident, are they checking hospitals?" Worry tumbled off her tongue.

"Yancy, I'm sorry that I don't know more but Sawyer was cagey, said that he wouldn't be the one to compromise an investigation. I don't understand what he was talking about, but he sounded stressed and that's not normal, even for a tough S.O.B like him. I'm sorry I'm not much help." Cole wished he had anything other than what he'd learned to offer, which was almost nothing.

"You're kidding, right?" She stumbled over her words. "I mean, you found out what we needed to know. It's not what I wanted to hear, but there's nothing to be done about that."

"What are you going to do?" He would rather be there to give her the news in person, maybe soften the blow because this had been a week of trials for Yancy. He may have only met her a week ago, *has it only been a week?* but he felt something hum through him that he couldn't pin down. For some reason he cared about what she was going through.

"Well, I'm going to have to call Ell since she's the one who got this ball rolling, despite the nature of the news," Yancy inhaled and let the air escape slowly, trying to slow her heart. "I don't have a choice, she'll want to know. You'll keep me informed if you hear anything?" She asked, sounding almost pathetic to Cole's ears which were too sharply attuned to her anguish.

"Absolutely. S.A. and I may not be on the best of terms but I think he really cares about your friend and he will let me know as soon as anything happens. He doesn't break his word. Honor among thieves and all that," he said lamely.

"Thanks again." She'd almost hung up before she heard his reassurance.

"S.A. will find her and I *will* call you."

For some reason, she felt better.

Energy Barons

Chapter 60

Struggling to regain the ability to concentrate, bleariness kept settling over her mind like a fog, ebbing back and forth as the hours stretched by since she'd been rolled into this dark corner, shivering until the man came in to toss a blanket over her. Allie fought to focus on the noises and scents around her, the two senses that were left unhampered by her kidnapper. When he came with the blanket, she tried to distinguish the subtle differences in odor, cross-referencing them with her recent experiences. She had become accustomed to the gag's stale stink over time and could now discern the odors of the coverlet's mothballs and got a whiff of the man. Combing her recollections of the last two days, she finally concluded that it was the Middle Eastern intern who had physically loaded her into the dreaded trunk and dumped her here, where she was still virtually immobilized, her limbs having become leaden, circulation cut off by the bonds. Why she was here made no sense. Nor did she understand being trussed like an animal, chucked on the floor, denied food and water yet been covered by a blanket? In her semi-conscious state, nothing made sense.

And it was impossible to keep track of time. As far as she could tell, daybreak hadn't yet come. The blindfold could block only so much light, unless she'd been left in a room outfitted with blackout curtains. *Damn, now why did I have to think of that?*

She fought the grogginess, but was losing as much as winning. The drug was working its way through her system at such a slow rate, the residual effect would make her drift off when she was trying hardest to stay awake.

Emerging from one of those involuntary catnaps, she heard voices for the first time as a door closed. Drifting from an adjoining room, she could make out the tone of the two men, for they were male voices, and she recognized both A′zam, her abductor she was sure, and Toby, the apparently not-so-nice guy.

Great. Why didn't I have Debra run a check on that creep when I first met him? She berated herself for not pursuing her initial response to the guy, which, now that she thought about it, was definitely one of apprehension. *Too late now.*

She tried listening harder and could only capture a few words here and there. Nothing she heard reassured her that her predicament was going to improve anytime soon. In fact, it all pointed to them finalizing their plan, whatever that was, and "cutting their losses." She heard that one loud and clear, putting into perspective exactly what her own fate would be. She wasn't willing to lay odds on the fulfillment of the last Chinese fortune she'd dug out of her cookie at dinner a few weeks ago that promised a long and prosperous life.

If they had nothing to lose, she, on the other hand, had everything at stake.

The front door swung closed again with a bang that jarred her out of a doze. Allie was pretty sure it was still dark outside, not a peep of light filtered through the grungy cloth wrapped around her eyes. This time the conversation was a little easier to follow as yet another man seemed to have entered the picture.

Glass clinked and heavy porcelain clunked onto a hard surface.

Coffee, I'll bet. Allie thought wistfully that a cup of strong, hot coffee to rid her mind of cobwebs would be wonderful, then admonished herself for being stupid. *Better if they'd forget about me alto - gether and go on their merry murderous way.* Abandonment could spell rescue, recalling her presence would only mark her ultimate demise. She'd rather a tiny chance at freedom than none at all.

Snippets of sentences carried through the vents and under the door that heightened her fear. Whoever the newcomer was, he appeared to be in charge and was calling the shots. After a quarter hour or more of discussion, the 'big man' made the decision to continue on their course. At first he was angry with the two clods who had brought a hostage into the situation.

So much for 'out of sight, out of mind.'

The boss then softened his approach. It sounded to Allie like he was coddling the Arab or Pakistani or whoever he was, because she was positive he wasn't some Lebanese Christian or Druze, and if he was really a student… who knew? He had to have some kind of ties to powerful people. That was evident. How else could he have been hustled into this country through all the proper channels, just to perpetrate some terrorist scheme. Oh yeah, by now she was certain that this cell was behind the destruction of the power plant and the deaths of those men at the coal mine. What she had just heard confirmed it.

Pity I get my hands on the biggest story of my life and I'll never get these numb little digits on a keyboard to write it. She mentally shook off the thought and concentrated on their discourse.

What she heard next made everything fall into place. Sol was right. The boss was putting a call into the other 'Lebanese' student in Alaska. She heard that correctly, right? He was giving instructions to implement that end of the operation and she had no way of getting word to the authorities. How many more people were they going to maim and kill? How much were they going to be able to cripple the fuel delivery system down here and in Alaska? Because now that she knew what their intent was, she *really* needed to figure a way out of this hole.

Just receiving word of the execution of the next phase of planning, the billionaire leaned back in his chair and crossed one leg over the other in a purely European pose, savoring a cup of rich Turkish coffee. He'd acquired the taste while traveling as his father's errand boy years before. As much as he may have resented the shuffling between minor dignitaries, backwater operations centers and outposts, delivering important information and directions from his pater, he had always known that he'd been building his inheritance, the vast empire he now governed with the same iron fist of his predecessor.

Reminiscing about his visits to training centers in Iran, Afghanistan and North Africa, he recognized the competence that had been drilled into the operatives and fanatical volunteers. They didn't question authority. Only because they didn't know it originated from a Westerner, he added silently. Had these minimal minds any concept that the true motive behind their efforts had nothing to do with the pandemic spread of Islam, they would have revolted.

Then again, perhaps not, he thought. The mob mentality was ingrained in the culture. *In every culture, actually.* It was to his profit that their own religious leaders were corruptible. It was about power and control, not religious fervor, a twist of fate that placed them in his debt and ultimately handed the scepter to him, not some reconstituted caliphate.

Interconnecting the emotional causes of environmental activism and jihad was nothing if not the definitive manipulation of imprudent humanity. *One sham deserves another*, he thought with approval. The masses cried to be led to their own destruction, never learning to trust the exceptional judgment of men who have come before, particularly those masterminds who had crafted the Constitution of the United States and the federalist system.

Domination of weaker minds hadn't posed the challenge he'd hoped. Still, he derived satisfaction from duping morons such as Haggerty and even the smug *intelligentsia* in America and Europe to blindly institute his dominion. The sweetest factor was that they had no idea that their own power was tenuous at best as they delivered their countries into captivity, hostage to his expanding economic control of energy and wealth distribution.

Shortsighted fools.

Chapter 61

Tracing the willow-edged flow carved by the Sweetwater River across the high desert bluffs through the night, wasn't much of a respite from the miles of monotonously flat blacktop they'd covered most of the way from Cheyenne. Rain not being loquacious by nature and his companion unable to curb his thoughts from a much deeper, darker vale than the one they were traversing, the hours had passed in stony silence. Once they'd committed to their self-assigned duty, Sawyer knew he was digging his hole so deep with the SAC that he'd be lucky to see sunlight ever again. He was just sorry that he'd dragged his friend into the muck with him. Even that wasn't about to deter him now.

He'd experienced the single-mindedness of the Hezb'ollah, Al Qaeda and Taliban during his service overseas, which meant that of everyone involved in the current situation, he was one of the few who recognized the potential for failure. Allie's life was in peril, if she wasn't already dead. All Sawyer had to do was envision the kid who'd been dumped off the mountainside by his comrade in arms. And Sawyer had his suspicions as to the culprit who had inflicted death without a second thought. He'd seen it before.

Blocking the whirling premonition of imminent disaster was becoming more difficult as he and Rain approached their destination.

Both Sawyer and Rain were familiar with the highway and the land's rough features as they gained altitude, arroyos cutting swaths through the desiccated plain, creeks running unhurriedly at the tail of the runoff. Willows lined the gullies, stands of pines growing thicker the higher the eye climbed up the rocky ravines. Only a few roads crawled up the slopes, turning forward and back as they scaled the valleys upward.

Despite the darkness, Rain spotted the turn-off they'd been seeking. No traffic, no lights in the general area indicating a residence of any kind. As Sawyer made the turn, they couldn't see the county road winding around the hills beyond the scope of their headlights. As it ascended the rise, Rain recognized some of the landforms. He had been through the region many times with family who had access to traditional hunting grounds. The switchbacks tightened as they came around the base of the hill, making it plain their drive would be protracted, the turns limiting their speed to a bare creep in the pre-dawn hours.

"There are a few old hunting cabins miles up the canyon," said Rain, breaking the heavy silence.

"You figure they might have taken up in one of those?" The question was moot. They'd already committed to the assumption that this was where the baddies had holed up. If they were wrong, then Allie was dead. They'd have no opportunity to reevaluate their choices because there hadn't been any other options. But it bothered both Rain and Sawyer that their quarry could have been so lax as to miss a scrap of paper scrawled with a directional lead. Could be plans altered faster than they'd expected and they got sloppy.

Or Providence is leading us. Sawyer added a silent prayer that was the case and they hadn't just squandered their one opportunity to find Allie.

Shunting away the misgiving, he continued the arduous drive up the minimally maintained road into the wilderness of the southern reaches of the Wind River Range. Time inched by as the suggestion of twilight created the illusion of fading starlight and they rounded a rocky outcrop where a dirt road turned off to the right. An old marker stood by the track. Missing letters left a sign barely legible in daylight, let alone the vestiges of night. **Br k n Br h**.

"Looks like Broken Branch. You ever hear of it?" Sawyer asked Rain.

"Yeah. It was purchased some time back by an outsider who never came to see it. I heard the sale was made through an agent who bought it for a song from an Indian family in financial trouble. Its over a thousand acres."

"You have good information," Sawyer was impressed.

"Cousins," shrugged Rain.

"You think this is it?"

"Most of what's up here is BLM property. Indians have hunting rights in the area and keep camps, but this seemed the best shot from the info on the paper."

"I hope the feds come to the same conclusion," Sawyer muttered, turning his lights down to only the foglamps in hopes of keeping their approach low profile. "How far up the road, d'you think?"

"Maybe a mile."

"Good, we've got to hope they haven't heard or seen us yet."

More than one copse of intermingled pines and aspens stood along the washed out gravel drive. Sawyer chose one to duck his rig into, out of sight of traffic and any habitation that was further up the valley. They may have been on the edge of nowhere but Sawyer found that even here there was a faint cell signal. He checked his messages to see what was Esteban's plan of action.

If he had formulated one, he hadn't shared it with Sawyer. Instead the voicemail was an order barked to stay out of it and do nothing, the Fremont County sheriff was on his way.

"That ties it. We can twiddle our thumbs and wait for the Mounties or see what's what," said Sawyer, clicking off the phone. "I think it's inviting trouble to hope they arrive anytime soon. This message was left hours ago and no one's here but us. And even were the sheriff to make it up here, surprise is gone, assuming we still have it, and who knows if the locals have ever dealt with a hostage situation before." He threw back his head and took a deep breath weighing the options.

"You have," Rain stated impassively. He was well aware of Sawyer's experience in some nasty circumstances while in the service. It wasn't something he shared with many but Rain had heard enough to know his friend's competency in just such a situation.

"It could be a complete fubar and Allie could pay with her life."

Rain didn't disagree. Instead he reached for his Smith and Wesson 325. That was enough of an answer for Sawyer who secured his M9 Parabellum in his waistband at the small of his back where it was easy to reach with his right hand. He had his knife in its jacket on his belt and he grabbed the shotgun.

"Its time for a little recon."

Chapter 62

Touching down at Lander, Esteban was unclipping his seat belt and lunging toward the door before the pilot of the King Air C90GTi Turboprop had pulled to a stop on the apron. It had taken almost three hours to line up a flight from Cheyenne. Adding on the travel time, Esteban was pushing the limit to keep his frustration under control.

Time had slipped away and all he could do was pester the sheriff and resident agent to get their rears out to the location he'd supplied, not that it was really much more than a description of a hunting retreat. The aircraft was a compact business model that could seat seven, a roomy cage for the single passenger that was practically clawing to get out as soon as he'd buckled up. All that he could think about was how many hours jumpstart the suspects had. Granted, the drive would take time, but there was no knowing if the pseudo-Lebanese student would chuck Maitland off a cliff just like Esteban was certain he'd done to the dead kid the Johnson County sheriff had hauled back up the mountain.

He was here now. All he had to do was get out the door and on the ground.

The local agent was waiting for him looking the epitome of a cowboy in his denim jacket and workingman's ropers poking from beneath his jeans. No fancy snakeskin on this guy's feet. He looked the part of a cowhand all but for the shield clipped to his belt. Frankly, Esteban could care less if the agent had been dressed in a tuxedo, he just wanted to be where he could do the most good.

Hopping down the steps as soon as the door swung open, Esteban greeted Special Agent Torowski, a transplant from Wisconsin, with a snap of his head and a blunt, "Where's the car?"

"Howdy to you too," he replied, his eyes drooping from having spent the last twelve hours dealing with the biker brawl on the reservation. The push me-pull you between the tribal police, the sheriff and the FBI had drained him of any humor and left him sleepless and cranky. He wasn't in the mood for the Denver dipstick to be throwing his weight around on top of it.

Instead of making a stink about Esteban's lack of manners, he just tilted his head toward a crusty looking four-wheel drive. Esteban didn't blink an eye after what he'd been driving on the other side of the state. Beggars couldn't be choosers and all he cared about was whether or not the rustbucket would get them to their destination.

Climbing in he queried Torowski about the situation at the location. "Any activity?"

"The sheriff called in a few minutes ago to say that a vehicle registered to Sawyer Aleman is parked just off the county road. He couldn't locate anyone near the truck and a gun rack in the back was empty. Not that that means much," assumed Torowski as he peeled out of the dark parking lot. Dawn was still just an omen, the star-studded heavens not yet ready to fade into the rose and turquoise of sunup.

"In this instance, it does. Aleman had a shotgun mounted there when I last saw him. So we can presume that he's armed, wherever he is. How long 'til we get there?"

"An hour. This Broken Branch place is way off the beaten track."

"Shit. Call the sheriff and make sure he stays put until we get there." For the thousandth time, Esteban raked a hand through his hair. "Could anything else go wrong?"

"That depends on what you think has gone right so far," Torowski shot back.

Sawyer and Rain hiked the mile keeping to the side of the rutted track that passed for a driveway. It was a moonless night but the lack of light pollution aided their sight, starlight filtering through the boughs of trees clumped at intervals along the route. Reaching a flat, they saw a rustic cabin perched under the branches of a half dozen pines, shooting a good thirty feet into the air.

The surprise was seeing three vehicles pulled up in front of the house, they'd expected to see two at most. The odds against them had just increased. What had been an even match-up was now anybody's guess. The extra car could have carried one passenger or five. Not a happy thought for either man standing on the outside with their few weapons in hand.

Sawyer and Rain put their heads together to assess the situation after managing to peer inside the vehicles and check out the cabin, locating all egress points. They hadn't heard anyone else arrive at the bottom of the hill, but they couldn't be certain that reinforcements wouldn't show-up at an inopportune moment. Quiet as it was out here, they'd probably hear the cavalry coming to the rescue, which could only cause a problem. They agreed that surprise was all they had working in their favor.

Sawyer pulled out his cell phone only to find that the signal had disappeared once they had rounded the mountain.

"We've got one chance to make sure the sheriff and Esteban don't walk in and put these guys on their guard," he looked Rain directly in the eyes. "You've got to go down to where there's a signal and catch them before they come barreling up that road and endanger everyone, especially Allie."

Rain considered the suggestion in a flash. He knew that no way in hell could he get Sawyer to leave the cabin, he was emotionally vested in this, whether or not he'd admit it. And Rain knew he'd never admit anything of the kind.

He nodded to his friend and went back down the hill, leaving Sawyer in position for…? He wasn't sure what his friend would do, but he suspected it wasn't going to be to sit and wait for backup. When they arrived it was going to cause all hell to break loose rather than add to security because the bad guys would then be ready and waiting.

Rain turned and rushed cat-footed down the mountain while Sawyer hunkered down at his post.

On the way up to the property where they hoped to find their quarry, Esteban's phone vibrated in his pocket. He extracted it, recognized the number as that of the Cheyenne FBI office and answered the call.

"We got a hit on who owns that property you told me to check on." It was Debra, her nimble fingers flicking across the keyboard as she spoke.

"And?"

"The title was junked up behind two trusts within a dummy corporation."

"I'm not even going to ask how you found it."

"Good, because you don't want to know," she said glibly which made him smile despite the dire situation.

"Shoot."

"The title is tied to a 501(C)(3), a charitable corporation that is run by a board of directors which are, in effect, trusts. Two of those trusts are managed by the same trustee. Someone who serves on the board for EcoEarth Legal Center, which, it turns out, is the same person who is trustee of the holding company for one of the vehicles driven by your suspects. He's also a close advisor, or buddy, depending on how you look at it, to the main man. It all seems to be linked to Kraegen."

"Theo Kraegen?" Esteban was stumped.

"In the flesh. The dummy corporations and trust entities are many and convoluted but not an unbreakable chain," Debra stated matter-of-fact.

"Woman, you are in the wrong business," Esteban was amazed at the connections and the work that was accomplished to connect the dots.

"Is that a job offer?"

"Either that or a marriage proposal," he said before he could think better of it.

"I'll let you buy dinner first, but I won't bite until you bring Allie back alive and kicking, otherwise I *will* make your life hell." Debra slid from playful to deadly serious in a heartbeat.

He didn't doubt Ms. Chorister's ability to make good on the threat and, aloud, promised his utmost effort. He felt guilty enough for having drawn the feisty reporter into the whole tangle in the first place and he vowed to himself to bring her home safely if it was the last thing he did. And when it came to this job, it just might be.

Chapter 63

An argument was brewing in the kitchen. It was a boon to Allie because it meant the raised voices made it easier to pick out the words, get a better picture of what might be in store for her. Not that she was all that anxious to find out.

It sounded as though there was contention about who should handle what angle of their 'project.' The new arrival kept his voice more level than the one she knew as Toby. Considering the circumstances, Allie had come to the conclusion that nobody was who they seemed to be and the names were probably bogus as well. Although no one was actually yelling, the timbre of the voices indicated a thinly stretched veil of tolerance between the younger operatives. She was making an assumption, she knew, about the third man's probable age, but by the sound of him, his take-charge attitude and the others reluctantly deferring to his opinion, he had seniority.

Probably the local moneyman. All this has got to cost a fortune and someone holds the purse strings. She didn't figure it was either Toby or A'zam, they didn't fit the bill.

What she heard was the new guy cutting off the others' dispute. His voice lowered once he'd gained control of the discussion, so she couldn't hear all of the details, but it sounded as though Toby was to be sent to finish the project. As they entered the common room, a snippet of the conversation filtered through the hall.

"A'zam is too identifiable to be operating on his own. You'll have to carry out the plan alone," said the new voice, to which there was no quarrel.

"Not a problem." Allie recognized Toby's voice. "The gear's all ready. I can leave anytime."

There was no further discussion, just some boots clomping through the cabin and doors opening and closing. Including hers a moment later.

Uh-oh. Time to pay the piper.

She heard the door to her room swing open and footsteps enter her quarters, whatever it looked like. She'd been assuming that it was a bedroom, though she hadn't encountered any furniture. A´zam had just dumped her on the bare floor.

Two pairs of boots were heard halting just inside the door. They didn't say anything. It appeared to her that she was being examined and the decision as to her destiny was being determined nonverbally.

A few seconds later, one set of footfalls left the way they'd entered.

The other person moved close to her and appeared to squat down beside her. The next thing she knew the gag had been yanked down and an open water bottle pressed to her lips. Parched as she was she drank the liquid, letting it soothe her throat before she realized what she had done.

Oh well, she thought as she slaked her thirst. If they'd drugged the water there wasn't anything she could do about it now.

Removing the bottle as suddenly as he'd placed it there, not giving her time to prepare and causing the liquid to drip off her chin like an infant, her captor spoke.

"Do you need a bathroom?" She recognized A´zam's voice but his odor had already alerted her to the identity of the waterbearer.

Conjuring up more of a croak than anything else, Allie attempted to say, "Yes," barely making herself understood. Her immediate thought, while he replaced the gag over her mouth, was to try to use the opportunity when her plastic shackles would have to be removed to find a way to escape.

Before anything else was done or said, A´zam was called back into the other room, leaving her where he'd found her. Blind, mute, bound and frustrated.

Toby was transferring equipment to the Subaru from the Olds, the passenger door and trunk yawning wide as he swapped a couple of laden duffles from the car. Sawyer observed from his station behind a chokecherry, noting the weight and size of the bags the project manager from Green Grasslands slung into the muddy SUV, one hastily tossed inside and the other carefully placed.

Explosives? The guess wouldn't be too far off the mark, thought Sawyer as he remembered the shock of seeing the 360-ton hauler burst into the air as the blast rocked the pit. He just wondered what they planned to blow-up this time knowing that there wasn't anything he could do about it while Allie was still in the hands of the other members of this virulent terrorist cell.

Sawyer called it as he saw it. This crew was nothing more than eco-guerrillas, not that categorizing the beasts made it any easier for him to just let the bum drive off to accomplish whatever lethal task his blistered heart desired.

But that was exactly what Sawyer did. He was Allie's only chance for reprieve at the moment, and he wasn't about to abandon his post. He could hope that someone would flag the mad bomber before he got too far. Despite the dirt covering the license plate of the Subaru, he and Rain had managed to surreptitiously scrape some of it aside to get the number. Rain would report the vital statistics on all the vehicles parked at the cabin as soon as he'd contacted the authorities.

For now, Sawyer had to assume that he was on his own. He hadn't heard any other vehicles arrive yet, but the main road circled around the opposite side of the mountain. There was a slim possibility that the sheriff could make it in without signaling the outlaws of his arrival. All he could do was watch as the man slammed the hatch closed, climbed behind the wheel, and drove down the track.

A minute later, Sawyer saw A'zam opening the front door. A wobbly Allie was pulled through the entry by her bound hands, the captor's fingers wrapped around the cable ties encircling her wrists. Not to be caught completely off-guard, he gripped a gun loosely in his other hand. Sawyer surmised that her clothes were oil stained and grimy from traveling crammed into the trunk of one of the cars still in the drive. She had a rag tied around her head blocking her vision, and another one secured around her mouth preventing her from speaking. She stumbled behind the Middle Easterner, her legs unsteady, likely from disuse. Her trembling gait attested to a lack of circulation making Sawyer assume the rope hobble she now wore had replaced tighter fetters, allowing her to shuffle awkwardly behind A´zam.

He stashed the mounting anger at her mistreatment and concentrated on the tableau confronting him. Rain and he had seen an outhouse located back behind the cabin, far enough away to offer privacy and keep any stench at bay. It looked like A´zam was leading his hostage in that direction.

Sawyer slid silently around the opposite side of the cottage, his passage obscured by trees, berry bracken and bushes. He had no intention of letting them out of his sight for long, but he would take no chances of setting off any alarms by inadvertently stepping on a twig or rustling leaves in passing. He reached cover and he watched as, instead of opening the outhouse door, the man pushed her past the structure toward what had appeared to be middens when they'd checked the perimeter.

There was no choice left. He'd heard nothing from the base of the mountain. If the sheriff had stopped the Subaru on its way, Sawyer had no clue. The authorities were nowhere in sight and Allie was being dragged to a certain death, to be ignominiously buried in an ancient trash heap.

Allie shambled after A´zam as best she could, willing her legs to move when all they really wanted to do was dissolve beneath her weight. He pulled her up almost as much as he was pulling her forward. Although she had been told that he was taking her outside to relieve herself, she felt a quiver of irritation conveyed from his hands to hers. It didn't feel right and she was desperately searching her mind for a way to escape. All she had was her hearing and that was offering no help, aside from picking up a scrape that was probably some nighttime denizen of the forest. She could smell the fresh scent of pine in the air and knew that she was miles from civilization, which thought didn't curb her panic any.

She was left with nothing for it but to sidle along behind her impatient guard who seemed keen to be free of his ward.

The next thing she knew, she was being shoved to her knees in a pile of dead leaves. Bile rising in her throat, Allie tried to scream at her abductor, the sound garbled, choked back by the gag. She weakly tried to thrash out of his grip. She couldn't see him brandishing a knife with one hand, the gun now in his jacket pocket, and with the other he yanked on a clump of hair that was knotted up in the blindfold.

His hands full with a struggling captive, A'zam didn't hear the furtive movement as Sawyer flashed forward and pistol-whipped him before he could slash Allie's throat. He would rather have shot the bastard but knowing that there was still at least one man left inside, he didn't want the report of a gunshot to bring another adversary careening outside before he could cut Allie's bonds. As it was, he managed to keep the noise factor at a minimum. Allie, sensing that she'd been delivered from death, feeling the clutch pulling on her scalp melt in an instant, dropped into the mound of detritus, exhausted and scared spitless.

She lay there frozen by fear as she heard a whisper amid the rustle of clothing.

"It's Sawyer. Don't make a sound."

She wasn't about to argue, breathing heavy sighs of relief as she felt hands holding her own and cutting through the cable ties around her wrists.

"Pull off your blindfold and gag and give them to me."

With shaky hands, Allie undid the bandanna from around her mouth first. It wasn't caught in her hair like the blindfold and, although it prevented her from seeing, would be more difficult to remove. The gag came off quickly and after tying the new hostage's hands, Sawyer tied the cloth over his mouth.

The blindfold followed quickly and Sawyer handed his knife to Allie for her to saw through the rope hobbling her ankles.

Pulling Allie to her feet, they heard gunshots echo from down the hill. He grabbed the unconscious kidnapper and heaved him by his arms, face up, into the woods flanking the garbage dump just as the cabin door flew open. An older man thrust his head outside and calling for A'zam, rushed out the door, rifle in hand, heading toward the outhouse.

The sun had begun its ascent, twilight diffusing the deep shadows of pre-dawn. Morning glimmer was enough to see the drag marks leading away from the middens and, lifting his eyes, spot Sawyer pulling the Arab into the underbrush.

The man didn't miss a beat, leveling the rifle at Sawyer's heart the same instant he dropped A´zam and went for his gun.

Allie stood immobile, knowing for certain that both she and Sawyer were as good as dead. Her rescuer a second slower than the man with the rifle.

A shot fired, rapidly followed by another and Allie's eyes shut tight, unwilling to view Sawyer's dead body before receiving the killshot meant for her.

But she didn't hear her companion fall. Eyes blinking open, she witnessed the assailant go down as the third shot rang out.

Agent Esteban stepped forward, deliberately keeping his gun trained on the downed man until he could double check that the man was dead.

"You killed him with the first round," Sawyer said coolly.

"Wanted to make sure my aim was true. Couldn't take a chance I missed."

Sawyer turned to help Allie up from where she'd slumped to the ground, looking and feeling like a traumatized accident victim. Pulling her to his chest in an effort to offer what comfort he could, he matched Esteban's gaze. "Just a waste of good bullets. Cost of ammunition has gone through the roof, you know."

Chapter 64

Sawyer felt Allie shivering and removed his denim jacket, bundling her inside the shearling lining before encircling her in his arms again. She was a little unsteady on her feet still, but when asked if she could walk, she nodded numbly and he led her away from the dead body and the now semi-conscious A′zam who was awakening to find himself handcuffed, a sheriff's deputy on guard duty.

The police vehicles hadn't yet been repositioned up the drive. Esteban and the other FBI agent, Torowski, were conducting their initial inspection of the area, working with the sheriff to tape off the scene.

Sawyer ignored the police activity and assisted Allie, who insisted on walking down the hill, shaky as she was. She'd been tied up for so many hours that her circulation still hadn't returned to normal, but she was in a hurry to put as much distance between her and the cabin as possible. Nor would she allow Sawyer to carry her, she was determined to make it to the bottom under her own steam, though she accepted his supporting presence, catching her when she faltered.

By the time they reached the bottom of the hill, an ambulance was pulling into the drive. Sawyer watched as they attended to Allie who was shaken and a little dehydrated but none the worse for wear. *Unless you include shock.*

They checked her thoroughly despite her trying to push them away.

"Let them do their jobs," Sawyer said firmly. "The dead guy'll keep."

Walking over to the side of the road where Rain stood, a deputy hanging close by, Sawyer met him while keeping an eye on Allie, a blood pressure cuff wrapped around her upper arm.

"Couldn't have asked for a more opportune arrival of reinforcements," said Sawyer. "Damn near lost the race this time."

Rain turned his gaze onto his friend's bleak countenance. "There a story here?"

"Not unless you consider the good guys shooting the bad guys just before my ticket was punched a story."

Rain nodded in comprehension. "Good thing they were already on the way. I'd hate to have to break in a new roping partner. Too much trouble."

"Yeah. What *I* want to know is, who's the guy who lost the lottery."

Chapter 65

Yancy walked through the hall doors on the floor where Kara's room was located, worried about Allie. She hadn't wanted to believe that her friend was really missing, but after Cole's call, she felt burdened, hope beginning to fade again. She'd tried going home and catching some shuteye. She was certainly tired enough, but her mind just wouldn't power down. Tossing and turning had led to ending up twisted in her bed sheets and no more able to sleep than when she'd pulled them over her head hours before. Waking before dawn, she was dressed and out the door, heading to the hospital without a second thought, just knowing that was where she needed to be.

Rounding the corner, Yancy peered in the window of the unit, surprised to see the place packed with Kara's family. Puzzled by the crowd's presence and seeing the turn the previous day had taken thus far, her thoughts skipped immediately to concern that everyone was gathered because Kara was dying or perhaps had already passed. Praying that she was mistaken, Yancy went to the door and heard the tinkling sound of laughter tumble out into the hall.

What happened?

Mary looked up just as Yancy arrived in the doorway, catching her eye with joyful tears filling her own. Yancy's smile grew as she realized that something wonderful must have occurred.

Motioning for Yancy to join them, Mary made room for her by the bedside.

She came inside and was amazed to see Kara wide awake and talking to her auntie and grandmother as if nothing had ever happened.

Yancy reached over and squeezed Mary's hands in her own.

"When did she wake up?" Yancy felt a drizzle of wetness slide down her own cheek.

"An hour ago, just before dawn." Mary's face was lit with an almost ethereal glow.

"Is Key back yet? Does he know?"

Before Mary could answer, the auntie who had sent Yancy to Sun Dance explained, "He had Keith call us soon after Sun Dance was done. He knew Kara would wake soon and told Mary to keep watch, and call the family to stand by and guard her." Her voice cracked with emotion. "We stayed through the night, then Kara opened her eyes and started talking like she'd never left."

Overcome with gratitude for bearing witness to what she considered a miracle, Yancy felt that a greater blessing couldn't have been delivered for this family, rewarding their endurance.

Thank God for this little girl's recovery. She hugged Mary and backed out before she made a real fool of herself, and felt her phone vibrate in her pocket.

Leaving the family to their celebration, Yancy skimmed rapidly down the hall to face the outside window overlooking the parking lot now bathed in the growing light of morning. Extracting the phone from her pocket, she answered the call when she saw it was Cole.

He got straight to the point.

"They found her and she's okay."

Nearly collapsing with relief, she breathed aloud this time, "Oh, thank God." She hesitated for the briefest moment. "That's the second bit of good news I've received."

"Yeah? Tell me what happened."

"Kara came out of her coma," she told him immediately.

"Then it's my turn to offer up thanks. This has been a day for you."

"Not like it's been for Allie or the Lysanders. I'm just a bystander. But I need to call Ell, she's been beside herself with worry. Are there any details?"

"None that they're releasing," said Cole. "Actually, I got a call from Sawyer's friend and he'd been read the riot act by the authorities."

"That must mean that something big went down. You're sure she's okay?" Anxiety sneaking back into her voice.

"Yes. Rain doesn't say much but he was clear. Allie's fine."

"That's terrific news. Thank you for calling me."

"I don't forget a promise," he said with meaning. "Now you'd better get to Allie's aunt so she can quit calling you every twenty minutes."

"Ten. She calls every ten minutes," Yancy corrected him light-heartedly.

"Same dif. Talk to you later, then?"

"Yes. I'll definitely call you back later. I don't break promises either."

Esteban, was knee-deep in paperwork and dog-tired as he and Torowski conducted the clean-up operations of the eco-terrorism plot. Escaping the twin devils of the resident agent and sheriff to grab a cup of coffee, he finally called the Cheyenne office to talk directly to Debra about Allie's rescue.

Although the news had already been delivered to the office hours before, she was relieved to hear directly from the SAC that Allie was fine. He reassured the reporter's friend that Ms. Maitland had managed to come through the ordeal without any real harm other than having been scared out of her skull.

To that comment, Debra hadn't anything to say. She was happy beyond words that they'd found Allie and gotten her out of captivity unscathed, but she had to bite her lip not to give Esteban a tongue lashing for having put his informant in the line of fire in the first place. Allie was safe and, in the long run, that's all that really mattered.

"So, have you given some serious thought to making the jump to law enforcement?" Esteban baited Debra. "The FBI could use someone with your talents rather than wasting them on hunting up minor research for a newspaper."

She brought him back to earth. "Mmm-hmmm. And if it hadn't been for a pesky reporter, how long would it have taken you to break this case open? I was just the conduit to hunt down the hunches." Debra paused for a heartbeat, "So you tell me where I'm doing the most good?"

Exhausted as he was, he chuckled at her razor-sharp point.

"Check and mate."

The telephone tree was in full swing.

Sol had just landed at Albuquerque. As they walked to the baggage claim, her husband had been explaining the stranglehold Scirras was building on the gold market and why. She was having a little trouble concentrating as Toddy went through the reasoning of how the future of gold wasn't so much in its value as a commodity or holding wealth, but in its innate value as a conductor of electrical current and its role in energy transmission.

"If these massive gold reserves are kept bottled up underground and the metal above ground exchanging at exorbitant prices, then it effectually keeps it out of the hands of the people, where it could be most useful to make electricity far more affordable by being employed as a conductor for energy delivery. Gold doesn't oxidize like copper and silver and right now, forty percent of electricity is lost in transmission over copper wire. Gold wiring would *gain* forty percent more load over the current power grid."

"That's good, babe," Sol was keeping track of his monologue with half an ear.

"There's probably enough gold in these tremendous reserves to supply the use of government and municipalities, and from the power plants to the initial transfer points. Copper is fine for ten-mile stretches or less. If gold wire were utilized in the lines from the power plants to the big transmission stations the gain would offset the forty percent loss over the small distances, bringing the electricity loss to two percent overall. By using gold, which isn't magnetic, you'd improve efficiency and reduce electro-magnetic interference. Gold relays, solder and chips alone would increase efficiency hugely *and* drop the cost of electricity to almost nothing.

"So, by controlling the gold supply, which is what Scirras is doing by manipulating the market, keeping a lid on mining with the help of environmental activists that he sponsors with his billions, he minimizes the potential to realize gold's greater value, that of lowering the cost of electricity so dramatically that *everyone* could benefit. Cheap power means economic boom all over the world."

Sol's phone rang and she fished it out of her pocket. She was tired and queasy and Toddy's excited exposition about the importance of gold for the future of cheap energy was losing her attention.

"Hello?"

"Sol, it's Debra. I thought you'd want to know that Allie's okay and your information put the investigation over the top. They caught the guy in Alaska before he could do any damage and they shut down the terrorist cell Allie was monitoring."

"I am so glad to hear that. The waiting has been hellacious, particularly with this recurring nausea."

"Oh dear, don't tell me you're coming down with something," said Debra, concerned for Sol's health.

"No, not unless you consider an afternoon bout of morning sickness a disease."

Debra laughed as she hung up.

Toddy had just walked up rolling his wife's suitcases along, and was standing right behind her when she'd made the last comment into the phone. Sol just about jumped out of her skin when he spoke next to her ear, "You're pregnant?"

Sol shoved the phone back into her pocket and pushed past him as she ran for the restroom. He was right on her heels with a huge grin splattered across his face and practically followed her inside, bags in tow.

"*We're* pregnant…" she called as she dashed through the door.

Chapter 66

It took hours before the three civilians were allowed to leave the scene on the mountainside in southern Wyoming. As exhausted as everyone was, initial statements had to be taken after which Esteban agreed to release the former hostage and two would-be rescuers to their own devices. He had no interest in throwing the posse in the tank and adding to the paperwork colossus he was already staring down.

The first thing the trio did was crawl into Sawyer's truck and head back to town, register at a local motel and crash.

Sawyer wouldn't let Allie stay by herself. She'd been through too much already and he knew how devastating the plummeting dive from an adrenaline rush could be. Refusing to leave her alone in the room, even for the duration of a shower, he grabbed his things from the truck and pulled out a clean pair of sweats for her. They'd get her some new clothes after she'd rested and he was certain she'd be all right.

Sawyer tucked her under the covers before he got cleaned up himself. Sluicing off the grit of the last twenty-four hours in record time, he hiked up a fresh pair of jeans and slid onto the bed beside her, just holding her as she shivered in the aftermath of her ordeal, eventually slipping into unconsciousness.

Rain commandeered the adjoining room and ablutions accomplished, quickly gave in to fatigue. Both he and Sawyer knew they'd be under intense FBI scrutiny before long and lucky not to find themselves behind bars for interfering with an investigation.

Dusk had faded into dark and Allie had fallen into a fitful sleep, cradled in Sawyer's arms where he eventually succumbed as well. Each time she stirred, he was awake and checking her to be sure she was fine. He'd never thought that he would find himself this concerned about another person's welfare, particularly *this* woman, who epitomized everything he abhorred.

He reconsidered that estimation. She had embodied the mimicking, mindless press when he'd met her just two weeks before, but he didn't think Allie was as staunch in her ideals as she had been. Experiencing information overload had forced her to re-evaluate the research, causing her to arrive at a wider understanding of facts versus hearsay.

Sawyer realized that it didn't really matter one way or the other what Allie had concluded. He'd lost the battle. Allie had worked her way under his skin and, whatever she believed, he knew that he wasn't going to let her go.

He'd been exceptionally successful avoiding romantic entanglements for years, having learned his lesson the hard way. That one love of his past had played one brother against another, leaving Sawyer and Cole both anesthetized when it came to female influence in their lives. He'd been discarded to see his brother take his place, capitulating to a woman who thought she knew what she wanted only to pull the rug from under one then the other, leaving a trail of anger and anguish in her wake that hadn't healed in nearly twenty years.

His arms now enfolding a woman who should never have gotten through his defenses, he watched Allie slumber, peace slowly returning to her features. It made Sawyer think that maybe it was finally time to move forward and that she was becoming a vital part of the healing process.

The next morning, the phone in the room jolted both Sawyer and Allie back to reality. He answered the call as she opened her eyes to realize that she wasn't alone. Her initial reaction to Sawyer's cradling as she awoke was one of comfort, a wave of warmth flushing through her heart and limbs. Astonished and gratified as she was to find how right it felt, she had difficulty accepting that warmth, having learned to place faith in no one else. She'd learned to be self-reliant over the years and whether she was miffed or glad to be in the company of a caring protector was beyond her ability to decide at that moment. He had more than earned her trust and the glimmer of a future with Sawyer was tempting, even hopeful.

Instead of allowing herself to indulge in that tender turn of thought, she lay back, tuning in to Sawyer's half of the conversation. After all that had occurred in the last twenty-four hours, the gist of his responses didn't sound particularly promising.

That didn't keep her from immediately switching gears, her mind whirring as words fell into place. In a few hours she would be filing the story of her life, when all such considerations were put on hold as Sawyer hung up, his face grave. *Uh-oh, what'd I do this time.*

He caught her look and his expression changed immediately. "Don't worry, everything's under control... to a degree."

She quirked an eyebrow, puzzled, "What does that mean? I can go home and submit my story?"

"Not quite. We have to go to the local FBI office and make a statement, then you can go write to your heart's content," facetiousness stealing into his remark.

"Why don't I believe you?" she said warily.

"Because it's a bald-faced lie," he acknowledged. "You know Esteban is going to give you some kind of restrictions while they investigate the case. You're a material witness." He smiled at her frown. "But I did just hear that they shut down the terrorist cell."

Sawyer went into a brief description of the capture and jailing of the other 'Lebanese' student in Alaska, apprehending him before he was able to complete that end of the sabotage. Of course the local side to that story was the fact that Blaine had been killed as he attempted to get past the sheriff and his deputy on his way to plant explosives along the pipeline that carried natural gas from Wyoming to California. He ended up losing control of the car and driving off the twisting road, over the precipice and into oblivion, which left only the two so-called exchange students. Attempting to find out any one of the conspirators' true identities was going to be enough of a challenge, considering the cache of fake passports, drivers' licenses and visas they'd discovered at the cabin.

"Yeah, and a lot of luck they'll have getting anything out of them, now that the administration has shut down harsh interrogation methods," put in Allie.

"Somehow, I expected you to take the President's side on that issue."

"I might have a while ago, but not now," said Allie resolutely. "You might call this last episode a *"teachable moment"*," she said using the president's language flippantly.

Pulling her to him in an embrace that was revealing to both that their relationship had turned a corner, he rumbled, "Well, I'll be hornswoggled. There is a God."

Epilogue

Summer temperatures hadn't soared as predicted. As fall settled in so did blasts of frigid air, showing up with unseasonable snow that swept across the Rockies and plains only to disappear again for a brief revival of clear skies, becoming an azure scrim complementing the rust and ochre leaves of autumn.

Yancy had been laboring for weeks, embroiled in fighting the EPA's appeal to reopen the closed power plant. It wasn't yet a moot point since Flat Butte was still not scheduled to come back on line for months yet. However, it looked like the whole shebang was headed for the Supreme Court where Yancy had her doubts that there was much of a chance to gain justice in this instance. So much hinged on the language of the Clean Air Act, the intent of the Congress when it was enacted, and the ultimate interpretations instituted by the courts.

She was somewhat heartened, however, by the latest related ruling of the nation's high court. The Corcoran Creek case had been concluded in favor of the interests of the Yu'pik and the mining company in Alaska. The environmental groups that had forced the abandonment of the permits tendered by the Corps of Engineers via a Ninth Circuit ruling, had lost to a clarification by the nine justices over a conflict of language within the Clean Water Act. It had been a close decision.

Sol and Toddy had been keeping a close eye on the outcome as well. As far as they were concerned, it was a victory against the radically high unemployment rate suffered by Alaska Native corporations across the state. Yancy, however, thought that the case she was pursuing might open the door to revisit the 2007 ruling handed down regarding carbon dioxide being classified as a pollutant, despite the fact that the Court had not been asked to make that determination, but whether it was a greenhouse gas… two different things, the final ruling determined by politics and the actual question based on science.

Yancy wasn't harboring much hope for such a development, but considering the consequences that this definition had already imposed on innocents like Kara, who was lucky to be alive, she knew she had to continue wielding that fiery sword.

The fallout over the eco-terror cell in Wyoming and Alaska had been kept under the radar despite the best efforts of a few hardy journalists to break it onto the network news scene. The Post's exclusive was overshadowed by politically correct pressure, putting Allie on the opposite side of the fence for the first time, hampering but not halting her earnest pursuit to reveal the facts.

Theo Kraegen had deftly managed to extricate himself from any direct association with the debacle out west. The data Debra had supplied to connect the dots between Kraegen, EcoEarth, the dummy corporations and the perpetrators evaporated under the massive torrent of paperwork submitted on behalf of Kraegen to quash the admissibility of the evidence.

Kraegen may have slunk off to his stronghold with his legal kingdom mostly intact, but the issue did manage to backfire on the Van Schaal White House. Despite the administration's and the mainstream press' best efforts to whitewash the whole affair, the Cap and Trade legislation went down to defeat. The vote also affected the president's expectations to sign a planned treaty document at the Framework Convention on Climate Change scheduled for December in Copenhagen. Opposition was growing with every passing day and were he to yield and add his signature to the Kyoto Accord's replacement, which the United States had never endorsed, his tumbling poll numbers would take a meteoric plunge.

Ever a step out of touch with reality, none of that curtailed Rone Haggerty's bleating about global warming with far less effectiveness to a rapidly vanishing audience.

The word was out.

Scirras, on the other hand, continued on his sordid march, untouchable by virtue of his effectively distributed wealth, fingers stirring every pot around the globe to the boiling point. The coalition of eco and jihadist terrorism was an experiment that he believed had great potential for further development. Both factions were adamant about the destruction of modern Western culture, making them natural allies. The fact that the two world concepts were diametrically opposed only made it more of a challenge for him to promote. However, when both sides of the spectrum are so far removed from one another, their commonalities become an intrinsic draw. In this case, hate. And Scirras' power thrived on hate and deceit.

His clutch on the gold market hadn't lessened, nor would it as long as the sheep went calmly to their own slaughter, believing that energy production equals the death of the planet. The environmental lobby would continue to benefit from Scirras' largesse and play the devil's advocate against ethical resource development.

His ploy was a simple one in the end. Keep demand for the commodity of gold at an outrageous high, thereby denying access to efficient power transmission, which in turn would keep low-cost energy beyond the grasp of average people who depend upon it for economic growth and everyday needs.

As the coup de grâce, even though the Cap and Trade was dead for the time being, resurrection was in the offing. Scirras was forever fomenting dissent and discontent among the world's populace. Locating, targeting and exploiting every avenue possible to wrest political power into his own hands. Building the empire he deserved, brick by brick, body by body, nation by nation.

He was halfway there.

-30-

ABOUT THE AUTHOR

Former newspaper publisher and editor, A. Dru Kristenev has more than three decades of experience in periodicals. Kristenev grew up in the publishing industry working every angle of a paper, from ad sales and production to writing and overseeing editorial content. The author carries a Bachelor of Arts degree, a Master of Science and a California Community Colleges Lifetime Teaching Credential and taught at the foremost colleges and universities in the Inland Northwest.

Since 2010, Kristenev has been on the road as an independent Christian missionary, crossing the United States more than ten times. She has also been a columnist for CanadaFreePress.com since 2014.

THE BARON SERIES

Four books in the series of stand-alone novels based on current, factual occurrences, the relationship of characters leads from one story to the next, weaving an ongoing tale of journalists running across criminally tainted philanthropy and politics. Caught by their own curiosity to uncover the truth, they are pulled deeper and deeper into the investigations, unexpectedly putting their lives at risk…

Land Barons- the first book in the Baron Series of romantic suspense novels that rely on solid research of environmentalist influence on American lifestyles, touching on the long reach of government regulation and media/corporate power. Anthea Keller is seeking a peaceful place to ply her trade as a PR agent. Instead, she finds herself in the center of a land scam, drawn in by Gary Mathers, an ex-cop who just can't reconcile the deadly misfortunes of local property owners forced to sell off assets. And who is waiting in the wings to snap up the firesale deals?

Gold Baron- the second work in the series. Fact meets fiction in the election process of the 2008 presidential campaign season, drawing on the reality driving the candidacies - who's influencing who and to what end with global markets and politics as the backdrop. Solana Greyfisher returns home to Idaho only to be snagged by a fascinating story that leads her to Toddy Littman, researcher extraordinaire. Together they dig through the morass of campaign funding paper trails only to attract the murderous ire of power brokers working the system to their own benefit.

Energy Barons - the third novel, whirls around political manipulation of the environmental movement causing economic upheaval in the West and endangering lives of the innocent. Ambitious Allie Maitland is caught by surprise while investigating what appears to be anything but an accident at the new power plant. Sawyer Aleman, former marine, wheedles his way into the FBI inquiry, under Allie's skin and into the role of guardian. Before they know it, the story rolls from Wyoming to Alaska and everyone involved is walking a perilous tightrope of greed, murder and mayhem.

BLOOD BARONS - the fourth novel in the Baron Series brings the tale full circle.

NYC: a metropolis of 8 million people; 500 disappear each year. Of those, three dead end case files lie open on Special Agent Roy Esteban's desk. Who are they? Why doesn't anyone know they're gone and why does no one care?

Lack of leads and an ASAC that wants the cases closed drives the FBI agent to take on an unorthodox partner in Researcher Debra Chorister. Together they track an unwholesome alliance between corporate science and government healthcare. And those three lone individuals? They're not the only ones who can't be found.

UNKNOWN PREDATOR

Hands tied by regulations, what does a rancher do to forestall the concocted destruction of a traditional way of life by officials cowering behind an "unknown predator?" Not what you'd think.

When neighboring landowners take action, dropping them into the middle of a legal quagmire, individuals obsessed with their own righteous cause threaten the ranchers' livelihood… and their lives.

A. Dru Kristenev
ChangingWind Ministries
changingwind@earthlink.net

Scripture Led Politics:
Mutual Exclusivity Be Damned

Wonder how Scripture relates to the political atmosphere in which we live?

Numerous legislative, judicial and regulatory decrees have altered life in America to a degree that our parents' generation would find it unrecognizable. To what end? Who benefits from the draconian coding that now cages the free thinker, particularly the faithful?

As government draws each new line in the sand, Author A. Dru Kristenev has taken a scriptural view of the cascading legal enactments, noting how they are fundamentally changing the American Dream. These commentaries open a deep discussion of how believers must tap their intellect and view the shifting political landscape in the historical light of the Bible, contemplating its significant lessons and their application.

●●●●●●●●●●

Read all of A.Dru Kristenev's books available on Amazon.com...

THE BARON SERIES Political Suspense novels:

Land Barons

Gold Baron

Energy Barons

BLOOD BARONS

UNKNOWN PREDATOR

Non-fiction Books:

Scripture Led Politics: Mutual Exclusivity Be Damned

Pay Attention!! ...your life, family and nation depend on it